SOLOMON'S THRONE

A NOVEL

JENNINGS WRIGHT

DEDICATION

To my family,
Chuck, Ryan and Zeke,
my best gifts.

ACKNOWLEDGMENTS

A HUGE THANK YOU TO MY husband, who puts up with me and all my projects and loves me anyway. To my family and friends, who have supported me and cheered me on during this whole process (even when they were feeling skeptical). I wouldn't have written this book without Chris Baty and his wonderful, crazy idea called NaNoWriMo. Thanks to all my beta readers and Facebook cheerleaders, whose encouragement was amazing. And a special thanks to my daughter Ryan, who is my sounding board and editor, and tells it like it is.

CHAPTER ONE

LISBON, PORTUGAL

SEPTEMBER 1683

"**F**ORGIVE ME, FATHER, FOR I have sinned."

The Jesuit had heard it a thousand times before, so many times, in fact, that he had a hard time focusing on the penitent in the booth. It hadn't been the normal day or time for confession, but he had seen the old man stagger into the chapel, and had assumed he was drunk. The city had built up around the old stone church, and the ale house across the way often spilled out its patrons onto the sacred grounds. The Jesuit didn't mind. What better place to sleep it off than the safety of St. Anthony's. The streets of Lisbon, especially so near the wharf, could be rough even when one had his faculties fully intact.

He watched the man as he went about his daily tasks of sweeping and checking the many candles, and saw with relief that he had collapsed with his back against the chancel wall, long legs sprawled out in front of him, chin to chest. His knobbled hand clutched the hilt of a long dagger, and his face—what could be seen around the wild spray of whiskers and wiry gray hair—was scarred.

Soldier, thought the Jesuit. He had seen many in his day, and heard many of their confessions. Many terrible things had been done in the name of God, and the men suffered long after their missions were complete.

Returning from the ash heap outside the rear door, the Jesuit saw that the man was gone. Surprised that he was able to get himself up, he put it out of his mind and continued trimming the tapers. In the silence a *thud* suddenly rang out. Looking around, he realized that he could see the man's boots under the curtain of the confessional. He hurried over, and took his place behind the screen.

"Forgive me, Father, for I have sinned," came the gravely voice. "It has been thirty years since my last confession. I have killed many men. I have lied..." He broke off, coughing. "I'm sorry Father. I have lied to protect a secret, and I am now the last one to know it. But I made an oath that the knowledge would not be lost, and now time has run away with me."

The Jesuit heard the man shift position in the small booth, and then saw a leather pouch pushed under the dividing wall to his side of the confessional.

"Father, I am entrusting this to you. There are men who would kill you for it. They have chased me and... and caused me great hurt. But they have never beaten me! I have never told my secret, until now. Now, you must carry it. You must protect it. This letter... This letter would change the world. We can't let that happen...We can't..."

The man fell into a fit of coughing, and, peering

through the screen between them, the Jesuit realized that blood was spewing from his mouth and cascading down his chin.

"My son! Let me help you!" The Jesuit made to open his curtain to go to the man's aid, when the soldier rose up and roughly wiped his chin with his sleeve.

"No! Father, listen to me! I am dying. I make my final confession to you, and ask my God to forgive me. But you must listen! You must keep this letter from them, at all costs. And you must find the Throne of Solomon. I have led them away—oh Father, I have led them a merry chase!" The man laughed weakly. "But you must find it, and protect it. No one else knows... I am the last." The man slumped back, and the urgency drained away as he began to fight for breath.

"I am the last. It is in Goa. They will find it if you don't go... Father, you must go."

Frantically the Jesuit tore back the curtains and knelt down next to the man. His skin was gray, and his lips were turning blue. Blood ran freely down his chin and onto his tattered green cloak, turning it black in a widening stain. The man gripped the Jesuit's hand fiercely, and spat out one final word, "Run!"

The Jesuit performed last rites on the man, and then asked a novitiate to help him carry the body to their living quarters. The man had definitely been a soldier. His body had more scars than healthy skin, but he had been tall and strong, even in old age. The cause of the blood became apparent as the novitiate stripped the body: he had a ragged stab wound in his chest. There was no smell of ale or wine about the man, and although his clothing was old and worn, it was of good quality. He had a leather purse full of silver cruzados. His dagger was of fine make and design, and he had an ornate silver eating knife in an inner pocket. In another pocket was a small leather-bound book, full of scribbled drawings and strange phrases.

"Father Eduardo..." The novitiate nervously interrupted the Jesuit's perusal of the body.

"Yes, Paulo, I'm sorry. It's not every day we have a man die in confession, now is it?"

"No Father. What would you like me to do now? Do we know who he was, or if he has any family in Lisbon?"

The Jesuit thought for a moment. "He said he was alone. That he was 'the last.' I think we shall bury him in the cemetery at Jeronimos Monastery, and add his remaining effects to our fund for the poor. He was a soldier... We shall give him a soldier's burial."

Astonished, Paulo nevertheless nodded his head in obedience. There were kings buried at the monastery. Vasco da Gama was buried there. Who was an unknown soldier compared to these men?

"Please wash the body carefully, and have Liza clean the poor man's clothes. We will redress him in those, and bury him with his weapons. I will go to the monastery now to arrange the burial, but I will conduct the mass here." Once again the novitiate nodded, and turned to his task.

Father Eduardo Borges Santos, the Jesuit, rushed back to the empty chapel and picked up the leather pouch the man had left on the floor of the confessional. Hiding it within his robes, he left the building.

CHAPTER TWO

PORT OF LISBON

MARCH 1684

T HE JESUIT HUDDLED BEHIND THE foremast of the merchant ship Sao Miguel, avoiding both the wind and the strange men he seemed to see everywhere in Lisbon since the death of the mysterious soldier the year before. He was wrapped up in a rough wool cassock, with a cape pulled closely around his head and ears. He had been told that the wind would die down by evening, which was several hours away. In exchange for being allowed on board a day early, he had been barred from the shared quarters he would occupy during the voyage. The captain had intimated that the crew would feel uncomfortable spending their last night at home in the company of a Jesuit, although was careful not to spell out the implied debauchery that would take place.

He had found a crate, which smelled strongly of chicken dung, and had stowed his belongings under it. He planned to sleep next to the crate, out of the cold as much as possible, rising with the dawn and the tide to see the ship leave his beloved city. He looked out over the tiled rooftops of the Seven Hills and tried to make sense out of the last few months. How was it possible that one man, a stranger, had so dismantled his life?

When the soldier died in his chapel, the Jesuit had felt that he was an important man, a warrior of the faith, who had led a hard but honorable life. He had done his best with the funeral mass and burial, although he had had to...embellish his knowledge of the man to get permission for his burial at the monastery. He had repented of his dishonesty, but he had never actually felt badly about it. He had always acted on his impulses about people, believing them to be special knowledge from God, and felt that, in most cases, his small embellishments to the strictest truth were justified.

After the burial, the Jesuit had taken leather pouch out of his small chest of personal belongings. It was the first time that he had looked at it since the grisly death, and his mind ran over the words of the intriguing man once again. *Run, Father!* Surely he was in the delusion of imminent death, suffering from his grievous wounds. Father Eduardo was a man of God... he didn't need to run from anyone.

Carefully opening the ancient leather, which was smooth and soft from much use, the Jesuit pulled out a roll of parchment wrapped in a soft kerchief of fine weave. The scroll was vellum, apparently excellent quality as it had no cracks or tears. It was obviously very old, and the writing was still sharp and clear. The priest couldn't read the text, but he recognized the language as Greek. He sat for awhile on his small bed, looking at the letter and pondering. Finally he wrapped it up in the soft cloth, and swung on his cloak.

———————⊰•⊱⊰⊱⊱⊱•⊰———————

"But can you translate it?" The Jesuit was sitting on a hard chair in the bright autumn sunshine, overlooking the Tagus River. His host was peering closely at the parchment, squinting and mumbling as he turned it to catch more of the sunlight.

"Patience, Eduardo, patience. Don't they teach you that in your Society of Jesus?" Doctor Balsemao didn't look up from the scroll. "Where did you say you got this? It is most remarkable!"

"The man who died during confession gave it to me. He said he was 'the last' and that he had vowed to pass it on so that the secret wouldn't be lost. It's probably nothing but the ramblings of a very sick man, *Doutor*. But he was very earnest, and it does seem that we should take a dying man's declarations very seriously, does it not?"

"It is not ramblings, my friend. It will take me some time to write it out properly, but it appears to be quite an old letter of some kind. And I think... yes, I do think that it is signed 'I, Paul' and some other words that I believe mean 'and Achalichus, who wrote this letter.'" Looking up, Balsemao saw the shocked look on the young priest's face. "Now, Eduardo, let us not jump to conclusions. Greek is a troubling language, and I may be wrong. Or it may be an accounting of the shop of Paul the baker. Give me some time..." He bent over the parchment once again, a deep crease showing between his brows. "Yes, some time. Come back in two weeks, and I will let you know what I can decipher."

The Jesuit sat for a few more moments, finishing the deep red wine that his father's oldest friend had offered him. Sighing, he rose and bowed his goodbye. Doctor Balsemao never looked up.

———◦○⬤○◦———

Two weeks later, the Jesuit was sitting in the same chair. Cold had arrived, and a brisk wind was blowing across the river. Leaves had deserted the trees on the surrounding hills, and the grey sky looked flat and heavy. He kept his hands tucked into the arms of the cloak, and the hood over his head. He would have preferred to sit inside by a warm fire, but Doctor Balsemao was agitated, and had preferred not to speak in the hearing of his family.

"I did not begin this translation with any suppositions. I am sure you can see that one could slant one's work towards a particular outcome, which of course we did not want. Whatever the letter says, it is best to know this clearly." He swung his arms as he paced around the small area of grass, blowing on his hands and rubbing his ears, but not suggesting they continue inside. "I must confess to you, Eduardo, that I am most chagrined by this letter. If it is real, if it is nothing more or less than what it says, it is a letter that has the power to do much damage to the world as we know it..."

The Jesuit took in a sharp breath. "That is what he said. That is what the man who died said... He said it would change the world. I cannot see how a letter could do such a thing!'

The doctor sat down across the small weathered oak table from the Jesuit. He looked at him, then looked out over the gray river. He didn't move for a very long time, but a sudden gust of wind stirred him. Without looking at the young man, he said, "The letter is from Paul of Tarsus. Our Saint Paul. It was written to the church in Jerusalem, dictated to his scribe Achalichus just before he was executed in Rome. Achalichus was to deliver the letter to Jerusalem himself. There is no indication, however, that this was accomplished. It is possible, of course, that the letter is a forgery... We can pray that the letter was a forgery." He trailed off, staring out over the river once again. A few raindrops fell.

"Come, let us go in before the fire. I will tell you what your letter says, and I will give it back to you. I will try never to think of this letter again, and I will pray that you will have God's wisdom on the matter."

The two men went inside quickly, as the freshening rain began to slant towards them. The housekeeper had kept the fire high in the small room the doctor used as his study, and the Jesuit stood in front of it, hands as close to the flames as he could manage. Balsemao went to a heavily ornate chest in the corner and returned with the pouch and several sheaves of paper. He handed the papers to the Jesuit, and took a seat in front of the fire. He didn't look at the priest as he read, just stared into the flames, lost in his own thoughts.

Paul, a bondservant of Jesus Christ, called to be an apostle by the will of God, to the church at Jerusalem: Grace and peace be to you from our Father, in the name of our Lord and Savior Jesus Christ.

9

I always thank God for you all, for your faithfulness to our Lord in the land of His birth. We know that God has called and blessed the nation of Israel since the time of our father Abraham, and that He will honor your faithfulness in this time of affliction. I have longed to return to you, and to share with you all that God Almighty has done among the Gentiles. Alas I know from the Spirit of our Lord that my journey is almost at an end, and that I shall be united with my Father before the year is finished.

I am very pleased with the news that reached me through my son and friend Timothy, that you have elected Peter to be the bishop of the church in Jerusalem, and that James, the brother of our Lord, has become the bishop of Alexandria. While the Jews rejected Jesus, there are many of us following the Way, and we know that is it written, "The Deliverer will come from Zion, he will banish ungodliness from Jacob; and this will be my covenant with them when I take away their sins." Israel will be saved, and it is right and fitting that she should be the center of our work to spread the gospel of good news to the world. Would that I could come!

We know that there are many upheavals going on throughout the world. We know that you are persecuted by the Jews for your faith in Jesus Christ, and by Gentiles for your faith in Abba Father. Through all things, the God of Abraham, Isaac and Jacob will be with you. As the church grows and spreads from Jerusalem throughout the entire world, may you continue to see His hand on our own people.

Timothy, my brother, greets you, as do Justus and Priscilla.

Achalichus, who wrote this letter, will deliver it to

you with all haste, so that you may know that I have longed to come to you, and am keeping you before our heavenly Father at all times.

Now to Him who is able to do all things, may you find strength beyond your earthly bodies, and may His strength increase as yours decreases. To the only wise God, glory and honor forever. Amen!

———✦———

The Jesuit stood very still, the temptation to throw the pages and the parchment into the fire very strong. He reread the letter, hands shaking. He looked at his friend, who was still staring into the flames.

Finally he spoke. "Peter was the bishop of the church. In Jerusalem."

The doctor nodded. "Yes, according to this letter."

"Not Rome. Jerusalem."

Another nod.

"But..." He stopped. He was again tempted to throw the letter into the fire. He could pretend he'd never seen it, never read it, never... But no. He had seen it. Somehow, against all odds, this letter had survived for 1600 years. It had been hidden by the dead man, and those before him, to protect the Church of Rome... Well, that's what he assumed. But someone else knew about it. Someone else wanted it. Someone had killed trying to get it. Or get it back?

"Eduardo." The Jesuit realized that Doctor Balsemao was speaking to him. "Eduardo, I must ask you to go now. I do not want this in my house any longer. There is still a Court of Inquisition here; Antonio Vieira is in Rome trying to end the *auto-da-fe'*, but they still have power. I cannot risk my family, my lands... Please, you must take your letter and go!"

Fumbling with his cloak, draped over the chair to dry in front of the fire, the Jesuit stuffed the handwritten pages from the doctor into his undershirt, pulled the drawstring tight on the leather pouch, and ran outside, oblivious now to the wind and rain.

When Father Eduardo returned to his small apartments at St. Anthony's, he tucked the pages away in his small chest and put all his energies into forgetting them. Unable to destroy them, and unable to forget them, he stumbled through the next several weeks in a haze of duty and cold. Winter had come to Lisbon, and with it the poor and destitute seeking help. He kept busy visiting parishioners and helping with the smallpox epidemic that cropped up over the Advent and Christmas seasons.

From time to time the letter would force its way into his thoughts, and he would just as forcibly push them back. He had no idea what to do with the information that Providence had put in his path, and was well aware of the dangers posed by the Inquisitors. The five year suspension ordered by Pope Innocent XI had led to a truce of sorts in the country, and very slim tendrils of trust had returned. But this... this was catastrophic. This letter produced by a complete stranger had the power to undermine the legitimacy of the entire Church. What would Rome do to stop such a thing from happening?

After the Christmas season had passed, the Jesuit

noticed that a stranger had begun attending mass. Lisbon had many travelers, traders and people from the Empire seeking a new life in the cosmopolitan city. But this man did not seem to be a trader. He had dark hair and fair skin, and he did not have the hands or sun baked skin of a sailor. He did not worship, but sat in the back of the chapel, hands folded in his lap, staring at Father Eduardo with a stoic expression.

The Jesuit spent the cold wet weeks of January and February in his small room, fire in the inadequate grate, working on a calligraphy copy of the New Testament for the Abbot at the Jeronimo Monastery. He had trained in such work in his youth, and still enjoyed spending the cold winter months creating the beautiful books. His mind was consumed with the detail, and he did indeed forget about the letter hidden away in his chest.

———⋯⋯———

On the first fine day of the year, he took a chunk of bread and cheese, and set out to walk the wharf and enjoy the warm noonday sun. Seagulls fought over rotting fish carcasses, and stray dogs and cats lolled about in the unexpected sunshine. The strong smells of a working wharf washed over him as he strolled along, enjoying the massive nau in for the winter, and the smaller fishing boats tied up to unload their early morning catch. Finding a stone wall on which to perch, he turned his face to the sun and closed his eyes, saying a silent prayer for his meal.

"Good afternoon, Father."

The voice startled him, and he turned towards it.

Standing before him was the man from the chapel, the man who had been attending mass. He had been coming so long now that the priest had stopped wondering about him. And yet here he was, standing in front of him at the wharf, far from St. Anthony's. His dark eyes were squinting against the bright sun, but he was standing very still and straight, hands clasped in front of him.

"Oh! Good afternoon. I'm sorry, I didn't see you there." He tried a smile, but he was feeling very uneasy.

"Father, I believe you knew a friend of mine. Sebastian de Gois?"

The priest thought a moment, "I'm sorry, no. Was he a member of our parish?"

The man stared at the Jesuit. "At the end. He died in your chapel. In your arms, I believe."

"That was his name? I didn't know it. Well, now we can properly mark his grave. I'm sorry about your friend."

At the mention of a grave, the man's intensity increased. "He was buried? Where?"

"Yes, of course. Ah! I assume you thought he would have been put in a pauper's grave, since we didn't know who he was? Luckily he had some coin with him, and he seemed to be a gentleman soldier from the little we spoke. I arranged for him to be buried at the Jeronimo Monastery..."

He trailed off as the man spun around and stalked up the street, away from the wharf. The Jesuit still felt very uneasy, and decided he would return to his cell and vouchsafe his belongings. Sebastian de Gois. *What trouble have you wrought upon me, Mestre de Gois?*

When he returned to his small room, he was relieved to see that it was undisturbed. Feeling foolish at his increasing anxiety, he gathered the leather pouch containing the vellum scroll, the translation given to him by Doctor Balsemao, and the small handwritten journal that he had found in the dead man's pocket, and hurried with them into the chapel. Constantly looking over his shoulder for the man at the wharf, he scuttled to and fro in the small building, trying to find a hiding place both large enough to contain all his secrets, and small enough to be inconspicuous.

Stopping in the middle of the sanctuary, he closed his eyes and breathed a silent prayer. Taking a deep breath, he opened his eyes, and looked around him, pushing aside his fear. There. The small side altar. He knew from having conducted services there that, behind that small altar, on the old stone floor, was a loose paving stone. He had never tried to move or repair it. Hurrying over, he got down on his knees and pushed on rear edge of the rock. It wobbled just a bit. Unable to get any purchase with his shaking fingers, the Jesuit leapt up and rushed into the sacristy. There he grabbed the knife with which he trimmed the candle wicks.

Working quickly, he pried up the loose stone. There was only a very small concavity beneath the stone, probably the result of water in some bygone age. Using his fingers and the knife, Father Eduardo quickly dug out enough earth to fit the pouch securely inside. He placed the papers and the journal in the leather pouch, cinched it, folded the top edge over to discourage dust, and put it carefully in the hole. He replaced the rock, and used his cloak to sweep the dirt that he could not scoop up into the corners. The rest he dumped outside the back door, wiping his hands clean on his cassock. His skin was damp with perspiration despite the cooling winter day, and he leaned against the wall, trying to dismiss his overactive imagination.

⁂

The next Sunday, the Jesuit noticed that the dark eyed man wasn't in the congregation during mass. Feeling relieved, he performed the service with a much lighter heart. After greeting the parishioners and partaking of the Sunday mid-day meal with a local solicitor and his family, he returned to his room with no thoughts other than finishing his book. He opened the door and uttered one word. "*Bosto.*"

His room, with its few possessions and minimally adequate furniture, had been hit by a cyclone. A cyclone with knives. His only other cassock was shredded, the pieces of black wool scattered about the room. His small bed, with the hay stuffed mattress, was ripped down the center and emptied of all but a few scraggles of straw. His rough wool coverlet was in tatters. The wooden bedstead, stool and work table were kindling. The ashes from the fire had been thrown out and onto the rest of the mess, and water from the small clay pitcher had been poured on top, making a sodden, smelly mess. And his book for the monastery, his beautiful book, on which he'd spent countless hours... Each page had been torn into small pieces, and the tooled leather cover slashed and ruined.

The Jesuit stood, frozen. He was a priest, not a man of violence. He had been brought up by quiet parents on a farm near Doctor Balsemoa. He had been fortunate to escape the tentacles of the Inquisition unscathed. He had not yet been born when Portugal regained its independence from Spain, so his country had been at peace during his lifetime. He had early decided on a monastic life. He did not understand the anger expressed in the wholesale destruction of his room, nor the mind behind it. He just knew evil when he saw it, and he turned and ran.

Looking out over the harbor, lit up with the dawn, Eduardo clutched the leather pouch in his inner pocket. He didn't know what it was about, but he knew that, unless he left Lisbon, the man with the dark eyes would find him, and would make him surrender what Sebastian de Gois had died protecting. He wasn't sure why, but he wasn't about to do that. He would protect the letter, yes, and the Church with it. But he would also find the man's treasure. The Throne of King Solomon.

CHAPTER THREE

LISBON

PRESENT DAY

THE TREE LINED STREET NEAR Se' Catedral de Lisboa was dark and quiet. Little traffic used the roads surrounding the ancient building once the few small bars and restaurants in the vicinity closed for the night. Residences were dark and still. The three men, clad in non-reflective black, slipped along under the trees, lost in shadow. They stopped at a small building on Rue das Pedras Negras, the leader making a downward swipe with his gloved hand and dropping to one knee.

From a small ground floor window, a blue light flickered once, twice, then died. The lead outside man returned the signal, and the three separated, two men disappearing around corners, and a third aiming a grapple hook at the tile rooftop of the house. Compressed air fired the hook with minimal sound, and, after ensuring the hook was secure, the man rappelled to the chimney pot on the roof. A small access door opened from the inside, and the man slipped in.

The two men silently descended the stairs, turning on head lamps. The building, built as the home of a moderately wealthy sea captain in 1562, had been transformed into to an ultra modern office space. Chic minimalist furniture lined the hallways, creating cozy meeting places. Bedrooms on the top two floors had been converted into generous offices, each with its own keypad for security. On the first floor, a gracious dark paneled room with elaborately carved doorway arches functioned as a reception area, while a large oak paneled dining room off the modern kitchen had been converted to a conference room.

The men bypassed all of this, including the valuable art showcased on every wall. Top of the line computers, stereo equipment, and expensive sculptures were equally ignored. The men approached a thick wooden door to the right of the modern Subzero refrigerator, and studied the keypad. The leader clicked a button on his smart phone and studied the screen for a moment. He looked at his partner, crossed himself, and put his finger to the pad. Carefully entering a 14 digit code, he pressed "Enter." Green light, and *click*. The man gave his partner a quick thumbs up and opened the door.

The stairway was illuminated with blue lights, casting a hazy glow on the dark stonework. At the bottom of the stairs the room opened out into a single large square, separated by banks of climate controlled vaults. The floor was criss-crossed by moving red laser tracks. Over each vault was a single fish eye camera. The men stopped on the top step and looked at their watches. The shorter of the two held up three fingers. The leader nodded.

In less than a minute, there was the sound of

equipment powering down, and the lasers disappeared. In another minute overhead fluorescent lights came on, and the blue lights dimmed. The green lights on the side of each fish eye lens switched to red. The men moved slowly into the room, cautiously testing out their inside information. If they'd missed just one system... After five quiet minutes, they went straight for a small vault set into the back wall.

Carefully the leader withdrew a black box from his coverall pocket. He opened it to reveal a man's index finger. His partner made a face and the leader smiled and shook his head. *Not real.* The finger, made of a silicone polymer and kept warm on a battery powered bed of foam, was perfect in every respect: fingernail, hairs, knuckle wrinkles. And, most importantly, fingerprints.

The leader consulted his smart phone, and crossed himself again, to the amusement of his partner. He wiped his upper lip with his shoulder, steadied his stance, and raised his own index finger to the keypad. He began his series of punches. Fourteen numbers. Star. Fourteen more numbers. Enter. This time there was a yellow light, and another touch pad illuminated. Quickly taking the warm finger from its box, the tall man pressed the fingerprints against the screen. The screen flashed red; the man removed the finger, and glanced over at his partner. Both held their breath. Green light. *Click.* The vault opened.

Inside the lighted vault was a black velvet box. Carefully withdrawing the box, the smaller man pulled the tab and opened it. All that was inside was a leather pouch, tied with a drawstring, and a small leather bound book. The man gently removed the pouch and opened it. He gave his leader a thumbs up—*got it.* Picking up the book he raised his eyebrows at the taller man. The leader gave a shrug. *Bring it.*

Handing the velvet box to his partner, the team leader took a thick plastic bag from his pocket. He slipped the two items inside, and carefully sealed the opening with the attached tape. A stainless steel box, the size of hardback book, came out of the cargo pocket on his leg, and the plastic bag with its precious contents was carefully stowed inside. With the unplanned addition of the book, the box barely closed. It had been specifically designed for the pouch, but the leader didn't want to leave the book behind. Anything important enough to keep with his intended target was definitely important enough to steal.

The men replaced the velvet box in the vault, and shut the door. The leader turned the handle on the door, and a wild claxon began to sound. Shock widened their eyes, and they looked at each other in stunned disbelief. After a moment of frozen silence, the team leader yelled, "Go!" He shoved his partner through the room and up the stairs, frantically trying to stow the box of stolen artifacts back in his cargo pocket while racing up the stairs.

All pretense of stealth gone, the two men crashed out of the kitchen door into the landscaped back yard. The two sentries had come running from their posts on the front corners of the building, and the four men began running across the lawn, northeast and away from the water. And their boat. As they leapt over the small fence that separated the property from the small side street, one of the men caught his foot on a finial and fell, his leg breaking with an audible *snap*. The leader stopped briefly, made the sign of the cross with his forefinger on the man's forehead, and hissed, "Go!" The three men resumed running, leaving the fallen man to his fate.

CHAPTER FOUR

LONDON, ENGLAND

PRESENT DAY

THE LONDON OFFICE OF XAVIER International Ltd sat in Kensington, not far from Hyde Park. The streets for miles around were fronted with Perpendicular and Tudor style homes, many on the bustling main streets converted into offices and exclusive stores, with the occasional take away in between. Encompassing an entire renovated home on Gloucester Road, the normally restful rooms of Xavier International were currently a hotbed of chaos. Pacing up and down and yelling in a mixture of English and Portuguese, Luis Xavier had the office staff cornered while he rampaged.

"The system was *invencivel!* They told me, they swore that no *gatuno* could beat that system without cutting off my thumbs! Even if they did cut off my thumbs, they couldn't use the system, because it reads the *calor corporal,* the body heat!" He turned to his cowering secretary. "You call those *bastardo!* You tell them to call me *instantaneamente!* NOW!" He slammed his office door.

Once inside his office, the calm quiet decor seemed to take the fiery edge off of his temper. Still livid and pacing, he stopped waving his hands in the air and stood in front of the large window facing Gloucester Road. Across the street little St. Stephens Church sat, exuding 150 years of serenity. He stared at it for several minutes, until his intercom came to life.

"Excuse me, sir? I have Mr. De Castro on the phone in Lisbon." The secretary said hesitantly.

Xavier snatched up the handset. "Emil? *O que aconteceu?*" What happened over there?

"*As minhas desculpas, Luis.*" My apologies. "We don't know yet what has happened. The system should have been unbeatable."

"Yes, so I was told when I agreed to pay the outrageous sum you charged me."

"Well, um, yes. It does appear that we have had an internal breach—on your end possibly, although there is a slim chance it was on ours—which allowed the thieves access to your codes, and to have knowledge of the system. You know that, of course. We have not yet determined how they breached the biometric component. And of course, they were unaware of the failsafe alarm upon the closing of the door. That last minute backup system did allow the *policia* to capture one of the thieves, as you also know."

"Yes, I know all that! What I want to know is who these people are, who in your organization sold our codes—and yes, Emil, it was your organization. I am the only one in this company to know the codes, and I can assure you that I didn't steal from myself! And I want to know where my artifacts have gone."

There was silence at the other end for a moment. De Castro cleared his throat. "So we are working with the local police, but the suspect who was injured has said nothing. He is not in the system, either in Portugal or on Interpol. Nothing else appears to have been stolen but the contents of the one vault..."

"That was the only vault that mattered! *Bosto!*" Xavier slammed down the phone receiver, but still gripped it hard enough to turn his knuckles white. Picking it up again, he punched in a number.

"Gideon? Please come to my office. Now."

———⋙✦⋘———

Gideon Quinn knocked lightly on the heavy mahogany door, and entered when he heard *"Chegar!"* from the other side. He had been not yet arrived at the office when all hell broke loose, and had only gotten snatches of information on his way up: "Mr. Xavier's gone mad!" "There was a break in at the Lisbon office..." "I don't know what was stolen, they say it was something from his private collection."

Oh boy, thought Gideon. *My day is about to get very interesting.* As head of security for the London and DC offices of Xavier International, Gideon suspected he was about to walk into a maelstrom. Lisbon, the original headquarters of the firm, and the only office not under his control, was contracted out to the leading security firm in Europe. The security system was absolutely top of the line, and he knew that Mr. Xavier had paid more for it than the known pieces of art he stored there were worth. Obviously there was something else there that justified the expense... He suspected he was about to find out what it was.

Xavier was still staring out the window at the small church across the street, his hands gripped tightly behind his back, his posture rigid. When he turned, Gideon stifled a quick gasp of surprise. His boss was always impeccably attired and groomed, his clothing expensively tailored and cared for, his Mediterranean skin clean shaven, his thick black hair expertly cut and styled. Now, however, his tie was loose and flipped over his shoulder. His jacket was tossed onto a coffee table, apparently over a cold cup of coffee. His hair was spiked up on one side from running his hand through it.

"Sir?" Gideon stood just inside the door.

With a wild gesture, Xavier waved Gideon to the leather sofa. "Sit. Sit. *Meu Deus!*" He started pacing again while Gideon sat down.

"I understand the Lisbon office has had a burglary?" Gideon felt off balance at Xavier's obvious distress. He had never seen this man, normally a powerful, confident presence in any room, come unglued. He wasn't sure what to make of it, and what, short of the murder of a loved one, could have caused it. "Was anyone injured?"

Xavier sat in the leather armchair as if his legs had been cut out from under him, energy sapped. "No. No one was there. The system failed, but *felizmente* no one was at the office. It was quite early this morning..." He rolled his head back and forth against the chair, the disbelief and anger all too visible.

"I have not yet spoken to the police detective. They called, of course, to report the break in, and they have one of the thieves in custody. Emil de Castro has been at the office, and has talked to the detective in charge. Only one vault was broken into..." He stopped, words temporarily failing him. "The system was supposed to work! *Droga!* The vault that was hit has a 28 number code. The code is random, and is changed every week. I know it, and the security firm's computer that generates it knows it, and no one else is supposed to be able to discover it." He sighed. "In addition, my fingerprint is required. In order to thwart someone trying to remove my finger, the scanner requires that the finger exert a calibrated amount of pressure, as well as my exact body temperature. There is, of course, a randomized laser nest throughout the vault room, as well as a live camera feed over each individual vault, with a fish eye lens that can capture 18" around each unit. Each vault has its own keypad and code. To even enter the basement, which was originally a root cellar and is made of thick stone, there is a keypad with a 14 digit code. The rest of the house has a standard but high end system of glass break sensors, motion detectors, and door and window sensors. *All* of that was breached. All of it. *Inconvievable.*"

Gideon just stared. It was obviously an inside job. If the only person in Xavier International who knew the codes was Luis Xavier, then de Castro had a breach. But that alone couldn't be what had caused this earthquake in his boss's demeanor.

"What was stolen, sir?"

"Something that has been in my family many generations. It is...secret. I do not know how anyone could have known what it was, or that it was there. But they must have. They must have."

"Yes sir, I would say that is the only conclusion,

since that was the only thing taken. Someone knew something—at least that there was one vault with especially valuable contents. With the additional security on that vault... Well, it would be a logical conclusion."

Xavier closed his eyes. "I am praying that it was an educated guess by someone connected to the security firm. The only people, besides myself, who know what that vault contained are my own family... My wife. My son." He rubbed his forehead. "That is all. That is all..."

———— ∽∘≪∅≫∘∾ ————

"So he wouldn't tell you what was stolen?" Rei Quinn asked her husband, looking at him over her cup of coffee. They were sitting at a table at the Serpentine Bar and Kitchen in Hyde Park, taking their lunch hour together.

"Not yet. He wants me to talk to Emil de Castro, and to the police detective. He's trying to find out if the thieves knew what they was taking, or if they were just running a gamble that it was something big. He knows he'll have to tell someone eventually, if he has any hope of getting it back..." He forked some beef pie into his mouth. "I've never seen him like that before, I can tell you. He was devastated."

"Bless his heart," Rei said. She, also, was an employee of Xavier International, although in her job as an art restorer, she rarely saw the big man. "I hope it's not his wife or his son. Isn't he at university? That would be unbearable. Have you talked to anyone yet? What do you think really happened?"

"I left messages all over Lisbon, but no one's called

me back. Luis and Emil are heavy hitters there, with their old families and their old money... I'm sure there's a lot going on at the moment. Obviously it was an inside job. Theoretically we could say a hacker, but I doubt it. The codes are randomly generated by a computer. The computer is not connected to any outside feed other than power. The code is encrypted automatically, downloaded to a thumb drive, sealed in courier package, and delivered to the London office weekly. Luis opens it on a small laptop kept for that sole purpose. It isn't connected to the internet or a phone line, either."

"So far so good," Rei said. "Very cloak and dagger."

Gideon nodded. "Yep, so hacking is out. At least hacking from an external site. But it's got to be an inside job at Tavernier Security—the rest of the system was too complex. There was another keypad with a 14 digit code. A randomized laser nest on the floor. Live camera feeds that suddenly died without tipping off anyone in the monitoring station. The entire building's security was compromised, and no one would have known except for the one thing that is not in the original plan: the alarm that sounds *after* the door is closed, if Luis' fingerprint is not scanned within 5 seconds of the lock engaging. That was added as an afterthought, and never put into the file or even on the invoice."

"Is that vault checked regularly?"

"No, that's the irony, at least as far as the thieves were concerned. If they'd gotten away from the building, it might have been months before anyone knew a theft had occurred. Maybe even longer. With all the security, and with the biometric component of the system, Luis only checks the contents when he's in Lisbon, has extra time, and remembers... Whatever's in there isn't something he uses or needs, that's for sure. It's one of those 'my father's father's father' kind of things. Probably Luis thought it was kind of stupid after so many years, but he wasn't going to be the one in that long line of Xaviers to drop the ball."

"There's another irony—it wasn't stolen until he put it in that super expensive vault... Gotta hate when that happens." Rei tossed her crumpled napkin onto her plate and pushed it away, smiling.

Gideon grimaced and nodded. "Seriously."

Gideon sat back in his chair, his feet up on his desk, the telephone to his ear. He didn't have a nice little church to look at. In fact, he didn't have a window at all, since his office was on the inside wall of the townhouse style building. "So he hasn't said anything?"

"No, *nada*. He prays." The Portuguese detective sounded disgusted.

"He prays?"

"*Certo*... He prays. And I think he is speaking Latin when he is praying. He does not eat. He sleeps, and he prays. That is all he does. He does not even look up when we talk to him. Just praying."

"And there is nothing on him in Interpol? Maybe he's American?" Gideon tossed a pen onto the desk and closed his eyes.

"No, he is not American. He is from Europe, somewhere. Italy maybe. Portugal. I don't know. Bad teeth. Americans never have bad teeth. And how many of you Americans pray in Latin?"

Gideon laughed. "True. So you have absolutely nothing, except that you know he was one of the men who broke into office."

"Yes, we know he was there. He was dressed all in black, and had many ah...*maquina*... equipments for stealing with him. They ran out the back and he fell on his face in the street after he fell over the fence. Broke his leg, but it is not a bad thing, and he does not seem to be in pain. But who can tell with all the praying!" There were rustling sounds in the phone. "He does have a tattoo on his arm, between his wrist and his elbow. It is letters, CA, in a kind of circle. We can find nothing on Interpol or any other police service about it—maybe it is his wife's initials and means nothing."

"Will you email me a copy of that? And his photo? Maybe he was around the London office, too... Can't hurt to ask."

"*Certemente.* I will call you if he says anything, or if we discover who he is. But I am not very hopeful, *signor.*"

Gideon hung up the phone. Nothing. A tattoo, and a penchant for praying in Latin. Those do not an ID make. Sighing, he hit the speaker button and dialed again. His ear hurt.

"*Alo.*" The voice on the other end was deep, and obviously agitated.

"Hello, Signor de Castro. It's Gideon Quinn from Xavier's in London. Any news?"

"No. Nothing. We have determined that it had to have been arranged by someone at one of our offices, most likely here in Lisbon. We conduct background and financial checks on all our employees, and update them annually, and we have no one who stands out.

No one with too much money or a new car. No one is acting strangely. No one's computer has been sanitized. We will have to check our employees' home equipment ah... discreetly, of course, but I do not have enough manpower to do that quickly and I am afraid we have a big risk of our perpetrator cleaning up after himself before we get to him."

"Wonderful."

"*Si.* It is a very big problem, very bad. It is bad for my old friend, *certamente*, and it is very bad for Tavernier Security. And *si*, for me. Also for me."

"Keep me posted. Sure would be good to catch the bastards now, before they disappear completely."

"*Vai fazer.* Will do. *Tchau.*"

They disconnected. Gideon sat staring at his ceiling for a few minutes. Once again he punched a button on the phone. There was a beep, followed by a woman's voice. "Yes, Mr. Quinn?"

"Is Mr. Xavier available, Cynthia?"

"One moment...Yes, he says he has ten minutes if you come now."

"Great, be right there!" Gideon swung his jacket off the back of his chair and slid into it as he left his office.

"Mr. Xavier... I'm not seeing a lot of action in Lisbon. I know I'm not technically in charge of security there, but I'd feel better if I was on the ground, seeing what happened first hand. And it would probably be best if I knew what was stolen..." Gideon looked his boss in the eye. He knew this wasn't going to be easy. It wasn't easy for him to ask. But he took his job seriously, and he could see the obvious distress in his employer. If he could get the thing back? Well, one step at a time. But he was hoping Xavier would let him try.

"I don't know. It has been a secret for so long... Since 1683. And in my family alone. It is bad enough that I have failed to keep it safe." Luis Xavier looked exhausted, with purple smudges under his eyes and a drawn pallor.

Gideon was sympathetic, but impatient. "If I don't know what it is—if no one knows what it is except you and your family—we can't possibly get it back. Your son is 20 and a student; I don't think he will be able to find it, do you? Or your wife?"

Xavier just stared at Gideon. *He's losing it,* Gideon thought. *He's almost broken.*

"Sir. I know this is a terrible shock to you, and you feel responsible. I want to help you, and I would like to try to get it back. But "smaller than a breadbox" is not a description that could possibly lead to a successful outcome. You have trusted me with your business for five years. I'm just asking you to trust me with this, and let me help. Please."

Xavier scrubbed his face with his hands, and when he looked up, Gideon knew he'd made the decision. "There is a leather pouch. Inside the pouch there is a scroll, which they told me is vellum. A very fine skin, probably of a young goat. A letter is written, in ancient Greek, on this scroll, and it is a letter from the Apostle Paul to the church in Jerusalem. It is... highly controversial. It has not been authenticated by any scholars, but my ancestor into whose hands it fell believed it to be real for a number of reasons. Not the least was that the man who gave it to him was murdered for it, and my ancestor was chased halfway around the world himself." He went over to a built-in bar and poured himself a tumbler of mineral water. He looked out at St. Stephens, his anchor in the storm, then turned back to Gideon.

"There is a translation of the letter in the pouch, but the pages on which that was written are crumbling. I do not handle those pages now, and only with special gloves. The translation is in Portuguese. Also there is a journal, an old leather bound volume written by my ancestor. That has been kept out of sentimental value, and I am worried that the thieves might destroy it. But the letter... *Deus nos ajude.* God help us."

CHAPTER FIVE

LISBON

PRESENT DAY

GIDEON LEFT THE POLICE STATION, discouraged. Detective Azenha was right—the thief wasn't talking. He hadn't talked in two days, and showed no signs of weakening resolve. He sat in his cell, still, and to all observers appeared to be in a trance. When moved to an interrogation room, he folded his hands on the table and muttered prayers in Latin. When given a tray of food, in any location, he ignored it completely. He sipped water from time to time, and performed basic bodily ablutions. That was the extent of his cooperation.

Azenha had emailed a photograph of the tattoo the man bore on his forearm, and it was, indeed, unusual. Gideon hadn't found anything online that was similar to it, and seeing it in person hadn't shed any light.

It could mean anything. His mother's initials. A gang or other society name. It wasn't in any known criminal database, and with no further information—even a nationality—they were unlikely to solve the case with it.

Additionally, de Castro had found nothing in the investigation of his employees. No one had quit coming to work. No one was acting suspiciously. They had so far covertly visited the homes of over half the staff that had access to even a small part of the security system information for the Xavier International office building, and had found nothing unusual. In short, they were no further today than they were yesterday, and Luis Xavier was, by turns, sinking in despair and rattling the windows in rage.

Gideon's cell phone rang. "Hello?"

"Hi, it's me," Rei said. "Listen, Mr. Xavier just called me to his office. I don't know what's up, but since he pulled me out of the preservation room, it's got to be about whatever was stolen, right? The letters and stuff are old—maybe he's worried about the thieves exposing it, or handling it? I don't know—what should I do? What do I say? I hardly know the guy, Gid... He runs the company, but he doesn't actually handle the art."

"See what he has to say. Try to get him to tell you what was so important about the letter, for one thing. All he said was it was supposedly written by Saint Paul. Maybe you can reassure him that the parchment and book are probably ok."

"Yeah, ok. He kinda scares me, especially now... I'll call ya back."

Gideon strolled down the street, looking at the GPS on his phone to figure out the route to get him to the Cathedral. He was lost in frustrated thought, pondering once again the implications of such a targeted attack on a particular vault. Was it the vault or the letter? That knowledge was key to recovering the stolen property—if he could ever find out what significance the stolen property actually had. Right now, there was just no way to know.

He had taken an informal tour of the Cathedral, admiring the windows and stonework. His heart wasn't in it, as much as he normally enjoyed these amazing architectural tributes. The more he thought about it, the more he became certain that the theft had to be about the specific items in the vault. It was too much of a risk otherwise, when there was so much valuable art so much more readily accessible. In the time they took to rob one safe, they could have stripped dozens of canvases from their supports, rolled them up, and been gone. There were hundreds of thousands of dollars in paintings and sculpture in the Lisbon office, not counting the pieces stored in the other basement vaults. The company bought, collected, restored, leased out and sold art to businesses and individuals all over the world. It just didn't make any sense that all the easy money was bypassed for whatever was behind an unknown curtain. Then again, all that preparation and money to steal a letter didn't seem to make much sense either.

His phone rang again, and he hurried towards the main doors of the Cathedral as he punched it on.

"Yeah?" He whispered.

"It's me—what are you doing?" Rei asked.

"Sorry, hang on..." He got outside to the front steps. "I was in the Cathedral. Go ahead."

"Ok, so he is one flipped out guy."

"Tell me something I don't know." Gideon couldn't help but smile. His wife was very even keeled. She could hold her own if needed, but she was more likely to kill you with sticky sweet Southern charm than snap your head clean off.

"OK... So there were a few things in the box. Three different time periods, I guess you'd say. The first was the letter. This is the only significant artifact, both from a historical and a monetary point of view."

"The letter from Paul to Jerusalem?"

"Right. Supposedly, if the translation done by the great great great whatever was accurate, the letter was written by Paul, to the church at Jerusalem. The letter says how pleased Paul is that Peter has been made the bishop of the church at Jerusalem, and further affirms that the church there, in Jerusalem, is the center of the faith." She paused for a response.

"Uhhhh... I don't think I get it." Gideon slowly strolled along the tree lined street away from the Cathedral, listening.

"You wouldn't, since we're not Catholic. OK, so short version is, the Catholic Church has always claimed that Peter was the first Pope, because Jesus called him the "rock" on which He was building His church. And Peter was traditionally thought to have been the bishop of the Church of *Rome*, the Roman Empire being the dominant world order of the day. The Church has gained tremendous wealth and power— the Vatican is a *country*, for heaven's sake!—by staking its legitimacy on the Peter heritage. So if Peter was actually the bishop of the church in Jerusalem, and if Paul confirms in his letter that the church in Jerusalem is the base for this new religion of The Way, or Christianity..."

"Then the Roman Catholic Church gets the stilts pulled out from under their beach house."

"Exactly."

"But would anyone really much care about that these days?"

"Well, that's hard to say. The Catholic Church still has a tremendous amount of wealth, and there are millions of Catholics throughout the world who worship not just the Trinity, but the Pope, and Mary and all those saints they have. But the main thing is, when the great great great grandpappy of Mr. Xavier got hold of this letter, the Portuguese Inquisition was still technically in effect, and it would have been considered the greatest heresy. The Pope had issued a five year cease-and-desist in Portugal, to try to regroup and see what was what with those Inquisitors and all, but the five year hiatus had expired, and the whole infrastructure was still intact. And not just in Portugal—in Spain, in India, in all of the Spanish and Portuguese colonial holdings. This was not a safe thing to possess."

"Why on earth did he keep it, I wonder?" Gideon was amazed. Most people, he thought, would have burned it or thrown it into the sea.

"Mr. Xavier says that grandpappy was a Jesuit priest. Yeah, I know your next question—apparently he quit the priesthood a few years after he got this letter. Anyway, he got it from a dying confession, and the guy who died was killed by someone trying to get the letter. To me, that would have been reason number one to get rid of it, but I guess it was an honor thing. Anyway, he had a family friend, a doctor that could read Greek, so that's who translated the letter onto the pages that are in the pouch with the scroll. Of course, the Jesuit didn't know what it said til then, and apparently *Signor Duotor* told him to get out and stay out after they read it. Not long after that the priest was chased out of Lisbon, but he took the letter and a journal the dying man had tucked away. Mr. Xavier says his family never had that journal, but the book that was stolen was the Jesuit's journal, of his trip, and his life in India, and his return to Portugal as a married businessman."

"Wow." Gideon was trying to think it though from the thieves' point of view. How could this letter possibly have any significance or value in the twenty-first century? Well, he wasn't Catholic, so what did he know. But it seemed such an unlikely theft, especially if he was right, and the letter was the intended target.

"Yeah, wow. And here's the good part..." She paused for effect. "He wants us to find it."

"Us? As in you and me?" Gideon stopped in the middle of the sidewalk, causing an elderly man to nearly bump into him.

"Yep. You because you are the studly ex-military security genius, and me because I have a smattering of Greek, that expensive PhD, and the preservation knowledge to take care of the artifacts when we find them. And because I can read Portuguese."

"What difference does it make if you can read it now? We don't have it!"

"Aha! That's the even better part. When Mr. Xavier paid for that fancy new vault and security system, he also had all the documents digitally copied. Every word, crease, crack, and bit of leather. And those digital files weren't in the vault—smart man there, anyway. They're here. In London. He's hoping we can read them, and maybe figure out who would take the originals, and where they'd go with them. His grandpappy was chased for this letter, and the other guy was killed... Someone's wanted it for an awful long time."

CHAPTER SIX

LONDON

PRESENT DAY

GIDEON AND REI WERE LEANING into a 30" screen, squinting at the scribbles and drawings shown there. Rei punched a key and the picture changed, but still looked much the same.

"Jeez, this guy wrote small...." Rei mumbled as she adjusted her glasses. "It's giving me a headache."

"At least you can read it. And what's this, Latin?" He pointed to a small area of writing, boxed in by calligraphic design.

"From what I can tell, he wrote out little prayers in Latin. This one here..." She went back to the previous page and pointed to a small rectangle in the corner. "*Deus succurro mihi.* God help me. Cheerful guy, this Father Eduardo."

"So what have we got so far? Anything? I feel like the thieves could be in Timbuktu right now, and we've got nothin'." Gideon flopped back in his chair and ran his hand through his short blonde hair.

"Well, Greek's not my best language, but from what

I can tell, the doctor translated it right. Those pages are probably dust by now, if they've been taken out of that pouch or bounced around, but the vellum was really well made and seems to be holding up pretty well. So we can assume that the bad guys now know what it says, if they didn't already. What I can't figure out, though, is why they wanted it."

"Maybe we'll read about some big discovery in the Telegraph tomorrow, and the Catholic Church will start cracking up." Gideon leaned forward again, putting his face right up to the screen, looking at a drawing on the page.

"Maybe... I'm wondering about this book, Gid. I can't be sure, but it looks like the Jesuit transferred a lot of what was in the little journal he found on the dead man into here, and somehow followed in his footsteps. There's stuff that doesn't make sense, and a lot of little notes and drawings that seem connected somehow... But honestly, I think he had found something."

"Found what? He had the letter all along. I thought that was the important thing here." Gideon rubbed his eyes. He wasn't even sure why he was trying so hard with the book—he couldn't read Portuguese or Latin, and the little drawings didn't make much sense either.

"OK, here's what it looks like. Now, I've only skimmed through it—we've only had it 12 hours, and I did sleep some in there. Father Eduardo leaves Lisbon in a panic, but thinks he's escaped whoever is chasing him. He's on this ship, the Sao Miguel, and he's following the spice route, so he goes down along the tip of Africa, and up to India. Lots of stops along the way, and he kind of becomes a missionary of sorts, finding local Catholics and having mass and stuff like that. But on the ship, he realizes that the dead guy's journal... I think that guy's name was Sebastian or something like that... Anyway, his journal seems to be leading to some kind of treasure, or at least something important."

"Wait, it's a *treasure map?*" Gideon stared at her in astonishment.

Rei nodded, her hazel eyes brimming with excitement. "Well... yeah. I think so. About halfway through this book—Father Eduardo's journal, I mean—he gets to Goa, India. Goa was basically the capital of the Portuguese Empire in Asia, so it was big and modern. A big Catholic presence there. But it was old, too, a lot older than the Europeans. The Ottomans—the Muslims—had been there, for one thing. Father Eduardo stayed there awhile, but he seemed to do a lot of what we'd call archeological research. And then there's a gap in the journal of about a year. And when he starts writing again, he's on a ship called the Santo Antonio de Tanna, heading back to Lisbon the way he came... Only now he's a business man, not a priest, and he's got a wife. He doesn't say it in here, but we know from Mr. Xavier that the priest changed his name from Eduardo Borges Santos to Joao Pastorinho Xavier. He got married, and had several children. He lived out his life as a wealthy trader in Lisbon, and started this company. No one in the family knows where he got the money—Jesuits took a vow of poverty, among other things. And this journal doesn't say. So... what did he find?"

"Could he have inherited money?"

"There's no indication of that. And why change his name?"

"Maybe he couldn't leave the order without, I don't know, making the Inquisitors mad?"

Rei shook her head. "This was the 1680's. There weren't internet registries and telephones. All he would have had to do was leave Goa and go anywhere he wanted that he'd never been before, and no one would have ever known a thing. I think he found something, Gid. And I think... well, I think he left clues to it on his voyage back. Which means... I think it means the treasure is still out there."

<hr />

Gideon and Rei stood in front of Luis Xavier, shifting a little uncomfortably in the silence as he stared at them with a blank face, black eyes intense.

"So what you are telling me is that, all this time, my family has thought it was protecting the Catholic Church, but what we were really doing was hiding away a map to a *tesouro?* A treasure?" His voice rose on his disbelief.

Rei nodded. "Yes, I think so." She explained what she had been able to glean from the journal so far. "I do think that the letter, certainly at the time Father Eduardo, or Joao Xavier, had it, was political dynamite, and it was certain that he had been chased halfway across the world and back for it. But I think it's possible—in fact, I think it's probable—that the bad guys of his day also suspected that the dead man knew about a treasure. And that he had, or at least might have, passed that information on with his dying confession. And I think your old ancestor found it, Mr. Xavier. I really do."

Xavier looked at Gideon. "Can you find it? Can you and your wife find this thing? And my letter... I want the letter back, too."

Husband and wife looked at each other and Rei shrugged. "We can try, sir. That's all I can say. The thieves have this information as well, and if they knew about the journal... well, I think they're going to be going after it too."

"They seemed pretty organized and well funded." Gideon said. "But maybe now we can pry a little information out of the man the police are holding, see if they knew what they were getting into. I'll pass the info on to Detective Azenha..."

"No!" Xavier interrupted. "I do not want anyone else to know what was taken, or about this crazy treasure talk. You will have to speak to the thief yourself." He started pacing the soft carpet, some color coming back to his olive skin. "You will have whatever you need to find my family's belongings. Whatever it takes. You talk only to me, and I will arrange it. It is... it is *mais importante*. Most important. I cannot fail my family. I cannot be the last."

CHAPTER SEVEN

LISBON

PRESENT DAY

GIDEON AND REI SAT IN an interrogation room alone with the captured thief. The man had experienced a drastic weight loss over the four days of his incarceration, but his concentration on his prayers hadn't waned. Nothing, in fact, had changed, and the police had given up interviewing him. He had been arraigned by a magistrate, and a solicitor had been appointed to him, but no one was optimistic about a change of heart.

The man sat, hands folded on the table, muttering in Latin. "Ave Maria, gratia plena, Dominus tecum... Benedicta tu in mulieribus, et benedictus fructus ventris tui, Iesus. Sancta Maria, Mater Dei, ora pro nobis peccatoribus, nunc et in hora mortis nostrae. Amen. Ave Maria, gratia plena..."

"It's the Hail Mary," said Rei.

"That prayer they do after confession? With the beads?"

"Basically, yeah. Signor?" Rei tried to get the man's

attention. "Signor, we know what you were stealing. We know about the letter from Paul."

The man stopped praying, but didn't look up. His hands clenched together tightly.

"We know the letter could be very bad for the Catholic Church. That people have been looking for it for a long time. And that maybe they are looking for something else, too..." Gideon let that hang.

The man looked up, his face showing emotion for the first time since his arrest. He started to speak, and then hung his head.

"We have a copy of the letter. A digital photograph that was taken a few years ago. The letter can still be released to the public... or not." Gideon casually sat back in his chair.

"No!" The man yelled and jumped to his feet, his face a study in anguish. "No! This is not possible. It is not... it is not possible." He sat back down, weak and distraught.

"You did not think Mr. Xavier would take advantage of modern technology to safeguard and study the letter? Things happen, buildings catch fire, there are thieves... His family has guarded the letter for many centuries. He would not like the letter to be lost forever." Gideon watched the man. His dark hair was dank and unwashed, and his skin was loose and sallow from his self imposed starvation. The bones of his face were prominent. His hands were shaking.

"That's why you took the letter? To keep the world from finding out? Or is to tell the world, to destroy the Church? The Xavier family has never released the letter; they've never even let scholars study in secret. It has been safe for over four hundred years..." Gideon let his words hang, trying to goad the man into a response. A full minute passed before the thief spoke again, softly.

"We are pledged to search for the letter. We have been searching for the letter for eight hundred years, when it was stolen from our monastery by those soldiers, those knights." He spat out the word.

"Knights?" asked Rei.

"Templars. Thieves. They were killed and disbanded everywhere else, but in Portugal the King wanted them to remain. They were *desonroso*. Dishonorable. They did bad work for the king, and they amassed much power and fortune in secret by stealing. They brought *humilar*, shame, to my order. We will regain our honor."

Gideon looked at him in amazement. "You're a monk?"

The man sat up proudly. "We are a religious order. We have been in existence many, many centuries, nearly since the time of Saint Peter and Saint Paul themselves." The man, now divulging his secrets, looked inordinately exhausted. "It is all lost if the letter is released…"

"Mr. Xavier doesn't want to release the letter. His family has never sought to release it. But he wants it back, and the book that was taken with it."

The man looked confused. "I know nothing of a book. Our team was briefed on the security of the building, but my *irmao* and I did not go inside the building. We were to stay on the outside and arrange the power and video lines. Our *abade* told us we were recovering what we had sought for so long. We all knew this to be the Achalichus letter."

"That's what he said, 'what you had sought for

so long?'"

"*Sim.* Why should he say more? We are committed to this quest through our vows. It is well known among the brothers."

Gideon looked at Rei, unsure whether to tell this man about the journal or not. He would be going to jail, a fate that he seemed to have no interest in fighting. Or he'd starve himself do death. But it certainly seemed that he would be both isolated from his "brothers" and compelled to silence.

"What's your name, signor?"

The man looked at Gideon, and then Rei. He seemed defeated, both by his confession of sorts, and the failure of his sect to contain the information in the letter. Apparently it had never occurred to those in the order that the letter would or could be copied.

"Petros. I am Brother Petros. That is all. We die to our former lives when we join the order. We are only the brothers." He rubbed his fingers lovingly over the tattoo on his forearm.

"What is the name of the order?" Gideon asked.

Petros shook his head. "No. I cannot say that. We cannot ever say that. No."

Gideon looked at Rei. It was worth a shot... She flashed him a small smile.

⊸•⊂⟐⊃•⊂

Rei had her laptop open on the small table in the internet cafe they'd found a block from the police station. Espresso cups were scattered around, and Gideon was finishing a tortilla. He wiped his mouth and looked at his wife. "Anything?"

"Well, maybe. I have skipped all the way to Father Eduardo's conversion to Joao Xavier. What it looks like to me is that he found something in or around Goa, and he was able to cash in for a lot of money. I'm guessing he didn't expose the whole treasure, whatever it was... He seemed to have enough money to be considered wealthy, and to cover his new identity as a trader. But he didn't have fabulous wealth."

"The Xaviers have pretty fabulous wealth now," Gideon said.

"Yes, but by all accounts they've earned it. Father Eduardo may have been a poor Jesuit, but Joao Xavier had a mind for business. He started out in the spice trade, of course, and was able to purchase an entire shipload of merchandise to transport back to Lisbon with him when he returned. He came back and made a huge profit, and invested more in shipping. He didn't travel again himself, but he built up clientele, hired a manager, and expanded into wood products from Africa, silks from Asia, ivory, gemstones...Whatever he could sell."

"Slaves?" Gideon asked.

"No, it doesn't appear he ever sold slaves. I'm sure Mr. Xavier is glad about that, anyway." Rei reworked her unruly hair into a messy bun. "So the bottom line is, he had enough money to get started, but he did pretty well for himself after that. And had smart kids, apparently. So the question is, what did he find, and did he leave a way for anyone else to find it?"

"That's definitely the question... I think we have to assume that Brother Petros' order, or at least his abbot, is aware that there is more to this than the letter. I guess I can understand single minded obsession, but it's hard to believe that a secret order has been hunting for this letter, which, for all intents and purposes, had disappeared and posed no threat. Not for eight hundred years... That just doesn't make sense to me. These guys are like a cult, separated from their families and friends, single mindedly focused on this quest of theirs. The letter... it just doesn't feel like enough to motivate the people paying the bills." Gideon had a headache from all the possible permutations.

"Yeah, I agree. Someone knows there's a treasure. Someone has known all these years, since the Templars stole the letter. One of them must have said something to someone, or maybe bragged about it. Or maybe they just knew enough about the Templars to know there was probably treasure hidden somewhere. Who knows—people are always looking for the Templars' hidden treasure. But if we've managed to figured it out, they certainly have by no... We just have to beat them to it." Rei grinned.

Gideon smiled back at her. "They don't have you, the puzzle solver extraordinaire. And even better, they don't know we have a copy of everything."

"I think the latter is better for us than my puzzle solving prowess... So I'd better get on it!" She went back to the laptop, scrolling through the pages of the journal once again.

"Gid! I've got something!" Rei was yelling from the suite's living room to the bedroom. It was 2:00 am.

Gideon came out of the dark room in his boxers, hair spiked and eyes screwed up against the light. He staggered to the sofa. "What?"

Rei was hyper, a combination of copious amounts of coffee and the thrill of discovery. "OK, so I realized I had to start backwards. Father Eduardo found the treasure in Goa somewhere, but then he left Goa and came back to Lisbon. It looks like his route was exactly the same on the return as it had been going, only in reverse. The only place he writes about extensively is Cape Town, and he says he stopped there on both trips. See here?" She pointed to the journal page on the screen, "He says, 'The Cape of Good Hope has, indeed, given me hope that, beginning, our sons shall be blessed.' The beginning... It must be where the first clue is."

Still looking sleepy, Gideon nodded. "I'm with you so far."

"Right. Now, the Templars would have traveled an overland route to India—no one sailed around the tip until Vasco da Gama in the fifteen hundreds. But Father Eduardo was going by sea, and he knew his sons would go by sea because of the business he'd started. So we can assume that he left clues along the spice route, in the places he stopped on the ships. He wanted someone to find the treasure—he'd had to leave it in Goa for whatever reason, but he wouldn't have wanted it lost. Especially if it had some kind of religious significance. And I think he was still being watched, if not chased."

"Why? Wouldn't he have lost them with all that travel and changing his name and all?"

"Well, there are numerous mentions in the second half of the journal about seeing strange men, men who reminded him of the first one that had chased him from Portugal. He seems to elude them at times, but they always seem to be able to find him again, so they had some kind of funding that allowed them to travel, and to send spies, and communicate. Everything was much slower then, of course, but business was being conducted all over the Portuguese Empire and there were many ships and overland convoys traveling these routes all the time."

"Hang on a sec..." Gideon went over to the small coffee pot and got coffee brewing. "We know he was writing the clues for his future children, who he would have assumed would live in Portugal, so the clues would follow the shipping route that existed in his day. Africa, the Arabian Peninsula, and on to the capital in Goa, right?"

Rei nodded. She pointed to a map of the world displayed on her computer screen, and slid her pen from Portugal, down the west coast of Africa, to the very tip. She opened another window, and a satellite view of southernmost Africa appeared. She tapped her pen against the lowest point of land in the image. "There. Cape Town. Whatever he left, if it's still in existence, is there. Somewhere."

Excited, Gideon leaned over her and zoomed in on the Cape. "So where is it?"

Rei sighed. "I have no idea."

CHAPTER EIGHT

MALTA

AD 96

THE FAMILY HAD BEEN IN mourning for two weeks. The body had been washed, treated with herbs, wrapped in yards of white cloth, and laid in the tomb carved from the sandy rock. Achalichus' brother had put all of the dead man's belongings into a basket, and laid it aside for his children. There wasn't much, as Achalichus had been chased out of his homeland by the Romans, who were persecuting the followers of the new religion, most often called simply 'The Way.'

Eliyas sat on a simple wooden stool, and looked out onto the beach where his sons and grandsons were making a fishing boat. Shipbuilding, fishing, carpentry... These were good respectable professions for a Jew to follow. Following that Pharisee, Paul, around, being a scribe. Well, that was crazy. Achalichus had never been able to return to Israel, and had spent the remainder of his long life here on Malta, praying and teaching and converting people to his Jesus, until he lost even his memory and sat staring out to sea.

Eliyas shook his head.

Ah, but he was a good man, even if misguided. Perhaps God had welcomed him, perhaps not. It was not for Eliyas to say. He had missed his brother for many years, long before his physical body had died. He could feel nothing now but relief for his poor soul, which had been trapped for so long. He didn't know if all the controversial talk about bodies rising from the dead was true. He didn't spare much time for such thoughts. But he knew that his brother was free now, and that made him glad.

He had sent a letter to his eldest nephew with the news of his father's death. Residing in Sicilia, Antonius should arrive soon on a ship to reclaim his father's possessions. He had not seen Antonius since he was a boy, and now the man was a father, a fisherman, a husband. He was a follower of that Jesus, who some said was the Messiah, too. Bah... How can a Messiah die? He shook his head again. Ridiculous.

———————⊰•⊱———————

Three days later Antonius arrived at his uncle's home. He was welcomed with open arms by all of his family who resided in Malta, and spent a week being feasted and catching up with all of the births and deaths, triumphs and tragedies. Finally his uncle seemed to remember why he had come, and presented him with a large basket.

"These belonged to your father, to my brother. It is all he had, in the end. He gave up everything when he decided to travel with that Paul fellow, and he never seemed to have the heart to start again when Paul died and the Romans destroyed the Temple."

Antonius took the basket gratefully. He hadn't seen his father in many years, since before he had fallen ill. He remembered a man of joy, a hearty man with stories to tell and whose whole hearted belief in Yeshua had converted his children and much of their village. He had nothing of his father's, and was very thankful that his uncle had preserved these few possessions for him.

Much of the basket contained threadbare clothing, along with one pair of sandals. There were the tools of his trade as a scribe, the quill and wood pens wrapped carefully in a soft leather pouch, and tied with a leather strap. Several scrolls were nestled in a wooden box. Antonius removed them and started to read.

The first was a letter Achalichus had started to write to his wife, Antonius' mother, who was in Israel, still in their village. While he was writing the letter, it appeared that he received word that she had died, and the letter changed from a missive about his journeys with Paul to a sad and bittersweet goodbye to his beloved. He had not seen her in four years, but he still held love in his heart, and it brought tears to Antonius' eyes to read the heartfelt goodbye. Neither Antonius nor Achalichus knew if she had accepted Yeshua as the Messiah... and that familiar ache returned as he read the letter.

The second was an inventory of sorts, listing what supplies had been purchased, and for what cost, for one of the missionary journeys. He didn't see a reason his father had saved this scroll, other than as a reminder of those heady days of joys and persecution with Paul and Barnabas and Timothy. He smiled to think of them, traveling and making converts wherever they went. It must have been an amazing time.

He wondered at the third letter, as it was dictated by Paul himself, to the Church in Jerusalem. Apparently it had never been delivered, a victim of the persecutions no doubt. Written in Paul's clear voice, it was merely a congratulations on the appointment of Peter as their bishop. It was unfortunate that the letter had not arrived to encourage the people, as they were always sorely in need.

He rolled the scroll back up and opened the last one in the box, which was a sad reminder of the mental deterioration his father had undergone. It was written in the handwriting of a child, random words and symbols, with no meaning whatsoever.

Keeping the other three scrolls in the box, Antonius threw the last one in the fire. That was not how he wanted to remember his father, and not how he wanted his children to know him. He packed the basket back up, hefted it to his shoulder, and went out to the courtyard to join his cousins as they worked on their boat. He set it near the door, and put his cloak on it. Soon he would go home to Sicilia, but for now, he would enjoy his family.

ROME

AD 264

Camillus burst into the bishop's apartments, sweating and out of breath. He had walked as swiftly as he was able through the market crowd, fearing the dreadful temper of the man who was second only to the new Pope. In fact, the mood of Bishop Iraneaus had been made considerably worse by the election of Dionysius as the Bishop of Rome three months before. A man of power and grasping aspiration, Iraneaus had coveted the appointment for himself. After, that is, Emperor Valerian had been executed and the new emperor, Gallienus, had issued his "edict of tolerance." Increasing Rome's treasury was probably the motive for such permissiveness rather than religious generosity, but it had ended the persecution nonetheless.

"You are late," Iraneaus said, looking at the priest down his patrician nose. Camillus bowed and nodded his apology.

"Yes, your grace. I apologize." He kept his eyes focused on a cracked marble tile at his feet. A full minute passed, and the young man could feel the bishop's eyes on him.

"And have you no reason for this?" Iraneaus finally asked impatiently.

"It was a personal matter, sir. My brother had need of me, and his home is some distance from the city. It will not happen again."

"Indeed," Iraneaus said as he raised a goblet of wine to his lips. He tidied his already obsessively neat writing desk, putting a quill and parchment to the side. "We have much to do today, and now less time to accomplish it. Dionysius has thus far been unable to unite the bishops, and the Church remains in disarray, as you know." Camillus nodded his head at this oft-heard complaint. "Had I been elected, of course, I would have imposed much stricter discipline on the churches, and a great deal of the money that has been given by our patrons would have made its way here, to Rome. As it stands now, however, Dionysius has perpetuated his dictum of austerity, and is losing ground to the growing Church in the East. This is not acceptable." He slammed his fist down. Camillus did not start. He was used to such outbursts. "Power must remain here, in Rome, as God Himself intended. We must send a letter to those bishops who chose to elect Dionysius and inform them of his folly. He will be made to step down."

Camillus merely stood, hands clasped in front of him, his mind racing back to the visit with his brother.

———⊸∘⟨⟩∘⊶———

Anthony lived on a small estate outside of Rome. He had survived persecution by keeping his faith largely to himself, a sore point between the brothers. However, when Camillus received the letter of invitation, he had welcomed removing himself from the teeming city, and left in the mid-afternoon so as to arrive for supper. When they had finished an excellent—and, to Camillus, decadent—meal of hen with fresh baked bread and ripe grapes, Anthony sat back and wiped his knife on his trousers. He looked at his younger brother, the priest, and smiled gravely.

"Things have changed for your Church now, brother," he said.

"Indeed, but for the better, it appears," Camillus said. "Dionysius is trying to reignite enthusiasm for the Church now that the Emperor has granted us all clemency. He is a man unused to power, but he is respected by most."

"I suspect that he is not respected by those bishops who have used their position to gain wealth, to have children, even estates...?" Anthony ended on a question. Camillus looked embarrassed, knowing he was speaking of Iraneaus, among others.

"No, he is not popular with some," he agreed.

"And those who are wealthy are now powerful, and have garnered powerful friends." Anthony stated flatly. "You might find yourself on the losing side, my brother."

Camillus nodded unhappily. "I fear so, but I am not free to go where I choose."

"If you could help Dionysius, you could."

"What help could I be to him? I am a priest, that is all."

Anthony studied him for a long moment, then rose to his feet. He gestured for his brother to remain at the table, and left the room. Returning with a stout wooden box, he placed it in front of Camillus. "Open it," he said.

Obediently, the priest opened the box, and looked at the scroll nestled on a swath of fine cloth. He looked askance at his brother, who nodded. Camillus removed the scroll and carefully opened it. He knit his brows in concentration as he worked out the Greek. "Meu Deus..." he breathed, looking again at Anthony. "Where did this come from?"

"It has been in the family. The scribe was our ancestor, and when he died, his belongings were given to his son, in Sicilia. No one thought it important then, and indeed, it wasn't. But now... As the Church tries to regain its strength and power, it would be quite a blow, would it not?"

"It would destroy us," Camillus agreed.

"What would happen if you took that letter to Dionysius, and gave it to him to use against those bishops like Iraneaus who would seek to unseat him?"

Camillus looked confused. "I don't understand," he said.

"That letter would destroy the Church of Rome. Without the Church of Rome, those bishops who have no family wealth of their own would be left with no money, no power. They are doing things they have no right to do, they are a disgrace. And they are greedy. Dionysius, however, is truly a man of faith. He wants to spread our religion around the world as Christ commanded, through the Church. But I believe he would follow the Great Commission should the Church cease to exist. If Dionysius made this letter known to those who oppose him, and if he threatens to make the letter public should they continue to oppose him... Well, those men know that he serves God first, and the Church second. It is why they oppose him so strongly. I think they will have to support him, albeit through gritted teeth."

Camillus pondered. His brother was ten years older, and had amassed wealth against all odds by buying and selling goods brought to Rome from the far reaches of the Empire. He had friends in the upper echelons of Roman society, and consequently a much better understanding of politics than the young priest had. And if there was one thing that Camillus had learned during his time under the thumb of Bishop Iraneus, it was that the Church was rife with politics.

"If it doesn't work, you have lost nothing," Anthony said. "But I believe it will. I believe this letter has come down to us from Paul himself for just such a time."

Camillus nodded, and rolled up the scroll. "I will seek a meeting with Dionysius when I return. We can but try." Anthony smiled, satisfied, and poured them both more of the rich red wine that had been made from his own vineyard.

--------⊃°⊂∕∞⊃°⊂--------

It took five weeks for Camillus to attain an audience with the Bishop of Rome, and he spent the entire night prior to the designated time praying in his rooms. Dionysius received him graciously, one man of the cloth to the other, and the younger man relaxed at once. After the opening pleasantries, he came straight to the point, and handed the scroll to the bishop. With raised eyebrows, Dionysius opened the letter and read. When he was finished he looked up in dismay.

"And what do you propose to do with this letter, young man? Have you come to threaten me?" He sounded disappointed more than angry, and Camillus put his hands up defensively.

"No, sir! No! Let me explain," he said, and went on to lay out all that Anthony had said to him, including his own role as the secretary to Iraneaus. When he had finished, he clasped his hands tightly in front of him and said, "If you choose to do nothing with the letter, I will return it to my brother and say nothing. I have no desire to hurt the Church, nor you, your grace. It is to protect her that I have come to you with this."

Dionysius sat in a chair at his desk, deep in thought. "Please leave this with me. I will pray and reach a decision within a fortnight. I only ask that you fast and pray until you hear from me, that I might do the Lord's will in this matter." He nodded gravely at Camillus, who bowed and quickly left the room.

When Camillus next appeared before the Bishop of Rome, he felt like a condemned man facing the scourge. He had been fasting and praying diligently for two months, having had no word from Dionysius in that time, and was quite sure that he would be punished for stirring up a hornet's nest. The time had not been all bad, as Iraneaus had left, alone, for what he deemed "a necessary tour of the outlying regions". In other words, he had gone to shore up support for his upcoming effort to depose the Pope.

Dionysius was sitting at a small table in his simply appointed office. He had a meal spread out before him, and a place was set opposite. He waved Camillus to sit.

"Good morning, young man. I trust you are well?" Dionysius said with a small smile.

Detecting no anger in the man, Camillus nodded. "Yes, sir, thank you. And you?"

Dionysius smiled wider. "I am quite well, thanks to you." At Camillus' confusion, he continued, "Two weeks ago, I sent an invitation to Bishop Iraneaus and his supporters to gather here for a meeting. At that meeting, I read to them your letter…" He watched Camillus closely. The priest leaned forward in his chair. He had not seen Iraneaus for over a month, and had not heard a whisper of gossip about this gathering. Dionysius smiled.

"I presented the facts, as you presented them to

me, and I made it known that I would make the letter public should they continue to undermine both the Church, and my duly appointed election to this office. I speculated that, should that happen, of course they would continue to be the fine Christian men that they are, but perhaps their... influence would wane. Perhaps, in fact, they would be forced to return to families where they had no inheritance or wealth. Made to support the children they have produced on, let us say, a farmer's income. Of course, those children would be helpful in their fields and vineyards..." Dionysius stood up and clapped Camillus on the shoulder.

"I think we will find that, when Bishop Iraneaus returns to Rome, he will be working much more diligently to further the Church, and perhaps somewhat less diligently to further himself. After all, I am not a young man, and he is the next in line, should the other bishops choose to elect him after I am gone. I think he will bide his time, and amass more wealth, until then. And in the meanwhile, we shall continue to pray that a true believer is appointed to follow me when the time comes." He poured wine for both of them, and raised his glass. "I thank you, my son, for what you have done for the Church, for Rome, and for Almighty God." He drank deeply, with satisfaction, and set the cup on the table.

"Now, I am entrusting the letter back to you. Iraneaus will try to find and destroy it, of course, so we shall have to make that impossible. I would like for you to select a few young men such as yourself, and it will be your main duty to vouchsafe the letter, and thus the Church. You will be transferred from Iraneaus, of course. You will keep me abreast of your activities…?" he asked. Camillus, in shock at the turn his life had suddenly taken, merely nodded. "Good. Then we shall move forward." He raised his cup again. "To the Church," he said, and drank deeply.

CHAPTER NINE

GOA INDIA

JUNE 1687

J OAO XAVIER HURRIED DOWN THE narrow alley, keeping his dark cloak pulled around him, and his hat low. He had not been Father Eduardo for almost two years, but he was still not used to the fine clothes, the breeches and soft shirt, the wool cloak that didn't feel scratchy against his skin. What he was used to by now were the strange dark eyed men who always showed up, no matter where he was or how long it had been since he'd seen them last. Other than the one who had confronted him all that time ago on the Lisbon waterfront, he had never spoken to them. His rooms had been searched several times, in several locales, but it had never again been destroyed as it had been in his little cell at the chapel.

Looking back, that had been a blessing, he thought. Without that fear, he wouldn't have fled Portugal so quickly. He had never been on a ship until that fateful day, and he had rarely been out of Lisbon. Now he was a merchant trader, ready to travel the known world.

He was no longer a priest. He was, in fact, no longer himself... He hadn't found it difficult to leave Father Eduardo behind, in point of fact. He found that there was much more to the world than he had known, and that he was able to see the God he had worshipped all of his life everywhere he went. He didn't miss his order, and he was vaguely ashamed to admit that he most certainly didn't miss his vows of poverty and chastity.

His face flushed as he thought about his vows. Unless he was terribly foolish, he would never again be poor. Sebastian de Gois had given him an incredible gift, even if that gift came with what he saw as a curse. The letter. He tried, always, to ignore the letter. Even now, he was a devout Catholic, and he knew the danger of the letter. Yet he couldn't bring himself to destroy something written by the greatest apostle of all, Saint Paul. So he kept the letter, and the dangerous translation, in its leather pouch. He had had an ornate wooden chest made in Goa by a local craftsman. The chest had a false bottom, but it was perfectly weighted and proportioned, and completely invisible unless you knew the secret. The pouch had been in there, undisturbed, for a year now. Out of sight, if not always out of mind.

Chastity, though. That had also been resolved when he had taken a wife. Isabel Medrado was the daughter of a Portuguese magistrate who had lived in Goa for ten years. Her mother had died shortly after arriving, and she had become indispensable to her father. Joao had met her at a garden party hosted by a fellow trader, and the two had instantly been attracted to each other. This was a new experience for Joao, who, at that time, was mere months from having been a

Jesuit priest, and who had never been in the company of a woman alone. Isabel was funny and smart, and, as most women were in the colonies, a strong and confident woman. And she had decided, quite quickly, that becoming the wife of Joao Xavier was very much to her liking.

There had been some moments of discomfort during their courtship, as her father was from a large and well known Lisbon family. It was difficult to come up with a credible reason why he did not know them— the traders all knew each other, and attended the Cathedral together, their children intermarrying. After a moment of panic, Joao had concocted a childhood in the country, attending to an ailing grandmother on an estate. With his obviously healthy purse and his ease with people, the Medrado family had been happy to take him on face value.

After six months, Joao asked Signor Medrado for permission to marry Isabel. The match was approved, and they were wed this past March. Their wedding night was terrifying, exhilarating, shocking, and a joy beyond measure. Father Eduardo hadn't known such passion existed; he felt more blessed by God than at any time in his life.

Lost in thought, Joao almost missed the doorway. He quickly turned and entered, stopping just inside the door. The oil lanterns were lit, making the corners lost in shadow, but illuminating the large bearded man sitting at the rough table in the center.

"Ah, Signor Xavier. I began to think you were not coming."

"*Perdao, Senhor.* I was detained by my wife's excellent cooking." The man laughed, picking up his pewter goblet and bringing it forward as a toast.

"To all women, may God bless them for their many attributes!" He drank deeply. "So what can I do for you this time, *senhor*?"

"I am ready to return to Lisbon. I have found an *operador local*, a local tribesman, who can supply me with cargo. I need a ship, however, that will make the ports that I desire. I have promised to show my new wife the way that I traveled here, as she was but a lass when she arrived herself. I spent much time in several of the ports, and would like a ship that was rather more at my disposal than at the mercy of another's schedule."

"But you do not wish to purchase a nau?"

Joao laughed. "I am a fortunate man, *senhor*, but not that fortunate! I would like to... *contraer*... contract a ship and its crew. I will fill the hold with my own cargo, and pay the wages and provisions for the journey to Portugal. My only requirement is comfortable accommodation for myself and my wife, and that we make port in several posts that I wish to visit once again. Beyond that, I will make no demands on the captain or his crew, and I will pay a generous bonus should we arrive in Lisbon safe and sound, with our cargo intact."

The large man thought for a time. "I believe I know such a man. He is the captain of the Santo Antonio de Tanna, and he also happens to own a share of that ship. If he is able to make such an agreement on his own, I think that he will be willing."

"Is the ship here now, in Goa?" Joao asked.

"She is not here yet, but she is expected any day. I will speak with him when she has returned, and ask him what you want to know. Fortunately for you, I can vouchsafe your ability to pay him for this undertaking." He stared pointedly at Joao. This man had found buyers for the artifacts Joao had sold over the course of the first year, and he knew him as Father Eduardo, as well as Joao Xavier.

Joao smiled. "Yes, I can pay." He bowed. "We remain at the magistrate's estate, living in the small quarters beyond the orchard in the back. You may send word after you have spoken with this captain. Of course there will be a *comision* for you, and a bonus if you can convince *Senhor capitao* to leave as soon as his crew has been rested and the ship made ready."

Toasting again, the man took a long draught. "If it can be done, I shall do it. Make ready your voyage, Father. And God speed."

<hr/>

Six weeks later, Joao and Isabel stood on the foredeck of the huge nau, the Santo Antonio de Tanna, and watched Goa fade into the horizon. Isabel was a little teary, as she knew it was unlikely that she would see her family again. But the clear blue sky, the vast expanse of sea before them, and her husband at her side all served to soothe her spirit. She hadn't been outside of Goa since her arrival eleven years before, and Joao had told her so many fabulous tales of the ports in which they would stay that she felt like a young child again.

She turned to him. "I am so happy to be here with you! And to see all those places you have told me about... Shall we explore as you did when you were there before? Are there friends that we will visit?"

Joao smiled. There would be no visiting friends— he had been Father Eduardo when he had spent time at the outposts before. He was hoping, rather, that no one would recognize him, especially when they attended mass.

"*Sim*, my dear. We will explore many amazing things. I do not know if we shall see any friends—I did not spend much time in society, as I was so taken with the wonderful surroundings. We shall see, though, and maybe we shall make new friends." He squeezed her hand. *Yes, we will do much exploring...*

The Santa Antonio de Tanna entered the Persian Gulf on a warm breeze. Having watched the strange scenery on either side for some time, Isabel turned to her husband. "It is a very dry country, is it not? It is strange to see all this water, and yet much that is brown."

"Yes, it is a desert country, except very near the rivers. We shall travel up one of the rivers to visit Ctesiphon. It was a very great kingdom, before the Romans and the Arabs came. They were Persians. It is said that the Garden of Eden was near these lands."

Isabel looked around in amazement. There was nothing in view that would lead one to suspect God's perfect garden had flourished here. "How shall we get there, Joao? Will we take the ship?"

He smiled. "No, but we shall be on a small boat for some of the return journey, back down the river. We will have to ride on *camelo*. Camels."

"Camels!" She gasped. *"Meu Deus!"*

Joao laughed. *"Sim,* camels. It will be an adventure for you, my dear. It is very much like being on this ship, actually."

Isabel made a face at him, and turned back to the view in front of them. The small port town of Umm Qasr was getting larger as the big ship navigated the channel. The port had been friendly to Portugal from time to time over the last few decades, but the Ottomans were making themselves known about the whole region, so the ship was on alert. However, as they got closer it was apparent that no other vessels were moored by the tiny fishing village, and a general stand-down occurred throughout the crew.

The nau, a large 42 gun frigate built in Goa, dropped anchor in front of the village. Captain Tiago Querido came alongside Joao. "And we have arrived, *signor.* You wish to go ashore today? We can lower the boat."

"Yes, thank you, *capitao.* We will stretch our legs on land for a bit, and I will try to find a guide for our trek inland to Ctesiphon. But as I recall there are no rooming houses here, so we will wish to stay aboard until we have made our arrangements."

"Very well. And how long shall we remain, sir?"

"I should think we will be here at least five weeks. We will be exploring the ruins... It is a journey of some twelve to fourteen days with a small caravan, and not traveling to exhaustion. As Isabel will be making the journey, we will want to make sure not to tire her too greatly."

Isabel began to protest and then remembered... She would be riding on a camel! She shook her head in disbelief. Perhaps it was best that her father had not accompanied them back to Lisbon after all.

The journey to Ctesiphon had, in fact, been completed in eleven days. The Bedouin guides had spent a week provisioning the caravan, making sure there were comfortable accommodations for the Xaviers in the form of a flowing tent that would be assembled each evening. The floor was lined with carpets, and a small brazier by the bed roll kept them warm during the chilly nights. Joao sat astride his camel during the long days, swaying side to side and also with a strange front to back motion. He had made this journey before, but had conveniently forgotten how sore his hind parts were for the first several days. A litter of sorts had been made for Isabel, much to her relief, but the long days of lounging on the platform against rolled up carpets made her bones ache.

At noon on the eleventh day the caravan came in sight of the ruins of Ctesiphon. They had tracked up the Tigris River for much of the journey, except when it veered too far to the east, and had crossed it to the south of the ruined city. The days were monotonous, as the scenery did not vary from sand, stunted shrubs and trees, and more sand. Heading northeast, they could see the great arch in the distance. Joao turned back to Isabel and pointed.

"There it is! We're almost there!" Isabel smiled with relief. They would stay on the banks of the Tigris, near the ruins, for a week, exploring and enjoying the hospitality of the locals. Joao had camped within the ruins themselves on his previous visit, leaving it to the guides to procure provisions in the village as needed, so he did not think that he would be recognized.

In a short while they were in front of the colossal structure. The enormous arch, the Taq-i Kisra, rose dozens of feet above them, with the wings of the palace on either side. Made of baked bricks, it rose out of the desolate landscape, quiet and lonely.

"What happened to it?" Isabel asked in a hushed voice, sitting up on her litter atop the camel.

"The Taq-i Kisra and the Shahigan-i Sepid..." The guide pointed to a mound of rubble that could only nominally be recognized as a former structure, "... were burned when the last of the great kings was overthrown by the Ottomans, a thousand years ago. They burned the library, the palaces... but the people were not harmed. The Arabs stayed for a time, but there were stories of the ghosts of our Persian ancestors, of the great kings who searched for their palaces. Slowly they moved up river, or to Bagdad. There is no one left now."

Isabel shuddered a bit, but looking at the Taq-i Kisra with its magnificent arch, and the enormous blue sky, she felt nothing but peace. She settled back against the rugs as the caravan moved on, past the site.

Later that afternoon they arrived in the village of Hasuyn as Salih. The guide and his servants erected their tent on a hill overlooking the Tigris, and set about establishing a cooking area and the other necessities of camp. Village women arrived with dates and other fruits, as well as a flat fresh breads and cured olives. There was a fresh breeze from the river, and the air was cooling, as it always did in the evening. Isabel went to the tent to refresh herself before the evening meal, and Joao sought out their guide.

"*Meu senhor,* have you arranged the meeting that I asked for?"

"Ah yes, sir, yes! The *anciao* will come for you in the morning. I am happy to be spending the day with my sister here in the village, and the men will get rest, yes?"

"*Obrigado, senhor.* I will be very happy to explore the ruins again, and to show them more carefully to my bride."

The guide bowed, and went back to his men, who were now relaxing with a hot beverage. He said something to them and they all laughed. *He thinks I'm a bit eccentric,* thought Joao. He smiled. *If he only knew!*

⤝◦⟨⟩◦⤞

The next morning, after hot, bitter coffee and a mixture of sweet rice and bits of dried fruit, the Xaviers made their way back to the ruins of the Taq-i Kisra with the elder of the village, Aqa Rahimi. The elderly Rahimi was the only local man who knew all about the history of the Persians, about the ruins of the palaces, and about the various carvings and inscriptions that could be found on the walls and remaining columns of the structure. He had learned from his father, and he from his father, and on and on through the generations, in a strong tradition of oral history, and he would be their eyes to the past. And for Joao, a prophet of the future. Alongside him was his cousin Khadem, who had worked for the Portuguese during their brief occupation of the area and would serve as translator.

The palace continued to entrance Isabel, and she

sat with a small sketch pad under an umbrella while the men walked around the massive structure.

"*Aqa*, why is it that no one has lived beneath these walls all these years?" Joao asked.

Through Khadem, Rahimi said, "It is bad to live in the king's house if you are not the king."

"But there are no Persian kings now…"

"One day there may be a king again. It is bad to be in the king's house if the king returns."

Joao nodded. They walked around the rear of the structure, looking up at the towering wall. Joao touched an area of brick that had been scratched. "What does this mean?"

Rahimi looked closely at the graffiti. "It is a prayer. For the dead."

Joao kept walking. The walls were remarkably intact. The brick was barely crumbling, and, although the roof had been burned centuries before, and the center section seemed to have lost many of its walls, it was still a breath-taking site.

"Do you know what was here?" He waved to the area behind the arch, which was a large open space.

"The palace was very grand. The ceiling was…" He made a tenting motion with his hands. Khadem consulted and came up with the word. "Round. The roof was very high from the ground, and the king and his people did their business there." The king's court.

He walked through the center to the arch. It was well known through the building of the gothic cathedrals in Europe that arches were very strong. The wings of the palace were beginning to fall apart, but the arch… the arch would stand until the brick crumbled to dust in the winds. Judging by the solidity of the building blocks, that would not be for a very, very long time. He had his spot.

"I will get my wife, and then we would like to see the carvings, if you please." He strode to Isabel and helped her gather her drawing paper and pens.

"I'd like you to copy some of the carvings for me, my dear. Can you do that, do you think?"

"Oh certainly! That would be wonderful, Joao. We would have *lembranca*, souvenirs, for our new home." She walked along beside him, bustling with excitement. "I have never seen such a place as this, my love! I did not relish the camel journey, I must confess, but now that we are here I am ever so thankful to you for even those camels! *Obrigado, meu amor.*"

Inside the structure, they enjoyed the cool shade. The day had heated up considerably, and the cool brick and shadows were much welcomed. Rahimi showed the couple several of the carvings made by the kings' artisans, and they both went to work copying them. While they were thus engaged, the two Persian men went to the camels and brought back cool wine, fruit, smoked meats, and bread. The set out a rug and all of the delicacies, and called to the travelers.

The food and drink were marvelous, and much needed refreshment. They relaxed for an hour, watching the birds that flew over the ruins and the few clouds that appeared very high up in the rich blue sky. After each had gone outside to wash their hands and face with water from a clay pitcher, Joao and Isabel went back to their drawings. By mid-afternoon they were pleasantly tired, and agreed that it was time to go back to their new temporary home on the Tigris.

———◦◦◅◉▻◦◦———

That night, Joao was up until the early hours, working by the light of a small brazier. He sat hunched in the far corner, careful not to wake his wife. On a board on his lap were the tools of his former trade—quill pens, ink, parchment. He put all his skill into the letter, not knowing who might ever read it. He hoped it was a son. A son's son, perhaps. But, of course, he had no way of knowing who, or even if... The Throne of King Solomon might sit for endless millennia, never found, never freed. That wasn't his burden any longer. He had found it. He had known when he saw it that he couldn't do more than make a few hasty drawings. He was being watched and followed, and he didn't always know when or by whom. He could not take the risk.

Shaking his head at the memories of those strange silent men he wondered, *Where do they come from? How did they always seem to find him?* He didn't know. He continued to write on the small scroll, making ornate letters and small border drawings. It was in God's hands, and he could only do his best.

———◦◦◅◉▻◦◦———

The next several days brought strong winds which blew the sand sideways and into frightful swirling demons. The small party did not venture back to Ctesiphon. Isabel and Joao had strong hot coffee in the village, and Joao was reintroduced to the hookah. He wasn't sure if he enjoyed the sweet, fruity smoke, but he did enjoy the company of the smiling men who welcomed him. Sometimes Khadem joined them, and he could communicate. Other times, all was done with smiles and bows and hand gestures. But the goodwill on both sides was readily apparent, and the time was passed in satisfactory fashion.

Finally a morning dawned clear and still, and Joao and Isabel prepared to visit the Taq-i Kisra again. It had begun to greatly disturb him that he had withheld so much from his beloved wife. No, to be honest, had *lied* so much to her. He was not sure what to do to rectify this, and put it to the back of his mind until he had accomplished his mission here, and they were safely back aboard the Santa Antonio de Tanna.

They arrived at the ruins in short order, and once again the site took their breath away. *It is the stillness,* thought Isabel. *The majesty of the place...* Whatever it was, the lonely palace, with its soaring arch, seemed to point to heaven. Isabel dismounted and turned to Rahimi.

"*Aqa,* was the Taq-i Kisra built by Muslims?"

"No, *senhora,* by the Persians. They were not followers of Mohammed. They were Zoroastrian...We are still followers in our village. There are not many of us left, but we are the gatekeepers of the great kings... We await their return."

Isabel turned back to the ruins. Whoever built it, and whatever they believed, she could feel her God smiling on them.

Joao said, "Rahimi, we will be doing more drawings today. Perhaps we will do some digging, and discover a hidden treasure!" They all laughed. "If you would like to just prepare a place for our meal nearby, we will be happy to wander about *solitario.*"

Rahimi nodded his assent after the request was

translated to him by Khadem, and Isabel and Joao set off to the palace. Joao had made sure that their small caravan dismounted to the north side of the ruins so that the arch and interior of the ruins were out of site of their guides.

When he took out a small hammer and chisel, Isabel looked quizzical. "*O que e que voce esta fazendo?* What are you doing?"

Joao smiled at her. "We shall leave something here. If our children ever travel this way, we can tell them where to look, and they can find a letter from their parents when they were young... I do not know that this would be welcomed by Aqa Rahimi, so we shall make it a secret." He withdrew a metal tube from his robes, made to hold a small telescope.

Isabel laughed. "You are crazy!" But she clapped her hands and began to look around. "Where shall we hide it?"

"I think in the kings' court. The arch is the strongest part of the palace. I think it will stand for many years yet." They continued to walk, looking at the archway. The court was dozens of feet long, and Joao craned his neck to look at the top. "When we walked all around the palace before, I did not see any place where the walls seemed weak. They are at least twenty feet thick at the base, and the bricks appear to be well fitted. I think that we must find somewhere to carve a mark, and that also has perhaps a loose brick or other indentation where we can hide our letter."

Isabel nodded, eyes bright with the adventure. "Perhaps this corner, where it joins the back wall..." It was darker in the recesses, although the light still shone through the opening made by the missing roof.

She began rapping and pushing against the bricks as she walked along the two walls.

"Here! Joao!" She showed him a representational carving of a man on horseback, his enemies trod underfoot. The bottom of the relief was made of a row of smaller bricks, like a narrow shelf. One of those wobbled ever so slightly when she pushed down on it. "This one!"

The loose brick was directly under the carved, agonized face of a defeated Roman soldier. His helmet was still on his head, but his cheek rested on the ground, just above the ledge. Joao used his chisel carefully in the thin line of mortar between the bricks and pried it out. Because it was set along the top edge of the row making the wall, there was a recess between the back of the small brick and the next row of bricks. He grinned at Isabel.

"Brilliant, *meu amor!*" He put the small tube up next to the outer bricks and replaced the ledge stone. "How will we reset this?"

"We shall ask Rahimi about the making of the bricks and mortar. He will tell us more than we want to know, and we will come back tomorrow and repair it."

"*Brilhante!*" He kissed her soundly on the lips. "And I shall make our mark now. Pray that we shall not make too much noise! You go up towards the archway and draw one of the carvings there. If Rahimi or Khadem comes to investigate, yell for me. In this corner I should be hidden in shadow, and my mark should not take very long to create. *Deus seja com nos!* God be with us!"

Isabel gathered her small satchel and went fifty feet towards the opening of the arch. There she set to drawing. From the back she could hear scraping and an occasional *tap tap* of Joao's chisel on the brick. It was not overly loud, and she hoped it was muffled by all the towering walls. In any case, no one came—the Persians were probably laughing at the crazy *Portugues* newlyweds. She had just completed her drawing of the bas relief bust of a king when Joao ambled over to her, slightly dusty, but smiling broadly.

"*E acabado.* It is finished."

CHAPTER TEN

CAPE TOWN, SOUTH AFRICA

PRESENT DAY

REI'S NOSE WAS LITERALLY PRESSED against the plane's window as they approached Cape Town. Table Mountain rose from the city in glorious green, looking for all the world like a giant had swiped off its top in one clean cut of an axe. The water around the horn was green and blue, with long white cresting waves along the shore. The bay was enormous, and one could see the east and west coasts of the great continent all at once. It was the most breathtaking sight Rei had ever seen.

"Gideon, my God! It's stunning! Can you imagine being a sailor and seeing that great flat mountain rising out of the sea? And what a welcome sight it must have been. It's just amazing."

Gideon leaned over his wife and peered out the window. "It's sure beautiful, but I have to say, I hope we aren't spending a lot of time here."

"Oh..." Rei's disappointment was brief. "You're right..." She turned away from the window to look at her notebook, open on the tray table. "I have some ideas, and I've been studying Father Eduardo's journal since we left Lisbon. There really aren't that many places that he could have hidden a clue, at least not that's still here. So if we're going to find it, we don't have that far to look. The main problem, as far as I can tell, is that if this clue is gone, the hunt's over. He only wrote about this one location in the journal. We know that he followed the spice route, but that could be dozens of places. Portugal had lots of outposts, both for trading, and for provisioning ships who were traveling. And also to try to expand the Empire. So if we don't find this one, we could literally look for years and not find the next one..."

"Great..." Gideon grumbled.

"We just have to pray that he chose well... I do think we can narrow it down some, with what we already know about him."

The captain came on the public address system and announced their imminent landing and preparations. The weather in Cape Town was 69 degrees and sunny, which was good news to the sun-loving Rei. The couple began to put away all their electronics, put on shoes, and wrap up their headphones.

"Sucks that my Kindle is considered an electronic device... I doubt it could crash the plane," Gideon complained. He pulled out the South African Airways magazine once again. "I've read all this, and it wasn't so great the first time."

Rei handed him Sky Mall. "Here ya go, hon. Do some Christmas shopping."

Gideon flipped through. "Ok, for your mom, we'll get this zombie rising up out of the ground...."

Rei whacked him with her paperback. "Keep it up, funny man. You might have nose hair clippers in your stocking." She leaned over and kissed him on the cheek. "At least Mr. Xavier popped for first class. My butt hurts from these seats, but they're pretty darn comfy."

"First class treasure hunting all the way... If we don't find the first clue, I hope he doesn't make us pay him back!"

"We're gonna find it." She ran her fingers through her auburn hair, and put it up in a messy bun. "If we can find this one, we will. I just feel it."

"Well feel this one then, because I won't be real happy if we have to report back that Cape Town was a dead end. Short of tearing Goa apart, which would be about as successful as following the entire spice route, we're going to have to piece it together from here."

Rei blew out a sigh. "I know. I'm feeling a lot of pressure on it... but when we get to the hotel, we'll look at the places that are old enough, and try to figure out a plan."

"How will we know if we've found the right place, though?" Gideon asked.

Rei smiled. "Our Senhor Xavier had a sense of humor—apparently, X marks the spot."

"What? You're kidding?"

"Nope. X for Xavier. Quick, easy and inconspicuous." She grinned.

"Holy cow."

"I know! It'll make the best treasure hunt story ever if we find it, and if Mr. Xavier makes it public. Anyway, we've got a few scribbled notes, but the descriptions aren't going to help us much til we find the right structure. You can't exactly Google 'where's the small crack near the carving in Cape Town.'"

"Is that what he says?"

"Pretty much. He didn't want it to look like he was leaving clues, so he just made quick drawings, and short notes. I'm trying to read between the lines, so to speak. We know he did want someone to find it, so we just have to assume we'll figure it out when we have more information."

"Alrighty then..." Gideon sighed. The wheels touched down.

The drive from the Cape Town International Airport through the bustling city kept Rei in amazed silence. She was from Beaufort, North Carolina, which was a tiny seaside town, had gone to college at UNC Greensboro, and graduate school at Duke. Until she moved to DC for a job with the Smithsonian, she had never lived in a big city. She thought DC was an insane place to live, and she and Gideon escaped to the Outer Banks whenever they could get away. When Gideon had been promoted to head of security at Xavier International, they had moved to London, which was, of course, huge and crowded and damp and confusing. Cities, in her experience, were not beautiful. But Cape Town had captivated her at first sight.

Cape Town snaked around Table Mountain, which was the defining feature of the tip of Africa. It could be seen from anywhere in the city and gave one the feeling that no matter where you drove, you were simply orbiting the mountain. Driving first on Airport

Approach Road, and then west along Settlers Wy from the airport, they passed the beautiful King David Golf Club, and then the Mowbry and Rondebosch Golf Clubs.

"Shoulda brought my clubs..." Gideon muttered, gazing longingly at the immaculate courses.

"You better hope we don't have time for a round!" Rei said.

The Mount Nelson Hotel was off Government Avenue. Between them and the sea was Signal Hill. Their taxi delivered them to the front of the pink hotel, with its spectacular gardens and lawns.

"Wow!" breathed Rei.

"Put this on the bucket list, honey," Gideon whispered back.

They checked in and were taken to a lovely garden cottage by the pool. The Afrikaans porter opened the curtains as he checked the room. "These cottages were renovated in 1990 and added to the property. You have your own rose garden out here," he gestured out one window. "And an enclosed patio. There is a stocked bar, and of course, we can provide anything you need. Just press the Front Desk button on the phone." Again he pointed, this time to the phone on the ornate desk. Gideon tipped him, and they stood, a little dumbfounded, in the middle of the cottage.

"We owe Mr. Xavier a bottle of champagne," Rei said.

"It's pretty amazing," Gideon agreed. "Unfortunately, we really need to get to work. Here, I'll set your laptop up on the desk and get your Internet connection going."

"While you're doing that, I'm gonna have to try out this tub." At Gideon's scowl, she made a face of her own. "We've been traveling fourteen hours, and I haven't slept in two days. I'm going to take a bath, and put on clean clothes. And *then* I'll get to work. This ain't the Army, son." She winked at him, and flounced into the marble bathroom.

———◦◦⟨⟨⟩⟩◦◦———

Rei had long abandoned the towel she'd wrapped around her wet hair, and was frowning at her computer screen, scribbling notes on the hotel note pad. "OK, so here's what we've got to choose from, and it's not much." She flipped through her pages. "The oldest building here is the Castle of Good Hope. It was an active fort run by the Dutch both times Father Eduardo was here. The pros are that it was obviously built to last, and had very thick walls. It was a working fort, meaning there were a lot of activity by civilians as well as employees of the Dutch East India Company and the soldiers here. And there were always ships in Table Bay. So he would have had any number of excuses to be there... The question is, could he have found the privacy to carve a mark and leave a clue?"

Gideon got off the bed and came to stand behind her. He leaned down over her shoulder and looked at her scribbled notes. "How can you read that?"

She reached back and slapped his leg. "Shush! Really, our only other options are one of these surrounding hills or Table Mountain itself."

Gideon groaned.

"I know. But it's not as bad as you think. When he landed here first, he was a Jesuit. The Dutch hated the Catholics, and didn't allow any mass to be said on land. So Eduardo might have sought out somewhere he could go to worship in private, and there was only one place he could have gone…" She pulled up a Google Earth satellite image on her computer screen.

"Cape Town was originally called the Cape of Storms, the *Cabo Tormentosa*. Great name, huh? Anyway, it was renamed the Cape of Good Hope, *Cabo da Boa Esperanca*. Much better. In 1503 Antonio de Saldanha, a Portuguese sailor, was the first European to land here, and he is the one who named Table Mountain. Not a lot of imagination there, but I guess it was a pretty obvious choice. So he climbed up to the top of that other mountain, the one with the funny top we saw coming in, between Table Mountain and Signal Hill. Lions Head. And he carved a great big cross up there. It's still visible today…"

"That must be some cross…" Gideon said.

"Yep. So. I think those are our only choices. Nothing else is old enough. The Castle is not far from our hotel, so we could go check that out first just because it's probably easiest. But I have a feeling it's up at Lions Head." Rei closed her laptop and stood up. "Now I need food."

⊸◦⫘◦⊷

The Quinns enjoyed a lovely dinner at the Planet Restaurant in the hotel. The monochromatic color scheme and crystal studded entrance was soothing, and the ambiance of the quiet gardens and cool breeze had relaxed the couple. They shared a bottle of South African wine, and Gideon chose the smoked crocodile for his main course, with an avocado salad. Rei, with a look of disgust at his taste, ordered a roasted kabeljou, after determining that this exotic sounding creature was actually a fairly common fish. She added a spring salad, and corrected the waiter when he thought she said the springbok. Her Southern accent was causing a bit of confusion, but she explained with a laugh that she wanted a salad and not an antelope.

"I don't feel like I'm working," Rei said, sipping her perfectly chilled chenin blanc. "This is pretty darn fabulous."

"Don't get used to it..." He winked at her. "But we might as well enjoy it." They clicked glasses and laughed.

As they walked slowly back to their cottage in the cool evening, Gideon abruptly stopped and grabbed Rei's arm. "Shh!"

"What..." He clamped his hand over her mouth. Rei's eyes went wide, but she could see the still seriousness on her husband's face. He shook his head, and removed his hand. He put his fingers to his lips and gestured for her to stay. She shook her head and grabbed his hand. He put his hands on her shoulders and leaned in to her ear.

"Someone is in the cottage. Stay here!" he hissed.

"It's housekeeping!" she whispered back.

"No, it's not. Two men. Only penlights. Stay!" He moved off the Syndenham Terrace pathway and disappeared in the shadows. Rei stood stock still on the path for two seconds then quietly followed him.

Gideon slowly moved through the shadows, and Rei could only see him because she was concentrating so intently. He had on dark slacks and a lightweight black sweater, and he moved slowly enough that the movement itself was unremarkable to the casual observer. She tried to mimic his movements, and was thankful for the burgundy dress and black wrap she'd packed. Her high heels weren't doing her any favors, though, so she slipped them off and carried one in each hand. She didn't know about snakes in South Africa, but she figured no self respecting snake was in the middle of the city and left it at that.

Gideon had reached the side of the little cottage, and looked quickly in the window. He glanced back up the path, where his wife was supposed to be, and grimaced when he realized she wasn't there. *Of course she's not there,* he thought. He shook his head. Not time to ponder his independent wife. He looked in the window quickly again, then pressed back against the wall.

Two men. Black hair, dressed in black, with pen lights. They were working at Rei's laptop, but he'd set up a pretty good password system on it, so they probably wouldn't get far. The danger was them taking it away. Rei had put a digital copy of the artifacts on another thumb drive, and stored it in the hotel's main safe on special request from Mr. Luis Xavier. Since Xavier International supplied all the artwork for the hotel, the management was happy to accommodate him in any way possible. But it would be time consuming to have to find and purchase a new laptop, and install all the programs and safeguards they needed; time they apparently didn't have. *How did they find us?* Obviously, his first course of action was to protect the computer.

A hand clamped on his arm, and he almost gave a shout.

"Shhhh!" Rei hissed.

Gideon shook his head in disgust, then pointed in the window. He held up two fingers, and mimed typing on a keyboard. Rei vehemently shook her head. He patted her arm and signaled her, once again, to stay put. *Fat chance*, he thought. But one had to try.

He crept slowly around to the enclosed patio. He knew that they had left the door open to catch the cool evening breeze, and unless housekeeping actually had come to their room while they were at dinner and closed it, it should still be open. He put his hands on the top of the wall and quietly vaulted over. *At least she can't do that...* He smiled a little to himself. He landed silently on the grass verge surrounding the patio, and determined that the door was still open. The gauzy curtain was billowing slightly inwards with the evening air. He crouched low and stopped to listen just outside. The noise of fingers on a keyboard, clicking a few times, punching a button, and waiting. A whispered invective. Obviously trying to break the password. Most people used ridiculous things for passwords... but Gideon wasn't most people.

Thinking about the layout of the room, he realized that the patio door was in the bedroom. The desk was through a large doorway between the bedroom and the living area, which could be closed with two pocket doors. Those doors were open, and the desk was at a three quarters angle away from the opening. Gideon risked a quick look. One of the men was sitting in the desk chair, the other looking much as he himself had looked earlier in the day when he had been reading over Rei's shoulder. He rolled into the room and stood up beside the armoire, which blocked any view the intruders might have of him.

He looked around the room. He had no weapon. One couldn't bring weapons on planes anymore, unless it was a private jet, and they certainly hadn't thought that necessary. On the dresser to his right was a dark wooden tray with a bottle of water on it. Thank God, San Pelligrino. Glass. He eased over slowly, keeping his eye on the men. He grabbed the neck of the full bottle and turned it, making a heavy, and effective, club. It would be sufficient, if he could sneak up behind the men. If either of the men had a gun, however...Well, he'd seen Indiana Jones, and knew what happened when you brought a knife—or a bludgeon—to a gun fight.

He took a deep breath. He could hear his heart beating, but tried to tune it out so that he could hear any changes in the cottage. What he heard was someone fumbling with the lock. *Rei.* The men looked up from the computer, panicked. They had become immersed in the problem of cracking the password, and had let their watchfulness lapse. In that moment, Gideon rushed forward and swung the bottle at the man standing. The man heard or felt him at the last minute and began to turn, but the bottle still cracked on his skull behind his ear. He fell to the ground, and Gideon turned to the man who was seated. With the desk in front of him, and his fallen comrade beside, he had very little room to maneuver, but he jumped up and over the desk in a quick, acrobatic movement.

"Stop!" yelled Gideon. Just then Rei managed to open the door. The man swerved to the open patio door in the bedroom, and sprinted. He put his hands on the top of the wall as Gideon had done, and vaulted. Gideon swung his bottle and let it fly just as the man's feet came off the ground. The bottle hit his leg and then shattered on the wall, and the man fell awkwardly over the top of the wall, momentum carrying him. Gideon ran for the door and vaulted the wall again, a few feet to the left of where the man fell. He fully expected him to be laying on the ground in the grass, but no one was there. He looked around but saw no movement. He held his breath and listened. Nothing. *Damn.* After standing still for several minutes, he gave up and walked around to the front of the cottage.

Rei was on the phone when he came in. "Yes, he went over the patio wall! I don't know—wait, hold on a sec," she put her hand over the mouthpiece. "Which way did he go?" she asked Gideon.

"I don't know—he was gone. Bastard was quick. The other one still here?" He had forgotten about the other man, unconscious in the suite with Rei, and had a moment of panic. She nodded and went back to the phone.

"We don't know... I think he's hurt, because my husband beaned him with a glass bottle in the leg, and he fell over the top of the wall. But he's gone. The other one's still here, though." She cut her eyes to the man on the floor, and then to Gideon. "Yeah, we'll manage." And she hung up.

"The front desk is appropriately horrified, and has already called the police. They should be here any minute, and would we be pleased to make sure this man doesn't go anywhere until they arrive..." She smiled at him. "That's your department, hon."

The police had come and gone. Gideon gave them a modest explanation, explaining about the burglary in Lisbon, and the monk with the tattoo that the police there had in custody. While he was tying the intruder up with strips of the high quality hotel towels, he had seen the tattoo on his forearm, identical to the one that Brother Petros had. That should keep the cops busy for a bit, and add a bit of excitement to Interpol's data collection department. No one knew who these people were yet, but they had more information now than a week ago, and now they had another man in custody. It was a pretty good bet that the South African police knew how to conduct an interrogation, especially when they were armed with the information from Petros. Gideon would check in with them in the afternoon.

The management apologized profusely, and offered to move them to the Presidential suite. Rei really liked the small row of cottages, however, and Gideon thought that the odds of another break in that night were slim, so they opted instead to move to a different garden cottage under an assumed name.

London was two hours earlier than Cape Town, so Gideon decided to call Mr. Xavier on his cell.

"*Alo?*"

"Mr. Xavier, it's Gideon. I'm sorry to call so late, but I wanted to give you an update."

"Yes, Gideon. Have you found something?"

"No sir, but I would say that we're on the right track. Two men from the same order as our Brother Petros broke into our room tonight. The police have one in custody, but the other escaped. They were unable to get into Rei's computer, and fortunately didn't think to—or maybe didn't want to—steal it."

"What do you mean, didn't want to?"

"Well, I was thinking. If they didn't want us to know they'd followed us, or found us, or whatever they did, they might not want to steal it. We'd be bound to be suspicious, and report it to the local police. Of course, we might see it as a random crime, but with all that's gone on, that wouldn't be my first guess, and I think they'd been told to avoid stealing it if at all possible. They weren't exactly computer geniuses... I think they were counting on the fact that most people use pretty simple passwords. From that, I'm assuming they don't know who I am yet. If they'd known I was your head of security, they could have guessed it would be a bit more complicated than Rei's birthday."

Mr. Xavier grunted. "*Sim,* I see that. So we are learning more about them, as they are learning about us. But why would they care what is on the laptop? They have the original items."

"They've always known about the letter, and we are speculating that they at least suspected a treasure. But it's doubtful that they're flush with cryptographers or intel specialists, especially since it appears that only the abbot knows there's more than a letter out there. These are monks. Maybe militant monks... A few obviously have some skills, and they know how to get information. But I don't think they're a big worldwide group... so we're going to be stretching them thin, and they're probably thinking it's easier to follow us, or steal Rei's work, than to try to take guys out of the field to do it themselves."

"I am worried about that word 'militant,' Gideon," Xavier said.

"Yeah... me too. I'll keep you posted, boss. Good night." He rung off and looked at Rei. *Yeah, me too.*

CHAPTER ELEVEN

T HE TAXI DROPPED THE QUINNS at the entrance to the Castle of Good Hope, off Strand Street, at exactly 9:00. The plan was to get there when it opened, take the first guided tour offered in order to get an overall picture of the huge fort, and then explore anything they saw as a potential hiding place. Arriving at the enormous structure, however, was quite discouraging.

"Holy cow... We are never going to be able to look at all of this place! It would take weeks!" Rei stood with her arms stretched out sideways and her head tilted back to look at the flags flying over the entrance.

"Yeah. It's... wow." Gideon just shook his head. "It didn't look so big on Google Earth."

"Okay. Deep breath." Rei closed her eyes for a few moments. "So we need some kind of map, like one that shows where things were when the castle was first built. We'll have to try to eliminate. Or use logic, anyway."

Gideon took her hand and led the way to the ticket booth. They looked up at the pediment over the entrance.

"Are those Greek gods?" asked Gideon.

"Sure looks like it...Or the Roman equivalent. I can

never tell them apart. That would be Poseidon—or Neptune—with the trident. And, hmm. Who had that thing with the snakes around it? Hermes? I think that's it. So that would be Mercury. Not sure what the deal is with all that stuff in the middle, though." She pointed to another figure, smaller and flatter than the two gods, who was surrounded by weapons and baskets and what looked like drums. "I don't know if that's old enough anyway, but I'm sure Father Eduardo wouldn't use pagan gods for his landmark."

They kept going, purchasing their tickets for twenty-eight rand, and getting a map of the layout of the castle. After studying it, they decided they would try the church first, but would need a plan B.

"The de Kat balcony has a lot of carvings and reliefs, but it wasn't built until 1695. So that's out." Rei pointed to the map. "There are five bastions—those five points of the star. They were named for William of Orange's titles—I guess that was one way to come up with names. So we have Leerdam, Buuren, Catzengellenbogen—wow, that's a mouthful! Then Nassau and Oranje. This one on the right is Leerdam... This part we're standing in was a courtyard to protect the citizens if there was a disaster or invasion or something." She sat down cross legged on the green lawn and spread the map on her lap. Gideon joined her and adjusted his sunglasses.

Rei skimmed the historical section of the brochure. "The entrance was moved just before Father Eduardo came—or maybe in between his visits. It used to be over there, between Burren and Catzengellenbogen. So let's figure we can rule out both of those sections of wall... And I don't see him being able to gain entrance into any of the military fortifications or the town's administrative sections. The forge has been redone and is working now, with demonstrations... But when would he have had access to a forge when the blacksmith wasn't there? No, the more I think about it, the more I think it would have to be the church. It was a Protestant church, of course, but I think that's our best shot." She folded the brochure.

Gideon said, "I say we check out the church, every square inch, inside and out. If we don't find anything, we go to Lions Head. If we strike out *there*... well, I think we'll have to come back here and start looking again. You have your stuff?"

Rei nodded. She opened her backpack and took out a sketch pad, a box of watercolors, and a bunch of pencils held together by a rubber band. "I'll move around and do quick studies while you play the bored husband and look around. I'll call you back to me every once in awhile, so you have a reason not to go too far afield in the castle. You know what you're looking for?"

"An X." He laughed.

"Scoffer..." She stood up and wiped the back of her jeans. "Yes, an X. I think we look first at areas that had original carvings, because it would be easier to hide his mark where there were already things on the stone. Also, it would have to be near something that could be moved, so if it's a huge sheet of solid rock, I don't think that'll be it. Smaller stonework, ledges, stone benches, a dirt floor, that kind of thing..."

She and Gideon had the same thought at that moment. Gideon said, "How are we going to start chiseling the bits out with all these tourists around?"

Rei looked around her, at the two or three dozen

people already milling about, and the school groups filing in. "That's a problem... But Gid, it would have been Father Eduardo's problem, too. This was a working fort when he was here—it was the hub of the whole town! There were stores, and the church, and the governmental stuff, and the offices of the..." She consulted her brochure. "The Vereenighde Oost-Indische Compagnie."

"The what?" Gideon didn't know what she had said, but was pretty sure she'd butchered the pronunciation.

"The VOC. The Dutch East India Company, basically. They ran pretty much everything around here back then. My *point* is, Father Eduardo had to figure out a way to hide his whatever it was in at least as big a crowd as we're going to have today. So that's another thing we need to consider—somewhere in or around the church that's kind of hidden away."

"We might have to try to figure out how to get locked in here tonight, if we can't," Gideon said.

She grimaced. "This says the place is full of the ghosts of those who were tortured in the dungeons..."

Gideon laughed. "Rei! You don't believe in ghosts!"

"No... but it'd be pretty creepy in here alone at night, just the same." She took his hand and started toward the church.

———◦◦◦———

They stood at the doorway of the small church. It was fairly dim inside, and there wasn't much to the outside, as it had been built into the main structure of the castle. Inside there were a few windows on the outer wall, hanging lamps that gave off little light, old wooden pews, and a small altar. Bas relief carvings decorated a good portion of the walls, including behind the altar. There was only one person in the church, an old woman who was sitting with her hands folded in her lap, head down in prayer. There were candles on the altar, but they weren't lit, and no clergy seemed to be in attendance.

Rei glanced at Gideon, and put her backpack on the last pew. Withdrawing her pad and pencils, she began to move slowly from the rear to the front, up the right side. She gestured to her husband to do the same up the left. She studied all of the carvings carefully, and realized that this was going to be a good deal harder than she had anticipated. While the church had been carefully preserved through the years, and the carvings had never been exposed to rain or the elements, the lighting in the church and the years of people touching the walls made it difficult to discern much detail.

All of the themes were religious, which, of course, made sense. But unlike those in Catholic churches, these did not depict angels and demons, or halos, and most contained regular people and pastoral elements. This meant that there were natural features like grass and trees represented by hash-like marks, many of which could be construed as an X. Rei walked over to Gideon, who looked equally frustrated.

She whispered, "We have to keep assuming Father Eduardo wanted someone to be able to find the clue. These carvings were all here in 1687 or 1688 when he came back. So he didn't hide his X so well that we'll think it's grass. I just can't believe that."

"If we find this first one, at least we'll know what to

look for next time. Let's start over, together," Gideon whispered back.

Just then, a small group of tourists came noisily in, chatting and gesturing. Rei took a seat sideways on a pew and started drawing the closest relief, while Gideon did his best to look like the long suffering husband and walked towards the altar, looking for an X.

The tourist group left, and the old woman was still sitting in the same position. Rei thought she'd gone to sleep, but she didn't really want to find out. She put her pad and pencil down quietly on the pew and joined Gideon, who was now on the left side of the altar.

"Anything?" she asked.

"Not yet…Still working on it. But up here would be good, especially behind the altar. The stone and wood blocks the view from the whole chapel, if someone was squatting or sitting down…" Rei looked out over the church and saw he was right.

"Are there any carvings up here? It's not exactly out where people could appreciate it."

Gideon slowly moved around the corner. "There are some up here, from the floor to the window. But there's not a lot of light down low… Do we have a flashlight?"

"I have that little LED light on my keychain, but that would seem kind of suspicious, wouldn't it?"

"To who?" Gideon stood up and looked out again. Only the old lady, still praying, or sleeping. Must be sleeping, she hadn't moved at all. "Go get it."

Rei walked quietly to her backpack on the back pew, and unzipped the front compartment. She withdrew the car keys she'd stashed when they'd left their car in the Heathrow long term parking lot, and unclipped the purple LED flashlight that had been a stocking stuffer from "Santa" the Christmas before. As she was walking back to the front of the church, the woman stirred. Rei stopped dead in her tracks, looking at Gideon in a slight panic. *Chill girl, we're not doing anything wrong.* She stopped at the pew with her drawing supplies and sat down with them in her lap. The woman gathered her light coat and handbag, smiled to her, rose and left.

Rei hurried to the altar. "Oh my gosh, I'm a mess! I feel like we're breaking into Fort Knox or something!"

"All we're doing so far is looking. The breaking comes later, we hope."

Gideon shined the light on the large carvings along the back wall, and Rei crawled along on the floor, her nose six inches from the images. No one came in to break the quiet, and every sound they made seemed deafening in the still, quiet church. Finally they came to the right corner. Nothing.

"Oh Lord, I'm a wreck. What time is it?" Rei asked, looking at her watch. "We've been in here two hours! I'm starving... Let's go find that restaurant and get some lunch. I think I'm going blind, anyway."

Gideon helped her up off the stone floor. She groaned as her sore knees straightened and popped.

"Old lady!" he laughed. She punched his arm.

"I'm still your young bride, old man," she said as she walked back to the pew to gather her belongings.

He joined her and they walked out, blinded by the bright African sunshine as they left the building.

The De Goewerneur Restaurant had a view of Table Mountain, and, best of all, pizza. They got two slices each, and a Coke, and went to a table outside. They chewed, both lost in thought. Finally Gideon spoke.

"OK, so nothing so far. We still have the wall on the right hand side, though. At least it's a lot more lit along that side, with the windows opposite. I'm not really feeling it, though. How 'bout you?"

Rei shook her head. "Nope, not really. I think it's at Lions Head. I was thinking how nervous I was feeling just looking around in there, and I just can't see Father Eduardo taking the risk. And he wouldn't have been able to see the church on his first visit, since he was a Jesuit then, so how would he have known there was anywhere in there to leave his clue? The journal seems to indicate he went back to places he'd already been... they barely let Catholics off the boats at all, and certainly not into their Protestant churches." She took a sip of Coke. "I say we finish looking... we'd feel pretty stupid if it *is* on that right wall after all. But I think the castle is a bust."

"Yeah. Me too. Well, what else do we have to do in Cape Town anyway, right?" He smiled. Then he remembered the man captured in their suite, now at the police station. "I need to talk to that detective. What was his name again?"

Rei fumbled in her backpack and came out with a business card. "Van Rensberg. Adelbert van Rensberg." She handed him the card. "You gonna call?"

"Yep. Time to see if our brother has talked." He dialed the phone.

"Detective van Rensberg? This is Gideon Quinn, from the Mount Nelson Hotel last night? Yes, that's right. Xavier International." He listened for awhile, shaking his head at Rei. "Ok, will you let me know when he comes around? Thanks." He punched off his cell phone. "Still unconscious." He sighed. "Shouldn't have hit him so hard, but I didn't know if they had guns, or how fast the other guy was gonna react."

"You did what you could with what you had. Actually, it was pretty awesome." She smiled at him. "Like being married to Jason Bourne or something."

"Yeah right. But thanks. Anyway, the doctors expect him to come around. All his vitals and scans are fine, just a heck of a concussion, I guess. So van Rensberg will let me know when he does, and hopefully he'll be able—and willing—to talk." He gathered their trash. "Ready to go look at that chapel again?"

"As ready as I'll ever be. But if there's any crawling needed, you're doing it this time. I'm gonna have bruises!"

———◦◦◦◦———

Back in the church, they found a group of school children being given a history lesson by a their teacher. They fidgeted and giggled and generally ignored everything the teacher said, like school children the world over. Rei and Gideon sat in the back pew, Rei drawing another carving. They were really quite nice, these carvings, but it was pushing the boundaries of her patience to sit still and draw while the clue might be in the room somewhere.

At long last, the teacher wrapped up her talk and the kids all popped up as one and ran for the door. The teacher, accompanied by three or four moms, hustled outside so as not to lose track of any of her charges. The sudden quiet was unnerving.

"Here we go," Gideon said, his voice seeming very loud in the still room. He started at the back of the right wall. Rei joined him, and they worked slowly forward. The carvings began to look alike after awhile, but there was no discernible X anywhere.

"I'm licked," Rei said, sitting down on the step to the altar. "And blind."

"Nothing." Gideon sat down next to her. "So it's not the castle, or it's not the church. Or it's not the *inside* of the church..."

"Uh huh. Very helpful."

He got to his feet and hauled her up. "Well, at least we've eliminated something, right? And you can have antelope for dinner, so that's good news."

"Oh yeah, best news I've had all day. Don't they have a Bambi story or something here? I only like to eat ugly critters, like chickens."

They left the church, and the Castle of Good Hope. It didn't live up to its name on that day, but tomorrow was still out there, holding its promise.

———⊶∘⊲⋙∘⊳———

The evening had been uneventful, and they had, indeed, opted to eat once again in the hotel restaurant. Rei once again passed on the springbok. The detective had called to report that there was no change in their prisoner, and the leisurely walk back to their new cottage had been much less exciting than on the previous night. They had enjoyed an after dinner liqueur from the stocked mini bar, and sat on the patio enjoying the sounds of the city, and of the unknown birds nesting and flitting around in the garden.

Early in the morning, a taxi drove them to Lions Head. Turning off Kloof Nek Road and onto Signal Hill Road, they could see the small parking area. To their left was the strange shape of Lions Head. Only one car was in the parking lot, and the day was shaping up to be overcast and a bit gloomy, so they hoped that no more tourists would show up. They arranged for the taxi to return at 2:00, and swung their full backpacks on. The hotel had provided bottled water, packages of nuts and dried fruits, and boxed lunches for them to eat on the trail.

Looking up at the mountain top from the start of the trail, Rei was doubtful.

"Jeez, Gid, that's steep!"

"It'll be fine... You work out." He tightened the shoulder straps of his pack.

"I work out? I don't work out. I walk to work through Hyde Park when it's not raining. I run to catch the Tube. Occasionally I take the stairs instead of the lift. I lug groceries. That's not working out! *You* work out, and I talk about working out with you."

"Come on, babe, it'll be fine. I'll help you if you need it. You want to put some of your stuff in my pack?" They had packed their bags pretty equally that morning, but looking at the hike ahead, Gideon agreed, secretly, that it was going to be tough on his wife. She *did* walk a lot, but London was fairly flat. This was steep. In fact, he wasn't completely sure how they were going to get to the cross carved on the seaward side at all, but he kept this doubt to himself.

They rearranged the packs so the water and food

was in Gideon's, and Rei had only her hat, sunscreen, and the chisel and small trowel she'd borrowed from a grounds man at the hotel before their unsuccessful trip to the Castle of Good Hope. Giving her a thumbs up, Gideon started up the trail. They wound around to the southwest, and hiking up a mild incline. The trail turned back towards the mountain, to the northwest, and began to get steeper.

"Hang on a sec!" Rei said. She removed her backpack and took off the light jacket she'd been wearing. "Jeez, it's getting hot! And don't walk so fast—my legs are a lot shorter than yours." She got a bottle of water from Gideon's pack, took several long swigs, and handed it to him. He finished off the water, and she put the empty bottle in her own pack. "Least I could do," she said to his raised eyebrows.

"Good of you."

They set off again, Gideon trying to shorten his naturally long stride, and keeping an eye on his wife without seeming to hover. She was red in the face and breathing hard, but was doing fine so far. He looked up and thought the real trouble was probably not too far ahead.

The car park had been on the other side of the mountain for most of the hike, and they had seen no one on the trail. As they came around to the east side, a lone middle aged man was making his way back down from the right-hand fork in the pathway. He smiled and waved cheerfully, and said, "You probably want to stay to the left. It's a little longer but there's some chains to help you up the last bit." He passed them with a purposeful stride.

"If he can do it..." Rei muttered. "Wait, did he

say chains?"

They could now see the car park. The original car, presumably belonging to the hiker they had just passed, was still there, as was a small black SUV. No one was visible, so Gideon assumed that whoever the car belonged to had already started the hike. If they were younger, or in better shape, they would likely overtake them. If they were monks... Well, they didn't want anyone to see their hunt for the clue at the cross, whether brothers, tourists, or local hikers, so they'd better hurry it up.

"Rei, we need to speed it up..."

"I'm going as fast as I can!" she snapped.

"There's another car down there." He pointed it out to her. "Whoever that belongs to, we don't need them up at the cross when we're there."

"Whoever...You mean it could be Petros' friends?" She quickened her pace. "Crap! If I make it down from here, my butt's gonna hurt."

<hr/>

The last section of the trail did, indeed, have chains along it, to help hikers pull themselves up. Rei stopped and stared at them.

"You've got to be kidding me..."

"Come on, we're almost there. You can do it!" Gideon was getting more frantic to reach the cross all the time. He knew Rei had done her best, but she was no match for motivated young monks, if that was, indeed, who the SUV belonged to.

"I know, I know... keep your hat on." Rei fiercely grabbed a chain and hauled on it, muttering under her breath.

"I'm assuming you're giving yourself a pep talk?" Gideon joked. Rei just glared at him.

"You're barely even sweating! What's wrong with you?" She asked.

"I. Work. Out. Plus I *was* in the Army, you know. It wasn't that long ago." He kept going, feeling dread building up in his muscles, adrenaline starting to pump. Finally, they reached the top.

"We're here! Oh, thank God!" Rei plopped down on the ground. "Wow... look at that view! That's that island where Nelson Mandela was a prisoner... What's it called? Robben Island? Incredible."

"Yeah, gorgeous. Now come on, Rei! We have to look *now.*" He had seen a glimpse of three men about a third of the way up the trail as they had rounded the last corner. They all had dark hair, and were all dressed in black cargo pants and black tee shirts.

"They're right down there." He pointed vaguely to the trail below them.

Rei scrambled up and started scouring the rock face. The cross, carved so long ago, was huge and weather worn, but still visible. On the ground under it were ancient stones, covered with lichen and soil, having stood the test of many millennia. Gideon decided he should stand guard, as there was only one way up to the top, and they had the advantage of height. What they'd do if and when the men arrived... that was another story.

"Gideon! Gideon, look!" Rei was trying to keep her voice low, but the excitement was unmistakable. "Here!"

Gideon ran over to her and looked where she was pointing. Sure enough, under the downward stroke of the ancient cross, weathered dark like the rest of the stone, was an X carved deeply into the surface. It no longer stood out, although when it was first made it probably showed white against the weathered rock face.

"This is it!" She said. She slouched off her backpack and withdrew the chisel and the trowel. "It's got to be somewhere under these rocks. See if any of them move!"

Gideon got down on his hands and knees and started pressing the rock face. The stones had all obviously been there for years upon years... Would anything be loose after four hundred and fifty years? He didn't know, but he did know they were running out of time.

"Gideon, stay around the cross... He must have used it as a true 'X marks the spot' mark, don't you think?" She was tapping her chisel against the rock face, and peering closely to see if she could see any seams or gaps. Gideon was right beside her, trying to lift the large stones out of the way.

"Here!" He was rocking a stone the size of a shoebox. "This one!" He continued to push the rock back and forth until he could get hold of the back edge. He wedged the fingers of both hands under the stone and heaved. It fell forward and down the solid pile of stones, landing at the bottom with a crash.

"Jeez, loud enough?" Rei hissed. She got out her small LED flashlight and peered into the hole the rock had left behind. "There's something in here!"

"I hope it's not a snake..." Gideon mumbled as he reached his hand in. The hole was deep, deeper than the stone had been, and his arm disappeared to the elbow. He fumbled around, then came up with a metal tube the size of small telescope. Rei reached for it and started to open it.

"No! Not here, they're coming! Put it in my backpack and let's get out of here!" He turned so Rei could unzip the pack, and she buried it under all the food and supplies. Zipping it up, she got to her feet.

The two hurried back to the trail.

"We're going to have to take that path the other guy was on... These guys won't come that way, they'll follow the official one. I hope." Gideon said. He went as quietly as he could on the loose pebbles at the base of the rock face, Rei following behind. They could hear the men coming up the trail now, because they were using the chains to pull themselves along. The rattling rang out through the otherwise quiet day.

Gideon and Rei scooted along the secondary trail, crouching low and trying to take cover behind the inadequate scrub marking the very top of the path. As they went farther, smaller trees and shrubs provided more cover, but there were sheer drops off to the side, and the path was very narrow and steep. Adrenaline kept them going, and they got to the fork and veered off to the left. Gideon started to run, looking back and gesturing to Rei. *Hurry!*

They could hear yelling by the black clad men, now at the top of the trail. Gideon hadn't had time to replace the rock that had covered the hiding place, and it would be obvious to the monks that, not only had Gideon and Rei eluded them, they had found something. Gideon didn't know if they'd seen the secondary trail—he and Rei wouldn't have known about it had they not seen the man descending from the top earlier—but he didn't wait around to find out.

He stopped, grabbed Rei by the hand, and ran full out, dragging her behind him.

Fortunately it was all downhill. Unfortunately, it was rocky and steep and winding, and they were already tired from the hike up. Rei felt like she was disconnected from her legs, and her lungs had long ago given up getting sufficient oxygen. Her heart was pounding, and she couldn't hear anything but its beat, and the sound of their footsteps pounding on the path. *At least we haven't been shot at,* she thought, and then gave up thinking and just concentrated on not falling down. They reached the bottom of the path, and realized that it was too early and their taxi hadn't returned. They stood, confounded, for several seconds, until the crashing of the men descending the mountain stirred them back to action. Gideon knew that, if the men had rounded the last bend, they could probably see them in the car park, and, if they had guns, would be able to use them soon. They had two options: first, they could follow Signal Hill Road to the right or to the left. If they went south and made it to the crossroads, they could take any of four roads that went off that intersection. But they would be on the roads, and there was no traffic at all that he could see. So the men could get in their black SUV and catch up to them in no time.

The other option was another secondary trail. Looking at the hasty map the concierge had drawn for them, they could go north on the secondary path, and that would fork two different times, giving them the option of going back up to the top of the trail head, west to Clifton Beaches, or either of two trails to continue north. Along the way there were patches of thicker trees, and he felt that they could hide more easily on any of these paths than on the road.

"This way!" he whispered, and led Rei north, along the trail. He knew she didn't have much more energy left, but he had no idea what their alternative was. It was keep moving or get caught. All he knew was that he absolutely didn't want to lose the clue.

Racing down the secondary trail, it was apparent that it wasn't hiked nearly as often as the main trail up to Lions Head. This was good news in that it offered more cover. It was bad news because it was more difficult to have good footing as they plunged ahead. Gideon was trying to listen behind them to see if they were being followed, trying to keep Rei going and on her feet, and also trying to review the map of the trails to determine a course of action.

They were still heading north, running parallel to Signal Hill Road. There was a tree line in between, but if the men got in their SUV and followed the road they would be seen. Gideon felt it was imperative that they get away from the road, but he knew that the first fork wasn't for quite some distance. They had gone uphill from the parking lot, so would be much less visible from anywhere but the top of the mountain, but the road was really bothering him. He decided that they needed to turn to the west, towards the beach. They would hit the first of the secondary trails eventually, or could keep heading west and hit the second one. Further still, they'd hit two roads and then the beach. Certainly some opportunity would present itself by then.

He veered sharply to the left, pulling Rei with him. "Come on!"

They plunged into the thick growth, and went ten yards or so before Rei stopped, bending over and gasping for breath.

"I've got to stop. I can't breathe! And my heart is about to explode..." She had sweat dripping down her face, and her shirt was soaked through. She went down to her knees, head hanging.

"You ok? You don't look so good." Gideon asked.

Rei glared at him. "Uh, no. Not too good. Thanks for asking..."

He looked behind them anxiously, but didn't hear anything. He quickly slipped off his backpack and pulled out a bottle of water. He unscrewed the cap and handed it to her.

"Here. I think we can walk through these woods. In fact, we'll be a lot quieter if we do. I don't know how far we'll have to go, but hopefully we can lose them in here."

Rei gulped the water, then handed it back. "Walking I can do. I honestly just can't run another step. Not right now. Now if they pull guns on us...ask me then." She got to her feet.

———⊶⊶⋐⊷⊷———

They had crossed the first trail cautiously, but didn't see anyone in either direction. Gideon knew that the terrain was going to start sloping down from there to the next trail if they stayed due west, so he turned to the southwest to stay on higher ground. They couldn't see Lions Head, so he was counting on no one up there being able to see them. He could see the water occasionally between the trees, and he knew there were roads along the four Clifton Beaches. It was a week day, but maybe there were tourists, and the accompanying taxis, down there.

They crossed the second trail, and the land flattened out. In front of them was the water, and white beaches with big granite boulders. They risked a glance up on Lions Head, and saw a lone man in black, looking east over the parking lot. They kept moving toward the water, heads down.

They crossed the first road, and saw no traffic in either direction. Just a few feet further on was Victoria Road. They could see a few bathers on the beach, a few surfers out in the water. They slowed down and looked both ways. To the north, they saw cars parked along the side of the road, and turned right to make their way to them.

"Maybe there will be a cab," Gideon said. Rei merely nodded, head down, close to exhaustion.

They walked a hundred yards to the cars. Most were empty, obviously belonging to the people on the beach, but the final car in the line was a cab. His "on duty" light was off, but the driver was sitting in the driver's seat, reading a newspaper. The window was down, so Gideon leaned in.

"Hey! Can you give us a ride? We were up there," he pointed up to Lions Head, "and got off the trail somehow. We've got a cab supposed to come back to the car park for us, but my wife isn't gonna be able to make it. Can you just take us to the Mount Nelson Hotel?"

At the mention of the nice hotel, the driver perked up a bit. He looked at Rei and saw her bedraggled state and smiled. *Tourists.* "Sure, climb in. Do you want to go back to the parking lot and see if your cab is waiting?"

Rei and Gideon responded at the same time, "NO!"

The cab took off south down Victoria Road, and the couple collapsed against the back of the seat in relief.

———————⇒∘◁▱▷∘⇐———————

Back at the Mount Nelson, the Quinns packed up all their belongings in record time. They'd tipped the cab driver very well, and told the front desk as they passed that they would be checking out. Something had come up, Gideon said to the front desk manager, and Mr. Xavier would be very pleased if they would email him the receipt for the room to the address on file.

"Of course, sir! We hope you have enjoyed your stay in Cape Town." The young woman smiled at them.

"Oh yes, we hope to get back one day." Rei smiled back but kept walking.

They gathered their bags, not waiting for the bellman, and went back through the lobby to the front drive. The valet whistled for a cab, and soon they were driving away from the lovely pink hotel.

"Where are we going?" Rei asked.

Gideon thought for a moment. He leaned forward to talk to the African who was driving. "Say, is there a hotel at the airport?"

The man shook his head. "Not really at the airport, sir..." He thought for a moment. "There is a nice hotel not very far from here, though. A Radisson. And they have a shuttle to the airport."

"That will be fine. Thank you."

The driver nodded his head. *Tourists.* He had always thought the Mount Nelson was a very nice hotel, but you never knew what went on, he supposed. He drove to the Radisson, and helped to unload the small bags. He received his generous tip with a smile, and thought, as he often had, that Americans were crazy.

Gideon checked them into the hotel on their personal credit card, afraid that the Xavier International accounts might be monitored. For all he knew, his personal ones were too, but he had no other option. He didn't have a lot of cash in rand, and he knew that they had to produce their passports book a room in any event. Hopefully they would be able to decipher the clue—if this really was a clue—and make arrangements for the next location quickly. Until then, they absolutely needed food, water, baths and rest, and this was going to have to do.

Their room was spacious, on the top floor and facing the water. Rei didn't go to the window as she usually did to check out the view. She collapsed on the bed.

"I have never been so exhausted in my life. I am pooped. Really. I don't think I can even take a bath, I'm so tired."

"I don't know that I've ever known you to be too tired to take a bath!" Gideon leaned over and kissed her forehead.

"Tell me about it..." She closed her eyes, then suddenly sat up. "Oh my God! The clue! Tell me you still have the clue!"

Gideon reached over to the dresser and got his

backpack. He patted it. "Right here." He dug it out and laid it on the bed. Rei sat cross legged.

"Can you hand me my carry on bag?" When Gideon gave it to her she pulled out her notebook, then gently picked up the metal tube and looked at it. It was made of thin, hammered metal, about a foot long, and several inches in diameter, but not heavy. The top fitted on well, and there was a decaying leather strap that had sealed the top onto the base. When she began to untie the strap, it fell apart and dirt particles sprinkled the bed covers. She looked at Gideon, and then gently removed the top. She peered in, then tipped it over.

Onto her hand fell a rolled parchment, a scroll with a red blob of wax. On the wax was pressed a seal, which consisted of a simple solid cross topped with a crown. Rei used her fingernail to very gently pry off the wax seal, and set it on top of her notebook. Taking a deep breath, she gingerly unrolled the scroll.

The original vellum had been of very good quality, and Gideon thought that it was very lucky that Father Eduardo hadn't used paper. Paper would have been a lot more readily available than an old fashioned vellum parchment, but the good priest apparently knew something about longevity, and sincerely wanted his treasure found. On the scroll was writing, a dull rust color, in the form of a letter, with calligraphic letters at the start of each paragraph.

"The ink had lead in it. That's why it's this rusty color. It was originally black... I can tell it's in Portuguese, but the ink has migrated a bit so some of it's fuzzy. Hang on." She carefully put the wax seal on the bedside table and opened her notebook. She began to slowly write, four or five words, a pause. A few more words. Another pause. Gideon saw that she was deep in the translation, and he started taking off his filthy clothes.

"I'm going to take a quick shower. Let me know what it says when I get out." Rei just flapped a hand in his direction and kept reading.

———— ⊸∘✐∘⊸ ————

When Gideon returned to the bedroom, his wife was sitting back against a pile of pillows leaning against the headboard, eyes closed.

"Well? Did you figure it out?"

"I translated it... I'm not sure I figured it out. I'm going to have to do some internet research, but I am just brain dead. And I have a heck of a headache." She handed the notebook to him, and slid off the bed. "I'm going to take that bath now, and a whole bunch of Advil. After that, I need to eat. I'm going to let this sit on the back burner for awhile, maybe even til morning. Then we'll see where we get with a fresh mind." She slowly walked to the bathroom, shedding her filthy clothes.

Gideon took her place among the pillows and read the translation of her letter.

Dear Son,

I am imagining that this letter is being read by my son, or his son's son, and I am thankful that I have made it to this, my last planned stop on our journey back to Portugal. When I was in the Cape of Good Hope previously, I did not know that I would ever be anything but a Jesuit priest. I did not know that God would bless me with a treasure, a wife, and now a new life. It is my hope and prayer that this quest will bless you and our progeny in equal measure.

We have traveled far, and have met our enemy many times since leaving Goa. I do not know how they are able to determine where I am going, or if they are, rather, following me. All I know is that my Isabel and I have risked much, and I have despaired of being able to finish the task that I feel my God has put before me. I have been entrusted with both the letter that greatly disturbs my spirit, and with a treasure that I am unable to own. But I have been given all that I could ever require, and, I believe, the ability to grow that blessed seed into a treasure of my own. God alone knows when the Throne will be found, and by whom. I can only pray that it falls into the right hands, the hands of honorable men, and not the hands of those who have hounded me like ambassadors from hell.

My original journey took me from Lisbon, around Africa, and finally to Goa. My country has been great in these areas, and her Empire has spread, although now she faces many difficulties and perhaps her influence wanes. As always, I worry that my choices have not been correct, and that the clues that my Isabel and I have left will not remain for you to find. I can only go forward in hope...

From the Cape of Good Hope, I traveled around the Horn to the Land of the Good People. There my brothers had an outpost, although it was sadly abused by the time I arrived there. However, it was situated very well, beside a large rock, and its rear wall was built into that rock. It is my prayer that these will survive until God should bring you to the place.

May God give you wisdom and peace. In the name of our Almighty Lord, Jesus Christ.
   Joao Xavier
   X
   Written in the year of our Lord 1688.

———————⇒◦⟐◦⇐———————

Gideon was flipping through the channels on the television, unhappy with the choices of football or an incomprehensible game show, when Rei emerged in a fluffy white robe and wet hair.

"The Land of the Good People? What the heck is that?"

She sat on the bed next to him. "No idea. And even though I don't feel quite so much like road kill, my brain is still not working. You need to feed me. And put me to bed." She winked at him.

"You're not afraid of the bad men?" He pulled her close and kissed her.

"Not tonight..." She got up and rummaged through her suitcase. "But I am afraid of starving to death."

———————⇒◦⟐◦⇐———————

They slept like the dead, putting all their trust in the multiple locks on the hotel door. They were too tired to do much else, anyway, and the wine and an after dinner scotch helped them unwind enough to sleep through the night. When the light began to come through the crack in the curtain, though, Rei's first thought—after coffee—was the letter. She quietly got out of bed, not wanting to disturb Gideon until she had some information, and pulled on knit pants and a sweatshirt. She grabbed her laptop, the room key, and her notebook, and quietly snuck out of the room.

While she was having coffee and breakfast and surfing the web, she got a text message. "Where are you??" Gideon. She texted back, and finished off her orange juice. Five minutes later Gideon slipped into a chair.

"Sorry, didn't want to wake you up. I think I've found our good people, though."

Gideon signaled the waiter for coffee. "Oh yeah? Who are they?"

"Where. It's what Vasco da Gama called Inhambane, Mozambique. The Land of the Good People."

"Mozambique? Isn't that..." He waved his hand vaguely northeast. "Up there somewhere. By Kenya or Tanzania or something?"

"Yep. Tanzania. I was worried about visas, but it looks like we can get them at the airport there... There's not a whole lot of info online, though. They had some kind of uprising or war or something..."

"Of course they did," Gideon interrupted. "It's Africa."

"Whatever. Anyway, tourism hasn't really taken hold there. There's not much information on things like historical landmarks and stuff. I think we're gonna have to go and wing it."

"Wing it?" Gideon asked.

"Yeah. Like, get there and say, 'Can you tell me where there used to be a Jesuit outpost?' Like that." Rei licked her finger and pressed it onto a tiny piece of bacon.

"Uh huh. Great. I'm sure that'll go well. Maybe we

just need to find the oldest guy there, and see if he's, you know, four hundred years old." Gideon looked at her as he blew on his coffee.

"Smart ass."

Gideon smiled at her. "I'll call Mr. Xavier, and he can have Callie arrange the tickets. Hopefully we can get out of here today... I feel like I'm being hunted, and I don't like it."

Rei agreed. "We could drive..."

Gideon shook his head. "The roads here in Cape Town are good, but I doubt they're much to speak of when you get to the countryside. Plus I think it's probably dangerous. And long. And there's not a Motel 6 anywhere to spend the night."

"Ha." Rei stuck her tongue out at him. "Fine, we fly. I think you fly into Maputo and drive to Inhambane... But there aren't a lot of flights, I don't think."

They returned to their room, and Gideon got out his cell phone and dialed. He went over to the window and talked to the office, updating Mr. Xavier on their progress and on the letter.

"Yes sir, we're very excited, too. I'd be a lot more excited if these monks stopped showing up. No sir, actually, I forgot to call him yesterday, but I don't have any messages from him. Yes, I'll try him again before we leave the country. Yes, Mozambique. Next country up, I think. No, east coast... Yep. Can I speak to Callie, so we can get on the tickets and arrangements? I'd like to get out of here as soon as possible... Oh right, it's only 7:30. Can you have her call me when she gets in then? We'll see if we can find anything here in the meantime. Thanks. Yep. Bye."

He hung up. "Forgot about the time difference.

He was in early, though. And I totally forgot to call Detective van Rensberg."

"I'll go get some sodas from the machine. Be right back." Rei left the room with the ice bucket and her bag.

Gideon got out the crumpled business card and dialed. "This is Gideon Quinn. Is our friend awake yet? He is? Is he talking?" Gideon listened awhile. "Basically they're tracking us. So we need to do a better job of laying low, I guess. And what was the group called? I want to write that down... Hang on a sec." He grabbed Rei's notebook and pen. "*Congratio a Achalichus?* What does that mean? Really? Weird. Ok, well let me know if you find out anything else. I think we will be leaving the country today. No, I'm not sure where we're going, but you can always call the London office. Yes, thank you." He hung up.

Rei came back in the room with 4 cans of Diet Coke and a full ice bucket balanced precariously in her arms, key card between her teeth. Gideon jumped up to help.

"So the guy is talking. His name is Brother Dimas. No last name, of course. And van Rensberg found out the name of the order or whatever it is—the Society of Achalichus. The CA tattoo is from the original Portuguese, which is *Congratio a Achalichus*. Who is Achalichus?"

Rei put the ice bucket down and shoved two of the Diet Coke cans down in it. She replaced the lid.

"I think... wasn't that the name of the guy who was Paul's scribe? He was supposed to take the letter to the church in Jerusalem, and then something happened and it didn't get there. So maybe someone else got the letter later on, after the Temple was destroyed and all that, and they started a society in the early days of the Church to protect it."

"Makes as much sense as anything else." He popped a can of Coke and picked up the remote. "I just love waiting..."

CHAPTER TWELVE

INDIAN OCEAN

DECEMBER 1687

ISABEL HAD EXPERIENCED A PERIOD of seasickness after leaving Umm Qasr and the calm Persian Gulf waters, but recovered her strength and enthusiasm within a week. The Santa Antonio de Tanna made port in Mogadishu, the prosperous Muslim city. The couple explored the brightly painted streets, with their narrow three and four story houses, and gardens overflowing with flowers. They made friends with the locals, and Isabel was enchanted by their colorful dress, courtly manners, and hospitality.

The ship stayed in port for a month, repairing sails and rigging, securing provisions, and eating good, fresh food. Joao traded a quantity of spices for ivory and gold, and a quantity of fine wax. The local merchants assembled an abundance of fresh meat, fruits, and grains with which to make bread, and the nau left with its galley full of these fine victuals, more than enough to take them to their next port.

After a couple of weeks of uneventful sailing, for

which Isabel, especially, was grateful, they made port in Mombasa. A bustling Portuguese colony, Mombasa offered the couple a return to society. Many of the settlers there knew Isabel's father or his family, and made them most welcome. Joao transacted to trade more spices for sesamum and millet, and a crate full of intricate carvings made of ivory. It was a most satisfactory stay, and the couple were quite sad to wave goodbye to their new friends.

The next stop, and one that was on Joao's list of mandatory ports, was *Terra de Boa Gente,* the Land of the Good People. A Jesuit mission had been built here in the 1500's, and, as Father Eduardo, he had visited the declining outpost and the priests still living there. The Arabs had been increasing in the area, and most people felt that it was only a matter of time before the area returned to their control. But for now, it was still in Portugal's hands, and safe for his personal mission.

As they came into the bay, they were met with the site of graceful dhows carrying fishermen coming in with their day's catch. The white beaches were lined with delicate palm trees. The air was warm, with a slight breeze. The protected bay offered calm blue water. Block and clay buildings were set side by side with wooden structures topped by reed roofs. It was a charming scene.

"Oh, Joao, it is *tao bela!* I did not remember how lovely all these ports were when my parents and I traveled to Goa. I was so young... All I cared about was a place to run and play, and other children to meet. It is *maravilhoso* that God has allowed me to see them again!" She kissed his cheek.

"We will spend time in town, but we are also going

to go far inland. I am going to show you something very old... You will be amazed!" He laughed at her apprehensive expression. "I do not think we shall have to ride camels again, my dear, do not fear!"

She squeezed his arm. "I did not love those camels at the first. But I did love our trip to Ctesiphon, and that made the camels worth all the pain in my *nadegas!*"

"I have talked with the captain, and he knows that we shall be here for several months. He will arrange for a smaller vessel to take us south to the mouth of the River, which we will follow for some time to the northwest. Then there shall be some trekking across the land, I'm afraid. But you will find the result to be quite satisfactory, I feel sure. And that is all I shall say—it is to be a surprise."

———⊸∘⊲⊘∘⊳———

Because they would be leaving again on a small sailing ship, Joao and Isabel decided to stay aboard the Santa Antonio de Tanna rather than take rooms in town. They spent several days exploring, getting their feel for land again, and enjoying all of the fresh local and Portuguese cooking, teas, and coffees they could find. Joao was constantly on the watch for anyone who might be following them, but it seemed that they had, at least so far, kept ahead of their pursuers. It wouldn't be difficult to ascertain where he was going, as the possible ports along the east coast of Africa were not so numerous, but he was in a good fast ship, with an excellent captain and crew, and they had made good time while under way.

After a week in *Terra de Boa Gente*, Joao and Isabel

were enjoying a walk along the quay. He told Isabel they would visit the Jesuits on the following day. She could accompany him to the chapel, but the living quarters would be off limits to her, as a woman.

"But I do not understand why you wish to see these men, my love. Did you know some of them in Portugal? Surely there are more interesting things to do than visit Jesuits?"

An honest man at heart, Joao had been struggling with his lies to Isabel. He did not feel that this journey, as arduous as it surely would be, was the right time to confess his past life to her. And yet people did fall ill, or become injured, or even shipwrecked, and he would not wish to face God with this lie on his conscience. He did not know how to start, and so he hadn't, and had left it too late to avoid hurting her.

"Isabel..." He faltered, and stood looking out over the calm water. He could feel the breeze in his hair, the warm air around him. *God, please forgive me for these lies, and give me strength to confess them to her.* She was looking at him expectantly. He sat her down on a flat rock, and knelt in front of her.

"You know that I was here before. I was, in fact, in most of the places that we are staying on our journey back to Portugal." She nodded. "Well... When I was here before, I... Well, I looked different." He stopped. This was not going very well. Isabel laughed.

"You looked different? What kind of problem is that, silly man!"

Joao shook his head and blew out a sigh. "I *was* different. I was a different man. I was not Joao Pastorhino Xavier." He took a deep breath. "I was Father Eduardo Borges Santos. I was a Jesuit." There.

He'd said it. He had no illusions that he was done talking, but the worst was out in the open now, and he would have to take whatever came.

Isabel just sat, staring at him, mouth open. She started to laugh, as if he had been telling her a joke, but then saw, from the look on his face, that it was true.

"I... I do not understand."

Now that it was out in the open, Joao felt the words tumbling out. "I was a Jesuit priest, in Lisbon. A man, a stranger, came into my chapel one day, and he died while giving confession. He gave me a letter before he died, and told me that something was in Goa. After he died, we discovered that he had been stabbed. I didn't really understand all that had happened, but I took the letter to an old friend of my father's, who was able to read Greek, and he translated it. That letter... that letter is very dangerous. To the Church. It was written by the Apostle Paul, and it would have been seen as heresy by the Inquisitors. I hid this letter, and tried not to think of it. But the men who had killed the man who died—I found out his name was Sebastian de Gois—found me. They suspected that de Gois had given me the letter before he died. They followed me. They ransacked my rooms. Finally they chased me away from Lisbon, and I left as a missionary on the Sao Miguel, heading for Goa. I was in fear for my life, Isabel... I had no choice."

She was still sitting, shocked and still, but listening. Joao took that as a good sign and continued, pulling out de Gois' small journal from his pocket.

"I had this, too, and on the long journey from Portugal to India I began to study it. The man, de Gois, was a Templar knight, Isabel. Maybe the last. And he

137

knew of a treasure that the Templars had hidden long before, near Goa. He left clues in here, and during those long days and nights, I tried to figure them out. I... I found it, Isabel. I found the treasure when I got to Goa."

"What?" She was still in shock. "You have a treasure of the Templars?"

"No. I don't have it. But I took a small portion of it. The men from Lisbon had found me in Goa. They wanted the letter most of all, but they suspected there was a treasure. They followed me for days and weeks. Finally, out of desperation, because I felt that I could follow de Gois' book and find it, I changed my appearance. As a Jesuit I was easily found and followed. As a sailor, I was not. So I dressed in the clothes of a deck hand, and I moved to a boarding house near the water. I said that my name was Afonso Borges. I frequented the ale houses of the sailors, and I kept watch for many days. When I determined that the dark men had not found me, I purchased a horse and supplies, and set out to find the treasure. I explored the countryside all around Goa, looking for the places mentioned in the book. De Gois had arrived in the area by land, not by sea, so I spent half of the year out there looking for his landmarks, alone except for when I needed food or provisions. I grew out my hair and my beard. I dressed as settlers did who lived and farmed nearby. When the shopkeeper asked me where I lived I would wave to the north and change the subject to the weather or the crops..." He stopped, remembering the lonely time, and his despair of ever finding the end of Sebastian de Gois' trail.

"Go ahead..." Isabel finally said. Joao looked at

her and realized she didn't look angry. She was not happy, of course, but perhaps she was finding a way to understand. He touched her arm gently.

"I found it. I finally found it, Isabel. And it was the most magnificent thing I have ever seen...."

"What is it?" She asked, some excitement in her voice.

"The throne of King Solomon himself. It is not just a chair, mind. It is gold, with precious stones all over it—rubies, sapphires, emeralds. There are golden heads of beasts on each step leading to the seat. A lion, an ox, a wolf, a lamb...Above the throne is a golden dove with a golden hawk in its mouth. There are gold decorations all over. Fruit. Flowers. Even a menorah. There are other chairs, and branches, and vines. A crown. It is all, everything, in gold! And there is some wonderful mechanism that makes the creatures move... It is beyond imagining, really, and it is his throne. King Solomon. The richest king to ever live." His eyes shone at the memory.

Isabel grabbed his hand. "But where is it now?"

"I couldn't move that myself, of course, and I wasn't sure, anyway, that I wouldn't be found by those men. Nearby the throne there were golden bowls full of jewels, and many kinds of gold coins. There were more vines and leaves made of gold, which must have come from some other part of Solomon's palace or from the Temple itself. I spent many days with the treasure, and I prayed to God for wisdom. Finally, He gave me a plan. I took several of the leather bags that I had been using to transport grain and dried meat, and I filled them with small items from the cave. The ones not part of the throne—jewels, pieces of gold, coins.

Whatever I could put in the pouches that I thought could be sold. I left the throne as I'd found it, and I did nothing to disturb either the entrance nor any of the landmarks that I had used to find it. And I returned to Goa."

He rubbed his face with his hand, and finished the tale. "When I had been acting as a sailor, I met a man who the captains and other officers said could arrange anything. Shipments. Cargo. He had a reputation as a scoundrel, but also for being discreet should one want to bring things out of Goa that perhaps weren't strictly counted by the shipping company. I sought him out, and over two months time he was able to sell half of my treasure. For a large commission, of course, but I had expected no less. He was also able to help me become Joao Pastorhino Xavier, with letters of patent, and references from far flung merchants. He is the only one, until now, who knew my secret..." He tapered off, unsure, now that he was at the heart of the matter of his lies directly to her, how the remainder of his tale would be received.

"I didn't intend to marry, Isabel. I was a priest! I didn't know I would meet you, would fall in love with you. By the time that happened, everyone was accepting me as the wealthy merchant, Joao Xavier. Your father... he would not have given me permission to marry you if he'd known I was just Father Eduardo of Lisbon, from no prominent family. All I had was the money God had provided me through Sebastian de Gois, and a plan to make a business, to become the wealthy merchant through my own work and ideas that I was pretending to be. I know that I should have told you sooner... I do know that, and I have wrestled with God for many many months now. I hope that you will forgive me, but I know that you might not. My heart is breaking because I have hurt you, and I know that I cannot make that up to you. But *voce e o amor da minha vida*—you are the love of my life. And I will do whatever I can to earn your forgiveness." He hung his head. It was all out now, and there was nothing more to say. It was no one's fault but his own. If she left him now, he deserved it, and he would give her a sizable sum to get her back to her father in Goa and allow her to live her life in comfort. He couldn't even pray now. He, of all people, understood reaping and sowing.

Isabel didn't say anything for a long time. She was still holding his hand, and he felt tears dropping on it. He looked up at her. She looked peaceful, but tears ran down her face. *It is over,* he thought.

"I love you, Joao. You have brought more joy into my life than I knew was possible. And you are right, my father would not have assented to your proposal of marriage if he had known who you really were." She stopped and withdrew a delicate handkerchief from her sleeve. She wiped her face gently, and lifted his chin. "I love you, Joao. Eduardo. Both of you. And I am pleased to be your wife, and share your adventure with you. I wish you had told me before... But I understand why you did not, and I forgive you."

For a moment Joao didn't understand what she had said. He was so sure that she would leave him and return to her father that he couldn't make sense of her actual words. But he saw her smile, and he felt her hand on his face, and he knew that, beyond all hope, she was still his.

———————— ◦◦◡◦◦ ————————

The following day they went to the Jesuit outpost. It was, indeed, a crumbling pile. There were many Portuguese in the town, of course, but many had left their devout Catholicism back in their homeland. The small outpost received little support or help from the Pope, and struggled along with the small tithes, donations, and occasional offerings they received.

"Will they recognize you, Joao?"

"I hope not. No, I think not. I do not look the same, and I am, of course, no longer dressed as they. I am now married, and a merchant trader, and I will speak as such. I will say that you are devout, and wished to see their small chapel, and that I would be happy to merely explore until you have finished your devotions. I know that they must tend their small herd of goats, and their fields, as they must provide their own food. It is my hope that they find me respectable enough to be left to my own devices..." He grinned at her.

"If they only knew!" Isabel laughed.

"Indeed... Well, we shall continue to pray for God to be with us." He patted his pocket where his telescope case encased the letter, and felt the small chisel.

Father Gustavo welcomed the couple, and enthusiastically accepted the generous donation Sinhor Xavier made to the small outpost. He listened to their plan with obvious relief, as he and the other two priests who lived at the outpost had many duties to attend to keep their basic needs met, as well as to provide for the spiritual needs of their few regular parishioners. Additionally, tomorrow was his day to visit the local village. Their missionary work was slow and discouraging, and his departure each week put an added burden on the small household.

Isabel went into the small, spare chapel and knelt to pray. She actually did pray, seeking God's wisdom and protection for her husband, and asking Him to bless these tired and cast down monks. Meanwhile, Joao did his best to appear the waiting husband, wandering around idly, killing time until his devout bride should be ready to leave. In truth, he knew where he wanted to go, and casually made his way towards the second building.

The back wall of the living quarters was actually the face of a rock. The outpost had been built up against this rock as a way to both fortify the structure in case of wind, rain, or native attack, and also to capture the coolness of the rock by night. Because the rear room tended towards damp, the library had been moved from there quite early on, and now it housed the general living area, with a fireplace, rough hewn table and chairs for meals, and oil lamps for reading. There were small windows on the south side, opposite the open fireplace, which provided the only natural light.

No one was in the small building, and Joao had seen Father Gustavo hurrying back to the fields to help with the ever present weeding. He scanned the rock wall. Over the decades rough shelves had been fashioned and hung, as well as iron hooks. Some had obviously also been removed or had broken off. But the wall didn't have any carvings or other obvious features in which to hide his X. He looked at the fireplace, but it was made out of locally fired brick, and they did not have the look of longevity. He went back to the wall, and got down on his knees on the dirt floor. He crawled from the corner by the fireplace all along the rock, to the opposite corner.

In the far corner there was a small outcrop. A small, rough wooden cross was perched on it. Underneath, the otherwise smooth rock was creased and folded, like the rock had been liquid at one point in time, and it angled backwards. It was his only option. He quickly carved his X, scattering the chips of rock across the floor, and putting the larger pieces in his pocket. Directly underneath he used the chisel to dig a hole as close to the rock as he could. He discovered that the rock continued angling back under the surface of the soil, and he dug as far back as he could with his chisel and his hands.

When the hole was large enough, he took out the metal tube holding his precious letter. He spared a quick prayer for the man who would find it, then took out a square of leather in which he wrapped the tube completely. He placed all this in the hole, and covered it up, carefully tamping down the dirt and smoothing it to look like the rest of the room's floor. He stood and stretched his back and knees.

Looking down, he realized he was filthy. His hands and nails were reddish brown, and the knees of his breeches had dirt ground into them. Glancing around, he saw no pitcher of water, so he quickly went outside. Beside the building he found a small rough well, and pulled up a bucket of fresh water. He laved his hands and cleaned his fingernails as best he could. Looking at his knees he decided there wasn't much he could do about them except use his handkerchief to brush away as much as the dirt as possible. His breeches were dark brown, and the soil was red, so when the surface dust was removed the stains could not be readily noticed. He suspected Isabel would never allow them to be worn again.

Hurrying around to the chapel, he found his wife sitting anxiously. She had heard the door and lowered her head to her hands in prayer, but when she saw it was her husband she jumped up and ran to him.

"Oh my goodness, I was getting so *impaciente!* I thought that perhaps Father Gustavo had returned. Oh my..." She sat back down.

"I am sorry I was so delayed. There was not a very convenient place to leave my mark, but I think that I have hidden it successfully. It is in God's hands now." He helped her up and kissed her. "Come! Now we have the journey of a lifetime to prepare for!"

CHAPTER THIRTEEN

INHAMBANE, MOZAMBIQUE

PRESENT DAY

THE QUINNS HAD FLOWN FROM Cape Town to Johannesburg on a small commuter flight. Apparently not many people traveled to Mozambique, as they had to wait two days for the next flight out. They spent that time holed up in the Intercontinental Hotel at the airport, watching bad television, paying the equivalent of twenty dollars each to watch bad movies on pay-per-view, and eating from room service.

By the time they got on their puddle jumper to Maputo, they were both ecstatic to be out of the hotel and moving once again. The flight was short, and they had no problem with the visa process and immigration. They had scanned, copied and printed off two copies each of their passport photos, and had everything ready to go at the visa counter. It cost more than posted, and the Australian man behind them said, "TIA... This is Africa. That's how it goes here!" They laughed, paid, and went in search of a car hire.

This was their first snag, as they were unable to locate an official rental car firm. But after realizing what they were trying to do, and being happy to have a tourist who actually spoke Portuguese visit his country, their driver took them to a small mechanic shop. He accompanied them inside, and quickly arranged the hire of a somewhat ancient Toyota Prado at the equivalent of $150 a week.

"But you must return to Maputo, madam. My cousin will take a credit card number from you but he does not wish to try to charge for the whole car!"

Rei laughed and assured them that they would return the vehicle to the garage. Gideon raised an eyebrow at her, and she just shrugged. "We'll have to leave eventually, right?"

Turning to the owner of the garage, she thanked him in Portuguese, and assured him that they would do their best to return the car in short order. He happily told her to keep it as long as she wanted, while carefully putting the scribbled copy of the Xavier International American Express Centurion card number in the bottom of his money box. He handed her the keys, and led them outside and around the building.

The Prado was long past the warranty period, dented and beaten up from the poor roads and driving conditions in the country. But it was shining clean inside and out, and was full of petrol.

"Is diesel," the owner said haltingly in English to Gideon. Gideon nodded his understanding. He noted that the vehicle was four wheel drive, and had obviously been mechanically maintained, if not, otherwise, so loved. The seats were covered with native kikoi fabrics thrown over to cover splits and holes in the leather.

The jump seats that should have been in the very rear were missing. There were tie downs in the cargo area, however, and the taxi driver and his mechanic cousin helped Gideon tie their luggage down.

"Is bump," said the driver. He made a wavy motion with his hand. "Bump."

Looking out over the road they had driven to get to the garage, Gideon nodded. "Is big bump," he agreed.

∞∞∞∞∞

The driver had recommended that they stay at the Hotel Avenida Maputo on Nyerere Street. It was a busy street and a large hotel, and the odds were reasonably good they could get an internet connection. The food and bar were well liked by locals able to afford them. They were only spending one night in Maputo, planning their drive to Inhambane and getting whatever supplies they felt they needed after getting some local information on the roads, availability of food and fuel, as well as water and other necessary facilities. Rei was already worried about the necessary facilities, and Gideon secretly thought her fears were probably well justified.

Their room had a lovely view of the Indian Ocean, and the bar was situated on the seventh floor and also had a wonderful view. They had a local beer, which was almost cold, and enjoyed bowls of fried bananas and ground nuts. Gideon asked the bartender about driving to Inhambane while Rei tried to locate an internet connection.

"Ah, very far." He nodded his head as he waved up the coast. "Ahhhh, *wingi* kilometers. Many. Six hundred kilometers, I think. *Ndiyo.*" He nodded again.

"And how is the road? Is it a paved road?" Gideon asked, afraid of the answer.

"*Tarikishupavu.* Hard road. Yes. *Magumu.* Difficult."

Gideon thanked him and returned to the table by the window. "Good news, bad news..."

"Of course," Rei said.

"It's about three hundred and seventy-five miles, and the road is paved. Theoretically. But he says it is a difficult road, so I am thinking that the paved road is not in very good shape. Normally—in the States—three hundred and seventy-five miles would take less than a day of driving. Five or six hours. But I have a feeling we're talking a couple of days, at best. Or one very long day. I'm not sure it would be prudent to drive after dark, though, so let's count on two days of tough going."

"So probably there's no Holiday Inn along the way, then." She made a face.

"Uh, no. We'll ask the manager or someone who might have a little more English where we can count on finding some kind of room. Somewhere reasonably safe."

Rei raised her eyebrows.

"We're white, we're American, and we'll be driving out in the middle of nowhere. And TIA, as the guy at the airport said. Keep your purse close!" He ate a handful of nuts.

"Gid! Are you serious?"

"Of course I am... But keep your camera handy, too. Just don't hang it out the window."

After a long conversation with the hotel manager that afternoon, which involved a fairly complicated social exchange that they were entirely unprepared for involving tea and discussion of relatives and a long history of the country, they determined that their best choice for a place to spend a night was in the port city of Xai-Xai. A little less than halfway, it was a newish city which had a few modern hotels in which they could safely spend the night, as well as plenty of petrol stations. Since they were using diesel, they would probably not really need fuel, but the manager impressed upon them the importance of getting it when they found it, as there were not always facilities, and what facilities there were did not always have fuel on hand. The port cities were most likely to have it, and Xai-Xai should be able to accommodate their needs.

They arranged for a bag of food for the morning, including chapatti, fruit, more of the chips and ground nuts, bottles of water, several glass bottles of Coke, and fresh coconut and sugar cane. Gideon realized that they were taking nothing for protection from malaria, and got directions to a clinic where they were able to get two weeks of doxycycline very cheaply. There was no medicine they could take would be effective immediately, but they agreed that something was better than nothing.

Next they walked along Nyerere Street and picked up supplies that they thought they might need. Canvas "safari" hats. Extra sunglasses. Supplies for a simple first aid kit: adhesive bandages, alcohol, pain relievers, a native remedy for itches and stings. Work gloves. A roll of very bad quality toilet paper. Two rough blankets. A five-kilo bottle of water. They carried this back to the Prado and put it in the back, covering it all with the blankets. They had been warned that cars were frequently broken into for possible valuables, so they hoped their small ruse would encourage thieves to look elsewhere.

"Can you think of anything else?" Gideon asked.

"No. But I'm sure we'll think of something obvious once we can't get it! At least we have food, water and medicine. And I speak enough Portuguese to get by."

"Swahili?"

Rei laughed. "Nope, no Swahili. Practice your sign language!"

<hr>

They left the hotel early in the morning with their bag of food and directions from the manager, who was again on duty and saw them off. They maneuvered out of the Maputo, amazed at how many people were out and about. People of all ages were walking along the roads. Children were going to school, outfitted in their uniforms of bright colored shirts or dresses, each school represented by a different color, all shod with black, ill fitting shoes. Women carried babies wrapped on their backs with kikoi, baskets of items for the market on their heads. Men rode or pushed bicycles laden with charcoal or firewood, dozens of crates of eggs, a multitude of paint cans or cleaning brushes, or even large pieces of furniture. Others walked more slowly, shuffling on bare feet, with a hoe over their shoulder.

Rei looked at her watch. "Holy cow, it's seven in the

morning! I've never seen so many people out at seven in the morning in my life!"

"I guess if you have to walk everywhere, you have to get started early. Look at all those kids going to school... Can you imagine American kids walking however many miles to go to school?"

Rei shook her head. Most of the kids' uniforms were dirty and threadbare. But they chatted and joked as they walked along, breaking out in little chases and giggles. There were very small children, six and seven years old, walking alone. As they passed houses, toddlers were wandering around naked and unsupervised, waving to cars and standing right on the verge of the road.

Most of the motorized vehicles were either motorcycles or dirt bikes, which appeared to provide a sort of taxi service. It was quickly apparent that these drivers didn't know, or chose to ignore, any rules of the road. They weaved in and out between cars, buses and sports utility vehicles; they carried two and three passengers at a time, many of the women riding side saddle in their traditional dresses. No one wore a helmet. None of the vehicles used directional signals, so it was a complete free for all until they got out of Maputo and its surrounding small villages.

"Well!" Rei said, sitting back. She didn't realize how tense she'd been until they got out of the crush of people, traffic, chickens, cattle and goats. She looked over and realized that Gideon was still gripping the wheel with white knuckles. "You can release your death grip now, honey."

Gideon laughed. He, too, hadn't realized how stressed and tense he had been. "At least we didn't mow anyone down. That's a plus." He relaxed back against the seat. "That was... intense."

Not long after they had left the city, the road, which had been old and studded with potholes before, became an obstacle course. Large pieces of macadam were gone, and the red dirt had washed out, leaving deep gaps that had to be carefully driven around. There was virtually no shoulder, so they found themselves sloshing through filthy puddles where trash had been dumped and goats were scavenging. The couple of times they met a large bus, they had to move over off the road so far that the Prado was leaning at a thirty degree angle and Gideon had to hold onto the ceiling handle to keep from landing in Rei's lap. They began to think that two days was an overly optimistic estimate.

After five hours they had traveled about one hundred and fifty kilometers. The posted speed limit was fifty kilometers per hour, but there was almost nowhere that they had been able to move above thirty. Both of them were frazzled and frustrated. They arrived at a tiny village which had a petrol station with a small outdoor seating area, and decided to stop. Rei looked forlornly at the small building.

"I need to go to the bathroom," she said sadly. She got out of the car and Gideon saw her ask a uniformed attendant a question. The attendant pointed several buildings down, to a low rectangular structure open on both ends. Rei nodded, and returned to the car. She opened the back, took the roll of toilet paper, and headed to the latrine. She looked like she was walking the plank.

While she was gone, Gideon got out their basket of food and two of the Cokes and took them to the table and chairs. The attendant came over and said something in Portuguese. Gideon shook his head and spread his hands.

"English?" He said.

"You buy?" She asked.

"Um, buy what?"

"Petrol. You buy petrol." She pointed to the pump. "You sit, you buy."

Sighing, he nodded. Of course, there was no one else sitting at the tables. In fact, there was no one around at all, except for an emaciated dog sleeping under one table and a couple of scrawny chickens pecking in the dirt. He withdrew 500,000 in 500 metical notes. The attendant took the wad of currency, smiled, and went to fuel the vehicle.

"Receipt, please!" He yelled after her.

———— ⌗◦C▱◦⌗ ————

After a few minutes, Rei walked back, looking ill.

"Oh. My. Gosh." She sat down in the chair next to Gideon and grabbed her Coke. "That was the most positively disgusting thing I have ever seen. Really." She drained half the bottle.

"Do I want to know?" Gideon asked.

"No. But I'm gonna tell you. You walk over there," she flapped her hand, "and you can smell it long before you get there. One side is guys and one side is ladies, although I can't see it makes much difference. It's a couple of brick stalls, with a tin roof and no doors. And a hole. Just a hole, and apparently people have bad aim around here. And you squat." She finished the Coke. "I had to stand there for good while before

I could even do it, and I thought about going out in that bush over there, but what if some local guy was wandering along, or some creature or something." She looked at the Coke in disgust. "I just swore to myself I wasn't drinking anything anymore, too. Next time, you're gonna stand guard over me while I find a tree!"

"With what, my trowel?"

"Find a big stick! I don't care! You'll see..." Then she glared at him. "Or maybe you won't. This guy thing isn't fair."

<hr/>

They arrived in Xai-Xai in the late afternoon. The roads hadn't improved, and they were most thankful that it wasn't rainy season. Rei had refused to stop at any other facilities, and Gideon had further annoyed her by stopping on the side of the road several times.

The Zongoene Lodge was about eight kilometers from the Indian Ocean, and on the mouth of the Limpopo River. It was quite beautiful, with mahogany furniture, thatched roofs, a swimming pool, and two bars. The Limpopo was wide and the beaches lovely. Unfortunately, the Quinns were too exhausted from the drive from Maputo to appreciate it.

They checked into their small cottage and were thankful for running water fed by a cistern on the roof. They showered and changed into clean clothes, enjoying another Coke while sitting on the small patio overlooking the coastal forest. The feeling of life began to return, and they toasted their success in arriving at their first destination. They had a wonderful meal with a bottle of South African wine, and felt much better as they walked to their cottage. The power was provided by a generator, and when the generator turned off for the night, the couple fell asleep immediately and slept soundly until the first light of the morning.

After a simple breakfast, which that was supposed to be quick—and perhaps was, by African standards—they checked out. The African woman at the front desk told them how to get back to the main road, and assured them that the road, at least for the next thirty kilometers or so, was maintained rather well to support the large semi trucks that transported fuel and other goods from the port. Armed with this good news and another box lunch from the kitchen, they alighted the Prado once again, and set off.

The second day was much like the first, but they were prepared for it. Gideon did, in fact, stand guard for Rei at an isolated section of scrub, and they ate an unexpectedly delicious fresh cooked lunch at a village near Quissico. They were making better time today, which Gideon attributed to both the better road condition and a better mental condition on his part, so they took the time for hot meal. They had fresh fried fish and chips, and a pineapple and papaya salad that was absolutely wonderful. Feeling much better, they finished out their drive in good spirits, and arrived in Inhambane in good spirits, in time to cruise around town before settling on a hotel.

They decided to stay at the Barra Lodge, which was an unpretentious grouping of cottages on the beach. They didn't know if they had been traced yet. Having to use their real names and passports presented a problem, but they hoped that the brothers of the *Congratio a Achalichus* weren't so tech savvy as to have instant access to passenger or immigration control lists. There wasn't much they could do about it, anyway... In real life it was not exactly easy to get false identification or cross borders illegally.

They followed the bellhop to the beachfront cottage and stood for a long moment outside the door, appreciating the view. The African pointed down the beach to a larger open air cottage, "This is the bar, and food also. You can watch the fishermen come to the beach with their catch. If you buy, we cook." He entered the cottage and put their bags on the dresser. He showed them the en suite bathroom, and pointed to the bottles of water on the small desk. "This water good. No drink," and he pointed to the bathroom.

Gideon tipped him, and they flopped on the large bed. After several minutes, Rei sat up.

"You suppose they have wifi?"

Gideon laughed.

They did not have wifi in their cottage, but they did find a place to connect to a very slow dial up internet connection in the main lobby. After ten minutes, Rei was scrunching her hair on the sides of her head in frustration.

"I'd forgotten how slow the internet used to be! Oh my Lord, we'll be here all night!"

"I thought you said you couldn't find out anything online about Inhambane anyway?" Gideon asked.

"I can't. We'll have to start asking some questions tomorrow. I thought I could find out a little more about the country though... It's mostly Muslim around here, and I don't want to get in any trouble. I saw a few women with head coverings, but I didn't see anyone wearing a burka or anything, so we're probably ok. We'll have to use Xavier International as our cover, I think... Archeology and all."

"Xavier *is* our cover." Gideon laughed. "We really are doing research for the company... Well, for Mr. Xavier, so it's the same thing."

"True. It feels really cloak and dagger, though, doesn't it? I mean, who gets chased around by monks in real life, anyway?"

"Us, apparently. But let's try to keep religion out of it tomorrow, shall we?"

"Sure. Unreligious Jesuit research. Happens all the time." She smiled and closed her laptop, having never made a connection.

⸻ ⌖ ⸻

They slept soundly, lulled by the sound of the waves lapping on the beach. They were awakened early by people chattering in Swahili and Portuguese and other languages Rei didn't recognize. Apparently the beach was used as a roadway, as well as an unofficial port for the fishing sailboats that headed out early each morning. The birds were communicating in raucous squawks, and the couple found themselves smiling at the unfamiliar but peaceful sounds around them.

"Coffee." Rei finally said, and took her clothes into the bathroom. Gideon, not as addicted as his wife to morning caffeine, lingered in the bed awhile longer. He wasn't sure what the day would hold, but he wanted to fully appreciate this moment of rest as long as he could. When Rei emerged, hair in a pony tail, and in modest slacks and button up shirt, he sat on the edge of the bed.

"You go order. It'll take forever, so I'll just meet you there. I'll have eggs, potatoes, toast, fruit, coffee, milk, juice... Whatever they have!"

"I'll say!" She kissed him and left.

Rei was sitting in the shadows of the beach front restaurant, staying out of the sun so she could see the screen on her laptop. She had gotten her strong, delicious African coffee, with hot milk, and was spending the time before the food came reading over Father Eduardo's journal again. She finished a page and looked out to the ocean, enjoying the clear blue water and the fishing boats' sails out along the horizon. She was daydreaming and relishing the peacefulness of being the only patron in the restaurant when a man walking alone down the beach caught her eye. She put on her sunglasses and looked more carefully, then drew in her breath.

He was dressed in black, with short black hair. He had a cell phone to his ear, and was looking up and down the beach, then up to the houses and trees along the shoreline. Rei shrank back into the shadows, although she knew that she couldn't be seen. She was afraid to move, as that might catch his attention, so she sat very still, the black laptop open in front of her to shield her pale face. The man was agitated and shaking his head. She knew that the open building was empty except for her, and the lone server had long been in the kitchen, probably taking a rest while he waited for her food to be prepared.

She moved her hand to her pocket but realized

she didn't have her own cell phone with her. Gideon was coming to meet her, and she hadn't thought she needed it. Now she had no way to warn him to stay where he was until this monk passed by.

The man stopped just past the restaurant, and looked up the pathway that led to the main lobby. Most of the cottages were off this pathway, except the three that were on the beach. Their cottage was one down from where the man was standing. He was not talking, but had the phone to his ear. Finally he turned up the beach and kept walking, passing their cottage with a bare glance. Rei slowly closed her laptop and put it in her backpack. She backed out of the dining room and into the kitchen, where she sought out the waiter.

"We can't wait, I'm sorry. But we will pay for the food, if you will please put it on our bill." And she left through the back door.

———⊶∘⟋⟋∘⊷———

Rei followed the staff pathway that twisted through the hibiscus and bougainvillea, and wound her way around to their cottage. Gideon was locking the door when she got there. She put her finger to her lips and waved him back inside.

"They're here! There was one of those guys in black on the beach. He didn't see me—I decided to sit in the back by the bar to cut down on the glare on the laptop, thank God. And he didn't come into the resort, but I think there's someone else checking front desks, because he was on the phone. We need to leave. Now!" She began throwing their belongings into bags. Gideon ran into the bathroom and gathered all their toiletries, grabbed the rest of the bottled water from the table, and threw it all in his backpack. He zipped it up, saw that Rei had stuffed all their clothes in the suitcase. He hefted that while pulling a carry on. Rei grabbed her purse, backpack and the other carry on, and they cautiously opened the door.

They decided not to check out. The front desk attendant had taken their credit card information when they checked in, and they didn't want to alert the desk to their departure. Perhaps thinking they were still on the grounds would slow the monks down long enough for them to get into town. They used the staff walkway again, and skirted around the resort to the car park.

Gideon was thankful then for the older car, as it didn't have an alarm system. He used the key to quietly open the rear cargo door, threw all their bags in, and opened the driver's side door. Rei was bouncing up and down with impatience beside the passenger door. He pushed the unlock button to let her in.

"Go! Go go go!" She yelled after slamming the door, and grabbed the handle over her head.

Gideon, however, proceeded at a normal pace. He didn't want the sound of tires screeching, or of gravel being strewn all over the other vehicles, to give them away. He sedately backed out and stopped fully before entering the roadway. He glanced at Rei and tried to smile.

"Which way?"

"Crap, I don't know! I'm about to burst an aneurism here! Just drive. We don't even have a map!"

Gideon decided to drive south, as the peninsula eventually petered out at the point to the north, and he didn't want to get trapped. On the other hand, it was possible that their Jesuit mission had been up there... There was just no way to know, and for now his instinct was to be closer to the mainland coastline if they needed to get lost.

They drove around for fifteen minutes, trying to keep a map in their head of the roads they'd driven down. Gideon had a compass on his watch, and figured that they could always head east and hit the ocean. When they were sure they weren't being followed, they turned up a rutted red dirt road which seemed to have some businesses as well as shanties and lean-to shacks. About a quarter of a mile up, there was a bar and coffee shop, which also sold bottled sodas and chapatti. A small road ran between it and a house, and he pulled the Prado in there, as out of the way as he could squeeze.

Rei grabbed her purse, Gideon his phone, and they walked cautiously to the bar. It was open air, but with a rusted tin roof, and they chose a seat in the back corner, partially hidden by the Merinda soda refrigerator. Rei's hands were shaking as she picked up the laminated paper menu.

"We're just getting soda, Rei. Nothing we have to wait for."

"I know. I'm just... I need to do something. That really freaked me out. How are they finding us?"

"They have the journal. They know where Father Eduardo went. It could be just a matter of elimination, or putting men in all the possible locations. And if they have some way to get flight manifests, they'll always be able to find us eventually as long as we fly commercial. We have no way of knowing exactly what they're doing at this point. Driving was probably a bad idea. It took too long, and gave them a chance to catch up."

"So what do we do now?"

"We find the outpost. We try to get to it before they do. But without the letter, I think they're counting on us doing the work for them, just following us to see where we go. I don't think they know what we're looking for. So if we can stay hidden..."

"Yeah, that's easy. A *wazungu* couple in Inhambane. And they'll find out about the Prado from the hotel..."

"Ok, so we need a different mode of transportation... We can't do much about being white."

A very pregnant young woman came over to take their order. "*Posso adjudar?*"

Rei held up two fingers. "Coke, *por favor. Obrigado.*"

Gideon was watching the road, and a motorbike went by with a woman sitting side saddle, a toddler on her lap. The driver had on a helmet, which was unusual.

"What about that?" He pointed. "We can use a motorbike."

<hr />

In the end, they had to buy one. The pregnant woman's brother had an old one, which ran fine, but he used it as a taxi so he wasn't keen on renting it to them. There was no such thing as insurance on the bikes, and he didn't trust them not to steal or wreck it, thus depriving him of his livelihood. He negotiated a deal which would allow him to purchase another, slightly better one, and sold them two helmets as well.

Gideon was happy with the deal, because the bike was small, only a little bigger than a dirt bike, and would fit into the cargo area of the Prado if they put the rear seat down. It seemed a good bet that they would need it again, and they could sell it later if it survived the trip.

They left the Prado tucked away in the alley, and paid the young woman's nephew, who was twelve years old but not in school, to watch it. They put on long sleeves and gloves to hide as much of their white skin as they could, and donned the helmets. The owner of the motorbike had drawn a crude map for them, and they headed north once again, to a secondary road that paralled the main road. They stopped at a government office, parked the bike, and Rei went inside.

She went up to the desk of a very bored middle aged man. "*Perdao, senhor*, can you help me? I am here doing some research for my employer, Xavier International," she handed him her card. "I was told that there was once an outpost for a Jesuit mission here. Perhaps it is now ruins? Could you tell me how to find it?"

The man thought for awhile, and then shook his head. "*Nao.*" He went back to reading a government publication.

"Um, *senhor?* Do you know anyone that might know? I would really like to find it."

The man thought for another long moment. "*Sim*, there is a lady at the store on the corner. She is very old, and she used to be a teacher, at the secondary school. She might know. If she does not know, then it might be lost to time..." He shook his head at the realities of life, and went back to reading.

"*Obrigado.*" Rei left the building, pulling on her helmet.

———————— ✤ ————————

"Well, there's a store 'on the corner.' I don't know what corner. And an old lady who might know. And if she doesn't know, it's lost in the mists of time, or some such thing." Gideon started the bike and drove away slowly in the direction Rei thought the government man had pointed.

On the next two corners there were no stores. On the two after that, also no stores. They were about to turn around, when Rei spotted a small store selling airtime cards, bags of fried chips, and a few other sundry items. She touched Gideon's shoulder and pointed so he could see. He came to a stop in front of the curtained door.

Rei jumped off, and stepped inside the dark interior. It wasn't much bigger than a large closet, but it was lined floor to ceiling with toiletries, snack foods, fresh tomatoes, dried fish, second hand clothing, and bottles of water and soda. An ancient woman was sitting on a stool in the corner, looking like she was taking a nap.

"*Perdao?*" Rei spoke softy, as she didn't want to startle the woman. "*Dona?*"

The woman came awake in that slow way the elderly sometimes do, and blinked a few times. Then she smiled at Rei.

"Can I help you, Mama?" She asked.

"Yes, please. I am looking for the ruins of an old Jesuit mission here in town. I was told it was here at least until the end of the sixteen hundreds... but I don't know where it was located. A gentleman at the government office that you were a teacher, and would know." She smiled, and pulled out a three 500 metical notes. The woman smiled more broadly.

"Ah yes, Mama, I do know where that is! I did not take my students there, of course, as many were Muslim, but we did study the history of our country, and that included the Portuguese and their Catholic church. I do not know what is left of the place now, but it was built of brick and stone, so there might be something. No one has built on that site, out of respect for the God of the Portuguese, but I do not know if the path is remaining."

"We have a motorbike." She waved to Gideon sitting out front.

"Ah, that is very good. Yes, you can get there on a motorbike, I am sure." She took out a scrap of paper and found a pencil in a box next to her chair. Quickly she drew a simple map. "You will go north, to the point of the bay and the ocean." She looked at Rei to make sure she understood. Rei nodded. "The mission was built halfway between the two waters, where there is a large pile of stones. It was built into those stones, mama, so that it was strong in the wind."

"And how will we know where to turn off the main road?" Rei asked.

"If you go up the smaller road, the one on the bay, you will see a motoke plantation. It is small, owned by a family up that way. Just past the trees you will see a pile of stones about this high." She held her hand up about 3 feet. "That was the marker for the small path. I believe it is still standing there, as it is the boundary marker also for the plantation. You will have to turn there, and go east towards the ocean. I do not know how far. But if it is there, you will find it. There was a small church, and another building where the priests lived. Something should remain, I think, but I do not know what."

Rei thanked her and slid the money across the counter. She also bought two oranges and two more bottles of water. Putting the helmet over her hair once again, she went outside with her purchases in a battered plastic bag and climbed behind Gideon. She flipped up her face mask and told him the directions, showing him the paper map. He nodded, and they headed north.

They took one turn to the left, and another to the right, and were on a rutted dirt road about one and a half car widths wide. If they had been in the Prado it would have been a challenge to navigate the giant holes, but on the bike Gideon was able to stay almost on the shoulder and pick out a reasonably smooth, straight route. They were motoring beside the plantation, with the bay on their left, and Gideon slowed down. As the old woman had said, there was a pile of stones at the edge of the field, entangled in flowering vines, but just visible if one knew what to look for. They turned the bike inland.

They only got a dozen yards before there was no more path for the bike. Gideon stopped.

"We can either skirt over to those bananas or whatever they are, and try to follow along the edge under them, or walk."

"I think we'd better walk," Rei said. "We don't know if the plantation goes straight east, and we also don't know that the owners would be too keen on us wheeling through their plantation. I don't really want to meet some mad farmer who has a machete in his hand, so you?"

They agreed that wasn't an ideal scenario, but Gideon was still loathe to leave the bike. After wandering around the area, they decided to hide the motorcycle in a thicket near the edge of the motoke trees. It wasn't invisible, but it wouldn't been seen at a glance, and they felt that was the best they could hope for.

They shouldered their backpacks and walked to the original path. Gideon had driven as dead east as he could from the marker, and following a straight east west track would help them find their way back to the motorcycle. After a few hundred feet, Rei began to wish they had their own machete. The African vines had taken hold, and the thorn bushes crowded the rest of the unused area.

"Holy cow, these thorns are about three inches long! One just made a rip in my pants!" She fingered the hole. "That sucks."

Gideon was more worried about missing the ruins for the vines and termite mounds. He knew the peninsula wasn't very wide here, and didn't think their chance of getting lost was high. But he thought they could probably walk right by a one story house if it was covered in vines and half eaten by termites and never realize it. He was starting to sweat from his long sleeves, long pants, and the lack of breeze inside the jungle.

They stopped and drank from one of the water bottles, and Gideon made sure the compass on his watch was still pointing east.

"I feel like we should have dropped into the ocean by now!" he said. "It can't be much further, or else we've passed it."

"I haven't seen any rocks yet. It sounded like a big landmark, from what the lady said. Let's just keep going. If we hit the ocean road... well, we'll have to come back and try again."

Gideon put away the bottle and picked some broken thorns from his jeans. "After you..."

Rei set off. Gideon got snagged by a tangle of thorns and stopped to disengage, while Rei went on. He had just untangled himself when he heard her yell for him. "Gideon!"

He jogged ahead, and saw that she was standing in a clearing, a huge rock on the left and the obvious ruins of buildings scattered around. Near the rock wall was part of a fireplace and chimney, the lower half of a wall connecting the two. The church's rock altar was still upright in the ruins, the walls of which were mostly reduced to rubble.

Rei looked at him. "I think we're in trouble... There's almost nothing of the walls left at all!"

"Let's look at the church first. That altar looks like solid slabs of rock, and it's sitting on what looks like paving stones, not this brick." They wandered through the piles of broken bricks to the altar and each took a side, squatting down and running their hands along the stone. They checked the inside of each leg, and the stone pavers it stood on. Nothing.

"Ok, let's think it through. He comes here." She started pacing, and picked up a brick. "These bricks are fine... but they're made mostly of this red soil and reeds. So he can't imagine that they're substantial like stone would be. And I don't know what the mortar was... It obviously didn't hold up that well. And anything wood... well the termites have taken care of that." She pointed to a large termite mound in the center of the clearing.

Gideon walked over towards the rock face that had been a part of the living quarters. He stood near the fireplace, looking at the remains of the brick wall.

"This is all the same brick, except for the stones that line the fireplace. But they're just loosely fitted in here... and I can't see any X." He started to move the stones. After he'd picked each one up, looked underneath, and replaced it, he looked at Rei and shook his head. "Just dirt."

He walked to the rock and ran his hand along the surface. Rei joined him.

"There are holes... Looks like they somehow hung shelves or pegs or something on this wall. I don't see any carvings..." Gideon continued to scan the face. "But there are some rougher areas that might hide our X."

Meticulously they covered the wall. Nothing. Frustrated, Rei stood looking at it with her arms crossed, tapping her foot. She spotted a small ledge that was near the ground level. She couldn't tell if it had been inside or outside the structure. But thinking about it, she didn't see any reason that it would have had to be inside anyway. The last clue wasn't. She walked over and got down on her knees, leaning over to see underneath the ledge. She brushed away dirt and mud that had splashed up on the rock during many a rainy season.

"Hey! Here! I think it's here!" She used both hands to brush at the dried mud. "Bring me some water!"

Gideon came over and handed her the half full water bottle. She couldn't pour it directly on the wall, since it sloped back and away under the ledge. She handed the bottle back to Gideon and cupped her hands.

"Pour some in my hand and I'll splash it up there." He did, and she tried to throw it on the wall. "OK, that was a complete fail... Try again." She cupped her hands again, and this time had better aim. After three more handfuls of water, she had the mud off and an X was clearly visible. She grinned at her husband.

"Ta da!" She made a game show sweep of her arm. Gideon pulled the small trowel out of his backpack and started to dig under the mark. He realized that the rock continued to angle back under the surface of the now wet soil, and quickly dug a hole about ten inches deep. He was about to give up when the trowel hit something hard, and rang out. *Clang!* He reached in with his hands and dug around the spot, coming up with the now familiar telescope tube and strip of leather.

"Excellent! Now let's get out of here!" Rei said.

———◦◦◦———

They found their way back to town uneventfully, if driving in Africa can ever be said to be uneventful. They got the motorbike into the Prado with the help of the young car sitter, and paid him handsomely for his apparently great work. Upon being asked, he had assured them that no one had come asking about the vehicle or the *wazugus*. They had no idea where to go for the night, and had a feeling that they were going to need an internet connection to help them decipher the next clue. That was not an easy task in a country like Mozambique where even power was scarce, much less an internet connection.

Rei opened her phone. "You know, it's so weird. I have a better signal on this iPhone here than most places at home! No 3G, though, just phone. But we could call Mr. Xavier to do the internet searches, if worse comes to worse."

"Let's not talk about worse! Let's just figure out where we can spend the night, and then go from there. It would sure help to have a map."

Rei pulled out the crinkled map that the hotel manager in Maputo had drawn. She flattened it out on the dashboard. After studying it a few moments, she pointed north of the dot that represented Inhambane.

"Here. He put another dot." She brought the paper close to her face. "I think it says... Massingo? Massinga? Something like that. It's not too far. Ok, with the roads... it's kinda far. But it's out of Inhambane, and if it's big enough for a dot, maybe it's got a hotel. Or maybe we'll pass something else on the way."

"A Motel 6?" Gideon put the car into gear and headed south.

CHAPTER FOURTEEN

AS IT TURNED OUT, THE Quinns only had to drive an hour and a half north before they found a suitable bed and breakfast. They saw a sign for the Kingfisher Resort as they went through a medium sized village, pointing east.

"Should we take a look?" Gideon asked.

"Why not? Although it's hard to imagine much of a resort way out here."

After ten kilometers of badly rutted road, over which they were extremely thankful for their four wheel drive, they saw a grouping of thatched roofs in the distance, right on the beach. As they pulled into the gated drive, passing under an old weathered metal sign that said "Kingfisher Resort" in faded blue letters, they were amazed to find that it actually was a resort.

Directly in front of them was a two level swimming pool, a small waterfall slide connecting the two. A bridge crossed over it to the left and led to the open air boma that housed the bar and restaurant. To the right was an enclosed traditional round house that had "office" painted on the side with a painting of a kingfisher next to it. The door was open. Gideon turned off the car and they got out, looking up at the tree full of weaver birds overhead, and they walked slowly to the office.

"Incredible!" Rei breathed.

"Talk about the middle of nowhere. Wow." Gideon said.

The African woman at the desk was most happy to offer them a double room, with an en suite bath. The hot water would be available from 6:00 to 8:00 in the morning and evening, when the fires were lit to heat a large cistern. Generators ran until 11:00 at night, and resumed at 7:00 in the morning. There was no internet on the property, and when Rei checked her phone, she had no signal. A bellhop helped them retrieve their luggage, and other than raising his eyebrows at the motorbike in the vehicle, said nothing. He led them to a round thatched cottage about halfway down the row. It was named "Eagle."

He unlocked the door with an old fashioned iron key, which he handed to Gideon. He opened the frowsy curtains and cranked open the windows to let in a fresh breeze.

"They will put down the mosquito net while you are at dinner, *rafiki*. You ring this bell if you need anything, and someone will hear." Gideon gave him a tip, and the young man bowed. "*Asante!*" He left them alone in the room.

Gideon and Rei just stared after him, shell shocked.

"How did we land here? And where the heck are we, anyway?" Rei finally asked.

They wandered around the resort, relishing the quiet. Small dhows were beached on the sand. The pool was cool and refreshing. The bar served brilliant drinks in whole pineapples. The staff was all smiles, helpful but unobtrusive. There was only one other cottage occupied, by a Dutch family with two small children.

Before dinner, they returned to their room and pulled out the new clue. It didn't appear that the brothers of the *Congratio a Achalichus* had managed to follow them, and they hadn't seen anything to cause alarm during their stroll. Rei sat on the edge of the bed and removed the shade from the small bedside lamp. She removed the familiar leather strap, and the top, and handed them to Gideon, who placed them carefully on the floor. He moved to sit beside her as she unrolled the scroll.

The vellum, ink and handwriting were all the same.

"Well?" Gideon asked after they'd both stared at it for a long moment.

"Hand me my notebook. It'll take me a little while. I should have done it earlier—it's going to be dark soon, and this handwriting is so scritchy!"

"Scritchy? Is that a technical word in the art preservation world?" Gideon teased. He handed her the notebook and a pen. "I'm going to go sit out by the pool and have another adult beverage. Let me know when you're done."

Rei didn't answer, immersed in the translation. Father Eduardo had what was probably fabulous penmanship for 1688, but not so fabulous from her point of view. The letters were rather tall and elongated, and the script bunched together. The capital letters at the start of the sentences were quite elaborate, and hard to read. Then there were the differences in spellings that four centuries brings. She reached for her purse and pulled out her reading glasses and the flashlight.

After an hour, she wandered out to the pool, notebook in hand. Gideon was lying, in the dusky light, on a large hardwood lounge, looking up at the stars. She sat next to him and looked up. The sky, even while not yet completely dark, was ablaze with lights.

"Did you finish?" he asked.

"Yep. And we're going to need help. I have no idea what he's talking about... but if someone can figure it out, we know the next location." She clicked on her flashlight started to read aloud.

My son,

I pray that this letter finds you in continued good health and spirits. You have come far from Portugal now, and there remain two more letters for you to find before you arrive in Goa, and the Throne. I continually pray that our choices are wise, and that these letters will withstand the test of time. Knowing not when you are making this journey, nor whom God has appointed to the task, I can only do my best. Pray God it is enough.

From the Land of the Good People, I traveled inland, following the great Save River for much of the time. Many Portuguese were exploring the inner reaches of Africa, looking for the lost city of gold. There was gold to be found, to be sure, but perhaps not such a thing as a city made from it. I visited one ruin that was long rumored to have been the site of King Solomon's mine. I did not realize the significance of such a name until I made my great discovery in Goa, of course, but our Lord does lead us on His divine paths.

The Munhumutapa people near the place of the great Stone Houses. They traded with us for gold, and were *a most civilized people, granting us much hospitality. They laughed at our inquiries of a great gold city, but were gracious to show us the home of their lost ancestors. It is a vast place, and upon returning, my task of discovering a safe hiding place has been the most difficult yet. But I pray that God will give you guidance, and that my choice is inspired by His Spirit.*

Your mother Isabel and I are well, and have had continued favor against our unknown enemies. We pray for your success each night, in the name of our Almighty Lord and His Son, our Savior, Jesus Christ.

Joao Xavier

X

Written in the year of our Lord 1687

"Wonderful. Stone houses somewhere in Africa. That's very helpful," Gideon said disgustedly.

"It can't be somewhere in *all* of Africa, because neither of his voyages lasted more than a year. If they traveled up the Save River for some of the way, that goes into Zimbabwe. Surely Mr. Xavier can find out some options from that information."

Gideon pulled out his phone. One dot. "No signal, except one speck of a bar... Let's go see if the office is still open."

They walked to the office and found it locked tight. It was time for the dinner service, so they made their way to the open air boma and sat. When the waiter came with the short menu, they asked him about telephone service. He shook his head.

"*Hapana bwana.* No sir. No telephone. You must go

179

to the *kijiji*. The village." He pointed inland.

They thanked him and gave their order. When he came back, however, he had better news.

"*Bosi,* he says Bwana Wandere have phone. Tomorrow." He nodded and left.

"Guess we find Mr. Wandere tomorrow morning, then, and wake up Mr. Xavier again," Gideon said, tucking into the hot chapatti the waiter had left.

At 8:00 the Quinns were at the office, pacing before the still locked door. Finally a young woman opened it, looking surprised to find guests standing outside.

"May I help you please, *bwana?*" she asked Gideon.

"We would like to speak to Mr. Wandere, if he's available," Gideon said.

"Bwana Wandere not here yet, please. Will he to find you there?" She pointed to the restaurant.

Gideon sighed and nodded. "Yes, we will have coffee. Thank you."

She nodded. "Thank you, please." She smiled.

They had had their coffee, eggs, toast and fruit before Mr. Wandere found them. He bowed and smiled.

"My lady said that you need help, *bwana?* I am Wandere." The tall African man grinned at them with dazzling white teeth.

"Yes, thank you! We need to place a call to London, and we do not have any service on our phones." Gideon held up his iPhone. "We were told that you have a phone? May we pay you for a call, sir?"

Mr. Wandere's face lit up. "Ah yes, indeed! It is very much to call to the London, you know. But I have much air time on my phone, and you are most welcome. Please to come to the office when you have done?"

"Yes, we'll be right there." They signaled to the waiter, the same one as the previous night, who came forward, proud to have the one to provide Mr. Wandere to them.

After a couple of "we are unable to connect your call at this time, please try again later" messages, they had finally reached Mr. Xavier and explained the situation to him. He agreed to do the internet research himself, and not assign it to his assistant, although he was skeptical of the need for quite that much secrecy. He was not the most prolific web surfer, so they expected it to take at least an hour, although they had left him with a list of specific search options to use.

Mr. Wandere assured them, happily, as he was making quite a large profit on the entire enterprise, that he would find them wherever they were should Mr. Xavier call back. They determined to be back at the office within an hour, and stole a half hour to walk the beach and take some photos on their respective iPhones. It was a gorgeous location, right on the Indian Ocean. Dhows were sailing far offshore, fishing. There were paths down through coastal forest to the beach, but no other buildings, as far as they could see in either direction. They walked, hand in hand, in the warm water, pants rolled up, stealing some quiet time.

They were sitting at a table, shaded by a thatched umbrella, when Mr. Wandere came running out of the office waving the phone over his head.

"*Bwana! Bwana!* Telephone, sir!" He handed the phone to Gideon with a flourish and a grin. "Thank you, please!"

Gideon took the phone. "Mr. Xavier? You found it? Great! Hang on a sec, let me get Rei's paper." Rei passed him the notebook and pen, and she and Mr. Wandere both stood by as he talked, nodded, questioned, took notes, and ended with, "I'm not sure, probably have to fly. Let me discuss it with Rei and see what can come up with. I'll call you back... If Mr. Wandere doesn't mind?" He looked at the manager, who nodded eagerly.

After Mr. Wandere took his phone back to the office, promising that they could use it any time at all, Gideon explained what Mr. Xavier had discovered.

"Good news, bad news, I guess. Apparently the "stone houses" are in Zimbabwe. Something called Great Zimbabwe. And as an aside, the word Zimbabwe actually means "stone houses", if we'd only known. Anyway, it's 175 kilometers from Harare, where the main airport is. And Zimbabwe's not exactly stable, so we don't want to go driving alone through the countryside. There is a small airport at Masvingo, which is only 10 miles away from Great Zimbabwe, though. The bad news is that we're going to have to go back to Inhambane to fly out. Mr. Xavier has a membership through the AmEx card that gives him jet hours. So he can have a plane get us tomorrow, and take us to Masvingo."

"Back to Inhambane, though? That makes me nervous..." Rei chewed her lip.

"I know, honey. But we can't drive to Great Zimbabwe; it's just too far, and even more unsafe than our friends the monks. Otherwise, we'd have to drive back to Maputo, and that's two days. I think we're going to have to risk it. We can stay here tonight, leave at first light, and go right to the airport. And that lets us put the Prado in the airport parking lot—I'll call the mechanic and tell him, and leave some more money in the glove box. I don't see that we have much choice..." Gideon shrugged.

"You're right. I know. I'm just fed up with those guys making everything so complicated! OK, call Mr. Xavier and tell him we're going."

———◦◦◦◦◦———

Mr. Wandere was very sad to see them go, as they'd paid him for the air time and a ridiculous "general use fee" for his phone, as well as giving him a huge tip. However, he made sure they had a good breakfast, hot coffee, and some fruit to take with them. He gave them directions directly to the airport, and promised the utmost in discretion should anyone ever come and ask about two *wazungus* in a Prado.

They made the drive back in good time, and left the Prado in the lot. They had called the mechanic who had rented it to them, and told him where it was, and he'd assured them he had a spare key. They told him that he could keep anything they had to leave behind, and imagined he'd be quite pleased to find that included a motorbike and two helmets. They made sure, however, that there was nothing that could be traced to them or to Xavier International anywhere in the vehicle.

The word 'airport' was perhaps a bit extravagant for the actual facility. It consisted of a tin shed, mostly rusted out, a rickety wood tower with a shredded wind sock, and two runways. As they walked through the building to the table that served as the desk, they saw a gleaming jet sitting on the runway. The young man sitting at the desk, in a very official looking uniform for such a small airport, looked up at them.

"May I help you?"

Gideon nodded to the plane, while Rei took the immigration exit cards and quickly began to fill them in. "That's our ride. Will you please tell the captain that we are here?"

The man nodded and got up. He walked outside, consulted with another African standing outside the shack, and then walked to the plane. He went around to the other side, and up the steps. After a moment he descended and returned.

"The captain says he will do the pre-flight check. You may stay here and he will come for you. Twenty minutes." The young man rather nervously looked out the window. Following his gaze, Gideon saw that the older man he'd spoken to was on a cell phone, facing away from them.

"I think we'll take a seat on the plane and wait, thank you. It's been a long day already, and we'd rather relax."

Looking somewhat disconcerted, the young man asked, "Papers, please?"

Rei and Gideon withdrew their passports, and opened them to the Mozambique visa. Rei laid the exit cards next to them. The man made a show of looking them over, but in the end there was nothing he could do but stamp them and point them to the door. They gathered their bags and hastily walked to the plane. Gideon saw the man with the cell phone look at them, and then to the window of the building, in surprise.

"Hello?" Gideon called out as they ascended the plane's stairs. The captain came out looking surprised.

"They told me you wanted to go in twenty minutes. Sorry—I was just finishing my sandwich." He held it up apologetically.

"Interesting, since he told *us* you had to do a pre-flight check. We need to go now, though, if we can."

The captain shrugged. "Sure. We just got here—no need for a pre-flight." When the Quinns had gotten themselves and their bags into the plane he pulled shut the door. "Hey Jimmy!" He yelled forward. "Start 'er up. We're a go!" He got their gear stowed, showed them the seats, and told them to buckle up. The plane's engines started, and he went to the cockpit.

Looking out of the window, Gideon saw a Toyota Land Cruiser screech to a stop in front of the tin terminal, and two men in black jumped out, in time to see the airplane start its taxi down the runway.

CHAPTER FIFTEEN

THE FLIGHT IN THE CESSNA Citation took only an hour. They landed smoothly at another small, two runway airport in Masvingo. Looking out, Rei saw that the other runway was grass, and couldn't help feeling glad for the asphalt one they were using. The terminal building and tower looked interchangeable with the one in Inhambane, down to the rusted roof and the wide open doorway. The petrol tanks were placed under a thatched roofed building off to the side. It was, overall, a run down but adequate stopping place.

Not used to much traffic, the couple of workers at the airport made them feel most welcome, with bottles of water and sweet biscuits. Their captain, an American named Joe McMillan, told them that he was instructed to wait for them, and that he and the co-pilot would be staying at a local hotel. He gave them his cell number, and told them to call with a head's up when they knew when they'd want to leave. He started to go back to the cockpit.

"Wait, Captain. How about we go with you? We probably can't get to where we're going at this point, it's a bit late in the day. Maybe you can book two rooms at the hotel Mr. Xavier suggested, and we'll start first thing in the morning. Hopefully it'll just be the one night, and we'll be on our way this time tomorrow..."

McMillan amiably agreed, and they gathered their bags and went to wait in the terminal. A taxi had already been called, a small old van that had seen many better days. The old driver was sitting in a rickety folding chair next to the vehicle, dozing. When they came out he awoke, and helped them put their suitcases into the van, where they sat to wait.

"Those monks will be able to find us, because Captain McMillan would have filed a flight plan..." Gideon said morosely.

"Yeah. I know. I think maybe we need to go on out to the site, even if it is the afternoon... If they can get their hands on a plane, they'll be right behind us."

Gideon sighed. "Probably. Getting your hands on a private plane isn't as easy as it sounds, but you're right." He climbed out of the van and went inside to speak to the driver. A few minutes later he came back.

"The driver said that the site is open until 6:00. We're about a half hour away. So we'll have a couple of hours, but I don't know how we'll find anything in that time. He said the place covers almost 1800 acres!"

Rei's face blanched. "1800 acres? We'll never find it!"

"Maybe we just need to get a map. They must have some kind of guide map for visitors. And then we'll have to figure out the most likely places, like we did in Cape Town. I don't see anything else we can do... We can't wander around looking for a big X. We'd be there for months!"

Rei nodded, discouraged. They didn't know anything about the site except the location from Mr. Xavier, and now this disconcerting news about the size and scope of it. How would they ever look over that much land? It was impossible.

"There is some good news," Gideon continued. "The African Sun has internet..."

They arrived at the African Sun Hotel, and realized that it was actually called the Great Zimbabwe African Sun, and was adjacent to the site. Hence the front desk was more than willing to supply them with a site map, and instructed them on the satellite internet connection, available in the lobby area only. Rei took her backpack and sat in a comfortable chair while Gideon was shown to their room by a uniformed attendant.

After much surfing, Rei realized that she wasn't going to get very much information online. Most was supplied by either the World Heritage Sites website, which was largely an overview, or by tour companies, which offered much the same. Wikipedia, not necessarily the most reliable source, listed eighty-five references, but most weren't available online. Sighing, Rei closed her computer.

She was having a cup of hot African tea and studying the site map when Gideon returned. "The rooms are in Captain McMillan's name, not Xavier or the jet company. Hopefully that'll slow them down, although it's obviously the hotel closest to Great Zimbabwe, so if they assume that's where we're headed, they'll figure it out soon enough. Whatcha got?"

"Not much on the internet... But I think I can narrow it down. Not that I'm right, obviously, but we have to start somewhere. Here look..." She turned the site map so he could see it clearly.

"Now, Great Zimbabwe has absolutely nothing to do with Christianity or the Catholic Church, so we don't have any hints there. But now that we know what he's hiding and how, we know he needed privacy to do it, and would choose somewhere he thought would last for a long time." She pointed to a circle on the map. "Here, there's a conical tower. It probably didn't have anything to do with religion in any way. But the walls are twenty feet thick, and it's fifty-six feet wide at the base. The tower is still standing today, thirty-six feet high, so it's obviously solid. I think that's a good possibility, probably on the inside, as they would have been hidden while carving the X and digging.

It's part of an area called the Great Enclosure, which is the most preserved part of the ruins. It might be wishful thinking on my part, though. I'd say the second choice would be here," again she pointed. "The Hill Complex. This is the oldest part, and there were a lot of artifacts found there, including the soapstone birds that are on the Zimbabwe flag. Supposedly this was the home of the kings, and of King Solomon's mines, and we're looking for King Solomon's throne, so that might have appealed to Father Eduardo, if he even knew it. It's hard to know what those early explorers knew or understood about the site, though." She shook her head.

"Those both look good, Rei. At least it's a start..." Gideon put his arm around her.

"I know. It's just so huge! If I'm wrong—even if I'm right, really—there is so much ground to cover. Literally."

"We'll start there, at the tower. Because we'll be hidden, too. And then we'll go to the Hill Complex. And if we don't find it... we'll just try to think it through again." He folded the map. "Fast."

———————◦◦⊂⊘⊃◦◦———————

After dropping her laptop in the room, Rei found the room attendant and asked directions to the site of the ruins. They thought it was better not to telegraph to the staff at the front desk that they were already exploring, so they made sure to go around and out of sight of the main hotel buildings as they walked. The African sky seemed huge and almost white, acacia trees dotted here and there. There were many kinds of birds that they had never seen before, and they could see small groupings of duiker and warthog. While they were not alone at Great Zimbabwe, the tourists seem to be on the way out, rather than on the way in.

They purchased tickets, and quickly followed their map to the Great Enclosure. It was amazing sight, and must have been quite shocking to stumble upon when the Portuguese first found it in the 1500's. Huge stone structures, of indeterminate but obviously ancient age, rose up out of the grass. Complex buildings, still in remarkably good shape, dotted the area in three distinct areas. Of course, the brochure pointed out, the Europeans had assumed that white people had been here before them and built it, as they couldn't fathom the native Africans having such skill.

Parts of the enormous wall had tumbled down, and candelabra trees and acacia had invaded the buildings. The grass was brown, awaiting the rainy season. The large conical tower was shaded by a large narrow tree that seemed to have placed its entire canopy over the gap left by the missing roof. They walked through a long corridor between the outer wall and an inner wall, both twenty feet high and at least ten feet thick. Rei felt a bit claustrophobic, and was glad to come out in the small courtyard where the entrance to the tower was.

They hadn't met anyone inside the Great Enclosure, but now they encountered an elderly couple who seemed to be examining the tower brick by brick. Rei looked at Gideon, eyebrows raised. Her question was clear, *"Are they looking for it, too?"* Gideon shrugged and went to make conversation.

"Hello! This is amazing isn't it?" He swept his arm to encompass the tower.

"Oh indeed!" said the man, a strong South African accent apparent. "The wife and I have been wanting to come here for ages, and finally we just said, 'why not, we're not getting any younger!' And besides it's not that far from home. Of course you can hardly get into the country, with this crazy government, at least if you're white. But then we've been on the other side of that coin, so I suppose we can't complain. Isn't this just magnificent? Margaret and I are trying to see how many stones and bricks were used to make this tower. We thought we'd count them within a cubic meter and multiply, but the wall's so thick it's impossible. Probably been done already, of course, but we amateur archeologists like to check the professionals' work, you know." The man laughed and took a deep breath. "Oh, my, look at the time! I think our driver was coming back twenty minutes ago... Margaret, dear, we must go. We shall reevaluate our plan and return tomorrow.

Good bye now!" And he turned to walk off, his wife in tow.

The Quinns watched them walk away, and laughed. "At least we're not counting bricks!" Rei said.

———————⌁———————

Once inside the tower, they stood in the center and looked at the walls in the filtered light coming down from the roofless top. The floor was dirt and scattered stones. The stones in the wall were laid well, with no mortar between. There did not appear to be any original carvings, although there was the sort of carved graffiti that all such sites seem to attract. They still only had the one small flashlight, so they decided to start at the entrance and work around counter clockwise. They looked up and down, from head height to the floor.

Halfway through they found a mark that appeared to be the bottom "V" of an X. Excitedly, they began digging into the dirt directly underneath, but found nothing down to a depth of eighteen inches. Rei examined it again.

"This doesn't look the same as the other X marks we've seen. I mean, it's hard to know, it's so old. But Father Eduardo seemed to make a deep center mark and the edges sloped up. The other marks were about four inches tall. This one is more squared off, fatter, and taller."

Gideon filled the hole and tamped down the soil. "Onward..." he said, and brushed off his pants.

They didn't find anything else in the tower that pointed to Father Eduardo's clue. The sun was much lower on the horizon and it was getting dark inside the tower. Standing outside in the fading light, Gideon looked at the outside wall.

"Should we take a quick tour around the outside? Can't hurt... "

Rei said, "There's enough light if we split up and go fast. But I don't really want to walk across that bit of flatland back to the hotel in the dark!" Gideon thought he heard her mumble, "Creatures..." as she jogged around to the back of the tower.

They went as quickly as they dared, trying to balance speed with careful searching. Neither found anything. When they met in the middle, they were discouraged. While not having said it, both had felt that the tower was their best bet, and finding nothing was very frustrating.

"Damn." Gideon put his hands on his hips and looked around. "It's just so freaking big!"

Rei pulled on his arm. "I know. We'll go back to the hotel and look at the map again. But can we please just *go?*"

They hurried along the path that linked the World Heritage site to the hotel. The sun was almost gone, and the stars had come out in great array. Rei didn't notice. She had her little flashlight out, and was shining it back and forth in agitation, talking to herself.

"What animals live in Zimbabwe? Do they have lions? Of course they have lions, it's Africa... And probably hyena. God, I hate hyena, they freak me out... What else? Leopards? I'd like to see a leopard. From a car." A bat swooped down, chasing an insect, and Rei let out a shriek. "Oh my Lord! Run!" She started off down the path, but Gideon grabbed her.

"Rei, chill. Just keep walking, keep talking, and

use your light. Look up there, see? The hotel. Don't run and look like some kind of antelope... Just walk." He didn't trust her to listen, however, and kept a grip on her arm.

When they entered the lobby, Rei was so relieved that she sunk into a chair. "I swear I heard a hyena out there laughing. I hate that sound they make..." She put her hand over heart and tried to breathe.

"I don't think it was a hyena. It sounded more like a warthog to me."

"Warthogs don't *laugh*, Gid."

"Yeah, and they don't eat people, either. We're safe now, Rei." He leaned down and kissed the top of her head. "Let's get some dinner. I'll even get you a glass of wine. And maybe a back rub later."

CHAPTER SIXTEEN

ZIMBABWE

1687

IT TOOK A WEEK OF preparation, during which time Isabel and Joao stayed aboard the Santa Antiono de Tanna. Joao hired a native guide, and agreed to pay for a dozen men to accompany them as porters and, if needed, protection. Two African elephants were pressed into service to carry supplies and tents, and the porters also were to carry food, weapons, cooking equipment, and other necessities.

"But Joao, where are we *going?* And please tell me that I do not have to ride upon those beasts!"

Joao laughed. "No, my love. You do not have to ride upon the *oliphants*. For some of the way we will be able to use a cart and oxen. Some of the way, I'm afraid you will have to walk. But we will also have small ponies with us, and you will be able to ride on those, as well. We are going far inland, to a great ruin of an ancient people. We will follow the Save River part of the way, but much of the way we will walk across grasses and through forests. We shall see a great many animals, and I think you shall find many things to draw on the way."

Isabel was most pleased with everything except the mention of walking. "We will be walking?"

"Yes. There are times when that is the only option. I have had some proper shoes shod for you, and for myself as well. And you might... well, you might want to consider wearing my breeches when we come to it."

Isabel was scandalized. "Your *breeches?* Joao! What would people think?"

"I don't know what people would think if they were to know, and the natives will not care, as their women are largely naked." He laughed at her further scandalized expression. "You do not have to decide now, *meu amor.* You will know the land before we must walk, and you can choose what to do with your skirts." He kissed her. He didn't think he'd mind seeing her in breeches, but it didn't seem like the time to mention it.

They left after first light. They followed trails used by the natives, and although these wandered and meandered between homesteads and villages, in general they found themselves heading northwest. Isabel was settled comfortably on a narrow cart drawn by two large cows whose calves were tied to the cart. Isabel had seen a lot of Africa on their travels, but mostly coastland. She was entranced by the brown grasses, the huge red mounds that the natives had told her were made by *mchwa.* As best as she could gather, these were a white ants with wings, and, to her disgust, the men seemed to view them as a delicacy to eat.

As they got away from human settlements, they saw more and more animals. Four legged creatures that looked like exotic deer, which the natives taught her were *swala*. Wild hogs that got down on their knees to eat and drink, and which were remarkably fast, called *mbango*. Small weasels called *nguchiro*. On the fourth day out, they saw a pride of *simba* resting on a rock outcropping. She knew these from drawings she had seen in books, although they looked much more majestic and imposing in real life. *Leao* in Portuguese. Lions. The guide told them that they were very sleepy in the day, and not very dangerous if not disturbed. But at night they hunted and could be heard across great distances, and that keeping fires lit and men on watch was necessary to keep they, themselves, from being eaten. She shuddered, and was glad for the munitions that the men carried.

As they made their way to the Save River, there were, indeed, times when it was unsafe to ride in the cart, and Isabel and Joao walked side by side along the trail. The first time this happened, Isabel refused to remove her skirts. However the heat, once she was exerting herself, and the thorns along the path which grabbed and ripped her clothing, made it nearly impossible to keep the pace of the rest of the party, and she quickly realized the wisdom of breeches. Joao held up a blanket for her, and she traded her skirts for a pair of his fawn colored breeches. She was immediately struck by the comfort and practicality of the garment.

"I do not know why women must wear skirts!" she exclaimed. "These breeches are so very much more *util,* practical!"

Joao kissed her. "And they show your form very well, *meu querido.*" She blushed, but squeezed his hand at the compliment.

———— ⋅∘⋖⋗∘⋅ ————

They reached the Save river after two weeks. Because it was the dry season, water had been scarce in the dry landscape, and they were almost out of the now stale tasting water that they had brought with them. Bathing had been non-existent, so when the flowing river came in sight there were many reasons for excitement and cheering. They set up camp on a bank, not too close because the guide was concerned about *mamba,* or crocodiles. This led Isabel to a moment of panic about their eventual crossing of this river, but Joao told her that they would follow it on the south side for some time, and by the time they needed to cross it, it was little more than a stream. She put that eventuality out of her mind, and concentrated on the lovely sound and feel of fresh, cool water.

In the event, no crocodiles were spotted. The guide positioned his men at both ends of a fifty foot stretch of beach, armed with loaded muskets, and the oldest one, who was apparently well versed in the ways of the creatures, scoured the water and banks for them. When none were spotted after some time, water casks were refilled, clothes were washed, buckets were brought to the *wazungus* tent for bathing, and the animals were temporarily pegged where they could drink their fill.

Several of the natives took sharpened spears and waded knee deep into the water. Joao, standing watch outside their tent while Isabel bathed, watched the men stand very still, looking at the water. With a quick flick of their wrist, they stabbed downwards, and many times came up with a wriggling fish. Joao remembered this from his initial trek inland, and knew that a delicious dinner of fresh fish wrapped in aromatic leaves would be on their plates that very evening.

Also that evening, the men built up a large fire and brought out homemade instruments. They played lovely, plaintive music; dancing music with a strong, warlike beat; and songs that they joined with singing, with whoops and ululations and tribal languages. It was exciting and disconcerting, and Isabel and Joao felt privileged to be witnesses to it. When several of the younger men laid down their instruments and began to dance, Joao joined in. Isabel shook her head at their insistence that she join the dance, but laughed and clapped to watch her husband cavort and hop around with the smiling men.

Their journey upriver was beautiful, but held its own challenges. Many animals had gathered by the river as the dry season continued, and they had to be constantly on guard against the various wild cats that had also gathered where the food was plentiful. At night the sounds of lions hunting and eating could be heard across the flatlands. The frightening laughing sound of the *vikuto* never ceased to inspire terror in Isabel, and she often clung onto Joao in the night. On many occasions they did see a crocodile, looking like a log floating in the water, or sunning itself on the bank of the river. Once, they watched as a particularly large creature, which had apparently been lying in wait under the water, rise up in front of a young *swala* and carry it away, causing its herd to scatter in fear.

The elephants in their party seemed to do as good a job as the fires at keeping the predators away, but they did not seem to be too discouraging to the black faced monkeys that were everywhere. These monkeys were not afraid of the men, the fire, the elephants, or anything else, and frequently tried to steal things from their camp. Their particular favorite, aside from any kind of food, was anything shiny, so Isabel quickly learned to keep her small mirrored glass, and her silver comb, hidden away, well inside her bag of sewing.

After another ten days, the river became noticeably narrower, which meant that the animal populations were thicker. Hunting was good for the men, and fresh meat was plentiful. The leader instructed the men to smoke some of the meat over the fire each night, and to fill up the water casks to the top each morning, as the river would soon become narrow.

They were not surprised, then, when he announced one morning that they would cross the river that day, and leave its side. Isabel, especially, was sad to see it go, and watched behind her as the cart carried them away. Joao, walking beside her, reached up and grabbed her hand, kissing her fingers.

"It's all right, *meu amor*. You will see a very great wonder, and not too long now. And you know, we have to get back to the ship again, so you will see your beloved river."

"Ah, Joao!" She clapped her hands. "I forgot we must go back again! That is wonderful. I have fallen in love

202

with this..." She spread her arms wide. "This Africa!"

⸺⸻∘⊂✺∘⊂⸻

A week later, they arrived. The sight was called *zimbabwe*, or *dzimba-dza-mabwe*, "large houses of stone," to the local Shona tribe. They made their camp in the valley, which contained some crumbling stone walls and other ruins. Joao knew that this was the least of the ruins, but enjoyed Isabel's fascination with them, and walked around them with her as the porters set up the cooking area, the best hunter went to find fresh game, and the animals were taken care of.

"Who lived here?" Isabel asked.

"It is somewhat of a mystery... the Shona say that the Munuputapa lived here, the great kings. No one really knows, or knows why they left. There is much more, which we will begin to see in the morning, my dear. It is lovely out here, in this Africa, is it not?"

The next morning, Isabel was rendered speechless when Joao took her to a grouping of structures on the top of a hill. Most appeared to have been small houses, although there was a larger structure on the edge of the hill. Inside one of the dwellings, shards of broken pottery and rotting pieces of baskets could be seen in the dirt. Exploring one of the farther dwellings, Isabel spotted what appeared to be a smooth black rock in the ground, and reached down to it. When it didn't come up readily, she bent over and tugged on it.

"Joao, can you help me get this stone? I fancy the smooth black surface, and would like to have it for our house in Lisbon, as a reminder of *zimbabwe*."

Joao knelt down and tugged on the stone. It didn't

move. He took his chisel out of his pocket and carefully displaced the dirt around the rock. He tugged again and it rocked slightly, but was still not loose.

"It must be quite a large rock. Do you still want it?" Seeing Isabel's nod, he went back to carefully digging around the stone. When he had dug a hole almost ten inches deep around the smooth black rock, he finally felt it release. It was surprisingly heavy, and he used both hands to pull it out. When it emerged, he was astonished. It was a bird!

"Oh my!" Isabel exclaimed. "It is lovely! It is a bird, is it not?" Joao nodded and used his sleeve to wipe most of the dirt off. When it was clean, it was obvious: it was a black, delicately carved bird, with a solid base adorned with a geometric pattern. It was all one piece, and weighed several pounds.

"You have quite a reminder now, Isabel!" He wrapped it carefully in his waistcoat, and they went back to their tent.

When Joao showed the statue to the guide after dinner that night, the man was stunned. "This is a very great blessing, *bwana*. It is said to be very good luck to find an object of the great kings, and the birds were sacred to them. You have the blessings of the gods, *bwana!*" He enthusiastically bowed to him.

"I believe in one true God, *o meu amigo*. But He has, indeed, blessed me mightily, and we will cherish this treasure always."

Later that night, as he was putting the final words on his letter to the progeny that would follow him on this quest, he thought that it was truly a sign. He didn't know if the crumbling valley dwellings were the right place for this clue, but he knew beyond a doubt that God had confirmed his choice of the *zimbabwe* for a hiding place.

———◦◦———

The following day, Joao, Isabel, and an armed porter explored father afield, into more of the ruins of the stone houses. There was a large structure with a great, thick wall. The stone buildings were connected, with passageways winding through the thick walls. At one corner was a tall, enormously thick tower. The roof had fallen in, and was littering the floor. The gap let in light, and they could see that the walls were at least twenty feet thick. Building it was quite a feat, and Joao wondered at these natives who had contrived such an amazing thing.

They wandered through the complex, and Isabel drew the likeness of the characters over the entrance. The porter shook his head when Joao asked if he could read the letters carved there. "*La! Iko Shona.*" When they returned to camp, their guide also shrugged and shook his head in the universal gesture of not knowing.

"It may be Shona, *bwana*. But the meaning is lost, even to those people. It is not known what those words say. It is lost."

That night, Joao and Isabel discussed where they should leave their clue. Joao felt that the tower was the best choice, as it was so obviously substantial and able to withstand the trials of time. Isabel felt that they should honor God's gift to them, and leave it in one of the structures on the hill. They could not reach an agreement, except to agree that they would spend more time exploring the site before reaching a decision.

The following morning, Joao awakened before first light. He knew that it could be dangerous to wander about alone, but he felt that he needed to see the sun rise over the *zimbabwe*, and thank God for their safe passage, for the stone bird, and for this beautiful creation that was Africa. He saw that there were two men still on guard by the fire, and, feeling a bit foolhardy, but also compelled, he moved to a site that was invisible to everyone at the camp, facing east towards both the sun and the ruined stone houses.

As the sun rose, it illuminated the hill first, before he could actually see the orb. Soon the light of the sun's rays came through the dwellings themselves, seeming to set them alight from the inside. As he prayed and thanked God for all the provision in his life, the sun continued to rise, and soon there was just one structure in his vision, ablaze with the first morning light. Isabel was right. *It will be there.*

CHAPTER SEVENTEEN

ZIMBABWE

PRESENT DAY

THE MORNING AFTER THE FALSE hyena scare, Rei and Gideon set out for the ruins. Both of them felt the pressure of time, as the likelihood of the monks chartering a plane increased with every passing hour. They knew that, if they didn't find the clue this morning, they would be in a situation they wouldn't like and may not win.

They hurried along, and even Rei wasn't thinking about creatures. She kept mumbling, "It's got to be the Hill. It's just got to be the hill..." under her breath.

When they arrived once again on the site, they immediately made their way to the Hill Complex. There were only three other people about, as they had arrived exactly at the 9:00 opening time. None of the three visitors was dressed in black, so they felt safe for the moment. The hike up to the structures seemed steeper in practice than in observation, but they kept up a brisk pace, Gideon leading the way. When they reached the top, they realized that there were a number of small structures, and one larger one. And once again, it was much larger than they had envisioned.

"Oh Lord, how will we search all this? It's huge!" Rei's face showed her pessimism.

"Let's just be systematic. It'll be easier and quicker to look in all these houses first. There's enough light, so we can split up. That's, what, three or four each? We can do that. If we come up empty... We'll have to go in there." He pointed to the walls of the large structure. "Let's hope we don't. Come on, I'll take every other one. You start here."

He steered Rei to the first house, and he jogged ahead to the next one. They both employed the same strategy—start at the door, work around counter clockwise, searching from the floor to the top of the walls. There were no roofs, so the light was good. There were animal carvings and the remains of primitive paintings on some of the walls, so they paid attention to the existing carvings first. They were mostly of birds, and Rei recalled that the famous black soapstone birds were found in these houses, and on the hill. Some of them were taller than a man... She brought her mind back to the task at hand.

She didn't find anything in the second or third of her structures either. She was entering the fourth and final one when she heard Gideon yelling her name. She couldn't tell where his voice was coming from, so she exited the house and stood looking back the way she'd come, head cocked.

"Rei!" From her left. She ran over to the fourth house in the group. Ducking inside, she saw Gideon frantically digging in the dirt in the far left corner.

"Did you find it?" She ran over to him.

"I found an X," he said. He pointed quickly to a spot just to the right of the corner. There."

Rei peered over his shoulder. Sure enough, there was a four inch high X, carved in what she had come to think of as Father Eduardo's signature style. She heard a *clink* and saw Gideon reach into the hole, coming up with the prize.

"Here it is!" He held it up to her like he was passing a baton. He quickly filled in the hole and swept his hand over the dirt so it didn't look recently disturbed. "Let's get out of here. I feel like I've got a dragon breathing down my neck!"

Rei stuffed the familiar metal tube into Gideon's backpack and held it up to him. He slid both arms in, brushed his hands on his pants, and led the way out the door and down the hill.

—⊸∘⋙∘⊶—

Back at the hotel, they threw their belongings into their bags. Gideon had called Captain McMillan on the way back from Great Zimbabwe and told him they wanted to leave as soon as possible. The captain assured them that he would get a driver right away, and meet them at the airport. They would handle all the paperwork and preflight, and have the plane ready to go.

As they were packing, Gideon's phone rang. He snatched it out of his pocket and yelled into it, "Hello!" as he kept stuffing things into his carry on bag.

"Gideon, it's Captain McCallister. We've got another jet here. Maintenance guy says it's been here an hour, and there were three men on board. There's no crew, so I can't get any more information. But I saw three guys pull up to the Inhambane airport when we were taking off, and seems to me maybe they've come here to find you. Be careful."

"Crap." Gideon said, and punched off the phone. "We have to go *now*. If you haven't packed it, you don't need it, unless it's a passport, laptop, or phone. If those guys aren't here yet, they're on their way. *Go!*"

Rei zipped the last bag, threw all the shoulder straps over her arms, grabbed the handle of a rolling bag, and cracked open the door. Twenty feet away and headed her way was a man, dressed all in black. She slammed the substantial mahogany door, threw the bolt, and ran smack into Gideon.

"They're out there." Gideon grabbed Rei's hand and went into the bathroom. Like many hotels in the bush, there was no hot running water. When you wanted a shower, an attendant brought a five liter bucket of hot water to your room, climbed a ladder over your open air shower, and poured the hot water into another bucket that was attached to a shower head. It made for a delightful shower, and also a good escape hatch, if they could climb the stacked rock walls and jump over the top.

"Take your backpack and your purse. That's it!" Gideon grabbed a wooden chair and put it against the shower wall. "Up! Now!" He was whispering frantically. They heard a knock on the door.

Rei dropped everything not draped over her shoulders and climbed. She popped her head up, and didn't see anyone. None of the cottages actually had a back door, which the monks had probably ascertained, so they were concentrating on the front. For the moment. Rei dropped as lightly as she could to the ground. When she looked up she saw that Gideon was already dropping onto the grass. He crouched low and crab-walked to the side of the building. A hedgerow of bougainvillea separated their cottage from the neighboring one, and they pushed their way through the vines and thorns to the other side.

Gideon stopped her and leaned in to her ear. "I need to call our driver. He gave me his card. But I can't talk here. I'm going to go up there," He pointed to the shower on the cottage. "I can call from inside. Then I'll come back out. You stay here."

Rei got a look of panic on her face and grabbed him, shaking her head. Gideon just nodded at her and took off for the shower. He climbed up the rocks that made up the outside wall, and dropped down out of sight. Rei pushed herself back into the bougainvillea, feeling very exposed.

While she was trying to calm her breathing and heart rate, she heard murmured voices. She couldn't tell for sure, but they seemed to be coming from the side of their cottage. She pressed further into the bushes, knowing that if anyone came around the back of the buildings, she would be visible. And that if Gideon chose that moment to climb over the wall of the shower, he was toast.

The murmuring got closer, but then moved off. She breathed a sigh of relief. What was taking Gideon so long? Finally she saw his head pop up quickly over the top of the wall, go back down, then his whole body vault quickly over and onto the soft earth. He ran back to her.

"The driver will be here in fifteen minutes…"

He whispered.

"Fifteen minutes? They'll find us before then!"

Gideon was concerned as well. There was not a lot of cover at the hotel, and he didn't know how long the two of them, hiding together, could avoid three men who could split up and cover more ground. He had told the driver to pick them up at the staff quarters, which he had noticed on the drive in. But for him to get there with Rei, they had to traverse an open area of lawn. He didn't know the place well enough to get around it, and he didn't see any way they could get across it without being seen.

Grabbing her wrist, he pulled her to the shower wall, which bulged out from the back of the round building. He stopped and did a quick look around. The coast seemed clear, so they ran quickly to the next group of shrubs separating this cottage from the next. There was one more cottage before the lawn, or they could go to the front and risk the pathway to the hotel's main building. Neither seemed like a great option. He sat still in the prickly bushes, thinking.

As he was weighing the options, he saw a very young man, all in black, walking behind the remaining cottage. Very soon, if they moved he'd see them. If they didn't move, he'd see them. They needed a distraction. Pushing Rei gently back into the bushes, he took off towards the front of the cottage. He grabbed a stone from the row lining the front path, and went around, past the front door, and to the other side. He hurled the stone as far and high as he could, then ran back to Rei. He heard the stone hit something loud—another rock, a tree, something with substance.

As he skidded to a crouch near Rei, he could see the

man turn quickly towards the sound, and pulled Rei out and around to the front. He now felt that getting around other people might be their best option. They ran, flat out, for the main building.

They were twenty feet from the back entrance of the lobby, near the bar, when two of the monks stepped out from behind a hibiscus and into the pathway. One of them had a gun, and it was aimed directly at them. The Quinns slid to a stop on the gravel, and Gideon put his arm protectively around Rei.

The man with the gun gestured for them to approach. They did so, slowly, looking around for the third man. Gideon was looking for an opening, or for a way to cause enough of a ruckus to draw other people to the area. He didn't know what the rules were about guns in Zimbabwe, but he thought it was illegal for most people... But the hotel had a guard, armed with an old AK-47, if he could get his attention.

They stopped five feet in front of the two men. The third man had not joined them, and neither of the monks in front of them had used their phones. Both men had the CA symbol tattooed on their forearm. Both men looked pissed off.

"We want the letters." The man with the gun said in Portuguese.

"You have the letter," Rei said.

"No! The letters from the Jesuit. The letters about the treasure. We want those letters."

"I don't know what you mean," Rei said. She knew Gideon wasn't understanding the conversation, but she squeezed his side to let him know it wasn't going too well. Which of course he had figured out by the gun still pointing at them.

"I do not want to shoot you, but I will. I am a man of God. I am following my orders to bring a treasure of the Church back to the Church. I want the letters." The man was agitated. He was not a soldier, he was a monk. He wasn't sworn to find a treasure, only the letter from Paul. Although he had been in the army for his two year of mandatory service, and knew how to use the gun he held, he did not want to use it on these people.

"The treasure never belonged to the Church. If anything, it would belong to Israel." Rei said.

The man's face turned rigid. "The Church is the repository for God's treasures. It is not for Israel, it is for Rome. We will find it, and we will give it to the Pope himself. Our order will finally be recognized." He motioned them to come closer, which was the opening Gideon had been waiting for.

They slowly walked up to the men, Gideon keeping his left arm around his wife. He carefully reached around the backpack and gently pulled the chisel out of the elasticized pocket meant for water bottles, and held it firmly in his hand. The man with the gun waved at them to hurry, and whispered something to his compatriot, who turned and hustled through the door. At that minute, Gideon lunged at him, chisel held like a dagger, plowing him into the wall and plunging the tool into his right shoulder. He didn't want to kill the monk, but he needed to make sure that he was incapacitated, so he turned the handle around and brought it down hard just behind the gunman's ear. The man dropped like a rock, and Gideon quickly pulled him farther from the doorway.

"Come on!" He grabbed Rei and ran. He didn't

know where the third man was, but he assumed the second one had gone to get a vehicle, so he ran away from the car park and away from the road, behind the kitchen and cisterns. He kept running, glancing back to make sure Rei was able to keep pace, until he got to a row of primitive brick barracks that appeared to be additional staff quarters. They ran quickly behind them, startling some women washing clothes in bright, shallow plastic buckets.

They came out at a dirt service road that appeared to skirt the main entrance. Gideon didn't know where it ended up, but the farther away from the crazy monks, the better. Rei was starting to gasp for air, and finally she pulled her hand from Gideon's and stopped, holding her side.

"Stitch!" she panted.

"Stretch to the other side. We've got to keep going." Rei nodded and put her right arm over her head and leaned to the left, grimacing. After thirty seconds, she took a tentative step, and then started jogging. Her face was grim, and Gideon knew she was using all her strength just to keep moving ahead.

"Hang on, Rei, give me the bags," he said.

Rei stopped, shoved her purse into her backpack and swung it over to Gideon. She gave a weak smile and started off down the road again, Gideon jogging by her side.

———— ⋙≪ ————

The road ended at a tall trash dump. Goats were standing on the pile of garbage, rooting around for delicacies, and a small herd of cattle were grazing in the dry grass to the side. There was no more road. The two just stood there, looking at the goats and breathing hard.

"OK, this isn't good." Rei finally said. She started pacing, as was her habit when she was stressed.

"We can figure it out, let me just see..." He looked at the compass on his watch. "OK, the ruins are that way, to the southwest. We can go there, where there are people..."

Rei cut him off. "We can't go there without crossing that big grassland. There's nowhere to hide, and it's way too far to run." She started walking around the trash heap, stopping to stretch her tired legs. She continued walking, shooing away a black and white goat who nibbled at her pants. She spotted something and called to Gideon.

"Hey! Come over here. There's path through this grove of...whatever these trees are. Maybe it goes to a village or something."

Gideon jogged over. Sure enough, there was a path. Whether it was a game trail or a path made by people, he didn't really care at the moment. He started down it, grateful for the shade of the trees. He thought they were eucalyptus trees, and they were quite tall but had no foliage at the bottom. That left them somewhat exposed, but it was a lot better than open plain.

The path meandered side to side, made inexplicable turns, and seemed to be leading nowhere. Gideon had just about given up, thinking it must really be a game trail, when two small boys appeared on the path, walking in the opposite direction, with the ubiquitous yellow water jugs on their heads. Smiling shyly, they giggled as the *muRungus* passed by.

Bolstered by their appearance, Rei picked up her pace, and in five minutes they were in a small, four hut village. Old women sat at the doorways, tending small fires topped with cooking pots. Naked toddlers with beads around their waists played with rocks and sticks. One very elderly man was napping on a woven reed mat. When the Quinns walked into the center of the encampment, all but the sleeping man looked up in surprise.

Rei smiled and waved. The women nodded at her, but didn't rise.

"English?" Rei asked.

The nearest woman shook her head. "*Kwete.*"

"Is that Swahili?" Gideon asked?

"I don't think so. The people here are Shona... But I don't speak Swahili anyway."

Rei pantomimed driving a car. "Car?" She asked hopefully, although she didn't see one, and there were obviously no roads. The woman shook her head again, starting to get amused.

"Airport?" Rei stuck her arms out and swooped around like a child playing at flying. The woman burst out laughing, hiding her mouth behind her hand.

"*Kwete.*"

Several of the toddlers came over to join in the game, and a young girl grabbed Gideon's hand and watched solemnly. Rei stopped in front of Gideon and shrugged.

"I'm out of ideas."

"You're pretty good at charades, though," he said.

"Funny. So what do we do now?"

Gideon took off the two backpacks and set them on the ground. "We wait, I guess. There aren't any young men or women here now. Someone is bound to come back, maybe for that food they're cooking. There must be at least one villager who speaks English—it's the official language of the country!"

Rummaging through the pack, he brought out two bottles of water. Immediately they were swarmed by the children calling, *"Chokunwa!"* One of the old women had gotten to her feet and was trying to shush them. Laughing, Gideon handed her one of the bottles and tried to repeat the word.

"Chokunwa!" he said, and the woman laughed behind her hand again, her eyes crinkling.

Gideon and Rei rested for an hour on a reed mat given to them by the laughing woman. It was quiet and pleasant in the shade, and they were exhausted from their escape, so they dozed and chatted and tried to determine what to do next. Gideon knew that both Captain McMillan and the taxi driver would be concerned, the captain rather more than the driver, who would probably just shake his head at the crazy Americans. They had eluded the *Congratio a Achalichus* monks for the time being, but they still had to find a way to their plane, which was almost certainly being watched. Gideon had checked his phone and Rei's, but they no longer had a signal. There wasn't much to do but wait.

Finally, two young men walked into the village from the opposite direction of the trail that had led the Quinns there. Both had hoes over their shoulders, and they were talking and laughing as they came into the common area between the huts. When they spotted the *muRungus* they stopped and looked at the old woman, still sitting in the doorway. They conversed for minute or two, and then approached. Gideon and Rei stood up and nodded their heads in greeting.

"English?" Rei asked. One of the men nodded.

"Small English, from school."

"We need to go to Masvingo. To town. Yes?" The young man consulted his friend.

"Masvingo far by walk. One day." He held up a finger to make sure they understood.

"Does anyone have a car nearby?" Here Rei once again pantomimed driving, and the men laughed. Then they consulted again.

"Wife she work at hotel. Hotel have car. We go."

Gideon and Rei both shook their heads, and the men looked confused, not sure if they had misunderstood the question.

"To town, not to hotel. Another way?" Rei asked hopefully. The men chatted for several minutes this time, one gesturing back towards the hotel, and the other to the north. Finally they seemed to reach a decision.

"*Hurudza*...farmer there." He pointed to the north. "He have truck, many truck. We go." He smiled. This time the Quinns both nodded agreement.

The young man said, "Shumba," and pointed to himself. "I am Shumba." Gideon and Rei introduced themselves, and gathered up their few belongings.

Shumba called to the grandmother in the doorway and said something, accompanied by arm waving towards the north. The woman smiled, without showing teeth, and waved at the Quinns.

"*Oneka!*" she called out.

"We go!" Shumba said happily, enjoying this change of pace.

CHAPTER EIGHTEEN

SHUMBA WALKED EASILY DOWN THE trails, moving at a comfortable pace. His shoes were two sizes too large and had holes in them, but he didn't seem to notice. Warthogs snuffled along and crossed the trail, never getting very close, but not seeming to be disturbed by their presence. Small antelope could be seen grazing, and several dozen had gathered at one outcropping, where they were licking what seemed to be rock.

"*Munyu.*" Shumba said when Rei pointed. "Salt. They lick for to be strong."

This trail was much like the first, although it meandered through open plain and acacia more than through tall trees. The sun was hot, and even though their pace was measured, both Rei and Gideon were sweating. Rei had taken back her backpack, although Gideon had her laptop in his own, and sweat was running in rivulets down both of their backs.

After two hours, Shumba pointed to a thin line of smoke in the sky. "Farm." This news gave the Quinns a second wind, and they arrived at the farm twenty minutes later in good spirits. Shumba went up to the stone house, which sported a blue tin roof, and called out. A middle aged woman with an elaborate head cloth but otherwise drab clothes came to the doorway. The two conversed for several minutes, and the woman nodded and went inside.

"Farmer come home soon. *Ngosikadzi* give us something to eat, and tea. We wait." He indicated an area under the one acacia tree nearby which had been covered with reed rugs. Rei and Gideon removed their burdens and sat down, stretching their backs. In several minutes the lady brought out a carved wooden tray with hot tea and sweet cookies on it. They took both gratefully and smiled at her.

After another hour long wait, they heard men's voices and the sound of a vehicle with a serious exhaust problem. Looking towards the road they saw an old pickup truck crest the small hill, with about a dozen men sitting in the back talking and laughing. When they saw the *muRungus* they all laughed, but it seemed good natured. They waved, and all piled out of the truck as soon as it stopped. The driver exited also, and walked over to them.

"Good day," he said in accented English, and nodded his head. Shumba beamed.

"Hello," said Rei. "We have come from Shumba's village..." At this Shumba nodded enthusiastically. "And we need to get into town. We can pay you for your trouble, of course."

The man frowned a bit. White people were always rushing things, and talking of money. "You come." He waved them inside. When Shumba didn't follow, he turned and said something to him in Shona. Shumba grinned and followed behind them.

"Sit!" He waved to a table and four chairs. "*Funda,*" he said to the woman, obviously his wife. "We eat first. I have worked all day, and am hungry." His wife brought more tea for them all, and went out a back doorway where they could smell food on a charcoal fire. She returned with bowls of beans, rice, stewed meat, fried greens, and *chingwa* for sopping up the sauces. No one spoke until all the food had been eaten, and the cook had been thanked enthusiastically.

"I am Martin," the farmer said. He pointed to his wife. "This is my wife, Patience. My sons were on the truck, they are now at their own homes."

"Were all those your sons?" Rei asked, eyebrows raised.

The farmer laughed. "No, not all sons. Some are workers. Five sons. Three daughters." He smiled. "You have sons?" he asked Gideon.

"No sir," Gideon shook his head. "Not yet." He smiled at Rei.

Rei smiled back, but was getting impatient as the day was drawing to a close. "Martin, we really do need to get to town. Our friend will be very worried about us."

Martin sat back in his chair and folded his hands together across his stomach. "You got lost," he said. "From where?"

Rei glanced quickly at Gideon. "We were foolish... We were at the ruins of Great Zimbabwe, and we wandered off. It was so beautiful out there. We got turned around, and ended up at Shumba's village. But our phones don't work here, and we would like to go to Masvinga to find our friends."

Martin looked at them for a long moment. Gideon knew that the story was implausible, but he also knew the real story was implausible. He took Rei's hand under the table and squeezed.

"Yes. I will take you to the city tomorrow. We cannot go tonight, the road is very bad. Cattle and antelope on the road, and many holes. It is not safe. Tomorrow, we go."

They saw that there was no sense arguing for an earlier departure. The man's truck was obviously old, and they had no idea where they were. Gideon nodded. They knew it was unsafe to drive at night in Zimbabwe, and not just for the four legged animals.

"Thank you so much." Rei said, and Martin and his wife smiled, she behind her hand.

It got dark at 6:30 and Martin and his wife lit the few oily candles in their small home. Patience laid out two reed mats in the corner of the room near the fireplace, and brought over a half dozen brightly colored woven blankets, smiling shyly as she handed them to Gideon. Having no clothes and no toiletries, getting ready for bed was a quick affair, and by 8:00 the house was quiet. After their long day, Rei and Gideon fell asleep quickly, even on the hard ground.

At first light, the household arose, and the smell of coffee and sounds of cooking woke them up. Rei went out the back doorway to the open air cooking area and tried to offer to help, but Patience shooed her back inside with a giggle. Gideon found a pitcher of water and a bowl on a table, and washed his face, then went out to the outhouse. Rei wasn't overly fond of the outhouse, but had to agree that it was much better than her one other experience with a public toilet in Africa.

After a breakfast of fresh eggs and more *chingwa*, Martin took his men to the fields to work, then returned for Gideon and Rei. They set off down the dirt road, driving through Martin's land for a good distance, through fields of sweet potatoes, cassava, tomatoes, beans, pumpkins and a small banana orchard. The road was, as Martin had said, abysmal. They achieved a maximum speed of fifteen kilometers an hour for the first two hours of the trip, and Gideon repeatedly checked his cell phone for any signal.

Finally Martin turned his old truck onto a macadam road, one car width wide and in much disrepair, but better than the dirt road they had been on. After another hour, Gideon finally had enough cell signal complete a call Captain McMillan. He answered on the second ring.

"Gideon? Is that you? Where are you?"

"It's me. Sorry Captain, we got a bit diverted by our friends." He glanced over at Martin, who remained impassive. "But we're safe, and are headed into town. I'm not sure where we should meet, though... Surely not the airport?"

"No..." McMillan was silent for a moment. "There was one of those guys at the airport all day yesterday, watching our plane. It was creepy, to tell you the truth. He just sat and watched the plane, and talked on his phone every once in awhile. I'm guessing they're still there, although we haven't been out to the airfield today. Hang on a sec."

Gideon could hear mumbling as the captain talked to someone.

"Hey Gideon, my copilot here says there's a cafe

about a mile from the airport. Not on the main road. It's called ... Hang on." More mumbling. "He swears it's called Octopus." Gideon could hear laughing in the background.

"Octopus?"

"That's what he says. Are you driving?"

"We have a driver bringing us into town."

"Ok, ask him if he knows it."

Gideon put the phone to his shoulder and turned to Martin, "Do you know a cafe near the airport called Octopus?" He saw Rei's eyebrows go up, but Martin nodded his head.

"Yes, very good food there. An hour from here."

Gideon put the phone back to his ear. "Ok then, he knows it. And he says it's an hour from where we are now. So meet you there?"

"Yeah, but drive around first. You can't miss those guys, and I think one of them got hurt somehow yesterday. Was that you?"

"Uh, yeah. He ok? Do you know?"

"I heard from the staff that a tourist got hurt, and that he was one of those guys in black. That's all I know. For his sake, I hope he's not in the hospital here. I'll go by the airport and see if their plane left— maybe they flew him out. I'll see you at the famous Octopus, then." And he disconnected.

"Is the guy ok?" Rei asked.

"Don't know, but the captain thinks so." He lifted her hand and kissed it. "Actually, I hope we never get close enough to any of those guys again to find out."

"Agreed!" she said.

An hour and a half later the truck pulled to a stop across a narrow dirt road from the Octopus Cafe. They had driven up and down the road once, but hadn't spotted any other white people at all, so they asked Martin to park. He declined an invitation to join them for lunch, and also declined Gideon's proffered money.

"You used a lot of petrol, Martin, and you fed us so well!"

Martin shook his head firmly. "In Zimbabwe, we are happy to help a stranger, and to take him into our home. You are most welcome to come back any time, my friends." He smiled and shook Gideon's hand. "I hope you get back to your home with safety."

"And you... We can't thank you enough!" Gideon and Rei alighted from the truck, grabbed their backpacks from behind the seat and ran across the street to the dark cafe.

Captain McMillan waved at them from a table in the back corner. He had a map spread out in front of him. They sat down in the rickety wooden chairs, and Gideon signaled to the waitress. When she came over, he ordered two Cokes. After she'd brought them to the table, uncapped the bottles, and given them glasses and straws, Gideon looked at the captain.

"So how the hell are we gonna get out of here, Cap?"

McMillan touched the map. "I've been looking. There are two towns with airfields I can use. Here, at Chiredzi," he pointed to a dot southeast of Masvingo. "And here, at Zvishavane." He pointed to a town a little south and west. "Chiredzi is mostly a sugar cane producing region, and there aren't too many people. The airport is adequate. Just. Mostly it's used by the sugar cane plantation owners in small prop planes. And it's farther away and harder to get to by road."

"Wait, by road?" Rei asked. "Who's driving?"

"I think the only way to get you two out of here is with a pump fake..." Rei looked at Gideon, confused. The captain continued. "I think we're going to have to get you out of here by car, to somewhere that I can fly to. If we choose Zvishavane, I'll probably say I'm headed for Gabarone in Botswana. Then I'll have a minor emergency and have to land to check it out. You come aboard, and we head...wherever you're heading." He raised his eyebrows at them.

"Actually, we don't know yet. But we will soon..." *I hope,* thought Rei.

"Ok, so you get aboard and we leave. Even if we fly to Nairobi or Kampala or somewhere like that, I can say I have to go there for a part... In these small airports they're not paying much attention anyway, especially if you give them a little incentive not ask too many questions."

Gideon turned the map to face him, and studied it. "It looks like this road between Masvingo and Zvishavane is a main one. While it isn't exactly an interstate, it's sure better than anything that's *not* a main road. And it's closer. So between the paved road and the shorter distance... I'd say that's the best bet."

"That was my thought," said McMillan. "Jimmy, my copilot, has been making a show of getting the plane ready, and has told the officer in the terminal that you guys bailed, and we're headed to the next job. I got your stuff from the hotel, since the rooms were in my name, so all that's in the taxi with our driver friend, who'll be back here in..." He consulted his watch. "Oh, forty-five minutes or so. He's also agreed to drive you wherever you need to go, as long as the price is right, but in his brother's panel van, not his cab."

Rei sat back in her chair, rather breathless at this take-charge man who'd arranged their escape. "Wow! That's amazing! And you don't seem flustered by this at all."

McMillan laughed, his blue eyes crinkling around the edges. "Mrs. Quinn, I've been a pilot in Africa for fifteen years. I've transported all kinds of people, from politicians to plantation owners, and in a lot of countries. Most everybody is running from somebody. It may not be the most moral thing in the world, but I've learned that a bribe goes a long way towards getting what you want done, no matter which country you're in on this continent."

⟶ ⟿⟫⟸ ⟵

An hour later, the taxi driver picked McMillan up to drive him to the airport. Ten minutes after that, a panel van pulled up in front of the Octopus, and a tall man entered and looked around. He smiled and joined them.

"Hello! I am Tendai Ndava. John is my brother. He says to pick you, and take you to my home, so we go!" He thrust his hand towards Gideon, who shook it.

"Yes, we go!" Gideon said, laughing, and grabbed his backpack. Rei got up and followed them out the door, and they slid quickly into the back of the panel van.

There was nothing to sit on in the back, and the road was a typical African road filled with ruts and bumps, but they stopped in ten minutes, and the door slid open.

"Please come." Tendai gestured to his small house. "You wait."

He led the way into the two room house, and beckoned for them to sit on the wooden bench near the cooking area. The walls and ceiling were stained black from smoke and soot, but the dirt floor was recently swept, and the room was clean. A crinkled photo of two children in front of a large cow was tacked to the wall. Tendai left them alone to wait, and went outside where they could hear him filling a tin bucket with charcoal. He returned, and started stacking the charcoal in the fire pit.

"I make tea. My wife is not here now."

Looking at the evidence of many hours of smoke on the wall, Rei quickly said, "No, please, don't go to any trouble. John should be here soon, and we will need to be on our way. Thank you though, you've been so helpful!" She smiled at him, knowing she was being rude by refusing the hospitality, but not wanting to be forced outside into the open by the smoke. Hopefully he would put her rudeness down to being a *muRungu*. Whatever he thought, he smiled, left the charcoal, and sat down on the floor, content to wait.

A half hour later they heard a vehicle come to a stop outside the house. John Ndava came in, smiling and holding out his keys. He and his brother conversed for several minutes, and John gave Tendai a small handful of bills. Tendai left the house, and they heard doors opening and closing on the vehicles. When it was quiet again, John started out the door.

"We go!" he said over his shoulder.

As they got in the van, they realized that Tendai

had transferred their luggage from the taxi to the van. He had also installed a box of food and drink supplies, a small pile of blankets, and a foam mattress. Rei was much relieved that they would have some cushioning from the roads against their backsides, and thanked both Tendai and John profusely. Both men grinned, and Tendai waved to them as he closed the panel door.

———————— ⇒◦❮❁❯◦⇐ ————————

The 75 kilometers on the Zvishavane-Masvingo road went relatively quickly, all things considered. They arrived just as the sun was setting, and went straight to the airport. To their great relief, their plane was there, and Captain McMillan was waiting for them in the small terminal.

"And away we go..." he said, leading them quickly out the door. "Paperwork's done, palms are greased, the runway lights will be on for another half hour, and I think we need to get out of here as soon as we can. The officer in charge here looks a bit greedy for my liking."

They piled into the plane, Jimmy closed and secured the door while McMillan went to the cockpit, and in a very few minutes they were taxiing down the runway and taking off, the few lights of the town winking on in the increasing darkness. As they circled around the airport, they saw the runway lights blink off.

———————— ⇒◦❮❁❯◦⇐ ————————

The flight to Kololo Airport in Kampala, Uganda was at the edge of McMillan's comfort zone in the plane he was flying, but he had a friend and co-worker who lived there and who had agreed to put them up for a day or two if they decided to head that way. Since the Quinns didn't actually know their next stop, and since Kampala was a large and reasonably modern city, he figured it was better than a hotel somewhere unknown. In Kampala, they could access whatever information they needed.

His friend made the arrangements for Kololo to keep the tower open until their arrival, and they landed without incident, parking the plane inside an open air hangar where Jimmy and a local mechanic would give it a once over and tune up before they took off again. Kololo was on the company's regular maintenance route, so the captain knew the jet was in good hands.

Jakisa, or Jack, Magara, met them in his Toyota Land Cruiser, and brought them to his gated house in Garden City. Traffic was bumper to bumper and side to side, and here also there appeared to be no one following traffic rules. Although Cape Town was pretty large, Kampala was the most crowded African city they'd been in, and they were dumbfounded at the amount of people and traffic and chaos on the road.

"Traffic's pretty light now," Jack said as he narrowly missed a *boda boda*, a motorbike taxi. "Tomorrow you will get to see the real thing. But where I live, it is not so bad. And we have power most of the time, so we are happy."

Jack was a tall, thin Ugandan with very close cropped hair and a lilting accent. He was nicely dressed in slacks and a starched white shirt, and the vehicle was immaculate.

"Are you from Kampala?" Rei asked, still staring

out the window at the endless stream of people walking down the sides of the road.

"Oh no, I am from Jinja. It is east, towards Kenya. I went to the States to university, and became a pilot at a flight school in Texas. Now I live in Kampala because Kololo is on our company's maintenance route, and I can jump off from here to anywhere in East Africa when I am on duty."

They weren't able to drive fast, so it didn't seem that they traveled far in the hour it took them to get from the airport to Jack's house. Once they turned into the district which was called Garden City, they could see that it was much more upscale than most of the city through which they'd driven. There was a large mall that had a New York Pizza Restaurant; Nakumat, a Kenyan store which Jack said was like a twenty-four hour Wal-Mart; and small, elegant boutiques. Nearby was a small but high-end hotel called Emin Pasha. The roads were paved and virtually pothole free. When they turned off the street and into Jack's drive, they were met by a large, solid metal gate. Jack honked once, and the gate was opened by a young Ugandan, who waved as they drove in.

The house was stone, two story, with a corrugated tin roof. The landscaping was lush. There were lights on in the downstairs windows. They parked next to another Toyota Land Cruiser.

"My wife's car." Jack said. "She is a lawyer. She is away in London, visiting her sister."

He led the way inside, and Captain McMillan started up the stairs. "Same room, Jack?"

"Yes, and the one next to it for the Quinns. They are all prepared." He smiled at Gideon and Rei. "Can I get you tea? Something to eat?"

Even though they hadn't had dinner, they weren't hungry, and were happy to be shown to their room. Rei saw a real toilet and a sink with running water, and grinned.

"Hallelujah!"

Jack smiled back. "We have a cistern, and even though it is the dry season, it is full now from the water trucks. The water heats from the sun, however, so you might wish to take a shower tomorrow, or it will be cold. Let me know if you need anything. Mac is next door to you, and he has been our guest often. Good night!"

He left them in their comfortable room. Rei sat down on the large bed while Gideon untied the mosquito netting. There was a knock, and the captain brought in their luggage.

"Here ya go! Thought you might be happy to have some clean clothes. If you leave the dirty ones outside your door, they'll get washed tomorrow. 'Night!" And he left.

CHAPTER NINETEEN

HE FOLLOWING MORNING, REI WOKE to the sound of birds in the lush trees outside the window, a rooster crowing somewhere nearby, and traffic sounds. The traffic wasn't terribly close, but the rumble and honking in the distance was ever present. She got out of bed without waking Gideon and washed her face. She desperately needed a shower, but thought she could wait for some warm water if she put her hair up in a bun. She looked at herself in the mirror and grimaced. She had bags the size of her carry on under her eyes, her hair was two days past dirty, and there were lines of grime caked in the creases of her neck. *Beauty queen,* she thought, giving up thinking about it until she could shower. She quietly left the room and found her way downstairs and to the kitchen.

A young Ugandan woman was standing at the granite topped island rolling out *chapatti*. She smiled shyly and nodded when Rei came in.

"Is there any coffee?" Rei asked. "And I'm Rei."

"I will put on the kettle, mum," the young woman said, checking the water level in an electric kettle, filling it from the tap, and plugging it.

"Thanks," Rei said, and leaned against the counter, looking out into the walled in back garden. It was full of bougainvillea, which cascaded over the walls, as well as trees she'd called powder puff trees when she had visited Gideon's family in Florida.

The kettle began to whistle, and the cook poured it into a coffee press into which she had spooned ground Ugandan coffee. "Hot milk or sugar, mum?" She asked.

"Hot milk would be lovely, thanks! What's your name?"

Getting a glass jug of milk out of the fridge, the woman said, "Jenneth," and smiled again, covering her mouth with her hand. *They all do that!* thought Rei.

Jenneth put the milk in a small pot and lit a gas burner with a match. When the milk was hot, she gave Rei a mug, the coffee press, and the hot milk in a small pitcher. Rei made her coffee, and drank it gratefully.

"Delicious!" she said. "Is anyone else up?"

Shaking her head, Jenneth went back to making the *chapatti*. "Would you like breakfast, mum?

"I'll wait for everyone else. Thanks though!" She left the kitchen through the garden door and found a seat under a shade tree.

Gideon found her there, his own black coffee in hand. He kissed the top of her head and then sat next to her. "So you ready to read the next letter from Father Eduardo? I'm pretty sure Mac said that there was some kind of internet here, and I would guess that hotel we passed, the Emin Pasha, has it, if not."

"Yeah. I was just enjoying not being chased or having to run anywhere! And I didn't want to wake you up. But I guess we need to figure out what it says so we know where we're going next. If we're really following the spice route, the last stop is probably Goa, India. So this clue might lead us there... but that's still pretty far. My guess is another stop or two first."

"Great. Well, we can only hope we've shaken our Catholic friends, anyway." Gideon put his arm around her.

"Probably. But they'll know we're going to end up in Goa, I'm afraid. It's in the journal they have. We might be ok until we get there... but I expect they'll wait there for us, now that they've botched stealing the letters outright."

"So we need a plan by then. At least we have some time." He squeezed her to him and kissed her neck. "You hungry? I'm suddenly starved, and I just realized we didn't ever eat dinner." He got up and looked at her.

"Can you just call me when it's ready? I'm so relaxed!" She leaned back in the chair and closed her eyes.

⋯⋯⋯

After breakfast, Jenneth told them that Captain McMillan and Jack had gone down to Kololo. McMillan needed to check on the maintenance of the jet, and Jack had a trip tomorrow so he was going to check on his plane as well. They wouldn't be back until the afternoon.

"If you want to go to a store, I can call a boda for you. Or you can have lunch at the nice hotel... It is very good." She smiled shyly, not showing any teeth.

"We would need to exchange some money, I think." Gideon said. He didn't want to use a credit card if he could avoid it.

Jenneth nodded. "Stephen can go for you. He can get take the money and get shillings. Good rate. I will tell him." She pulled out a cell phone and typed out a text message lightning fast, which made Rei laugh. Very soon the phone beeped, and Jenneth read the response. "He can go soon, when he goes for some service for the car. He will be back before lunch."

They thanked her, and went up to their room. Taking out the by now filthy backpack, Rei dug out the metal tube holding their next letter. The leather strip holding the top on was still intact, and the tube, aside from a few small dents, was none the worse for wear. She opened it and began the familiar routine of getting out her notebook and a pen, and propping herself up against the headboard to translate.

Gideon said, "I don't even have a converter to charge the phones... I'm gonna go ask Jenneth. Let me know when you're done!" He left with both of their phones and their iPhone charger in hand.

———◦◦◦———

Rei was accustomed by now to Father Eduardo's way of writing, and translating was becoming easier. She was, once again, stumped about the location, but felt sure that the answers would be at her fingertips once she was connected to the internet. She got her laptop and charger out of the bag and took it, with the notebook, downstairs, leaving the letter in the drawer of the dresser.

She found Gideon talking to the young man who had let them in the gate the night before, whom she assumed was Stephen. Gideon handed him British pounds, and the man carefully folded it and put it in his pocket. He left, and Gideon turned to her.

"That was Stephen. Apparently kind of the general dogs body, handyman, security guy. He's going to exchange the money, and be back in time for us to go to Emin Pasha for lunch. You got it translated?"

"Yep. Clear as mud again, though. Let's see if we've got internet." She looked at the outlets, which didn't match her American plug. "Crap, forgot about that. The hotels all had adapter strips. Let's see if we can find one."

They hunted around the house and couldn't find another converter besides the one charging their completely dead phones, so they went back to the kitchen. Jenneth was frying up *chapatti,* and the smell was delicious.

"Jenneth, is there another power converter somewhere? I'd like to plug in my computer," Gideon asked.

Jenneth flipped the *chapatti* in the cast iron pan and pointed to a drawer at the end of the counter with the spatula. "I think there is one in there."

Gideon opened the drawer, found the converter, and they went back to the sitting room where Rei had left her stuff.

"OK, so I've never heard of the place where Father Eduardo left the next letter..." She started powering up her laptop.

"What else is new. Is it another "land of the good people" thing? I hope it's not the "land of the bad people.""

"Funny." She made a face at him. "Nope. It's a place called Ctesiphon. I don't even know what country that's in, but it's between here and India."

"That narrows it down." Rei sat back in the

comfortable chair and rested his head on the back, closing his eyes.

Rei's Mac purred to life, and went through the start up. Once her screen saver and programs were up, she clicked on the wifi icon. No networks showed. Thinking maybe she hadn't let the computer load all its information, she let it sit another minute, and tried again. No networks.

"Damn. Back to Jenneth." Rei put the laptop on a side table and went back to the kitchen.

Jenneth told them that there was internet service and a router, but that the connection was not always reliable. There were many days, apparently, without Internet access, although when they did have it was reasonably fast. Having nothing to do but wait for Stephen to return with their money, and hopefully give them a ride to the hotel, they tried to relax, wander the grounds, and enjoy the quiet. But with the letter to try to decipher, they found it impossible. They walked to the big metal gate.

"There's a door in it. We could go out..." Rei said.

"We might get locked out, though. Let me go ask Jenneth if we can walk to the hotel. She can text Stephen to just meet us there." He left for few minutes, then returned. "Yep, we can. It's about a ten minute walk. She texted Stephen—I still can't get used to that!—and he will meet us there in about a half hour. He is on his way back now."

Gideon opened the door in the gate, and they walked out. The road was paved, and only had small potholes in it. They walked downhill on the right side of the road along a dirt path that bordered the asphalt, and Rei suddenly said, "They're driving on the wrong side like in London!"

Gideon laughed, "You didn't notice that last night?"

"I was tired!" she protested.

"Obviously," he teased.

They made the right turn that took them up another hill, and came to the hotel on the left. Emin Pasha was low and built into the side of a hill, with beautiful dark wood everywhere. Once they got inside and found their way to the restaurant and bar, they saw a half dozen green upholstered sofas with big coffee tables, under a roof but open to the landscaped yard. The restaurant was to the left and was also open air, and the bar behind. There were tables under umbrellas outside, and huge iron sofas with red upholstered cushions on the lawn.

"Wow!" Rei said, staring. "This is amazing!"

A waiter in white pants and a white tunic, wearing a red fez, came up to them. "Welcome!"

"We'd like to have tea now, and then lunch? Maybe on those sofas?" Rei said, pointing to the seating area.

"Yes, mum, you come." And he led the way. They sat and gave their order, and he saw Rei's laptop. "We have wireless internet for you, mum." He said, and went to fill their order. Rei found a plug, and once again gave the network icon a try.

"Yes! We're a go!" She opened her notebook and uncapped her pen.

"Ok, so here's the letter." She began to read.

My dearest son,

If you have retrieved this letter, you have just seen one of the greatest wonders on this good earth. Isabel and I have been in much prayer and discussion about where to leave it, as the great stone houses of the kings is such a large expanse. But I had wanted my bride to see this miracle, and her delight in the journey was a blessing from our heavenly Father on this poor man. I do not know, as I write this letter this night, where we will finally choose to leave it. I can only pray that we choose correctly, and you will find a way to pursue the next step of your quest. The journey is long, and there is much danger. But God will be with you, I am confident.

After visiting what the natives called the zimbabwe, I travelled back to the Land of the Good People. The Sao Miguel was not as fine or large a ship as the Santa Antonio de Tanna, and it had suffered much in a storm after we left the Cape of Good Hope. It was for this reason that I was persuaded to see the zimbabwe on my original journey. The ship was almost fully repaired, the injured men recovered, and the provisioning had begun. In three week's time, we departed and continued our journey north up the coast of Africa.

We stopped in Mombasa for two weeks, but did not linger there, and I did not find anything about it compelling so as to warrant exploration. There were no ruins, no churches of note, and I stayed on the ship for most of the time in port. We stopped likewise for a very short provisioning in Mogadishu, but the Ottomans did not welcome our visit, and we left in short order.

As we were journeying north, I heard tell of another ruin, north into the land that was once the Persian Empire. My captain had determined to stop for a trade of spices and silk at the port of Umm Qasr, in the gulf. He told me that he had once, when another ship had needed much repair, taken a journey of some two weeks to these ruins at the behest of a local sheikh, the Arabs *being now ensconced in the land. He encouraged me that I would have time, should I wish for such a journey myself, and knowing my interest in such things, as he had promised his merchant friend that we would remain some days in Umm Qasr.*

Consequently I found me a guide, and he took me by camel to Ctesiphon, a journey of twelve days. These are the ruins of great rulers, who did not worship my God but who were fierce and brave, and who led a kingdom through forty kings. It is there you will find my letter, my son, if it remains.

I wish you Godspeed. My Isabel and I continue to pray for you, and for your success in this quest. May God richly bless you and keep you safe.

Yours,

Joao Xavier

X

The year of our Lord 1687

"Cestis...what?" Gideon asked. "I've never heard of it."

"Me neither. Not that I'm up on my Persian history." She opened her browser and typed in 'Ctesiphon'. "Well, Google knows about it." She started to read. "And we've got a problem already."

"Is it gone?" Gideon asked anxiously.

"Nope. It's in Iraq."

Their lunch at Emin Pasha was wonderful but it was overshadowed by their dilemma. Gideon had been in the Army, but that wasn't going to do him any favors trying to get into Iraq. And even if they got in the country, it would be extremely dangerous to wander around alone in a remote location. Gideon wanted to go without Rei, who, of course, strongly objected. And she was most likely right, anyway, as Gideon wasn't sure he could find the next X and its accompanying letter without her.

They decided to put the problem on the back burner until they could talk to either Captain McMillan or Mr. Xavier, and tried to enjoy the setting. The food and service at the hotel was top notch, and the Ugandan beer Gideon ordered, Nile Gold, surprised him with its excellent flavor. They had eaten at one of the outdoor tables, under the red umbrella, and treated themselves to ice cream after the meal. Full, they decided to take a walk around the peaceful grounds.

As they strolled along, beside the tiled pool, along the Mediterranean inspired buildings housing the guest rooms and suites, they tried not to talk of Iraq. They recounted their adventures in Cape Town and Inhambane. They reminisced about their fortuitous rescue in Zimbabwe.

"Martin was amazing. Really. He wouldn't take a single dime for all the help, the food, the bed..." Gideon shook his head in disbelief.

"And Shumba, walking us all that way. We were really blessed. It could just as easily have ended with rebels or soldiers or something. We did everything you're not supposed to do, and lived to tell about it. We even got our luggage back! It's amazing, if you think about it," Rei said.

"No one would believe it. If we ever get to tell the

story, seriously, no one will believe it! Which reminds me, I need to call Mr. Xavier and tell him we're all right. And tell him about Iraq. I don't think he can do much for us there... and I doubt the jet company will let Mac fly us into a war zone."

They walked a few yards, and Rei said, "Guess we'd better get back to Jack's, and see if they're back from the airport. We're going to need advice, I think. And our phones should be done charging."

They wandered back across the beautiful grounds. The traffic noise was still out there. A big hotel was being built that was going to block some of the city view. But the birds were in the trees, the grass was green, the flowers were spectacular. Rei thought that she'd like to come back here one day, when life was a bit calmer. She took Gideon's hand.

"No one I'd rather almost get killed with than you, hon," she said.

—◦◦✐◦◦—

Jack and McMillan hadn't returned when they arrived at the house. Gideon got his phone and went to the garden to call Mr. Xavier. His boss wasn't thrilled about the Iraq angle.

"Can you skip it? You know you have to go to Goa, right?" he asked.

"No, I don't think so. For one thing, I think the clue that sends us to Goa will have a lead to other clues that are there. Goa is a big territory now. The treasure is probably not in the city of what's now called "Old" Goa, and how would we know even where to start? And there will be clues along the way. This guy doesn't seem to have been a map guy. He's a letter guy. I'd certainly rather have a big map with one X than fifteen letters and fifteen Xs. But that seems to be what he did, so we're going to have to follow him. And that's going to take us to Iraq, at least if you want us to continue."

"I do, but not at the cost of your lives. *Maldicao!* If you can get in and out safely, then do it. Keep the jet as long as you need. But if you don't think you can, then you must stop. One day it might be possible to go to Iraq without worry of being *explodir*." Xavier sighed.

"That's true, but probably not soon. I'll keep you posted. You might want to say a prayer!" He hung up.

As he was walking into the house he heard the two pilots come in. Rei met them all in the front hall, and Gideon asked them if they had time for a consultation. Jack led them into his office.

"What's up?" Mac said.

"We have to go to Iraq." Gideon said.

The two men stared at him, not sure if it was a joke.

"Yeah, I know. And to make it worse, we need to go to a place that's closer to the border with Iran than with any of the other bordering countries," Gideon continued.

Silence.

"Hence the need for a consultation..." Gideon said hesitantly.

Both the pilots started to speak at once. "You can't..." "It's impossible!"

Rei stepped in. "Ok, we know it's not...easy. But that's where we need to go. I don't think where we're going is near any big war zones or anything..."

Jack snorted. "Mum, the whole country is a war zone. And they do not take kindly to regular Americans these days. If you could even get permission to get in, you would have to have an armed escort, and you could only go where they let you go."

"So... I guess we need an unofficial way to get in, then." Rei said, furrowing her brow.

Mac spoke, "I think it might be time to tell us what's going on. We're just pilots for hire, we're not some kind of militia. But I've seen those guys that are after you, and I was in the Marines for ten years. If I can help...well, I'll help."

Gideon and Rei looked at each other for a moment, then Gideon shrugged and told the men the story, starting with the theft in Lisbon.

"If I hadn't seen those guys, those brothers or whatever they are, I wouldn't believe you for a skinny minute," Mac said. "But they're real, and they seem pretty dedicated. Jack, you know anybody in Kuwait?"

Jack thought for a minute, then opened his desk drawer and withdrew an address book. "I had a friend at university that went into the military after we graduated. He stayed in the Army ten years or so, then got out and has been doing consulting in the Middle East. I do not know where he is—I have not talked to him in some time. I have an old number..." He pulled out his cell and punched in the international code followed by the number. After a short wait, he spoke into the phone. "Richard! It is Jack Magara! I am needing some information, and I thought that you might be able to provide it. If you can, give me a call, please." He recited his number. "*Webele!*" And he hung up.

"I do not know where he is living. It is 9:00 in the morning in the States, but if he is in the Middle East somewhere, the time will be closer." He shrugged. "I do not know another person who could help you with this."

McMillan had been in thought while Jack was on the phone. Now he said, "How far in country to you need to get, if you can cross at the Kuwaiti border?"

"Two hundred miles... On the Tigris River," Gideon answered.

Mac grimaced. "Well that's certainly a challenge. Obviously, you're going to have to make an unauthorized crossing. You're going to have to have a local guide, and some protection. Two hundred miles in that terrain... I don't suppose you'd consider a camel?"

"That's not exactly the quick in-and-out I was hoping for," Gideon laughed.

"No. But it would be the least noticeable. So you need a truck that doesn't arouse suspicion, a driver, ditto. Somebody with a gun. Enough food and water to keep you away from people for a couple of days, and enough petrol to fill the tank. No problem..."

CHAPTER TWENTY

NEAR ABDALI, KUWAITI BORDER

PRESENT DAY

FTER A LOT OF PHONE conversations with Jack's friend in Qatar, the two pilots had pieced together the beginnings of a plan. Mac flew them from Kampala to Addis Ababa, then on to Abu Dhabi. From Abu Dhabi, they landed in Kuwait. Being on a private jet eased their passage, especially as they had their credentials from Xavier International. However, it was a long and exhausting trek, and they were very happy to finally stay on firm ground when they arrived in Kuwait.

Jimmy went to the Hilton and reserved two rooms in the jet company's name, and the Quinns arrived with Mac an hour later. They went straight to their room to shower and change, and met the two airmen in the hotel bar feeling much refreshed.

They ordered, and after the drinks came, Mac took out a small leather pad. "Jack's buddy Richard called. He's got a guy lined up to take you over in truck. The guy... his name is Abdul Bazzi, I think... Anyway, the guy has been getting intel for the US since the first time Iraq invaded Kuwait. He's got some family on both sides, people died, same old story. But apparently he's proven trustworthy, and he says he can get you in and out in a day if you can complete your business quickly. If you have to stay a night, he can handle that too, although the price doubles. Cash, of course. And lots of it, I'm afraid. Looks like the equivalent of about twenty-five grand, if you have to stay the second day. I think he'd rather cross back over at night anyway, so that should be your goal."

Gideon nodded. "And protection?"

"Bazzi's son is going to ride shotgun, so to speak. But they've got some kind of a rig built in, and hopefully no one'll ever know you're in the truck. You've got to dress in the native garb when you're wandering around your ruins. But sounds to me like, if anyone can get you in and out safely, this guy's a good bet."

Rei said, "I'm not going to ask what happens if we get caught."

"Better not to," Mac confirmed. "Jimmy and I will be staying here. We've got 3 days for R&R and plane maintenance. If you're not back by then I don't know if I can stay any longer. Depends on if there's another client. If Xavier will keep paying for the plane to be idle, I can stay. But otherwise, we're going to be on call."

"Thanks Mac, you've already done so much!" Gideon said, offering his hand. "I'm just going to say, 'See you Tuesday' instead of goodbye." They shook, and then toasted to the success of the mission.

<hr />

It was still dark when Gideon's phone rang. He and Rei had been up for an hour, unable to sleep. They had decided to write letters to their families and leave them in the room, just in case. This was their only acknowledgement of the danger—or stupidity—of their mission.

"Hello?" Gideon answered. He listened then turned off the phone. "Let's go."

He and Rei grabbed their backpacks and left the room.

They went down the service elevator and exited from the maintenance door to the side of the building. A beat up white pickup pulled up to the curb and they both got into the front seat, Mac first. The man driving nodded a greeting, but didn't smile or speak. He drove to an industrial area on the edge of the airport complex and stopped the truck. Another, identical, truck was parked in the lot, and a younger Arab man got out and ambled over.

He opened the passenger door. "I am Asim. That is my father." He gestured to the older man driving the truck. "We will go in that truck there. It will not be comfortable for you, I am afraid, but it will be safer. Come."

They got out of the first truck and walked to the second. In the bed of the truck was a hodgepodge of hay bales, oil drums, and assorted scrap metal. Asim went to the back, put down the tailgate, and tinkered with something in the pile. A small door opened, hinged invisibly at the top, and exposed a space just big enough for two people to lie down in. It was lined with blankets, with small pillows at the front. Rei looked at it in dismay.

Asim looked at her and smiled. "It is ok, miss. We have taken many people across the border this way. There is air, and it is not too very uncomfortable. Maybe you will sleep, no?" He laughed.

Rei gave a weak smile, but no laugh. She wasn't claustrophobic exactly, but this looked a lot like an MRI machine, and those gave her the heebie jeebies.

"Can I go to the bathroom first?" she asked.

<hr />

Rei and Gideon were stuffed into the hiding place, clothed in dirty white abaya, their backpacks on their stomachs. They had turned their phones off to save battery and make sure there was no unintended sound at an inopportune time. Gideon found the drive along the road relaxing, and drifted off to sleep. Rei just clutched her backpack and prayed. This was obviously the most ridiculous thing they had ever done, and she was sure they were going to be killed, beheaded, burned alive, or thrown into a stinking jail for the rest of their lives.

After an hour, the truck thumped off the pavement and started driving across uneven ground. Gideon woke with a curse and tried to get his hand up to rub his head. He couldn't reach and gave up.

"That was rude..." he whispered to Rei.

"Yeah. I doubt it's going to get much better. This is ridiculous! What are we doing? We're just regular people! We work for an *art* collector. You don't look anything like Indiana Jones!" She was starting to hyperventilate.

Gideon could only take her hand. "Honey, listen.

We'll be ok. I'm sure these guys have done this hundreds of times. And they're not getting paid the other half of their money unless we all get back alive, right? So that's some incentive, at least."

"Wonderful," Rei muttered.

———◦◦◦———

Gideon knew that Kuwait was very small, and he also knew that the truck hadn't slowed down in the three or so hours they'd been off the paved road, so he had to assume they were in Iraq. He didn't share this information with Rei, who seemed to be dozing off and on. Having been in the Army, although never stationed in a war zone, he knew only too clearly the real dangers they faced. Especially Rei. Abdul had given him a 9mm Glock with a full clip while he was putting on his abaya, and he had stowed it within easy reach. Or so he thought at the time. He couldn't reach much now.

Both of the Quinns lost track of time as the truck bounced and skidded on what was obviously sand. Occasionally they would drive across a smooth stretch of ground, whether tarmac or packed earth Gideon couldn't. He was hot and sweating and extremely thirsty, and his muscles had begun to cramp from being in the same position for so many hours. Rei seemed to go in and out of a restless sleep, moaning occasionally and trying to turn, unable to do so. There was adequate air flow, and enough light that he could dimly see their forms if he tipped his head up a bit. He should have brought an iPod, he thought. *I could have caught up with my audio books.*

Finally the truck seemed to slow. This made the ruts seem larger, and Rei came fully awake after a particularly large bump sent them both six inches in the air, only to crash back down on the metal truck bed. The truck came to a stop, and Rei started to say something to Gideon, when he squeezed her hand hard.

"Listen!" he hissed.

They could hear voices speaking in Arabic. They had no idea what was going on, but there were more than two men talking, which meant they had company. Rei held Gideon's hand tightly, and he awkwardly brought her fingers to his lips and kissed them. They could just make out each other's faces in the dark, and he smiled at her. She had tears in her eyes, but mouthed, *"I love you."*

The group of men conversed for over an hour. At first the conversation seemed heated, although Rei thought Arabic always sounded heated so she couldn't be sure. But after fifteen minutes they were laughing, apparently telling stories or jokes. The sound made the couple relax somewhat, but that made Rei realize that she really needed to go to the bathroom. She tried to think of other things.

"Ma'a as-salaama," said one voice.

"Allah yasalmak," replied a voice that sounded like Asim's.

They heard the truck doors slam shut, the engine fired up, and the truck started bouncing over the terrain once again. Both Gideon and Rei breathed out a sigh of relief.

"I have to pee!" Rei whispered.

⊸•〰•⊸

Another hour went by, and the truck stopped once again. This time they only heard two voices, those of their driver and his son. The car doors slammed, and the hidden door at their feet opened. The sunlight was blinding after their hours in darkness. The two men grabbed their ankles and hauled them out of the truck. It took several minutes for both their eyes and their muscles to adjust. Asim led them one at a time around a boulder so they could relieve themselves, standing watch with his AK-47.

"Oh, thank God!" Rei said, as she came around the rock, adjusting her abaya and hijab. "I feel so much better."

She and Asim joined Gideon and Abdul. "So is this Ctesiphon?" she asked.

"We call it Tasbun," Abdul replied. "We will need to walk a short distance. If we drive there, it will possibly draw attention. If we walk, we will look like pilgrims. Sometimes those of Persian descent still come here to the place of their ancestors. These days there is not much of that, of course, as traveling is very dangerous. But there is a village there," he pointed to the northwest. "Not far. There are still descendants of those people there. We will walk around and come at the site from that direction. It should be enough. If we meet anyone, cover your faces and hands." He turned to Rei, "You must keep your head down. Even if you do not see anyone about, keep your head down and walk a few paces behind us as a local woman would do." Rei nodded and adjusted her hijab to cover more of her face.

"Let us go," Abdul said, and began walking

westward. Gideon and Asim walked beside him, with Rei a few paces behind. Gideon wasn't happy with this arrangement—he wanted to keep his eyes on his wife. Asim reassured him.

"I will see if anyone comes. She will be safe. That is my duty."

They walked west for an half hour, and then turned north. The Tigris River was visible at times as a winking, sparkling line. As they got closer, they could see the trees and green that flourished along the banks, and farther north the smoke rising from the village fires. Small boats were fishing in the river.

After another half an hour they turned back to the southeast, and came across a hard packed trail through the hills and scrub. They went up a small rise, and from the top, they could see the ruins.

"Oh!" gasped Rei. "That's beautiful! Look at that huge arch!"

Their guides just nodded and kept walking. They had not seen anyone yet, and Gideon was praying that they would be able to get in and out of the site without encountering another person. His senses were on high alert, and he had the now familiar flood of adrenalin keeping his heart rate up. Abdul sensed it, and lay a reassuring hand on his arm.

"Calm now. I can see no one, and if we meet someone here, it is unlikely to be rebels. There are some places that are still sacred, even in Iraq."

⋙∘⋘

They approached the enormous arch from the front. Abdul told them that the right wing of the palace had collapsed in an earthquake in 1880, but that the remaining ruins had been stable since then, and largely exempted from the strife that had ravaged the country. There were rumored to be spirits about the place, and no one was keen to stir them up, no matter what else was going on.

Rei craned her neck as they passed under the entry of the arch. They wandered in the room that had once been the kings' court, enormous with its barrel vault ceiling. The left side of the palace still had rooms, although walls were crumbling and the roof was gone. Rei could see that there were carvings in the stone throughout the site, but that they were concentrated mostly in the kings' court.

"Asim, can you stand guard near the front of the arch? I think what we're looking for is in here somewhere. Gosh, it's just so huge..." She looked around at the enormous space. "What was this place called? Not the town, but this palace?"

"Taq-i Kisra. The Palace of the Great Kings."

Gideon and Rei started at the left side of the arch and began working their way down the wall. The Persian kings had apparently loved wall carvings, and it was a long, slow process. The sun was beginning to set, and the shadows were growing long inside the stone room.

Gideon said, "I *really* do not want to spend the night here, or anywhere near here. All the hairs on the back of my neck have been standing up for six hours. Let's keep going until we can't see a thing..." Rei agreed. She did not like being a woman—an American woman, at that—in a Muslim country illegally.

They got to the corner and could barely see in

the darkness.

"Do you have your flashlight?" Gideon asked.

"Yes, but I think it's almost dead." She unzipped a small pocket in her backpack and handed it to him. "Here."

The beam was indeed much dimmer than it had been on previous days, and it was doubtful that it would hold out much longer. It had just begun to flicker intermittently when Rei saw it.

"There! Look, Gid, there!" She pointed to a spot on the wall that the beam had just passed over. Gideon brought the light back to where she was pointing. An X was chiseled onto the helmet of a fallen soldier whose face appeared to be resting on a narrow brick ledge.

"Are the stones loose?" Gideon began to press on them. The light flickered and went out.

"Crap! Ok, we know about where the X is," Rei said. "Jiggle the stones on the ledge. If one of them isn't loose, we'll just have to dig. But don't take a step! If we lose it now, we'll have to come back tomorrow. We know from the other ones that he always puts them right under the mark... It's got to be here!"

They both planted their feet solidly so they weren't tempted to move, and began trying to rock the stones on the ledge.

"They're solid," Rei said. "Let's dig."

Gideon handed her the trowel but kept working on the stones. "You dig. I'll keep trying these. I feel like that X being right above this ledge must mean something..."

Rei carefully knelt straight down, cognizant of her position next to the wall. She put her fingers on the now invisible ledge, and traced a vertical line down to the sand. She carefully started digging with her right hand, her left resting on the wall for perspective. It was incredible how fast and how completely the darkness had fallen.

She had dug about six inches deep in the soft sand when she heard the stones above her head shift. Gideon grunted and then she heard the sound of a rock scraping against another rock.

"Head's up!" Gideon said.

A rock landed on her knee.

"Sorry, hon! I thought the rocks would be elongated, but they're really pretty short. And there's a big space behind here... Hang on..." She stood up and heard his robes scraping against the stones.

"Got it! Feels just the same as the others—metal tube, leather strap. Thank God our Father Eduardo was a creature of habit! Here." He handed it to his wife and slapped his hands together, trying to remove the dirt.

"I'd better try to put that stone back," he said, as he reached down to find it in the dark.

⊸•⇎•⊶

Walking back to the truck in the near total darkness seemed incredibly dangerous, not to mention impossible, to Rei. They had filled in her small hole and put the loose stone back in the ledge as well as they could, and groped their way to the opening of the arch, the now-dark sky giving only the barest outline of the roof line as they walked along the left wall. They could see a very faint difference where the arch was, and as they approached they saw the form of a man rise from the ground.

"Success?" Abdul asked.

"Yes. Thank you! Will we be able to get back to Kuwait tonight?" Rei asked anxiously.

"We shall try. We have diesel in the back of the truck to refill the tank, and we will have a small meal before we set out. I shall have to drive without lights, and that will be slow, but I believe we can still cross the border before it is light. Come."

He led the way to Asim, and the four started back the way they'd come. Since it was dark, Abdul didn't insist on Rei following behind. Gideon had already decided he wasn't leaving her to walk back there alone, so he was glad that the discussion didn't arise. Asim chambered a round in his rifle.

"Do you see someone?" Gideon asked in alarm, drawing his own pistol.

"No. There are jackals."

"Great. Creatures," Rei grumbled. She held Gideon's arm in a death grip as they walked.

———✦———

They didn't bother with the roundabout route they had taken to get to the Taq-i Kisra. Abdul led them unerringly straight back to the truck. The moon was a sliver, and the stars were bright. Their eyes had adjusted and Rei no longer tripped over every stone, but she was completely turned around and knew that she and Gideon would never have found their way back without the Bazzis. *I guess we'd just fall in the river, eventually,* she thought.

The truck was just as they'd left it, and the Quinns visited the makeshift privy again before being stuffed back in their hiding place. Abdul reminded them that they would be traveling at a slower pace than on the way north, as he would be running in the dark, without headlights.

Once they were as comfortable as they were going to get, Asim closed the hatch, the truck doors slammed shut, and the engine fired up. The first few minutes were on very soft sand, but the ride smoothed out as they reached a dirt road. Gideon and Rei both drifted in and out of sleep, awakened periodically when a rut threw them in the air and they landed hard on the metal truck bed.

Time seemed to move at a fluid pace. On one hand, it seemed shorter than the ride north to Ctesiphon. It was cooler, and the slower pace made a more pleasant noise inside the smugglers' hole. On the other hand, the coming illegal border crossing, their last known hurdle, made them much more anxious than on the outbound journey. They had the letter now. They didn't dare think about it being taken away by some authority claiming it was an antiquity of Iraq. Nor that same authority arresting them for all kinds of illegal activity.

<hr />

They had been on a fairly smooth road for some time, and both had drifted to sleep. Suddenly Abdul slammed on the brakes, sending their heads into the front wall of their chamber, and the truck slid sideways before bouncing to a halt. Other vehicle doors slammed, and they heard yelling in Arabic. The doors of their truck opened, but didn't close, and they could hear Abdul and Asim speaking in a conciliatory way. More yelling. More attempted appeasement.

Rei grabbed Gideon's hand. He squeezed it, and put his other hand on the butt of the Glock in the top of his waistband. He raised his head as much as he could to try to determine a line of sight, and realized he'd have to move his feet or he'd shoot them off. He experimented with pushing his toes to the side like a dancer, and thought he could probably get a couple of rounds off before he and Rei were either killed where they lay, or pulled out onto the sand.

The angry voices got closer, and they could hear people rummaging through the junk all around them on both sides of the truck. The doors squealed as they were pulled all the way open, and they could hear banging from the cab. Soon they heard knocking underneath the carriage. They barely dared breathe, and Rei had her eyes closed, mouthing silent prayers.

Finally, after twenty minutes, the search ended. One of the strangers barked something, and Abdul answered in a subservient voice. They heard the truck doors slam again. After an endless quiet moment, the engine turned over, and the truck started to drive slowly, gradually picking up speed.

"Oh, thank God! Thank God!" Rei said, tears running down her cheeks. Gideon couldn't agree more.

CHAPTER TWENTY-ONE

CAPE OF GOOD HOPE

APRIL 1688

JOAO AND ISABEL ENJOYED THE long winter stop in the Cape of Good Hope. Determining to wait for good weather to resume the journey up the west coast of Africa, the captain of the Santa Antonio de Tanna had given his crew some of their wages, and made berth until calmer weather could be relied upon. The Xaviers paid for the rental of a guest house on the elaborate estate of a merchant with the Dutch East India Company, and spent many weeks exploring the area and making new friends.

When Joao had been in the port city before, he had only rarely left the ship, as Catholics were not much welcomed, so he was seeing much of the town for the first time along with Isabel. He knew, however, that he would leave the final letter here, and they spent some time discussing what location would be the most prudent.

The Castle of Good Hope was the bustling center of trade and society in the Cape, and they considered it carefully. The church had some potential, and the fort in general was quite solidly built and looked built to last for many centuries. However, there were always many people about, conducting business, shopping at the markets, attending services in the Protestant chapel, and performing the tasks of the governmental. They could determine no feasible way to carve Joao's mark, much less effectively hide a letter without being seen.

They considered, too, Table Mountain. It was enormous, and would obviously be there until the Lord returned. However there were no distinguishing marks, or areas of prior habitation, that would allow their progeny to find the clue. It was not their intention that this letter, the first in the hunt, never be found, but they had run out of ideas for a suitable location.

One day Joao began talking to a man sitting at a neighboring table while he had tea in an inn. The old man had lived in the Cape of Good Hope all of his life, and was a natural storyteller. He reminisced about Vasco da Gama as if he'd been onboard his ship on that first voyage around the Cape.

"And then there was that other fellow... What was his name, another Portugee. Ah, de Saldanha, I believe. He named the mountain there. Not a lot of imagination, I must say. But a table is what it is, I'll be bound, so Table Mountain is good enough. And he's the one what climbed up Lion's Head over yonder and carved that big cross. Quite a Christian that man was, I guess. Still see it after all this time. I'd wager it would be a signal for Jesus Christ Himself to come to the Cape when the time comes for Him to visit us again."

Joao turned and looked out the window at Lions Head. "Where is this cross? I've never noticed it before."

"Tis on the far side. Looks out to sea, not over the town. Course the town t'weren't here then. Was quite a job, all that chiseling and carving..." He shook his head at man's folly. Joao continued looking thoughtfully at Lion's Head.

———⚬·◅✥▻·⚬———

A week later Joao rode a roan gelding around the city, and out towards the sea so that he could look back up at Lions Head. To be sure, there was an enormous cross carved in the rock. He wasn't sure how to get up there, but he knew that he had found the place for his final letter.

A big storm raged over the next several days, and Joao and Isabel used the time to plan their hike as best they could. Isabel, who had gotten very accustomed to wearing breeches on their journey to the *zimbabwe*, suggested that she could do so again, to aid their hike. While Joao enjoyed the site of her in his pants, he didn't think the Cape of Good Hope was the place to try the unusual fashion again.

"We shall have to try it in regular clothing, so we do not attract attention. If it proves impossible for you, I will have to attempt it another time alone."

"Darling," Isabel protested. "Who will see us on that far side? I can change into the breeches once we have begun. It would be ever so much more practical."

"And you are a practical, resourceful lass, I know." Joao smiled at her. "Well, let us come to a compromise. You may put them in the saddle bag, and if it appears that we will be alone, you may change into them. Is that satisfactory?"

Isabel smiled and kissed him. "Yes! It is most satisfactory. Thank you." Joao returned her smile, and went back to writing his letter.

The weather stayed very wet, so life returned to its usual pattern of tea, fires in the fireplace, and dinner at the pub with other transients who were waiting out the weather. One evening, as they sat enjoying a sherry with a group of fellow merchants, several men walked in. One was obviously a seaman, and the others likely merchants who had traveled one way or the other along the trade route. Mr. Brinkerhoff, a senior official at the Castle of Good Hope, waved over the seaman.

"Ah, Captain Roemer! How goes it, sir?" He heartily shook the man's hand.

"The weather is doing us no favors, sir, I'll be bound. We were delayed on our way down the coast, and have been beating against this wind and rain for almost two weeks now. My crew is tired, and many have taken ill. I have never been so happy to see that great Table Mountain as I was yesterday. We all were, even our normally quiet passengers. Once we had made berth, it was ale for all!" He laughed and sat down at the table.

"Aye, it's hard on those of us who don't make their living at sea, that's the God's truth," Brinkerhoff said.

"These fellows are a strange lot. Some kind of religious order, I believe. They don't talk, except among themselves. They're of the Church of Rome, so I don't know that they'll be able to disembark here. But they can do what they like on my ship as long as their coin is paid. At least they're not trying to tell me my business or drinking their weight in wine. Quiet is a blessing, after some of the Portuguese I've ferried."

Joao listened to all of this with growing dismay, as did Isabel, sitting to his left. They had assumed they were safe from the men, apparently some brand of monk, as they hadn't arrived in the Cape sooner. Now it appeared they would have to elude them once again. And with the final letter, too... It was almost too much.

Joao stood up quickly and pulled Isabel to her feet. "Gentlemen, ladies, we must be leaving. I'm afraid we have overstayed and my wife is feeling ill. Please excuse us."

The men and women all made sympathetic noises, and Joao escorted Isabel out before any introductions could be made. He did not need for Captain Roemer to bring back their names to his ship.

———⊶◦⊱———

The following day, he and Isabel rode to the base of Lion's Head. They had discussed it late into the night, and prudence dictated that they wait for dryer weather. But as of that morning, the brothers did not know they were in the Cape of Good Hope, which made it the only opportunity that was absolutely safe. The wet ground and cold wind would have to be tolerated as concessions to the safety of their final mission.

They tied their horses in a protected thicket at the base of Lion's Head, on the sea side. The weather was drizzly and cold, and Isabel had mixed feelings about putting on Joao's breeches. Her skirts were much warmer, but even standing in the thicket gathering their supplies had left them wet to the knee, and heavy. She quickly removed them and pulled on the breeches, catching Joao's grin.

"Quite the Jesuit you are…" she said, teasingly.

"If I'd ever seen a woman as comely as you in breeches, I would not have taken the vows, my dear." He kissed her soundly, then handed her the small shovel.

There was no trail or path up the mountain. Joao led the way, angling up and around to try to minimize the difficulty as much as he could. The soggy ground was slick where it was bare, and wet leaves made everything treacherous. They clung to trees and saplings as the climb got increasingly steep, until they were forced to stop a dozen yards from the rock topped summit.

"I don't think I can climb up there, Joao," Isabel said, gasping as she leaned into a scrubby pine tree. "It is almost straight up!"

Joao looked up and agreed. "*Senhor* de Saldanha did it, although I daresay not in the rain. I am going to continue. I believe I can get there… Will you be all right here? I do not expect that it will take overly long, but I do not want you to be afraid, or to slip again."

She looked around her. "If I sit on that rock there," she pointed, "I shall be safe. And there will be a little shelter from the wind. Pray you be careful, Joao. I do not wish to see you sliding down this mountain!"

She handed him the small shovel she had tucked under her arm, and he helped her to the rock. The view out over the sea was lovely in the dark silvery way it is with long rain. She leaned back and sighed.

"Tis good to sit, I must say. And I am thankful for these breeches. Now hurry on!"

Joao kissed her again and got his bearings. He didn't think he could make the climb straight up, but one more turn around the mountain should lead him to the top. He clung onto trees and branches, and used them to haul himself up each step of the way. He put his boot in a mass of wet leaves when he was almost at the flat ledge below the rocky top, and only just caught himself on a thin limb as his feet slid out from under him. He used all his arm strength to pull himself back up, and finally reached the even ground. For a moment he stood still, hands on his thighs and breathing hard, in front of the giant cross.

He called out, "Isabel? Isabel, can you hear me?" He felt like his voice was dropping straight down with the rain, but then he heard her reply.

"Yes! Are you all right?"

"I am at the top! I shall be back soon!" He got to work.

⸻⊸◦◖∅◗◦⊷⸻

The trip down the mountain was almost as exciting as the hike up had been. The rain was coming harder now, and the fallen leaves continued to create a hazard as they tried to stay upright. Never had two horses looked more pathetic, or more welcome, as their two, huddled and hunched against the cold rain. Isabel started to mount, but Joao grabbed her waist.

"Have you forgotten something, my love?" he asked.

She looked confused for a moment, and then looked down at her muddy boots and soaked breeches. She laughed.

"It wouldn't do to ride into town like this, I suppose!" She took her skirts out of the leather satchel and tried to get under a tree canopy to change. Her skirt quickly looked as wet and muddy as the pants had.

Joao helped her mount, sidesaddle, then mounted his own gelding.

"And we are done!" he said happily. "Now we have only to get to Lisbon, and start our life."

"Do you not think they will continue to hound us for the letter, no matter where we are?" Isabel asked.

"Oh yes, I do. At first. They will probably do as they did to me in Lisbon those years ago, and search our home. But there are many safe places to keep valuables in a city like Lisbon, and I think we will not keep that letter at our home. It will be safe, and we will begin our new business, our family... We will begin to live."

CHAPTER TWENTY-TWO

KUWAIT

PRESENT DAY

BDUL DROVE THE TRUCK OVER the Kuwaiti border at 5:47 in the morning, as the rays of the sun began to appear on the horizon. The vehicle bounced over the loose sand, miles from any road, and Abdul turned on the headlights and headed southwest. After twenty kilometers he came to a stop in a dry creek bed, protected on three sides by rock, and Asim pulled Rei and Gideon out of the truck. The almost collapsed, both with relief and with muscle cramps, and Rei started to laugh and cry.

"What happened back there?" Gideon asked Abdul.

"Rebels. They wanted us to pay them a bribe to keep going across their territory, but they thought that we were smuggling heroin also. So they searched the truck. It has happened before, and we have never had anyone found. But they were most thorough, and we had a fright while they were under the back and looking through the things around you. Praise Allah, they did not find you!"

Rei exclaimed, "I have never been so terrified in my whole life!" She wiped the tears from her face.

"I assume we're in Kuwait now?" Gideon asked, looking around at the sand and rock that looked just like the sand and rock in Iraq.

"Yes, and now you may sit in the truck with us. You do not need to hide in the back any longer, although I think that we will not be stopped anyway."

They all piled onto the bench seat, which at any other time would have been ridiculously uncomfortable, but, after the hours unable to move, seemed deliciously free. Rei sat half on Gideon's lap, and they sat next to the door, aware that touching an unrelated woman would make the Muslim men uncomfortable. Rei watched as the sun rose in yellow and pinks over the desert. Once they got on the paved road to the city, she rested her head on the glass and dozed.

———⇒∘⊂⊘∘⊂———

They arrived back at the industrial park at 7:00. They thanked Asim, and Rei barely resisted giving him a hug. She just grinned at him and said "Thank you so much!" over and over again. The took off their abayas and he threw them into the hidey-hole on his truck, and motored off with one last wave. The Quinns got in the plain white truck from which they'd started their journey.

Gideon sat in the middle next to Abdul, and they drove back through the city to the Hilton. They were filthy, exhausted, and half starved, but elated and still feeling a rush of accomplishment and excitement that hadn't worn off. Gideon turned on his phone and dialed the captain.

"Hey Mac, it's Gideon," he said when the man picked up.

"Oh, thank God!" McMillan said. "We've been up all night. I've been kicking myself three ways from Sunday for setting this whole gig up. I was sure you'd end up dead or in prison somewhere."

"We had a close call, but we're almost at the hotel now, so it's all good. We're gonna clean up, get room service and then *sleep*. I'll catch up with you mid-afternoon." He hung up.

<hr />

They hustled through the hotel lobby, careful not to attract any undo attention. With their backpacks slung over their shoulders, jeans and casual shirts, they hoped they looked like they'd been out for a stroll or for a cup of strong coffee. They endured an elevator ride that seemed endless, exited on their floor and entered their room.

"Oh my gosh!" Rei exploded. "Oh my gosh oh my gosh! I can't believe we didn't die. Really. I thought we were going to die." She danced around the room while Gideon laughed.

"Yeah. I actually did too. It's one thing to be in the military and get in hairy situations, it's totally another to be in them with your wife. I didn't like that... But you did great!" He wrapped her in his arms. He hadn't liked it at all, and hoped Goa would be a whole lot safer. "I'd better tell Mr. Xavier we're alive—I'm sure he's not sleeping either." He got the iPhone out of his pants pocket and dialed.

They bathed and ate a huge room service breakfast. They climbed into the soft bed gratefully and slept. When they awoke six hours later they were still sore, and Rei had the beginnings of bruises on her shoulder blades from bouncing around in the truck bed. They looked in the hotel directory and discovered a gem: a masseuse. They booked massages for before dinner, and called Mac in his room.

Five minutes later there was a knock at the door and Gideon let the pilot in. He shook Gideon's hand, but then gave him a quick hug.

"Let's not do that again, shall we? I aged ten years yesterday and last night. That was awful! So tell me about it—but first, did you find the letter?"

Rei lifted up the metal tube. "Yep. In the dark without a flashlight, even. Gideon was awesome."

"Abdul and Asim were awesome," Gideon corrected. "Jack can tell his buddy to hang onto those two. We got stopped by rebels on the way back from the site, and they searched the truck. Abdul said they thought he was smuggling drugs. But they didn't give us away, and the rig they have worked. It was a bad time, though. We couldn't move in there, and I wasn't going to get too many shots off before they had us out and on the ground..." he trailed off, reliving it.

"Yeah. It was bad," Rei agreed. "So let's not talk about that part anymore, OK? We're here, I'm sure Mr. Xavier has wired Abdul his money by now, and we have the letter. Everyone is safe. So why don't I work on translating it before our massages and dinner?"

―――――――⊶∘⊄⋙∘⊂―――――――

The masseuse worked out all the kinks from their confinement, and the hotel served them a superb dinner. Rei chose a decadent chocolate torte for dessert, and enjoyed every minute of it guilt free. Jimmy joined the party after a day at the airport with the plane, and they all retired for an after dinner drink in the bar. Finally they called it a night, and Mac came to their room with them.

"Can I hear what the letter says?" he asked. "I feel like I'm invested in this whole thing now!"

"Can't see why not," Gideon answered. "We're going to need your services awhile longer, I think."

Rei got out her notebook and read:

My dear son,

If you are reading this letter, you have made it to the location of the Taq-i-Kisra. I am sure that you have been through much to obtain it, and I pray that my Father in Heaven has kept you and anyone who has accompanied you safe through your trials.

The final resting place of the Throne of Solomon is near the great city of Goa, in the East. The Portuguese are well settled there, and you will find all you need to complete your quest once you arrive. It may be that you do not arrive at the right time of the year, so I pray that the rains will not delay you once you arrive.

When you have gotten settled in Goa, you will need to visit the great church there. You will find another, and the last, letter. That letter has instructions for you to follow, and shall lead you to the treasure that I have left for you. I do not believe, nay, I cannot believe, that anyone else will have discovered it by chance. I believe that it is by God's providence that you will find it, and that by His wisdom you will know what to do with the precious Throne once it has been found.

We continue to pray for you every day, and we count it all joy to have been part of God's great plan to free this great part of His people's history. Be safe, my son, and be ever vigilant.

In the name of our mighty Lord and Savior Jesus Christ, your loving father,

Joao Xavier

X

Written in the year of our Lord 1687

"We already knew the end game was Goa. Now we just need to find 'the great church', and the last letter. And then, I hope, a treasure map?" Rei said.

"Sure sounds like a treasure map. And he says 'near' Goa, which was a lot smaller area in the 1680s than it will be now. For all we know it'll be in the center of the city!" Gideon said.

Rei had opened her laptop, and was typing. She clicked a few links, and said, "Looks like there are nine churches old enough to be 'the great church' in Goa... I'll have to do some research to figure out if we can narrow down the options. We've got the Church of Our Lady of the Immaculate Conception—wow, that's a mouthful! Our Lady of the Mount. Chapel of St. Catherine. Church of St. Francis Xavier. Churches and convents of Saint Monica and Saint Francis Assisi. Our Lady of the Rosary. Church of Saint Catejan. Church of the Carmelites. The Professed House and Born Jesus Church...That's a weird name. And those aren't all that are old enough, but probably all that would be potentially called 'the great church.' So. Research time."

"In the morning," said Gideon. "I'm beat, and we can get a fresh run at it tomorrow. Mac, can you map out our trip to Goa, and let me know how many stops and how long it'll take? And I'll need to think about what to do about our *Congratio a Achalichus* friends, who are bound to be waiting for us. Maybe landing somewhere other than Goa would be our best bet—I'm sure they're watching the airports."

"I'm on it," said Mac. "See you in the morning. Maybe breakfast at 9:00, and we'll both have something?"

"Yep, see you then." Gideon closed and locked the door behind him. He turned back to his wife, who as still typing on her computer. "Bed now, love. There's plenty of time to do your research in the morning."

She smiled at him, and closed the laptop.

———◦◦◦———

Rei woke at 7:00 and sat quietly at the desk researching the churches in Goa while Gideon slept. It was obviously a crap shoot, and there were a lot more options than in any location the Jesuit had sent them before. He probably hadn't intended it to be so difficult, but a lot had changed in four centuries, including pet names like 'the great church.' She was able to make some logical deductions, and cross a couple of locations off to get a top three, but they wouldn't know how accurate she was until they got there. And then they would have the monks right on their heels.

They were enjoying their coffee when Mac joined

them. He ordered, and brought out a small notebook.

"I've looked at the airports we can get into, as well as the relative safety of the region we're in. Which is not very... I think our best bet is to fly from here to Sur Airport in Oman, where we do a quick refuel and then fly to Mumbai. The plane can make that trip over the Indian Ocean, and the weather the next couple of days looks okay for that, although I'd probably like to do it late at night or early in the morning for the smoothest ride. I looked at all the other airports outside of Goa, and turns out Mumbai is as close as anything, so we're going to have to drive from there if you don't want to fly into Goa directly."

"We?" asked Gideon.

"Heck yeah, you don't think I'm dropping out of this now, without knowing what happens, do you? And you're gonna need to get out of dodge when this is over—I'm the guy for the job." He grinned at them. "I was in the Marine Corps, that's where I got my wings. I'm thinking you could use a little help with these monks of yours, too."

"Absolutely! That's great! Thanks, Mac." Gideon shook his hand across the table.

"OK, so back to the plan. Mumbai is about 580 kilometers from Goa, which they say is eleven and a half hours not counting stops. You never know in those countries, though... Could be a lot longer. It's not rainy season, at least, so we can be thankful for that. I'd say we fly from here to Oman tomorrow morning. Have lunch, fuel up, rest, and head out tomorrow night to Mumbai. You guys can sleep on the plane, and we can all sleep in the hangar in Mumbai until it's light. Jimmy'll stay with the plane, we'll hire a car, drive part of the way, and find somewhere to stay... So we get to Goa in three days."

"Three days is a long time," Rei said. "But the longer those monks wait, the better. Maybe they'll get bored or careless. And I definitely don't think we should fly into Goa. I'd be watching the airport if it were me, so I'm sure they are. Of course, Mr. Xavier is so glad we're not dead, three days won't seem too bad to him!"

"Did you figure out where we need to go once we get there?" asked Gideon.

Rei took out her by now well worn notebook. "There are a lot of old churches in Goa thanks to the Portuguese... and we obviously hope we don't have to visit them all. My two best guesses are St. Francis Xavier's, and the Born Jesus, which houses Francis Xavier's remains. Father Eduardo was a Jesuit, and Francis Xavier was one of the initial seven men who founded the Jesuit order. When he first arrived in Goa, Father Eduardo was still a Jesuit. So I am guessing that he would have attached himself to one of these two churches. Afterwards, when he was looking to hide a letter, they would have been logical. But the other side of the coin is that people would have known him at whichever one he'd gone to or worked at. So it could be the *other* Jesuit one... Or neither, just to make sure he didn't run into someone who might recognize him."

"Great. That's not exactly narrowing it down!" Gideon said.

Rei shrugged. "Well, the Church of the Carmelites is probably out because they were Carmelites. But it's in ruins anyway, so if it was there, we won't find it now. The Church of Saint Catejan was either not finished yet, or had just been finished when he was

there, so I'm ruling that one out as 'the great church.'"
She consulted her notes. "For now I'm leaving out the
two with convents. Saint Catherine's is a chapel, so
we can assume it's not 'the great church.' That leaves
Our Lady of the Immaculate Conception and Our
Lady of the Mount. Our Lady of the Mount has been
reconstructed twice, but early on. I think that would
be our fourth choice."

"Bottom line?" Gideon asked.

"Saint Francis Xavier. Born Jesus. Immaculate
Conception. Top three." She closed the notebook.
"With the caveat that I could be totally wrong."

CHAPTER TWENTY-THREE

Mumbai, India
Present Day

I T WAS DARK WHEN THEIR plane landed in Mumbai, but they could see the lights stretching out on the peninsula and on the skyscrapers in the city. They slept in the plane after all the paperwork had been done, and ate a quick breakfast in the captains' lounge before getting a taxi to a car hire firm. Mac had decided to land at the smaller Juhu Airport, instead of Chatrapati Shivaji International, so they drove south along the coast and enjoyed the beautiful morning sun on the Indian Ocean.

Captain McMillan rented an SUV in his own name, and they were soon driving through the crowded streets. They went north on National Highway 3 to clear the peninsula, then turned south onto the Mumbai-Pune Road. They merged onto National Highway 4, which was the Pune-Bangalore Highway. The roads were decent, and traffic, outside of the city, moved along at a good pace.

They stopped for lunch in Pune, and enjoyed a veritable feast of local curries, dhal, coconut sauce, rice, na'an, and gooey sweet pastries for dessert. The food made them all sleepy, so Gideon ordered strong black coffee to go, and they piled back into the SUV. Mac consulted his map.

"We can stop in Satara, which is a bit less than halfway to Panaji, or we can go on to Kolaphur, which will leave us only a couple or three hours tomorrow. There are little towns along the way, but those less likely to have some kind of hotel. How're you feeling?" he asked Gideon, who was behind the wheel.

"I'm ok now that the caffeine has kicked in. That lunch just about put me in a coma! Let's see how we all feel at the first town, and if we're all right, I guess we push on. I'd just as soon get there on the early side tomorrow so we can check out at least one of the churches, and find a hotel or guest house or something. I guess we need to figure that out, too..." He settled back in the seat.

They decided to keep driving at Satara, and stopped in the late afternoon at a small inn outside Kolaphur. Having exchanged money in Mumbai, they paid cash for two rooms, which included dinner and breakfast. They bathed and ate, tired from long day of driving. As they slept they could hear the sporadic barking of a dog nearby.

Breakfast was light but delicious, and most importantly included copious amounts of strong coffee. They were back on the road by 8:00. They arrived in Panaji, a town nine kilometers from Old Goa where two of the churches they were visiting were located, at 11:00.

"We're too early to find a room, wouldn't you say?" Gideon asked.

"If we want an inn or guest house, we can probably do that now. If we want a hotel, maybe not," Mac replied.

"I've been thinking about it, and it seems like the last thing we want is to go out of our way to advertise that we're here. I don't know how sophisticated these guys are, but let's give them the benefit of the doubt and assume they can flag our credit cards. Not yours, Mac... At least I don't think they have your name, although they would have seen you at Great Zimbabwe. Anyway, let's just assume we have to use cash, and we need to try to be as incognito as we can."

Rei raised her eyebrows. "Disguises?"

"Maybe not disguises, per se. But you could wear a sari and a headscarf and some big sunglasses, and Mac and I can wear hats and those tunic things the men here wear. That white linen stuff. You know..."

Rei laughed. "Sherwani."

"How the heck do you know that? You are a repository of useless information, you know that?" he laughed. "OK, so we wear *sherwani*, and a turban or some kind of hat. We'll look ridiculous, I'm sure, but at least we won't stand out completely. They'll be looking for tourists, so we just need to look untouristy."

───◦◦◦◦───

They drove through the streets, and found a nice looking guest house in an upper scale neighborhood. The house was pale pink, with shade trees and a pink wall. The iron gate was open, so they drove into the parking area. There was only one car in the small lot.

"Wait here, I'll go check it out," Mac said, and hopped out of the passenger seat.

He was gone for ten minutes, and came back smiling. "Very nice lady! We have two rooms overlooking the back garden. No en suite baths, but we're the only ones here, so that's not too bad. She was happy to take cash, and breakfast was included. We can go on in now, and she'll feed us lunch, too."

"Great!" said Rei. "I'm sick of being in the car!"

They got their luggage and went in the house. It had obviously been the home of a well to do family, with a gracious, wide tiled hallway, and large arches leading to rooms off either side. The stairway swept up the right wall, and they found their rooms at the end of the hall. They both were large, with high ceilings and tall windows. French doors were opened to a small balcony which overlooked the walled garden. The trickling of a fountain could be heard, although the vegetation hid it from their view. The bathroom, across the hall, had been made from another bedroom, so it was also large, with a claw foot tub and intricately painted tiles. The Quinns took a moment to wash their face and hands, and plug in some of their electronics to charge.

Wandering down the stairs, they followed voices until they found Mac seated on a shaded veranda. He waved to a pot of tea, and they sat.

"I was talking to Mrs. Pandey, and told her that we'd like to buy some native clothes. She thought I was a bit nutty, but I told her we're doing some research, and wanted to blend in... I don't know what she really thinks, but she told me where we could go. The shop's not far from here. I think it's owned by a relative of hers."

Mrs. Pandey came out with a tray of food, which she put down in front of them, smiling.

"You please enjoy!" she said, and she left.

The food was simple but full of delicious flavors.

Having only had Indian food in London, Rei was already surprised at how many different curries there seemed to be. She wasn't a huge fan of the very spicy ones, although they were Gideon's favorite. But homemade na'an, melted butter, and coconut sauce managed to cool her tongue.

After lunch they followed Mrs. Pandey's directions and walked to a small tailoring shop on a quiet mixed street of residences and shops. When they walked in it was apparent that the innkeeper had called ahead, because they were expected, and didn't have to explain what they wanted.

Thirty minutes later they all walked out dressed in local garb, the men in white linen sherwani and pants called *churidars.* Mac had a simple boxy white hat on his brown hair and new large lens sunglasses. Gideon had a turban covering his blonde hair. Rei had on a colorful top called a *kameez,* churidars, and a yellow scarf called a *dupatta,* which she could pull over her head. She too had large sunglasses covering her face, and had put her hair in a tight bun.

"I kind of like this," Rei said, looking down at herself. "I have pants on, so I can run if I need to. And everything else is so loose I could eat a huge meal and not have to unbutton my pants!"

The men laughed, and the three walked back to the house. Mrs. Pandey greeted them with a grin, and complimented them on looking like natives.

"It's as close as we're gonna get, anyway!" said Gideon.

———⟶◦◅⟋▱◦⟶———

They left Panaji and followed Mrs. Pandey's directions to Old Goa. They had decided to try the Chapel of Saint Francis Xavier first, as it was the smaller of the two churches affiliated with the Jesuits. Located through the gates of St. Paul's college, down a lonely road, on the bank of the Mandovi River, it was a large brick structure, rather imposing for something called a chapel.

They went into the cool, dark interior and got their bearings. There was one altar. The rafters were exposed wood. The three stopped in the rear to read the information about the chapel.

"Damn!" Rei swore, then clapped a hand over her mouth.

"What?" Gideon asked.

"I didn't find this online. The original chapel fell to ruins. This building was built in 1884!"

"Crap. So if he did hide it here, it's long gone or destroyed, or buried under all this brick." He waved his hand around the interior.

"Yep. There's nothing to find here."

The three left the church, dispirited.

Outside on the steps Rei said, "Ok, so do we try the Born Jesus place today? Or head there first thing in the morning?"

"Let's go today," Mac said. "We can at least get the lay of the land, come up with an action plan."

They agreed that this made sense, and trudged to the car. They asked the guard at the gate of Saint Paul's College how to get to the Basilica of Born Jesus, and wrote down his rather rambling directions, which were punctuated with landmarks and vague hand gestures to the left and right.

"I think we'll have to ask along the way," Gideon grumbled as he powered up the window.

As it happened, the man's directions were impeccable, and before long they were parked in front of the west facing facade of the Doric inspired church. There were brick buttresses along the sides, and a row of round windows on the third story. The roof was lined with a balustrade.

They got out and entered under the large arched doorway. The interior was bright, and the walls painted white except for at the back, where the altar was. There, the wood carvings were ornate, with angels and columns, a huge sun and an ascending Jesus. The ceiling overhead was white and spectacularly arched. The building was obviously not a museum, but an operating church.

"We need to find the relics of Saint Francis Xavier. This floor is marble—there's no way anything is hidden underneath it. Or at least nothing we'll get a chance to dig out. And there are no carvings on these side walls, just up at the altar. I can't see us getting a shot at the altar... But probably Father Eduardo couldn't either." Rei started walking into the huge structure.

They came to the crypt of the saint, and stared at the elaborate mausoleum.

"This mausoleum wasn't here in Father Eduardo's day. But Saint Francis was in that silver tomb. And that cross and those angels were on top of it," Rei said.

"But this whole thing is marble!" Gideon said. "If they did that after Father Eduardo's day, they covered up anything he might have done."

Rei just nodded. When she was doing the online research, it had seemed possible that something could have been hidden and survived here. And it probably was possible in the rest of the church. But not in the mausoleum, which was a hugely elaborate and highly decorated mass of marble.

"So it can't be in here, unless it's in the silver coffin. A, I don't think Father Eduardo would desecrate a saint's casket, and B, it would have been found before now if it was in there. So it's got to be the main altar, or the other altar over there." She pointed to a chapel off the main knave.

They walked across to the small altar, noticing that there were several people quietly praying, and an elderly woman dusting in the main altar. Rei pulled her scarf over her head, as she noticed the other women had done. They studied the smaller chapel altar.

"This is a possibility, although I don't see any Xs at the moment. If he hid it here, it would have to be hidden in something besides the floor. Marble." Rei tapped her foot. "I don't see us getting up there any time soon." They all watched the cleaning lady at the main altar morosely.

They were turned towards the altar when light shined in from the main door, which opened and closed quickly. Rei glanced over her shoulder, more out of nosiness than concern, but drew in a deep breath.

"It's one of them!" she whispered. "Don't turn around! From the back we look like Indians."

They could hear footsteps going up the center aisle of the knave, casual, not hurried. The man had probably checked the church every day for a week, and had perhaps decided that they weren't going to show up on his watch. He walked to the mausoleum and looked inside, and while he was turned to the left side of the church, the three turned from the small chapel on the right and walked as casually as they could down the side aisle of the church and out the door. They were careful to keep backs to the man, and not show their Caucasian faces or hands.

As soon as they got outside they jogged to the SUV. Mac quickly started the vehicle and drove down the street the way they were facing. He had no idea where that road would lead, except away from the man in black.

———— ◦◦◦ ————

They finally made it back to the guest house after following more rambling directions from a man at a petrol station. They changed into their western clothes and sat in the garden.

"That sucked." Mac said.

"Yep," Gideon said.

"Well, we ruled out one, anyway. And confirmed they're here looking for us," Rei said.

"And we saw another place where it would be almost impossible to find a clue." Gideon countered.

"I've been thinking..." Rei said, "and I agree, Born Jesus is not going to be easy. And they're watching it. We don't know how many brothers this group has, so they might be watching all of the churches. But don't you think it's more likely that they're watching on a rotation, not sending one guy per place? I mean, that monk that came in wasn't there when we got there."

"He might have taken a potty break," Mac said.

"True. We can't know, I guess. But it would be suspicious for these guys to spend all day every day in a church, wouldn't it? Anyway, why don't we move Born Jesus down the list? We know there's only two places inside it could be. I didn't see any place outside, did either of you?" Rei asked.

"I wasn't really looking, but nothing jumped out at me. There were some carvings, but mostly high up, not down at...well, graffiti level." Gideon said.

"Right. So we know where it is, and we know they're watching it. We were there at what, 3:30? So if they're doing a route, checking several on a rotation, maybe they do it at the same time every day. Maybe once in the morning and once in the afternoon."

"That's possible," said Mac. "If we can learn the route we'd know when to be somewhere else."

"Yeah, but we don't want to waste time tailing that guy when we need to find the letter." Gideon countered.

Rei nodded. "So let's just go to the next one on the list. The tongue twister—The Church of Our Lady of the Immaculate Conception. The name alone could make it 'the great church!'"

CHAPTER TWENTY-FOUR

THE CHURCH OF OUR LADY of the Immaculate Conception was not in Old Goa, but was in the city of Panjim, just a few kilometers away. It was located at the end of a residential street, on the town square. A big blue statue of the Virgin Mary with a huge halo looked benignly out over the neighborhood. Under her was a blue iron lectern that could be used for addressing an outdoor congregation. There were old brick steps leading up to an elaborate whitewashed stairway, with zig zag portions leading up to the white church building. A great silver bell hung in a bell tower, a smaller bell to its left, and a cross sat high up at the top.

"This looks promising," Gideon said.

"And not crowded," Mac said.

They started up the steps. They zigzagged their way to the arched front door, and went inside. The two story knave wasn't well lit, although it had a row of windows running along the second story. The floor was stone, and the altar was an elaborate Renaissance style. There was no one inside, but candles were burning.

"Looks good so far!" Rei said.

They walked along the sides of the church, looking for any markings, but finding none. They stood in front of the main altar, which was below an elaborately carved wall. Two smaller altars stood on either side, and there were statues of Jesus and the Virgin next to them. Rei noticed three other marble statues, and went to investigate.

"Hey! Over here!" she called excitedly. "Look!" She pointed to the small plate describing one of the statues. Gideon leaned down to read it.

"Saint Francis Xavier!" he exclaimed. "Who are these other guys?"

Mac read the inscriptions. "Peter and Paul. Saint Francis was in good company!"

"Hurry, look around! With Saint Francis Xavier here, I think this church is a good possibility," Rei said.

They all took different sections of the altar and began combing the walls, floors, statues, and carvings. Rei was down on her hands and knees looking in front of the statues of Jesus and Mary when she heard Mac grunt in satisfaction.

"Here! I haven't seen the other Xs, so I might be wrong. But I've got something over here!" he said.

Gideon and Rei had run over to join him when they heard the vestry door open, and a young priest came into the sanctuary. He was startled to see them and stopped short, then smiled a welcome.

"*Shubhodaya,*" he said.

"Hello," Rei said in English. "English?"

He nodded his head. "You are visitor?" he asked, gesturing up and down to indicate their clothes.

Rei laughed. "Yes, visitors. We came to see your lovely church."

"Yes, much lovely! You wish to have a tour?" he asked.

"Oh no, we're just looking around. Thank you. Is it all right if we explore for awhile?"

He paused as he translated this in his head, then nodded assent. "You look. I have come for the candles. It is all fine." He gave a small bow, used a candle snuffer on the small stubs of candle that had still been burning, and removed them from their holders.

Once the priest had gone back through the vestry door, the three knelt down at the statue of Saint Francis Xavier. Mac pointed to a carved X on the base of the statue, on the rear near the wall.

"That's it! That's Father Eduardo's mark!" Rei exclaimed.

"So what's it pointing to?" Gideon asked. "We've got a marble statue, and a stone floor."

"And what if they've moved this statue in the last four hundred years?" asked Mac.

Rei sat back on her heels and looked around. "Let's think this through. Every other X has been above the letter. Some have been buried, some in a hiding place..." She felt around the statue's base. "There's nothing on the statue itself. A hidden compartment would have been nice. So it's got to be the floor."

Gideon looked at the floor around them. "It looks original. These stones are smooth and worn, and don't look at all modern era." He began tapping on the stones around the back base of the statue with his chisel. *Tap tap tap.*

"Stop!" Mac hissed. "That priest is going to hear that and come back! Look, the stones are set pretty tightly together, but it looks like there's no mortar or anything actually cementing them. None of them seem loose." He looked at the corner where the wall met the floor a foot behind the statue. "But if we can lift the stones out one by one..."

He shifted to the corner where the stones butted up to the wall, and used Gideon's chisel to pry up the stone that was directly in line with the X. It was thicker than he'd expected, and much rougher on the underside. It was sitting on dark, dry dirt. He handed the stone to Gideon, who put it face down on the floor. Working his way towards the base, he slowly pulled up the next stone. He had sweat running down his face, and Rei had started to rock back and forth on her heels.

"Hurry it up!" Gideon whispered. "That priest is going to bring new candles any minute!"

Mac clenched his teeth, and kept working patiently, careful not to drop the stone when he handed it to Gideon. He had begun to lift out the stone directly under the X when they heard the vestry door open again. Rei and Gideon stood up and feigned interest in the statue of Saint Paul, effectively blocking the short pile of stones on the floor as Mac pressed back into the wall. If the priest came out of the sanctuary, they would be found out.

Rei moved over to the altar rail and looked up at the elaborate carvings. The young man smiled when he saw her still there, and refilled all the candle holders. He began to putter around the sanctuary, apparently preparing for a mass. Gideon and Mac stayed by the statuary, trying to remain out of sight.

"Excuse me, Father..." Rei said. The priest turned to her. "Do you have any literature on this altar and the carvings? A book perhaps? It's quite amazing! The pamphlet in the back isn't very detailed."

"Ah yes, I do have a few things. This church is very old, no? We have some old letters, a few books. But they are in my private quarters."

"Oh, I would love to see them!" Rei said enthusiastically. "I am an art history buff, and I am just so impressed by this work..." She smiled.

The priest was torn for a minute, but after glancing at his watch, nodded. "Certainly. I will get them for you, but you must read them here. We do not loan out our historical materials, as they are irreplaceable. You will wait?"

"That's really great of you, Father. Thank you so much!"

The priest left again, and Rei hurried back to the men. "Hurry! I don't know where the parsonage or wherever he lives is, but it can't be too far."

Mac lifted the last stone. There, in a ten-inch deep hole, was a leather pouch. He lifted it and handed it to Rei, and as she opened it, he began to replace the stones.

"It's a letter!" she whispered. "We've got the last one!" She unzipped her backpack and put the pouch into it.

Gideon and Mac hastily replaced the stones, made sure they weren't loose, and all three left the building. Rei looked back, feeling a little bad for lying to a priest, but she said a quick prayer for forgiveness and followed Gideon out the door.

They gathered in the Quinns' bedroom at the guest house to open the letter. Rei would have to translate it, but Gideon and Mac were hoping there was also a map of some kind that they could start trying to match up to modern maps of Goa. While it was one of the smaller Indian states, the population had moved steadily inland from the coast and from Old Goa. However, when Rei pulled the vellum scroll out of the tube, there was only one sheet, containing a letter.

"Damn," said Gideon. "Nothing so simple as a map…"

"A map might not have helped much anyway. Mapping coastlines was one thing, but inland maps from the 1600s are notoriously wrong. I'll figure out what it says—he said there would be instructions, so we have to trust that we can still follow them after all this time. Y'all go get some tea or something—you're making me nervous," Rei said.

She set to work with her battered notebook, and finished quickly. She reread it, and shook her head a bit. The man certainly had a flair for mystery. Of course, a lot of things had changed since he wrote the letter, and it would be up to them once again to decipher what might have been a commonly known location in his day. She closed the notebook and went in search of Gideon.

The men were sitting on the veranda, a laden tea tray on the table before them. Mrs. Pandey had brought them a true British tea, with scones, cream, and cookies, along with hot tea, sugar and milk. Rei sat down and helped herself to a cup and plate.

"So?" asked Gideon.

"I've got it. I don't know what "it" is, but I've got it written down. We'll just have to do what we've been doing, and decipher the name."

"Well, let's hear it..." Gideon said.

My dear son,

You have arrived in Goa, and seen what a lovely city and countryside I have lived in for these last years. I continue to pray that you have not arrived with the great rains, as you will not be able to complete your journey until they have subsided for the season. But I am sure that, if this is so, you can take your ease with the society here, and enjoy the many delicacies and forms of culture that our Eastern capital city can provide.

While I spent many a week in search of the old Templar's treasure, following his journal and his wanderings, trying to make sense of his abbreviated prose, I will not require that you follow quite so closely in my footsteps as I in his. You must go to the Sea of Milk, and there, if the rains are not upon you, is the resting place of the Throne of King Solomon, the wealthiest king to ever live.

You will need to reach the top of the Sea of Milk, and search behind it. There is a great rock, appearing in shape as a bishop's mitre. If you start at that place, and head west to the sea, you must part the curtain at the midway point. There I have left you my mark.

Behind the mark, you will enter a large catacomb. You must be very careful not to lose your way. I have left signs, as I myself did, indeed, lose my way upon my first investigation, and was brought to the doorway only by the grace of God and His mercy. You will need torches to break up the interminable darkness. And you will be in there as Jonah was in the great fish. But you will come, in the end, to the greatest sight your eyes will behold until our Lord Jesus returns to this earth:

the Throne of King Solomon himself.

I know not how you will remove this treasure from its long resting place. But if you find it, I trust that our Lord will give you what is needed to complete the quest. I will pray every day of my life for you, my son, and give thanks for the Templar whom Providence used to give me a life of freedom.

In the name of our Lord Jesus Christ, blessings.
Joao Xavier
X
In the year of our Lord 1687

⸻

"So that's it. We just have to find a Sea of Milk, part the curtain, go behind the X, camp out in a catacomb, and figure out how to haul our treasure out of an enormous cave. No worries." Rei said glumly.

"Uh huh. Any ideas on any of that?" Gideon asked.

"Nope. I'm hoping the internet will at least give us the Sea of Milk. I'd say the Jonah reference means we're going to be underground for three days, which I don't find a hugely appealing prospect personally... And if we find the treasure, I'm leaving it to Mr. Xavier to get it out."

"I can get the camping gear, flashlights, all that." Mac said. "This is a pretty tourist-driven place, and there is apparently a big national park to the east somewhere, so surely there's somewhere that caters to adventure seekers."

"We'd better not ask Mrs. Pandey," Gideon said. "I don't want her to know more than is good for her..."

"We've passed about a dozen coffee shops that

said 'internet cafe' in the last two days, so Mac, why don't you drop Gid and me off at one of those, then get directions from someone for the supplies. Hopefully we'll figure it out while you're gone. And maybe get a map of the whole state of Goa, not just this city area?"

Mac nodded and stood up. "I'll get the keys, you get your laptop. Let's do it!"

———⊷∘❦∘⊶———

Gideon and Rei were sitting in the back of a smoky coffee shop, drinking tiny cups of espresso and surfing the web. There were a half dozen other patrons, all Indians. Still dressed in their local garb, they didn't feel too conspicuous, and, in fact, no one seemed to be paying any attention to them. They were only a couple of miles from the Basilica of Born Jesus, in Old Goa, and the cafe seemed to be surrounded by a good number of eco-tourist and adventure-tourist stores and tour companies.

"I think I've got something..." Rei said, not looking up.

"You found the Sea of Milk?" Gideon asked.

"I think so. There is a waterfall called Dudhsager Falls, on the border of the state of Goa, and the neighboring one, Karnataka... In Marathi and Konkani, the languages spoken around here, it means 'the mihir and Chandiveera Sea of Milk.' It comes from a legend about a naked princess pouring a jug of milk over herself so a prince can't see her body, and apparently when the water comes down during monsoon season it looks white and makes white foam in the pool at the bottom."

"Her nakedness?" Gideon asked.

"That was not exactly the most important part of what I just told you!" she teased.

"To you maybe..."

"*Anyway*...as I was saying," she said, making a face at him, "since we're not here in monsoon season, the waterfall is not very impressive. That's great for us, and must be what Father Eduardo meant by praying we weren't here in rainy season. The falls are naturally divided into four tiers, and it looks like we need to go to the top. That's going to be a bit of an issue, since there's not a trail up there. The two ways to see the falls are by a train that goes over the lowest tier, and by being driven in on jeeps from a nearby town, and then hiking the last kilometer. But that puts you down low, too."

"So we need to drive, find somewhere to leave a rented car, and hike through what, woods? To the top. Find a rock that looks like... what was that again?" Gideon rubbed his forehead.

"A bishop's mitre. That's the big pointy hat with the two tails that bishops wear in fancy services," Rei said.

"Right. A pointy hat. Then 'part the curtain'... I assume that's actually get behind the waterfall somehow. I'm sure that's safe. And then find the X and get behind that. Which might be a passage, or we might have to bust through some rocks. That sound about right?"

"Yep, and all while carrying enough supplies to be in the cave for a week." Rei smiled at him.

"A week? You said like Jonah, three days!" Gideon was liking this less by the minute.

"My interpretation is three days in, then three days

back out again."

"That's a lot of food and water to haul..." Gideon pondered.

"I know. We'll have to take the minimum of each. You were in the Army—what's the minimum water consumption for an adult per day?"

"I think three to four liters is the minimum. A liter is... jeez, about 4 cups, give or take. I don't know exactly. So that's about 2 regular bottles of water per day per person, which means we have to hump in at least 42 bottles of water. And that doesn't leave any for bathing, washing hands, brushing teeth..." Gideon turned Rei's notebook around, turned to a new page, and started making a list.

"Holy cow..." Rei said. After a silent minute, she said, "Let's think this through. Father Eduardo didn't have plastic water bottles. He might have had a clay or leather canteen. When he first went into the cave, he wouldn't have known it would take that long... and he got lost once, too, he said. So there's no way he carried his own water in there. There must be fissures from the waterfall, or springs or something. There's got to be! It doesn't make sense otherwise."

Gideon nodded slowly. "That makes sense. But Rei, that was four hundred and fifty years ago! Can we count on the conditions being the same now? That seems like a pretty big risk."

"What if we hedge our bets? We get a couple of cases of water, and we leave them in the car. We carry, say, five or six each. maybe 10. If we find the cave, and are able to get inside, we can certainly go back for the water if there's none along the way, right? And if there is, we'll have the bottles to refill, and we wouldn't have to do that too many times to make it."

"That should work. But where does the water for the waterfall come from? Is it clean? In the States we could get tablets to put in water to make it reasonably safe to drink... maybe Mac needs to see if he can find some of those while he's out. I'll text him." Gideon tapped out a text message while Rei searched the web.

"The water is from the Mandovi River. It provides water for Goa and Karnataka. I can't find anything that says it's polluted... But there could be parasites or things in it. So if he can find those tablets, that would be great. I don't suppose we can boil it, so if we don't find the tablets, I guess we just pray!"

They returned to the guest house, the back of the SUV laden with bags. On the way, Gideon had placed a call to Mr. Xavier. Their boss had been thrilled with their progress, but not very excited about their being out of contact for a week or more.

"If you don't hear from us in eight days, call the local authorities and tell them where we went. We will go to the closest town, Kulem, and stay tonight, and head to the Falls first thing in the morning. That gives us a week to get in, find it, and get out. It's going to take more than the three of us to get out whatever's in there, so we won't do more than take some pictures, maybe make a map, before we head back."

"Gideon, you and your wife are doing a great thing for my *familia*. I can't thank you enough..." Mr. Xavier said, his voice heavy with emotion.

"No problem, boss. It's been kind of fun." Gideon

disconnected and smiled at his wife, who was looking at him with her mouth open.

CHAPTER TWENTY-FIVE

THEY CHECKED OUT OF MRS. Pandey's guest house in the mid afternoon, telling her they would try to come back after they had explored the area, and they thanked her profusely for her hospitality and help. The drive to Kulem took two hours, over marginal roads that were still better the bests roads they'd traveled in Africa. In Kulem they found a guest house off of the main road, this one a lot more run down. Mac booked them two rooms, but warned them when he came back to the car. "One bathroom for all the guests, and this time it's full up. No dinner, no breakfast. Looks like even getting coffee is going to be a pain."

"We're giving up caffeine for the next week anyway," Rei pointed out. "Might as well start now!"

They drove to a local market and stocked up on high energy, light weight foods. They bought fresh fruit for the first day or two, but purchased dried fruit, dried beef, a nut paste that they assumed was similar to peanut butter, and roasted nuts. They bought paper goods too, reminding Rei of one of the less pleasant aspects of being in a cave for a week with two men. They stopped at a quiet side street and sorted their packs out. Lightweight sleeping bags. Memory foam pillows that squished down to the size of a large sausage. LED flashlights with lots of extra batteries. Whistles. Lightweight jackets, caps and gloves. A couple of changes of clothes and the few toiletry items they thought they might be able to use, even with limited water. Chamois for drying off in the event they were blessed enough to clean their bodies. A first aid kit. An extra bottle of ibuprofen. The bottles of water.

"I think that's the best we can do," Mac said. "Lift it up and make sure you can carry it."

Rei lifted hers and put it on her back. She grimaced. "It's ok standing here. But I don't know if I can carry it for a week, even figuring it's going to get lighter as we eat the food."

Gideon took her pack and moved some of the water and heavier items to his. "Try it now," he said.

She put it on and nodded. "Not gonna be fun... But this is ok. And we have the Advil, right?"

They stopped at a street vendor for a quick bite of grilled chicken on na'an, and went back to the guest house. Their rooms were next to each other, and the Quinns stopped while Mac unlocked his door.

"We haven't seen our friends..." Gideon observed. "That makes me a little nervous."

"I've been thinking about that, too. At this point, I assume they want us to lead them to the prize. So they're probably following us, and not pushing an encounter," Mac said.

"Not much we can do about it, I guess," Gideon said. "Just be on the look out."

"Yeah, and there's this," Mac said, and entered his room. His suitcase was there, on the bed. He unzipped the large compartment, and then peeled back a section of the lining. He handed Gideon a large knife, one of two hidden there. "I had no idea how to get guns," he said, "But I had a lot of knife training in boot camp. I assume you did?"

Gideon nodded. "Hopefully they couldn't get guns, either... the old 'knife to a gun fight' problem. But I feel better having this, anyway. Thanks, Mac."

Mac handed him a leather sheath that would slip on his belt. "Better get to bed. I think we're not going to sleep all that well for the foreseeable future."

<hr />

They woke with the sun and were on the road in thirty minutes. They stopped at another street vendor and grabbed some buttered na'an, and decided a last coffee wasn't such a bad idea. There wasn't much traffic on the road, and they didn't spot anyone following them, but Mac thought the monks could have stuck a GPS tracking device on the car. As soon as he said this, Gideon asked him to pull over, and they all looked under the vehicle for anything odd, but found nothing.

"Guess we'll find out soon enough," Rei said. She was the only one without a weapon, but since she didn't know how to use one anyway, that was probably for the best.

They drove the seven kilometers to the parking area used by the local tour company. They had purposefully gotten there well before the first scheduled tour, and backtracked down the rutted, bumpy, distinctly Africanesque road until they found a break where they could enter the woods. They drove parallel to the road, back towards the car park, until they found a clump of dense bushes, behind which they parked the SUV.

"At least it's black," Gideon said as they tried to cover it with vegetation. "I'm sure the rental company would be thrilled to know what we're doing with their vehicle..."

"No problem. They have your credit card number, right?" Rei teased.

They put on their packs, covered the rest of their belongings in the cargo area with empty bags and strewn clothing, and hiked to the lot. From there, they followed the path that led to the lower tier of the falls. In twenty minutes they were looking up at the steep hill they were going to have to climb to reach the top.

"Oh my gosh," Rei said, craning her neck. "I didn't know it was going to be that high! It didn't look that steep from the bottom."

"I definitely don't think we can go straight up it," Gideon said. "For one thing, when the train comes, or when the first tourists come, they'll be able to see us up there." He looked around. "I think we can go back this way, and then cut around the side. If we do what we did at Lions Head, and try to angle up, it'll be a lot easier."

"Easier. Not easy," said Mac. "But I think that's all we can do. You're right about being visible... no way to stay under trees all the way up to the top."

"I'll take easier any day," said Rei. "Lead on, honey." She adjusted her pack and tightened the strap across her chest.

Gideon took them back the way they had come for a few hundred yards, and then turned off the trail and started angling up the side of the hill that made up the base of the falls. It was still rough going, and the men kept Rei between them as they went single file so that they were able to help her, or catch her, as the need arose. None of them had on hiking boots, and their sneakers tended to slip and slide on the rocky parts. They clung to trees, went down on all fours, and worked up a sweat as they made their way ever higher.

As they came around the back side, they realized their only choices were go almost straight up, or go a long way out of their way towards the river feeding the falls, and then angle back.

"Can you do it?" Gideon asked Rei, looking at the shorter, steeper option.

"I think so. I'd rather do that than have to go all the way up there and back again. I hope we don't need to be on the other side of the river, though... I hadn't thought of that!"

"Me neither," Gideon said. "I guess we'll cross that bridge.. Uh, river... when we get to it." He once again led the way, this time heading for the top.

It was very slow going. Twice they all started to slide downhill, and had to catch themselves on saplings. They rerouted to the side as much as possible, but it came down to crawling on their hands and knees, and pulling themselves up with anything they could hold onto. Rei was about to call it quits when Gideon slipped over a ledge and out of sight. He leaned over and gave her a hand.

"This is it! We made it!" he said.

When all three were up at the top, they leaned against a large rock in the shade and drank from their water bottles. They were sweaty and dirty, and Rei realized how long a week was going to be without a bath, when they were starting out in such a state.

"Ok, boys. Let's find our bishop's mitre," she said. She left her pack where she'd been sitting and walked out in the open where she could get a better view.

She found herself standing on a large, gently rounded rock, looking out across the falls. She was able to see down them a very long way. After a second of vertigo, she enjoyed the view and the sound of gently falling water. She understood now what Father Eduardo was saying about not coming in the rains, though. The rock on which she stood would be under water, and the sound would be deafening. The men joined her.

"So, anyone see a big hat?" Gideon asked, looking around.

———⌖———

They finally decided that they must not be in the right location to see a hat in the rock formations, and debated the best way to change perspective. Going straight down would be very dangerous, and could probably only be done successfully with rappelling equipment. They could go back the way they'd come and angle over to come out by the third tier. But looking at the falls from this angle, Gideon realized one thing. All of the tier ledges were on the opposite side of the water. The side they were on was a sheer drop to the bottom.

"We're going to have to cross the falls. We either have to go all the way down, cross the railroad tracks at the bottom, and go up the other side, or figure out if we can cross the river up there somewhere," he said as he pointed back to the river.

"The water is low right now," Mac said. "But we

have the problem of the packs. We really can't get them wet..."

"And the current," Rei said. "I don't really want to get swept down there." She glanced down the steep falls.

"Right," Gideon agreed. "We're already at the river, so let's check that out first. If we have to go all the way down and back up the other side, this whole day will be shot."

They turned and edged along the side of the water, not close enough to be on the slippery rocks. After several hundred feet the rocky shoreline began to give way to trees and scrub, and the ground was firm but not rock. Further along, the river turned to their left, and the sound of the falls was diminished to a distant purr. Ahead the river turned again to the right.

"Maybe after that curve," Gideon pointed. "If it's this narrow up there, and we can get far enough from the falls to feel like we won't be swept over, we can give it a try."

They trudged on, growing sticky in the humid, still river bed. The bugs were biting their exposed skin, and their packs began to grow heavier.

"Our shoes are going to be wet going back," Rei said, to no one in particular. "But I'm not going in there barefoot."

The water in the river was moving and seemed fresh, but the color was dark from the shadows and the dark soil and pebbles that made up the bottom. Rei had visions of leeches and crawfish and all sort of creatures, and was regretting her vote to cross the river rather than go down the falls to the tracks.

They rounded the next bend, and the water in the river was only fifty feet wide. It was obvious where the high water mark was in monsoon season, but for now the water lazily moved downstream, and a crossing looked promising. Gideon took off his backpack and set it on the ground. He went into the woods, and came out with a brown, dry branch about five feet long.

"I'll go in, see how deep it is and how strong the current is. If it's not deep, I don't think we have anything to worry about. If it's deep... Well, sometimes there can be a strong current along a river's bottom. So we'll see."

"Be careful!" Rei said, and she kissed him quickly.

"Yep," he said, and he walked to the edge of the water. The bank was muddy, and his shoes sunk in, making a disgusting sucking sound. He grimaced and started poking the water in front of him, judging depth. He took his first couple of steps in the river, barely deep enough to cover his shoes. He poked and prodded, stepped, and repeated. Slowly the water level rose up his pants, and then over his belt. On the next poke of the stick the entire thing disappeared.

Rei shouted, "Did it get really deep?"

Gideon shook his head. "No, I can probably still stand. Barely. The stick is shorter than I am, and I can touch the bottom with it. It might be over your head, though."

"You gonna swim, or try to walk?" Mac called.

"I'm guessing five and half feet, so it would be chin deep, but I could stand. It's the step after that I'm concerned about. If it gets any deeper, I'll have to swim." He took the step, and plunged down until the water covered his shoulders.

"That takes care of the bath problem," muttered Rei.

"I'm ok. And it doesn't feel like much of a current

down there—my feet are solid," Gideon yelled over his shoulder. They saw him feel under the water with the stick, and then take another step, which brought him to chest level water. He quickly poked and walked until he was on the far bank.

"We'll be soaked, but we can do it. I'll come back and get my pack, and we can all cross." He made his way quickly back along the same line, and stood dripping in front of them.

"We're going to have to hold the packs over our heads though... I'll take mine across, set it down, and come back. Mac, you'll have to toss me yours and Rei's, and I'll take them across, then we'll span the deep part and make sure Rei gets across ok."

"Got it," Mac said. Rei nodded and swung her backpack in front of her.

———————— ✦ ————————

They made it across without the backpacks getting wet. The same couldn't be said for Rei's hair, but all things considered she was happy. And much cleaner than before.

"Thank God, no creatures!" she said happily, after inspecting her legs for leeches.

They trekked back to the falls, and began to angle through the trees rimming the side of the water, to come out at the topmost of the tiered ledges. With the water flow light, they could safely stand out on the ledge, and from there could not see the railroad track. They hoped that meant that no one could see them, as they doubted tourists were supposed to hike the falls. And they certainly didn't want to make tracking easy for the monks.

Standing on the rock, they could see that, while water went down only the far side now, in monsoon season it would also cross the rock and cascade to the next tier. As Rei studied the area, she saw that the seasonal torrent of water had gouged the surface of the rock and made channels where none had originally existed. Near the rock face, she saw that the eons of flooding water had carved large gaps on either side of a funny shaped rock.

"Hey Gid, what does this look like from over there?" She pointed to the rock sticking up like a lone tooth.

Gideon studied it, moved a step to either side, and motioned Mac over. They talked for a moment, which Rei couldn't hear with the falling water beside her. They both crouched down into a squatting position. At almost the same moment they saw it. From one particular angle, the rock was pointed to the sky, and two flat slabs of rock jutted out the rear to meet the rock face.

"That's it!" Gideon yelled. The men rushed over to her.

"Now what?" Mac asked.

"Now we 'part the curtain'. We have to go west, which is towards the waterfall. And go behind the water..." Rei said.

"You know, that sounded a lot easier when we were sitting at Mrs. Pandey's," Gideon grumbled, looking down at the long, long drop.

"Agreed," Rei said, trying not to look down.

Mac led the way, staying close to the rock face and away from the edge as long as possible. Rei, in the middle, could hear him grumbling, but she couldn't make out the words. She was pretty sure, though, that she shared his sentiments... *This is nuts.*

As they approached the waterfall, which even in the dry season was strong enough to sweep them all away, Mac noticed that the east side of it was diminished because of an angled overhang that seemed to direct the water more to the west side of the rush. He carefully got down on one knee and watched the water, then reached his hand out and through the flow.

"Hey! There really is a space behind here. I can't feel the back, so it should be deep enough to stand in... and the flow isn't very strong here. I'm going to step through it..." Mac said.

"Wait a sec," Gideon said. "We need some kind of safety system. I'm kicking myself for not bringing any rope."

"I think if I just take a quick step I'll be through it. Let's do this." He was psyching himself up. "I'll clip all the straps together on my backpack. I think you can hold that handle there above the pocket, and if I slip... well, I hope we don't both go over." He gave a weak smile.

"Don't even say it!" Rei said. She tried again not to look down.

"Let's do it," Gideon said. Mac snapped all the clips across his chest and waist on the backpack, and tightened the straps. Neither he nor Gideon thought there was much chance of stopping a fall if the water took him, but it felt better doing something, and certainly was better for Rei.

"Here goes..." Mac said, standing as close to the water as he could. Then he stepped through it.

"Hey!" he called. "It's a big space in here! The edge

is right behind the water—you barely feel it when you go through."

The Quinns stared at the water, hearing his voice but seeing nothing.

"Wow," breathed Rei. "That's amazing. Who's next?"

"You go next. Do the same thing with your backpack that Mac did, and step quick. He'll be there to pull you in. Then I'll go."

"Who's holding you?" Rei asked, concerned.

"Y'all will just have to grab me from in there," he said. "Should be ok. I'll get there, I promise."

"You'd better," Rei said. She secured all her buckles and straps, and followed Mac's footsteps to the edge of the waterfall. "Hey Mac! I'm heading through! On three..."

"Gotcha!" came the reply.

Rei took a deep breath. "One... Two... Three!" She stepped. Mac was right, she had barely felt the water before she was safely inside the large hollow in the rock.

"I'm OK!" she called to Gideon.

"Thank God! Ok, here I come... Ready. Set. Go!" He stepped through into the waiting grasps of both Rei and Mac. "I don't know how we'll get out of here, and I sure as hell don't know how we'll ever get a treasure out... But that was awesome!"

The light was very dim inside the cave, and they all broke out their flashlights.

"There's an X somewhere. And we 'go behind' it. So either there's some kind of opening already, or we do some demo," Rei said.

"I hope it's not a lot of demo... I left my jack hammer in the truck," Gideon said.

The three spread out along the back wall and began looking. Gideon found the mark on the curving left wall.

"Here! Got it!" he said.

"Any secret button to open a door?" Mac asked.

"Unfortunately no..." Gideon said. "But maybe..." He was running his hands along the uneven rock that made up the back of the cavity. "I think there's a narrow opening, here." He shined his flashlight behind a rock that jutted out about a foot.

Rei joined her flashlight to his, and they saw that it was, indeed, a very narrow opening.

"Can we fit through there?" she asked.

"Father Eduardo did it," Gideon said. "We'll have to take the backpacks off, and definitely suck in some air. Rei, I think you're going to have to be the trail blazer on this one."

"I wish we had those head lamp things... It's kinda creepy in there," she said, but she removed her backpack and handed it to her husband. "Can we tie a string around my waist so you can pull me out?" she joked.

"I wish," Gideon said. "I'll hold your hand on this side, and you can shine the light with the other hand. Hopefully it's not far til it opens out..."

"And hopefully no animals are living in there," Mac muttered, but low enough so Rei couldn't hear him.

Rei turned sideways, and held out the flashlight in her right hand so it illuminated her path. She reached back with her left hand and grabbed Gideon's. She gave it a squeeze. "I'm ok, honey. How lost can I get?"

Gideon, who knew she got lost in the Tube on a regular basis, refrained from comment.

Rei started to shuffle her feet, moving slowly sideways. The passage was so narrow she couldn't bend her knees more than a couple of inches, but she didn't touch either side. She tried not to think of MRI machines.

"I think y'all can make it—it'll be tight, but it should be ok," she called back.

"You're about three feet in," Mac answered. "Can you see anything in front of you yet?"

"Hang on... Yes! It opens up." She turned back to the crevice and shined her light back to Gideon. "Five feet or so. It's not too bad."

"What's there?" Gideon asked.

Rei turned and swept her flashlight slowly around her. The cave was much larger than the hollow behind the waterfall. Stalactites hung from the ceiling, and she could hear a faint drip drip of water somewhere. The roof of the space was at least twenty feet high.

"It's a big cave!" she answered. "Come on!"

Gideon tossed in the backpacks, and Rei scooted in to get them. She bent sideways, caught the handles on the top, and dragged them out into the open. She leaned them all against the interior wall. When they were out of the passageway, Gideon started through. His chest and back slid along the walls, and there were a few moments of claustrophobia, but then he was out on the other side.

"Your turn, Mac!" He shined the light and saw the captain, who was older, taller and bigger, barely squeezing through the narrow space.

"Just so you know, this sucks!" Mac said in a tight voice. Soon he, too, was in the cave, and they all swung their flashlights around, looking for a tunnel.

CHAPTER TWENTY-SIX

THEY FOUND THE TUNNEL JUTTING off to the left, heading further into the hill. Although it was slight, there was a downward angle to the floor, and they knew that they were descending behind the falls. Every fifty feet or so they saw another of Father Eduardo's marks. They remembered the Jesuit's admonition about getting lost and they were very glad for those Xs.

"I'm hungry," Rei finally said. With all the adrenaline and excitement earlier, she hadn't thought about food, but now she realized that they hadn't eaten in at least seven hours.

"Me too," Mac said. "And we need to keep to a regular eating schedule. In here it would be easy to lose track of days and times, with no natural light."

They sat down in the narrow tunnel, all of them leaning against the wall, and broke out their lunch. Fresh bananas. Nut paste. Water.

"Not very exciting," Rei said.

"Nope, but better than it'll be in a couple of days when the fruit's gone," Gideon said. Rei grunted.

"My watch has date and time, in twenty-four hour mode. We need to eat and sleep as best we can with the outside world," Mac said. "It's two o'clock now. Should we go another two or three hours and call it a day?"

"Probably start looking for a good place to set up after two. I'd rather not set up camp in one of these tunnels, if we can find a bigger cave. Just feels like a claustrophobic place to sleep," Gideon said.

In fact, the tunnel was warm and dry. While completely dark when their flashlights were off, the combined light of the three LEDs were enough to illuminate the path, and they hadn't encountered any other overly narrow or overly large areas. They hadn't yet encountered water, either, which was a cause for some concern, but they had a sense the tunnel system meandered back and forth inside the hill, which meant that they would come back to an area close to the falls before too long.

By the end of two hours, they were all exhausted. The walked another forty minutes before finding a small cave off the main tunnel. It was a dead end, but the size of a hotel room, so they used it for just that purpose.

"What about a latrine?" Rei asked. They had found some outcroppings of rock along the way, but there wasn't anywhere in the cave Rei wanted to use as an outhouse.

"I'll scout it out after we get set up," Mac said.

They got their sleeping bags fluffed up, and their dinner rations out. Mac took a flashlight and his knife, and left. Rei and Gideon sat side by side, leaning against the wall, his arm around her shoulders.

"I'm beat," he said.

"My butt's sore from all that climbing. And I'm a little worried about water..." Rei said.

"We have enough for now. Hopefully we'll find

something tomorrow." He kissed the top of her head. "Even though the floor is rock, I think I'm going to sleep very well."

"Me too," Rei said, and leaned her head back. She'd just started to doze when she heard Mac come back in.

"Good news, bad news," he said.

The Quinns stared at him.

"Good news, there's a good place for the privy just around the next bend, and more good news, I can hear water somewhere ahead."

"And the bad news?" Rei asked.

"There are three tunnels up there, and I don't see another mark."

⸺∘◦⊂∕∕∕⊃◦∘⸺

They all slept soundly, falling asleep not long after eight o'clock after telling funny stories about their childhoods. Rei woke up in the middle of the night and had to wake Gideon to accompany her to their latrine, but otherwise, they slept surprisingly well for being on solid rock, and woke refreshed. The realization of a day without coffee was depressing, but they ate a quick breakfast, brushed their teeth from the bottled water, and moved on to the cave Mac had found the night before.

"I didn't look everywhere, obviously, but I didn't see a mark at the mouth of any of the tunnels. This one in the middle is the one where you can hear water. I say we go down that one first for the water, even if we don't think that's the one the priest meant."

"I agree," said Gideon. "We drank a lot yesterday with all that hiking, and we lost a lot of fluid sweating out there by the river. We'll mark this one, find the water, and come back to look for the X. I can't believe Father Eduardo would leave us hanging... so it must be somewhere. We just have to uncover it."

Gideon opened his backpack and removed a glow stick, which he snapped. The green glow made his face ghastly. He took his knife and made a hole in the plastic, and marked the wall at the entrance to the tunnel with the fluid. Every few feet he made another mark. The sound of the water got nearer, and they sped up without realizing it. Their flashlights shone ahead on an open space, and Mac's long legs carried him ahead of the other two. He was looking straight in front of him, when his right foot stepped down on nothing but space.

He flailed his arms and tried to throw himself backwards, but he knew he was going to fall. His left foot slipped out from under him and he started to go down, when he felt a hand grab his backpack. He hadn't buckled all the snaps when he put it on, but the one across his chest had helped balance it, so he knew that one was tight. The one at his waist was unhooked, and he could feel his arms starting to slip out. He crossed them over his chest and held the straps tightly. He could hear Gideon groaning with the effort of hauling him back.

"Keep holding my belt, Rei!" he heard Gideon yell, and Rei let out a scream of effort at holding the weight and inertia of the two much larger men. He was facing away from the wall, so there was nothing he could do to help himself, other than keep holding the straps.

"I got you!" Gideon yelled to Mac as he strained with the one handed grip on the backpack. The pack kept catching on the lip of the abyss. He was lying on his belly, one knee bent around a rock protruding from the floor, Rei trying to hold him by his belt with her right hand and holding another rock with her left. He had very little leverage, but he could feel the adrenaline coursing through him.

He gave one vast heave, which lifted Mac up enough for Gideon to grab the shoulder strap. One more pull, and Mac was scrambling on his side, holding Gideon's wrist, pulling himself up.

They all lay on the floor, panting.

"Oh my God," Rei finally said. "Oh my God." She started to cry. "Oh my God!"

"I lost my flashlight," Mac said.

———— ⋘⋙ ————

They knelt well away from the edge and Gideon and Rei shined their lights along the ledge and below. Across the chasm there was a small waterfall flowing down from somewhere high up, landing in what sounded like a pool of water. It was too far down to see. There was no water on their side of the chasm.

"We're not filling our water bottles here," Gideon said.

"No, and I'm damn glad I didn't come down here alone last night," Mac said.

"Don't even say it! That was awful," Rei said, squeezing her eyes closed.

"Well, we should head back. We still have to find the X, and the right tunnel. Hopefully that was all the excitement we get for today." Gideon stood, stretched his shoulders, and put on his backpack.

Shaking his head at his folly, Mac followed suit. Gideon helped Rei up and held her pack for her to slide into.

"All buckles all the time," he said. The others agreed.

———— ⊸∘⊂⊄⊃∘⊸ ————

Thanks to the glowing green smears on the wall, they had no trouble finding their way back to the central cave.

"At least we know it's not that one," Rei said, looking around at the other two tunnels. "I know he left a mark. He always left a mark. We'll just have to look more closely at these two and find it." She headed to the tunnel on the right.

The three of them searched the walls and the floor around the right tunnel entrance, and went a dozen feet inside the tunnel, before deciding to try the other one. Near the entrance to the left tunnel a stalagmite had slowly formed, looking like a column. They had to squeeze around it to look at the wall, part of which was obscured by the column of hardened mud.

"Nothing," Gideon said.

"Nope," agreed Mac.

"There *must* be. He wouldn't have taken us this far and then stopped. We know we came the right way to this cave, because there was an X only a few yards from its mouth. What if there's another of those really narrow ones, like the one we came through behind the waterfall?"

This perked the men up, and Mac took one flashlight, and Gideon and Rei the other, and they began to search for a smaller opening in the rough walls. Rei walked ahead in the pool of light and looked behind every outcropping or jagged rock.

"Here! It's here! Well, something's here... Shine the flashlight in there, Gid," she said.

Gideon shone the light and Rei looked in. "I can't really tell for sure, but it looks like an opening... Should I go in?"

"Wait a sec," Mac said. "There's no X out here anywhere. I'd rather not split up, even on the other side of a rock wall, until we've found the mark. And if we don't find the mark... I think we have to call it a day. At least until we can come back with more supplies. We could die in here without those Xs to guide us out."

"He's right," Gideon said. "I think we have to know for sure... We can't afford to lose another flashlight, or a person—the last time we didn't follow an X was shaving it way too close."

Rei nodded, and stepped back from the rift. They all resumed their search, ending back at the left tunnel. Nothing.

"This isn't right. Let's think this through. He said he'd left marks all the way to the Throne. The last marked tunnel led to this room. So there must be a mark in here somewhere," Rei said.

"There's not. We've looked everywhere," Gideon said, sitting back on his heels.

Mac shone the light around randomly, thinking. "Wait. What if..." He got up and went to the stalagmite and looked at the wide bottom, which was formed to the wall. "What if this stalagmite has formed here since Father Eduardo made the mark. What if the X is on this wall," he rapped the rock, "but we just can't see it anymore?"

"Brilliant!" Rei exclaimed. "And we'll know if we go down the tunnel because there either will or won't be another X."

Gideon stood up. "Great work, Mac!" He clapped him on the shoulder.

"Let's wait til we find the next X to get too excited," Mac said, but he smiled, happy to redeem himself.

———————⌖———————

They decided to go down the tunnel to see if Mac's deduction was correct, but in either event, they would return to the open room for a meal and a pit stop. They walked two dozen yards, each flashlight scanning a wall, and there, on the right, was an X. They did high fives and laughed, but their relief was deep. The weight of being underground wasn't so bad as long as they were following in the Templar's and Jesuit's footsteps. Being at a dead end made the rock seem heavy and the tunnels more claustrophobic.

After an hour of rest, they returned down the tunnel and carried on. The rest of that day was uneventful, and they had decided to stop within the hour, when Rei stopped and cocked her head.

"Listen! Do you hear that?" she asked.

The men listened, but shook their heads. "Nope, what?" Gideon asked.

"Water!" she said.

They hurried forward, and this time the water was right in their path, a small stream trickling over the rocks on the left and hurrying across the slightly slanted floor to disappear through fissures on the left. The little bed was a couple of inches deep, the water cold and free of smell. They all knelt down and splashed their hands and faces, letting water run over their arms.

"I didn't find any purifying tablets," Mac said. "Should we worry?"

"I'm not. We need water, here's water. We'll die without it, so we just have to hope we don't die with it!" Gideon said, angling his empty water bottle as best he could into the flow.

It took a good while to fill the bottles, as the trickle wasn't strong and the stream wasn't deep. But when they had all drunk their fill, and replenished the bottles, they felt much better. Another hour hike brought them into a small cavern, and they decided to camp there for the night.

"Sometime tomorrow we should find it," Rei said as she smoothed out her sleeping bag. "The Throne of Solomon. I can't believe it!"

"What I can't believe," said Gideon, "is that those monks haven't caught up to us yet. I've been listening—I haven't heard anything. But they've got to be following us. I can't believe they gave up, or that we were somehow so good that we lost them."

"I've been thinking about that, too," Mac said. "If it were me, I'd let us find the treasure before doing anything. After all, we're doing the hard part, almost falling into crevasses and figuring out that lost X. There might be more of those tomorrow, none of us knows til we get to the Throne. That's when the real danger is, if they're back there somewhere."

"You guys are real party poopers, you know that?" Rei asked.

"Yeah. But we'll get there first, anyway. Probably a

good bit ahead, too, since we haven't heard anything. That should give us time to make some preparations, at least. Not much else we can do. I can't see us all making it out of here without a confrontation— we're going to have to cross paths sooner or later," Gideon said.

"Great," Rei grumbled. "I'm sure I'll sleep really well now, wondering if Gollum is on our tail." She flopped down on her back and jammed her foam pillow under her head, crossing her arms over her chest.

Despite her protestations to the contrary, Rei did sleep well. They all woke early, and completed their morning meal and ablutions quickly. Regardless of the coming confrontation with the *Congratio a Achalichus,* today they would find the Throne of King Solomon, and their excitement was mounting.

By lunch time, however, they had found nothing but more tunnel. Twice they had come to rooms with more than one passageway, but the X was always clear, and they didn't get lost. They found another stream, this time with a basin worn in the rock which made it easier to fill the bottles, and that made them feel refreshed. They ate their dried fruit lunch sitting in a line in a tunnel, drinking the cool, delicious water, not talking.

At four o'clock they still hadn't come to the throne room, and all three were beginning to have misgivings. What did they know about this Jesuit, anyway? He'd obviously been here, but what if it was all a huge practical joke? They weren't worried about finding their way out, but behind them somewhere there was probably a band of angry monks, who were certainly armed, and crossing paths with them in a six foot wide rat hole didn't seem particularly appealing.

At five o'clock they were completely dejected. Not finding it today meant extra time in the warren of tunnels and caves, and while they did have enough water, they didn't have a whole lot of extra food, and even less extra patience. Their feet hurt, they'd already changed the batteries on the flashlights twice, and the lack of the natural day and night pattern of the sun was making them cranky.

"Let's quit soon," Rei said. "I've had it. I'm sick of these tunnels."

"I agree. By six?" Mac asked.

"Works for me. This day is dragging on forever," Gideon said.

They trudged on, no one speaking. Mac was unofficially in charge of the time, as he had the most sophisticated watch, so the Quinns left it to him to tell them when it was time to think about setting up camp. They both just walked, Rei in front of Gideon, heads down, thoughts wandering to good food, sunshine, the beach, good food...

Suddenly Rei stopped short, and Gideon bumped into her backpack. "What?" he asked, frustrated.

"Look!" she said, and pointed the flashlight ahead at shoulder height. Something flashed in the light, just at the outer reaches of the beam.

"Come on!" Gideon said, and grabbed her hand. They jogged forward, shining the flashlights alternately ahead and at the uneven ground. The tunnel gradually opened out into a huge space, and they stopped.

There it was, in front of them. The Throne of Solomon. There was no mistaking the magnificence of it, or the greatness of the king that had ruled from it. The seat itself was at the top of six steps made of gold. On each side of each step was a golden animal. The throne glittered with precious gems. Over the throne was a gold menorah and a golden dove. There was a large golden chair on either side of the throne, and stacks of smaller chairs within the reach of their flashlight beams, also seeming to be gold.

Mac took his flashlight and began to circle around to the left, looking at the chairs, and the throne. Rei and Gideon walked slowly to the front, Rei examining the gold sculptures on the steps: lion, ox, wolf, lamb, tiger, camel... They were exquisitely and realistically formed, with jewels for eyes, and ivory teeth. Examining the seat, she realized it was ivory covered with gold.

"This is just...fantastic!" she said to Gideon. "I've never seen anything like it!"

Gideon stepped on the first step. As he did so, they heard a mechanism start. Gideon froze.

"What's that?" Rei whispered.

"I don't know..." Gideon said, standing still. Mac came running around to them.

"What's that?" Mac asked. Both Quinns shrugged, eyes wide.

The ox and the lion on the first step began to move. Both stretched out a leg, which Gideon used for support to the next step. When he put his weight on that step, the wolf and the lamb did the same thing. Tiger and camel. Eagle and peacock. Cat and rooster. Hawk and dove. He turned and sat on the seat, and heard the sound of another set of gears.

Rei pointed over his head, and he looked up. A gold hawk from somewhere above was descending with an elaborate crown in its talons. It stopped inches from his head, and stayed there.

"Incredible..." he breathed.

———⸘◦⸎◦⸙———

The three set up camp in the corner of the cathedral sized room, away from the treasures themselves. Rei would have stayed up all night exploring, but the men were cognizant of the danger behind them.

"They'll be as stunned as we were at first by the Throne, Rei. That'll slow them down. And they'll expect us to be near it, so we need to be over here, away from the reach of their flashlights when they first enter the cavern," Gideon said.

Rei stayed at the camp, alone in the dark, while Gideon and Mac set up diversions and traps with military precision. She could hear them murmuring, and every once in awhile something banging. Beams of light shot up and out at random intervals. She felt very alone and vulnerable, and sat with her knees up and her arms crossed in front of them, tense and watchful.

After an hour they returned. "Let's eat quick, and take care of any bathroom issues. I want to get the lights out for good as soon as we can, and Mac and I will pull watch duty, four hours on, once we're ready. I don't want anything to give away our position with Rei over here, so we need to be quiet, and dark. Got it?"

Rei nodded, and quickly got out dried beef, dried fruit, and some semi-crushed crackers, along with water. They ate in silence, washed up, and then made the world dark.

The cavern was black. Totally and completely without light, the only sounds those of the Quinns sleeping nearby. Mac had done watches at night in boot camp, and thought he knew what dark was, as well as loneliness and fear, but pulling watch in this cavern was unlike anything he'd ever experienced. The good news, he mused, was that unless the monk bastards had night vision goggles, he'd see their flashlights long before they got to the huge cave. If they had NVGs... Well, best not to think about that. He pushed the button on his watch for the hundredth time, the blue light illuminating the dial. Only halfway through the shift. He leaned his head back on the wall.

His mind was wandering, thinking about wide open skies and grilled steaks and maybe getting a massage to work out the kinks he'd collected sleeping on the rocky ground, when his eye detected a very faint change in the light. It was still too dark to see his hand in front of his face, and at first he thought he was imagining things, but no, there was a slight warming of the monotonous dark at the tunnel mouth.

He shifted slightly and toed Gideon. He could feel the man's body tense as he sat up, and he hissed ever so softly. Gideon crawled towards him, and put a hand out, touching his knee. Mac leaned over, close to his head.

"Light." He felt Gideon nod once, then crawl away.

Gideon felt for his wife, and then leaned over her, putting his mouth next to her ear. "They're coming," he whispered. "Stay here." She nodded, and he kissed her, and went back to Mac.

Both men had a knife in a sheath on their belt. Both had a flashlight in their jeans pocket. Mac had a long branch, which appeared to be made of gold, but wasn't heavy enough to be solid metal, that he had found near the throne. The end wasn't sharpened to a point, but with enough thrust it would penetrate. Gideon had gold arrow, which had a lethal tip. He had found no bow, and they had assumed the arrow was either ceremonial, or that the bow had been made of wood and was long since decayed.

They stood, shoulder to shoulder, as they watched the light slowly grow brighter. When it was still a mere inkling, their adjusted eyes could see enough to move forward towards the tunnel mouth. If there were more than four monks coming, the odds were against them, although they still had some surprises, and the benefit of knowing the layout of the cavern. If the monks were armed with guns, and they didn't act quickly enough, they didn't stand a chance.

Judging by the rate with which the light increased, the men were being very cautious. They had been smart to plan their attack for the wee hours of the morning, but were taking no chances with noise or a sudden burst of light, which, after so much darkness, would be as startling as a gunshot to their quarry. Gideon and Mac stood still, one on either side of the tunnel mouth, aware that any noise they made seem loud in the absolute stillness.

As they had hoped, the monks entered from the narrow tunnel in single file. The first one came into the space, swinging his light side to side, still walking forward. He stopped short as his light illuminated the throne and surrounding treasure. Behind him, two other men came in and stopped, gaping, at the mouth of the tunnel. When no further man appeared, Mac and Gideon lunged at the two in the rear.

Gideon put his left hand over the monk's mouth and pressed hard on the carotid artery in his neck. The man dropped in five seconds, without a word, and Gideon lay him quietly on the ground, removing his flashlight and feeling for weapons as he did. Mac had done the same with his man, and they both stepped quietly back into the shadows.

The lead monk said something softly in Portuguese. "*Voce pode acreditar nisso?*"

When no one answered, he turned back and saw his men on the ground. He didn't go to them. He shone the flashlight around in a wide arc, and then snapped it off.

———⋗∘⋖⋙∘⋗———

Neither Gideon nor Mac had seen night vision goggles on the monk, so they assumed that he was feeling his way slowly and quietly towards the treasure in the dark. He would have to turn on the light eventually, as he had no idea of the layout of the cave beyond the throne, and even if he wanted to retreat, he couldn't do it blind. Gideon and Mac had counted off paces to strategic locations in the cavern, and each made their way to their next vantage point. Gideon was worried about the two unconscious brothers reviving, but they had removed their flashlights and guns. There would be nothing for them to do but sit tight and wait.

When Gideon reached his spot, a large rock to the

right of the throne, he whisked his hand over the top. The quiet "shhiish" sounded loud in the silent cavern. Gideon quickly stepped off thirty paces backwards, and dipped down behind another rock outcropping. He heard the monk stumble, and then the light clicked on. The man shined it in the direction of the sound, and then down at his feet. He picked his way carefully, putting the light on a low, almost night light, setting. He got to the rock, and looked around it cautiously.

Mac's backpack was on a pile of gold chairs ten feet from where the monk stood. His light didn't illuminate it fully, but he saw it and walked slowly over. He took it by a shoulder strap, and lifted it. Suddenly he fell backwards, a gold arrow stuck in his right shoulder.

———⟡———

Gideon and Mac both turned on their flashlights and ran to the monk. They had not wanted to kill any of the men, but not knowing their height or build they had assumed 'average' all around and aimed the arrow accordingly. The man was lying on his back with his arms spread out, the backpack still clutched in his right hand. His left hand clumsily tried to reach the knife at his hip, but Mac put his foot on it, and took the knife away.

"Mac, I'll tie this guy up, and then we'll handle the other two. If they've come to, I don't want you having to deal with them alone." Gideon took out the remains of a sports bra that had been cut into strips, rolled the man on his side to bind hands behind him, and tied his feet. He stuffed a sock in his mouth. He looked at the arrow, but knew it was best not to try to remove it, or risk exacerbating the bleeding.

They made their way back to the tunnel entrance, and stopped short. The two men were gone.

"Crap!" said Gideon.

"At least..." mumbled Mac.

Gideon stepped close to Mac. "I don't want to lead them to Rei, and she knows to stay quiet as long as she's ok. They had to either go back down the tunnel, or towards to treasure. They hadn't seen anything else. If we turn off the lights and wait, we should hear them eventually, if they're still in here."

"If they went down the tunnel in the dark, they're either idiots, or they have more people or supplies somewhere down the line. I'm hoping they're still in here, and there're not more of these nut jobs back there," Mac said.

"Agreed. So we check the throne first," Gideon said.

Mac nodded. "Lights off. Twenty seven paces dead ahead." He clicked off his flashlight, and Mac followed suit.

They walked quickly and quietly, twenty-seven paces, then each turned forty five degrees to their respective outside wall, and walked five paces. They stopped. Waited. The soldiers knew that their training made them patient. But they also knew, Gideon in particular, that life in a religious order had made their opponents patient, too. What they hoped was that the two younger men would be disoriented and scared without their leader, and would either resort to calling out for him, or try to find him and make enough noise to pinpoint their location.

Time dragged on. Gideon thought of Rei, sitting alone in the dark, not knowing what was happening.

He prayed for her, and prayed that they would get out of this hateful tunnel alive. Periodically they could hear the injured monk shift on the ground and moan off to their far right. Then there was a small sound, from behind the throne. A little shuffling noise, not long enough to follow. Quiet. Mac thought about the area where the sound seemed to be coming from. There were gold chairs piled haphazardly all along the back of the throne.

Crash!

Mac and Gideon both snapped on their flashlights and ran, one around each side of the throne. They saw the two younger monks on the ground, entangled by upturned chairs. They freed themselves just as the older men rounded the corners, and looked indecisive. One turned to run into the darkness, the other took a stand to fight. Gideon and Mac drew their confiscated guns and pointed them at the monks.

"Don't," Gideon said.

When they had the two men tied up with the sports bra ribbons, Gideon called out. "Rei! Are you ok?"

"Oh, thank God! Yes!" she yelled. "Are y'all?"

"We're both fine. We'll be a little while longer. Sit tight!" He breathed a sigh of relief.

They walked the monks to the throne, and tied them to the base of it with strips of a windbreaker. While Gideon made sure they had no other hidden weapons and couldn't get free, Mac went to get the leader. He walked back, half carrying, half dragging the man, who even in the LED light looked ghostly pale. The arrow was pulling his chest down toward the ground.

"He lose a lot of blood?" Gideon asked.

"Not too bad. He can't afford to lose much more, and I'm sure he feels like crap, but right now I think he's stable. Not sure what we're going to do about this arrow though. If he can make it back through the tunnels, which I doubt, he isn't going to fit through that opening under the falls with three and a half feet of shaft sticking out of him."

"I was hoping it would go clean through," Gideon said. "But I don't know what else we could have done other than dropping a rock on him with a deadfall. Then he'd be dead or trapped, and we'd be in a worse mess."

Mac looked at the men. "They don't have packs. Must have left them back in the tunnel somewhere. I really hope they don't have friends with them..."

"We'll look in a few hours. I want to get back to Rei, and we need to get some sleep."

———————⌖———————

Five hours later they ate breakfast and checked on the men. Rei tried to speak to the two younger ones in Portuguese and in English, but they prayed quietly and didn't acknowledge her. The older man drifted in and out of consciousness, brow sweaty, and in obvious pain.

"Can't we take that arrow out?" she asked Gideon "He has to lie on his side, and that gold is so heavy it's pulling down on both sides."

"I've been thinking about it, and I don't see any choice but to remove it. You're not supposed to, and he might end up bleeding to death. But it seems like our other option is for him to have to stay in here and starve to death, because he can't possibly make it out with that in his shoulder. Mac, you up for it?"

"Not really," Mac said, making a face. "But I think you're right. It's going to be hard enough to get all of us out of here before we're out of food. He's going to slow us down either way, but I don't see how we even start with that arrow still in him. And we should probably worry about infection, too."

Rei got the first aid kit and one of Gideon's tee shirts. Mac took one of his own tee shirts from his pack. They studied the monk, who was barely conscious.

"Mac, you're going to have to pull it out the back. We can't pull that arrow tip back through. I think I can get the flights off, so it's a pretty smooth ride out." He plucked the finely made gold feathers out of the shaft. "OK, so I'll hold him down, and you pull. Rei, you be ready with the shirts. Put one on his back, and we'll lay him down quick, and then put the one on the front and I'll kneel on it, try to put pressure on both wounds at the same time."

Rei looked ill.

"Babe, can you do it?" Gideon asked.

She nodded, and gripped the tee shirt in her hand. Mac wrapped his tee shirt around the arrow tip in case his hands slipped down the shaft as he pulled, and grabbed the gold with both hands. Gideon straddled the monk at his waist, and pushed down on the side of his shoulder. The man groaned.

"Ready... Set... Now!" Mac said, and heaved the heavy shaft. The monk screamed, and then passed out. Mac landed on his backside with a crash. Rei paled, but stuck the tee shirt under the monk's shoulder, caught the tee that Mac tossed to her, and put it on the flowing blood on his front. Gideon pressed down with his hands as he rearranged his stance, and then knelt down on it.

No one spoke for several minutes. The two younger monks were on their knees, heads bowed, hands tied behind them, murmuring prayers. Finally Gideon risked a look under the tee shirt.

"It's not too bad on this side. Gravity is helping us. Can you tell if the one on the bottom is soaked, Rei?" he asked.

"Hand me the flashlight," she said. "OK, roll him a bit." She shined the light on the tee shirt. "It's red, but it's not sopping wet."

"We'd better keep pressure on. Mac, can you spell me?" Gideon asked.

Mac came and they quickly switched places. The monk was sweating and moaning, but didn't seem to be getting any worse, which was encouraging.

"Let's look underneath," Rei finally said. Mac got off the man's chest, and Gideon rolled him gently to the side. Rei looked at the wound. "It's ugly, but it's just barely leaking blood. I think if we can somehow sew it up, he'll be ok."

"Sew it up?" Mac asked incredulously.

"Watch this…" Gideon said as Rei took the flashlight and ran back to their original encampment.

She returned with her backpack, and unzipped a small front pocket. She removed a tin box and held it up triumphantly. "Ta da!" she said.

"And that is?" Mac asked.

"She doesn't go anywhere, ever, without that sewing

kit." Gideon said. "Her mama drilled that into her from a tender age. You never know when there will be a sewing emergency." He laughed, enjoying the release of tension.

"I've never sewn up a person, and this is just regular thread, so I don't know how well it will hold. I'll double it, of course. And I think it's gonna hurt like hell," she said with a frown.

"He's out, basically. Just do it now. We'll hold him down."

Rei tackled the wound on the front first, using the antiseptic from the first aid kit. After some thrashing around, the monk seemed to fall into a deeper state of unconsciousness. She found that if she thought of his shoulder as an inanimate object as she sewed it helped, but she still felt vaguely sick. When she was done, they bandaged the wound and gingerly turned him over. She repeated the process on the back.

"Well, that's it. We can give him ibuprofen when he wakes up, but that's about all we can do for him," Rei said. She looked up and saw the young monks looking at her with stoic expressions, and smiled at them. "We could all use something to eat, I think."

To allow the young men to feed and otherwise attend to themselves, they untied their hands, but tied one's right to the other's left. They tied the joined hands back to the throne's base. All of them ate sparingly of crackers and nut paste, chased down by water. The men drifted to sleep shortly afterwards, leaning against the golden throne.

Gideon decided that he would take Rei and back track into the tunnel looking for the monks' gear. They would need to pool their resources for the journey back to the waterfall. Mac agreed to stand guard over the prisoners. The Quinns found the stash about five hundred yards down the tunnel, three large black backpacks full of military rations, water bottles, ammunition for the two guns, batteries and communications equipment. There was a minimum of toiletries and changes of clothing.

"These guys humped in a lot of stuff!" Gideon said as he hefted one of the packs.

"I guess they didn't know about Jonah and the three days," Rei said. "We'll have to split the everything up from the third pack. The two younger guys can carry their own."

They took one, but left the other two backpacks where they found them. They could get them on the return journey, when the young monks could put them on. Gideon felt a lot better knowing how much food they had, as he suspected their trip back was going to be greatly slowed by the injured man.

They spent the rest of the day photographing the throne, chairs, and the small pots of gold and gems that they found under the seat of the throne itself. Rei used her iPhone and a flashlight, and Mac and Gideon also did their best to illuminate the site for her. She also took copious notes and made detailed drawings, adding dimensions.

"I don't know how they got this in here, or how Mr. Xavier will get it out," she said.

"My guess is, there's another way in. This cavern has other tunnels besides the one we came through. Father Eduardo found his way in because of the Templar's journal, but the throne had been here long before the Templar found it. With the right supplies and safety equipment, they should be able to find the original entrance," Gideon said.

Mac agreed. "Unless there was a rockslide a lot of years back, that stuff sure as hell didn't come in through the waterfall. That rock face seemed solid to me. So there's got to be a cave or mine entrance somewhere. This isn't man made, so somehow the people who hid it here already knew about it.

"I wonder who it'll belong to?" Rei mused. "India? Israel? It's probably going to be a big mess."

"Mr. Xavier's big mess. We found it, but he can deal with it. I hope we get a bonus, though!" Gideon laughed.

———⊸∘◅✦▻∘⊸———

They spent a final night in the cavern. The injured monk was able to drink some water, but he couldn't swallow any of the dried food or thick preparations of the MREs. Rei mixed some nut paste into the water, making a very bitter drink, but at least he got some nutrition. By the morning, he was able to stand up unassisted, although he was very shaky.

After breakfast, they packed everything up, donned their backpacks, and headed down the tunnel. The young monks retrieved their own packs, and their hands were retied in front of them. Mac walked behind them with the gun, and Gideon and Rei helped the leader. Their progress was painfully slow, as the injured man needed frequent breaks.

At the end of the first day, they had gone barely half the distance they needed to travel to be able to exit in three days. Secured to a stalagmite, the monks ate and drank, still not speaking, even among themselves. The Quinns and Mac sat off to one side.

"We need to move faster," Gideon said.

"How?" Rei asked. "He can't go faster."

"I think we're going to have to leave him. We've got enough food and water to leave some here with him. If we get back to civilization quickly, we can have help for him sooner than we can get him out of here at this rate," Gideon said.

"I agree," Mac said. "We leave him food and water and a flashlight, with extra batteries. We can have someone back to him in four days if we bust it."

Rei looked stricken at the thought of the man having to stay alone. But she saw that they were right, and slowly nodded.

The next morning Rei explained the situation to the monks in Portuguese. "We'll send someone back, I promise. It will be faster this way."

The leader nodded, but the two younger monks began to protest, "*Nao podemos confiar-los!* We can't trust them!"

The leader looked for a long time at Rei, and then nodded again. "*Penso que podemos...* I think we can."

"I will stay with you, father," one of the young men said.

"Yes, Eli, that will be fine. Thank you." He turned to Rei. "It appears that we have misjudged you. We have been searching for so long..." He closed his eyes. "I would like to tell you why."

CHAPTER TWENTY-SEVEN

"OUR BROTHERHOOD WAS STARTED BY a distant grandson of Paul's scribe Achalichus in the third century. He had become a priest, and was a secretary to a powerful bishop. By that time the Church had amassed much wealth, but there was a power struggle among those clergymen who sought personal wealth and those who sought the furtherance of the Church. When our founder realized what the significance of an old letter handed down without thought through generations, and that the letter undermined the entire claim to legitimacy of the pope's, he gave it to the embattled Pope, who used to solidify power. He founded a secret order charged with the protection of the letter." The monk seemed to draw strength from his story, but he still spoke slowly, softly.

"Why didn't he just destroy it?" asked Rei.

"The letter was written by Saint Paul himself! No good Christian would dare destroy such a thing. But he saw that, if the contents of the letter were to become known, the influence of the church in Rome would be diminished by those seeking only to grow wealthy, not live by her teachings. He felt that he could not let that happen, and allocated funds to recruit a few young men already in training for religious life. They were given the name *Congratio a Achalichus*, the Society of Achalichus, and a charter similar to other monastic orders: chastity, poverty, allegiance to the Church. And the perpetual task of protecting the letter. When the Templars looted their monastery in the early thirteen hundreds they found the letter. Thus began our eight hundred year quest to return it. We have continued to be funded as a long lived, but small order. We do not demand much from the Vatican, and our small budget is never questioned. We try to do good works in our community outside of Lisbon, but we have become soldiers in recent decades under our late abbot, Lucius. As he got older he was increasingly obsessed with finding the letter and returning it to the Society's protection."

"But the letter was never made public. It might even have been destroyed, for all you knew. I don't understand why you needed to get it back," Rei said.

"I do not either, looking back. I have been in the Society since I was seventeen years old. Since his death, I am now Abbott myself. I never thought to question him, or his obsession. He knew about the Xavier family. It has apparently been passed from abbot to abbot that Father Eduardo became Joao Xavier. All of the sons of that family have been watched since he returned to Lisbon is 1689. His home was searched many times, as was his business, and all of the Xaviers' homes and businesses since that time, to no avail. But the real obsession was the suggestion of treasure. A brother had written a letter in 1685 to the abbot, mailed to him from Goa, that the priest had disappeared. But when he reappeared as Joao Xavier, he had suddenly

348

become wealthy. Our order knew of the Templars and their treasure hoards. The Templars were alive and well in Portugal long after they had been wiped out elsewhere." The monk fell silent, eyes closed.

"So when you stole the letter and found the journal..." Rei prompted.

"When our abbot saw the journal, he became a fanatic. He said that God intended for our order to have the Throne. He disregarded the letter completely—the letter we had searched for all of these years. It had no importance to him in light of the Templar's treasure." He sighed. "I see now that he was insane, perhaps senile, but in such a small family of brothers, such things spread like wildfire. Suddenly we had a new quest, and we were to stop at nothing... *Nothing...* to accomplish it." He closed his eyes and sighed deeply.

"What does that mean?" Rei asked.

"Lucius said it was a Crusade. That taking lives in pursuit of this holy object was justified. He wanted you dead... He wanted anyone or anything in our way eliminated. And we just went along. We did whatever he asked. We hacked into computer systems. We bribed people. We hurt people to get information... I can say that we have not, thank God, killed anyone, but I think we would have. I think *I* would have." He sighed again. "Lucius is dead. While we were in Goa waiting for you the word came to us from the brothers still at our monastery that he had a massive stroke. I had already been appointed as his successor, so the 'crusade' became my own."

"Why are you telling me this now?" Rei asked.

"Your men did not kill us. Lucius knew that your husband had been in the Army. We found out that your pilot had also been a soldier. He told us that it would come to us killing you before you could kill us, that you would have no mercy in your quest for the treasure. He said you would sweep everything out of your path. But I see now that that was his own mind at work... *He* would sweep everything from his path. But you and your men have shown us mercy, and did not kill us, although they most clearly could have done so. As I lay in such pain yesterday, God showed me all the wrong we have done. And for what? A treasure that does not, nor ever will, belong to us. We have been led astray for many years—young men who have been recruited into a small and isolated brotherhood because of our zeal, and told delusions of old men who have spent wasted years finding nothing." He leaned his head back against the wall, exhausted, eyes closed.

The young monk who had been sitting next to the abbot, looked at him, his face anguished. "Father Thomas... is this true?"

Thomas didn't open his eyes. He nodded, and sighed. "I believe so, my son. I believe so. We have been told, and we have believed, lies. We have sinned... While we wait here for our rescue, we will put ourselves into the hands of Almighty God and His judgment."

———⌖———

The Quinns and Mac headed out first thing the next morning. Thomas had decreed that both of his men would stay with him, and adequate food and water had been left, along with two flashlights and a supply of batteries. They made good time going back, following the marks left by their ancient patron, and feeling the weight of the monks' lives on their shoulders. They spent a restless night in the cave with the stalagmite, and kept a brisk pace from early morning on.

Arriving at the cave mouth at dusk, they decided to spend the night there so as not to risk descending the waterfall and hill in the dark. They awoke at first light, a slight but welcome sliver of sunshine coming though the crack. They squeezed through, one at a time, and carefully stepped out from the waterfall and onto the ledge. They decided to descend on that side of the falls, which took them almost two hours of angling back and forth. They were hot and sweaty by the time they reached the railroad tracks that crossed over the first ledge to the other side.

Rei looked up at the trestles. "Anybody know the train schedule?" she asked.

Mac looked at his watch. "I did a few days ago... I feel like the first train arrives here around ten, give or take."

"What time is it now?" asked Gideon. His watch had been cracked in his rescue of Mac, which seemed eons ago.

"9:36," Mac answered.

"So do we wait, or go for it?" Gideon asked.

"Wait!" Rei said.

"Go for it!" Mac said at the same time. There was an awkward silence.

"Personally, I'd really like to get out of here, and get someone from Kulem on the rescue operation. If we can get up there fast," Mac pointed to iron steps leading up the stone bridge, "we should be ok."

"We'll be ok if the train is *after* ten. I'm not sure we'll be ok if it's *before.*" Rei said.

Gideon stood still and listened for a minute. "I don't hear anything but water. Let's just go." He put his arm around Rei's shoulder and kissed her ear. "We can do it, babe."

They all scrambled up the metal rungs and out onto the stone bridge holding the track. They walked quickly but carefully west, crossing over the last tier of the waterfall. They were still thirty feet from the next service ladder when they heard it: the train whistle.

"I knew it!" yelled Rei as she began to run.

"The train won't be going fast—it stops for people to look at the falls," Mac said as they jogged along.

"Is it legal for us to be up here?" Gideon asked.

"That I don't know..." Mac said.

"Then let's get down!" Gideon said, and sped up, holding Rei's hand and pulling her along behind him.

They took the rungs down as fast as they could, and as soon as Rei's feet touched the ground the engine of the train passed overhead. Mac was right, it was barely moving, bringing the viewing cars to a stop across the span of the falls. The three stayed under the bridge for fifteen minutes, until the train slowly moved off towards its next destination.

"Alrighty then..." said Rei as she started walking in the direction of the SUV. "That was about all the excitement I can stand in one week."

———————⊶⊙⫷⊙⊷———————

Getting the rescue operation started took longer than they could have imagined, as the authorities in the small town could not, at first, understand what they were saying about caves and an injured man. The head official kept shaking his head.

"We do not have caves in this region. No sir. We do not."

After nearly an hour, Rei asked to step outside, where she placed a call on her cell to Mr. Xavier. After explaining that they had, indeed found the treasure, and it was, indeed, King Solomon's Throne, she finally broke through his excited questioning to get to her immediate point.

"Mr. Xavier! Sir! I'll show you pictures and send you emails and everything as soon as we get to a hotel. But please, listen... One of those monks is injured, and he's still two days back in the tunnels, with two other men." She listened for a long moment. "Yes sir, but that's a long story. What we need is for the authorities here to mount a rescue operation for Thomas and his men. They're not near the Throne room, we can figure that out later. But they have a limited supply of food and water, and we need to get going to get them out. The people here just aren't seeming to get it!"

After another long pause she said, "Thank you!" and hung up. She ran back into the building and whispered to Gideon, "Mr. Xavier's on it. The phone here should ring soon..."

In fifteen minutes the head official picked up the phone on the second ring and barked a greeting, still annoyed with his crazy American guests. He listened for a long moment, his eyes on the tourists, his back straightening ever so slightly.

"Sir, yes sir. Consider it done, sir. Yes. Thank you,

sir." He hung up the phone. "It seems that word has come all the way from New Delhi that I am to provide rescue for men trapped in a cave behind Dudhsager Falls. A cave that I have never heard to exist."

He stood up and put on his hat. "You, sir," he said, pointing to Mac, "Will accompany our rescue team. You will tell us what we must bring to accomplish this thing, and you will lead us. There is not a question. You will come." And he walked out of the office.

———⊸०⋐⋑०⊸———

Five days later the Quinns were sitting on the veranda of Mrs. Pandey's guest house when they heard car doors slam shut. They looked at the patio door, expecting Mrs. Pandey, who had gone to a local bakery for pastries for tea.

"Glad you guys are kicking back, resting up. Some of us had work to do..." Mac said as he came through the door, followed by Thomas and the two young monks.

Rei jumped up and ran to hug him. "Mac! We didn't expect you til tomorrow! I'm so glad you're all ok!" She smiled at the monks and said, "*Bem-vindo de volta do escuro!* Welcome back from the dark!"

Thomas said, "Thank you, Mrs. Quinn. And thank you for assisting with our rescue."

"We would never have left you!" Rei said, aghast at the thought.

"No, I have come to know that. Please accept my apologies for my order, and for myself. *Tenho pena.* I'm sorry."

"It's water under the bridge...or over the falls," said Gideon, shaking his hand. "Come have some tea and tell us about Mac's heroics."

EPILOGUE

IT TOOK A CREW OF forty workers and six archeologists five months to extract the Throne of King Solomon from its long resting place. Luis Xavier hired an expert spelunker to discover a secondary entrance to the cavern, and after two weeks of exploration, they emerged through a diamond mine, long forgotten. Apparently the ancient miners had dug through to the cavern, following the alluvial deposits as they meandered under the hills. When the Throne and other artifacts were illuminated by generator driven lights, the workers also found ancient pottery and tools, indicating the miners had used the cavern as a primitive dormitory.

Under tightly controlled conditions, after analysis by the archeologists and two engineers, the Throne was disassembled, and it, along with all the accompanying artifacts were documented and crated. A half dozen shuttle cars, used in coal mining, and just small enough to traverse the tunnels, moved the crates from the cavern to the mine entrance, where they were loaded on trucks, taken to Mumbai, and flown to Israel.

KINGFISHER RESORT, MOZAMBIQUE

THREE MONTHS LATER

Rei was lying, eyes closed, soaking up the sun on a chaise lounge beside the crystal blue sea. She had been dozing, enjoying the sounds of the surf and the sea birds, and the delicious thought of having nothing to do for two whole weeks. Hearing a noise next to her, she opened one eye and saw Gideon settle down on the chair.

"Well?" she asked.

"It's all done," he said. "Mr. Xavier has agreed to present the Throne and all the accompanying treasure to the public at the Tower of David Museum in Jerusalem on the first of Nisan, which is the New Year for Kings. That falls on March 24. And we are invited as the official finders of record for the lost Throne of King Solomon. All expenses paid..."

"Wow, that's awesome!" Rei said, sitting up. "So we're going down in the history books."

"Something like that," Gideon said, adjusting his sunglasses and lying back on the chaise. "Oh, and we're getting a big fat bonus."

"What about the St. Paul letter?" Rei asked.

"Mr. Xavier agreed to let the Society keep it. He's quite happy with the treasure, and I think also happy to be relieved of the burden of that letter."

Rei took a sip of her fruity adult beverage, and kissed him. "I'd do it again, you know."

"Don't even say that!" Gideon pulled a towel over his face.

The Prime Minister himself opened the exhibit, and the Quinns, Captain McMillan, and Luis Xavier were feted all across the city for a week. Tales of their exploits were blown up to Indiana Jones proportions, and no mention was ever made of a letter written by Saint Paul, or a secret organization bent on finding it. Father Eduardo/Joao Xavier and his wife Isabel had an exhibit with all of their letters prominently displayed on a map of the Portuguese spice route.

Rei and Quinn stood at the foot of the throne, looking up.

"It was worth it," Rei said.

"Yep," Gideon agreed.

Mac joined them. "Pretty awesome, seeing it here with all the lights and fancy displays," he said.

"Better than in that cave!" Rei said. "But it was nice to have it to ourselves for a little while, wasn't it?"

The men nodded, still gazing up at the seat on which Gideon had sat, and the crown that had lowered onto his head.

"Hell of a job, y'all," Gideon said, raising his glass of champagne.

"And by Father Eduardo. Or Joao. Whatever we call him, he was an incredible guy," Mac said.

"And don't forget his Isabel... They had quite an adventure, too," Rei said.

They toasted, and drank, and each said a silent thank you.

LISBON, PORTUGAL

1704

Joao and his fifteen year old son Quico trotted along the busy street atop bay mares, heading to the wharf. Joao had promised his son an outing, and he always enjoyed the ships along the quay. A nau was in port that reminded him of the Santa Antonio de Tanna, which had been sunk several years before. They stopped at an inn, where a groom took their horses, and Joao told him they would walk a bit before coming in for their midday meal.

"Papa, why do you not go on any of the voyages anymore?" Quico asked as they walked slowly down the waterfront.

"I have done my share of seafaring, my boy. I have your mama and your sisters now to think of. And you, of course," Joao ruffled his head, which he knew annoyed the young man.

"I could come with you! I would love to go to Africa, to see all the places that you and Mama talk about in your stories at bedtime. The *oliphants* and the camels..." His eyes were dreamy and far away as he remembered the stories he'd heard all his life.

Joao laughed. "When you are grown and running the business, you may make those decisions. But I am done with that life, Quico. I am content."

They stopped at the wall where many years before a young Father Eduardo had been confronted by a man in black about a dead Templar. That life seemed to have belonged to someone else. And yet it was that day, and that life, that had led to this young man next to him. To his beautiful wife and three young daughters at home in their large home overlooking the river. Ah, God indeed moved in mysterious ways.

"Come, let us sup. I am famished, and this inn has very good bread. Maybe we shall take a loaf home to your mother, what do you think?" He began to walk along the top of the wall, arms out for balance.

Quico laughed, shaking his head at his father's exuberance and love of life. "I think, Papa, that you are *doido*, crazy!"

THE END

IF YOU LIKED THIS BOOK, YOU'LL LOVE:

THE HOARD OF THE DOGES

BY JENNINGS WRIGHT

TURN THE PAGE FOR A SNEAK PEAK!

AVAILABLE SOON!

VENICE, ITALY

1125 AD

"Y OU SHOULD HAVE SEEN IT, *signore*, truly, you would have marveled!" said Doge Domenico Michele to his oldest friend, Pepe Dandolo. The thirty-fifth Doge of Venice, newly returned from the Holy Lands and the First Crusade with the Venetian fleet, continued, "We could not contain all the plunder in the holds of the ships! And there was that fat William, Prince of Galilee or some such title, begging me—begging me, I tell you!—to help them attack Tyre. Out of the goodness of my heart, of course!" He laughed heartily and guzzled wine from a silver goblet. They were sitting in the Doge's private study, a warm, wood paneled room. Rich jewel toned tapestries hung on the walls, and an elaborately carved winged lion presided over the room from the stone fireplace.

"The goodness of your heart has been known to be expensive," observed Dandolo dryly.

"Oh, indeed, and it proved as much once again. Not only did we receive the majority of the plunder from the conquest, but they have given us what amounts to free reign in the entire Kingdom of Jerusalem, a quarter of the city of Acre, twenty-one villages in Tyre... And no taxes!" He laughed again. "Apparently, I can be quite persuasive."

Dandolo smiled. "And yet you did not return to Venice with ships overflowing with riches, my friend."

"T'would have been impossible to bring it all and yet still carry the men, who were, of course, most anxious to return to hearth and home. And it was also unnecessary. Venetian influence continues to grow, but that influence is expensive to maintain, and we were stretched thinly while I was away with the fleet. There is much unrest everywhere these days." He took a long draw from his wine, wiping his mouth with the back of his hand. "However much the Patriarch and William wish to believe it, the Holy Lands are not secure, and the sultans will fight to regain it. Our fleet conquered Samos, Lesbos... we even destroyed Rhodes on our return voyage, but the Greeks are resentful, as always. We must keep a military presence in the territories, and quickly colonize our new holdings in the Kingdom and Levant."

The Doge walked across the polished floor, his soft shoes barely making a sound. A middle aged man, but full of vigor, he had the swarthy complexion of a sailor from his time with the fleet. His dark hair had only a few strands of gray, and his patrician nose and high cheekbones gave him an unmistakable air of authority. He stopped at the window and looked out at the newly restored Church of St. Mark.

"So then, where is it?" Dandolo finally asked.

Michele turned and looked at him, then waved his arms in an expansive gesture. "It is everywhere.

I have left some of it everywhere we have influence. It will be under the control of the doges, allowing us to protect and defend and grow Venice in a way not dreamt of before."

"You will not keep some for your family? For all of our families?" Dandolo asked. The aristocratic families of Venice had ruled the city-state among themselves for generations, and their wealth had grown along with hers.

"Bah!" retorted Michele. "Have you not enough gold, Pepe?" He sipped his wine, and looked at his friend shrewdly over the edge of the goblet. "What we have now, my friend, is better than gold. Who do you suppose I will send to our new territories, to Acre and Jerusalem and Tyre? To rebuild Rhodes? It will be you, my brother, Giovanni Barbagio... It will be our families who will have a mill and a market in every town. It is the great Venetian families who will serve as magistrates and governors. It is we who will have *land*. More land than you can fathom." He grinned at his friend.

"I see that you do not yet comprehend. Ah, it is to be expected, you have not traveled to the Aegean, to the Holy Lands. But so you shall. I will, I believe, appoint you as the Overseer of these islands we have recently conquered. Then you will perceive things differently, I'll wager! And you will see why we have need of the funds that the plunder will provide." He drained his cup and set it on the hearth. Dandolo stood and bowed.

"Come, let us dine. My wife has arranged quite a feast for us, and we shall toast once again to Venice and her might." They headed toward the sound of merry voices down the long hallway as they exited the study.

ABOUT THE AUTHOR

BORN AND RAISED IN ROCKLEDGE, Florida, Jennings spent her early years reading anything she could get her hands on, when she wasn't spending time in and on the water. She won a prize in the 6th grade for her writing.

Jennings attended the University of Tampa, graduating with a B.A. in Political Science, and almost enough credits for B.A.s in both English and History. She spent time over the years doing various kinds of script doctoring, business writing, editing, and teaching writing, but mostly having and raising her family, homeschooling her children, owning and running a business with her husband, and starting a non-profit to Uganda.

Thanks to a crazy idea called NaNoWriMo, Jennings got back into creative writing in 2011 and hasn't stopped since. She's written three novels and a screenplay, with more ideas on the drawing board. She currently lives in North Carolina with her husband, a political writer, and two children, and travels extensively.

Web: www.jenningswright.com
Email: jenningswright@jenningswright.com